Advance praise for *Nesting*

"*Nesting* is a powerful novel. Brand-new, urgent and hugely satisfying."
—Roddy Doyle, author of *The Women Behind the Door*

"A gorgeous, maddening, thrilling and compassionate book. Roisín O'Donnell so expertly captures the dull thud of dread and the frailty of hope. *Nesting* shows us that the quietest voice in the room can also be the most powerful."
—Sheila Armstrong, author of *Falling Animals*

"*Nesting* is a haunting, deeply affecting debut—a gripping and unflinching exploration of coercive partner control, societal inequality, motherhood and the terrifying reality of a world closing in fast when you have no options left. An incredibly compelling tale of survival, it is as emotionally charged as it is brutally real. The writing is flawless. I was profoundly moved."
—Elaine Feeney, author of *How to Build a Boat*

"Clear, urgent and compassionate, *Nesting* will sweep you along, heart in mouth."
— Lucy Caldwell, author of *These Days*

"Tough and tender, urgent and finely nuanced, this is an addictive reading experience. Roisín O'Donnell has written a novel of undeniable power."
—Wendy Erskine, author of *Sweet Home*

"Roisín O'Donnell tackles the unsettling cruelties and manipulations of coercive control with insight and emotional complexity. The voice is authentic, vivid and important. Emotionally charged, psychologically nuanced and full of compassion and possibility, I read with my heart in my mouth."**—Una Mannion, author of *Tell Me What I Am***

"*Nesting* is a triumph in empathy. This novel is achingly beautiful and utterly necessary. The attentiveness to language shines from every page. A book to open eyes and hearts. O'Donnell imbues her characters' circumscribed domestic space with a page-turning emotional urgency."
—Danielle McLaughlin, author of *The Art of Falling*

"Such a moving, heartfilled, urgent book."
—**Jan Carson, author of *The Raptures***

"Persuasive and painfully real. Roisín O'Donnell writes with startling clarity and compassion."
—**Rónán Hession, author of *Ghost Mountain***

"*Nesting* is a triumph of a novel. A beautifully crafted, unflinching portrait of the lengths a mother must go to to make a home for herself and those she loves."
—**Louise Nealon, author of *Snowflake***

"A perfect portrayal of the insidious nature of intimate partner abuse where the bruises are not physical, but violently emotional. I fell in love with the voice of Ciara as she sets out to create a new life against all odds for herself and her children. A story of bravery, love and redemption, chock full of emotional suspense—I couldn't look away. A high-wire act of a debut."
—**Chelsea Bieker, author of *Madwoman***

"What an extraordinary debut! I clutched this book tightly as I read, and rooted for Ciara from page one. *Nesting* is an unputdownable story of love, courage and survival."
—**Mary Beth Keane, author of *Ask Again, Yes***

"Paced like a thriller, *Nesting* is a deep, beautiful, hopeful meditation on trauma, healing and love."
—**Jessica Stanley, author of *Consider Yourself Kissed***

"Such a beautiful and real portrayal of contemporary Dublin."
—**Ana Kinsella, author of *Look Here***

"A dazzling debut, pin-sharp in its depiction of the insidious hooks of behind-closed-doors coercive control. O'Donnell handles her heroine's pain and potential power with nuanced, page-turning aplomb. I was gripped to the end."
—**Cristín Leach, author of *Negative Space***

NESTING

Roisín O'Donnell

NESTING

ALGONQUIN BOOKS OF CHAPEL HILL 2025

Published by
Algonquin Books of Chapel Hill
an imprint of Little, Brown and Company
a division of Hachette Book Group, Inc.
1290 Avenue of the Americas
New York, NY 10104

Originally published in Great Britain in 2025 by
Simon & Schuster UK Ltd.

Printed in the United States of America.
Design by Steve Godwin.

Library of Congress Cataloging-in-Publication Data is available.

ISBN 978-1-64375-570-0 (hardcover)
ISBN 978-1-64375-572-4 (ebook)

Printing 1, 2024

First U.S. Edition

For Mary and Áine

At first
  I was land.
    I lay on my back to be fields
and when I turned
    on my side
      I was a hill
under freezing stars.
    I did not see.
      I was seen.
Night and day
    words fell on me.
        Seeds. Raindrops
Chips of frost.
  From one of them
    I learned my name.
        I rose up. I remembered it.
Now I could tell my story
  It was different
    from the story told about me.

"Mother Ireland," Eavan Boland

Contents

I

BEFORE THUNDER

SPRING 2018

1

Ciara steps out of the car and a cold sea wind catches her breath, whipping her hair across her face. After some maneuvering, ignoring tuts from the passenger seat, she's managed to squeeze her old silver Micra into a tight parking spot across the road from Skerries beach. The April afternoon sky stretches bright and clear. Above the rooftops of the seafront terraces, gulls glide as if manipulated by invisible wires, their taut wings motionless.

The passenger door slams.

Ryan rounds the car, and she hears him open the boot. Ciara turns, pushing her hair from her eyes. Struggling against the weight of the wind, she hauls open the back door to a torrent of "Me first, me first, me first!" Four-year-old Sophie has unbuckled her own seatbelt. She squeezes under her mum's arm and jumps onto the pavement, dark pigtails flying.

"Yes! The sea! Can we build a castle, Daddy?"

Ciara doesn't catch Ryan's reply. She's too busy grappling with the buckle on two-year-old Ella's grimy red car seat. This car needs to be cleaned. Deep-cleaned. Christ. That's why they always take her old banger to the beach instead of

Ryan's pristine jeep. Finally the buckle opens. "Wha-la! There we go, missus. Freedom."

"Up, Mammy." Ella reaches out one of her chubby arms, still so young that she has dimples where her elbows should be. Her other arm is hooked as always around Hoppy the blue rabbit with the love heart sewn on his chest. Threadbare in parts, stuffing gone lumpy, he looks somehow both careworn and wise.

"Come on up then." She kisses Ella's cheek and nuzzles her neck, inhaling the faint smell of bananas and porridge.

Sophie has skipped ahead into the sand dunes with Ryan. There's something comical about their mismatched figures. Her fluorescent orange cycling shorts, butterfly top and sparkly hairclips, alongside his black T-shirt, pressed jeans, dark gray hair combed neatly in place. Despite her father's grip on her hand, Sophie is still managing to dance.

Sharp blonde stems of sand reed scratch Ciara's ankles as she weaves through the dunes with Ella on her hip. "You see the sea, Ella love?"

The strand curves in a crescent around the bay, striated with bands of crushed shells, driftwood, seaweed. RTÉ forecast twenty degrees for today. An April high, which clearly didn't factor in the bitter gusts sweeping off the Irish Sea. Sunday afternoon, the beach is dotted with clusters of people huddling under coats or sheltering behind windbreakers, determined to make the best of it.

At the end of the boardwalk, her runners sink into the sand. When she's caught up with Ryan she puts Ella down and stands beside him looking out to sea. "Tide's out," she comments, for something to say.

Ryan turns to her. "I'm taking them swimming."

His gray eyes study her face, testing her. He was in such good form this morning, when he announced they were going to the beach, but already something has changed. What has she done this time? Her heart begins to quicken.

"Swimming? As in like, paddling? Sure they'll love that."

"I said swimming. Proper swimming. They're big enough."

"But they don't know how to swim?" She tries to laugh. "It's bitter, Ryan. They'll freeze."

He folds his arms across his chest. His lips set in a thin, determined line. She hears her mum saying, *Pick your battles, love.*

"Okay. Swimming. Why not. I'll stick the wetsuits on them there. Girls! Come here to me, will you?"

The wetsuits are from last summer. Ella's is so tight she can't bend her arms. Ryan stands watching as she hauls Sophie's back zip up, lifting her daughter off her feet. "Hey Mammy! Stop! You're hurting me!"

"There now hun, perfect." Sophie waddles away like a bad-tempered penguin. Imagine if Sinéad were here, how she'd laugh at the sight of her nieces.

Ryan is pulling off his T-shirt, frowning. "Did you not get them new wetsuits? I thought I gave you the money?"

She mumbles something about the suits being out of stock and busies herself unlacing her runners and rolling her black leggings up over her knees. Feeling his stare on her, she ties her hair back, zips up her pale-pink fleece.

Ella toddles up and grabs her hand. "Mammy, come!"

They leave their beach bags and rolled-up towels on the

dry sand, above the hungry creep of the advancing tide. Her daughters pull her over the harder, wave-rippled sand, onto the place where the wet beach mirrors the sky.

At the first lick of the frothy waves at their toes, the girls squeal and run away. Ciara curses under her breath. It's even colder than she expected. Waves slapping up her bare calves. The wind, menthol. What if there are jellyfish? Blooms of Lion's Manes, drifting in Dublin Bay. Stepping deeper, into the tug of undercurrents, she imagines tentacles lacing unseen between her children's bodies. God forbid any of them get stung. If anything happens to ruin this day, it will be her fault.

Ryan strides over, takes Sophie's hand. "Come on, we're going swimming. We're going deeper."

Sophie shrieks each time a wave hits her. Ella is pulling at her mum's fleece wanting to be lifted. She scoops her daughter onto her hip again. The wetsuit isn't making much difference. Ella's teeth are chattering.

"Cold, Mammy."

"It's okay love, you'll be okay. Isn't this great fun? Will we try to jump the waves?"

She eyes Ryan. How long do they have to endure this?

At the diving spot by the Martello tower, people are preparing to jump. Open-water swimmers, leaning against the rocks, wrapped in coats and towels. If any of them were to glance in her direction, what would they see? A happy family? Out near the horizon, Skerries Island looks like a sleeping giant with a friendly beer belly curving out of the water. She wants to point this out to Ella, to laugh about it together. But right now, there's no space for stories.

"I'm freezing! It's too, too cold!" Sophie splashes over and wraps her thin arms around Ciara's waist. "Can we get out now, Mammy? I want to get out NOW!"

Ryan is cupping water in his hands, tipping it over his shoulders. He fixes her with a look of contempt. "They just have to get used to it."

"They're cold, Ryan." She cringes at the pleading in her voice. "It's too cold for them. I think I'd better bring them in."

"Fine."

"I'm sorry it's just I don't want them getting—"

"I said that's fine."

He turns his back and dives in, muscular arms slicing into the water, swimming away from them.

Maybe he'll keep aiming for the horizon. Maybe he'll end up in Greenland.

Stop. You can't think that. Jesus.

The girls run back up the beach, Ella wailing "Cold, cold, cold!" One at a time, she peels off their wetsuits and bundles the girls into the bathroom towels she shoved in the beach bag this morning. Sophie howls when she rubs her dry. Suddenly Ciara is four years old again, sitting on Castlerock beach during those summer trips home to Derry, her mum rubbing a scratchy towel on her goose-bumped, sandy skin.

"How about some food?" Ryan's voice takes her by surprise. She hadn't noticed him getting out of the sea. He's always had this habit of appearing quietly, startling her. His question is directed at Sophie, who goes all shy, buries her head in her mum's chest.

There it is again, that voice in her head. *Haven't you got what you wanted? The thing you've been secretly longing for?* A lovely home in Ireland. Two little girls. Pigtails curling in the salty spray, jumping around in Minnie Mouse swimsuits with frills around the bums. Ryan, a loyal, hard-working husband. The type of man who other women sneak glances at, when he's pushing the swings or ordering lunch, or standing—as he is right now—bare chested, towel-drying his hair. And yet—on this bright day with seagulls screeching—there's a gathering weight in her chest, like the feeling before thunder.

Slides, see-saws and sea-rusted swings. The cold wind has died down, and there's some warmth in the late afternoon sun. Along Skerries Harbor, there's a festive atmosphere, couples and families walking along the seafront. A boy is flying a dragon kite over the marina, and a man is using a drone to film his kids, who are trying to down it with rocks. "I've told you," he is saying. "I have specifically asked you to please not."

At Storm in a Teacup, she orders ninety-nines for the girls and Ryan.

"Not having anything?" He speaks without looking at her.

"I'll share some of theirs," she says. "I'm not that hungry."

Soon, Ella has a dripping vanilla beard. Raspberry syrup oozes between Sophie's fingers. Ciara mops their chins with paper napkins, creating a shredded gloopy mess.

"Here, let Mammy have some of that." She takes a bite of Ella's ice cream, aiming to get rid of it before it melts completely. The sweetness makes her stomach turn. She can feel

Ryan watching closely. "Oh God. The state of them. Ice cream is never that brilliant an idea, is it?"

Ryan says nothing. *Here it is. The start of another of his silences.*

A headache is building at the base of her skull. Her body, flooded by the uncanny sense that she's trapped. Stuck in this bright day forever. She's invisible, walking unseen through the crowds. Other women are happily herding children, holding partners' hands or strolling with friends, talking. Her little meandering family blends in perfectly, so why are these dark thoughts swirling again?

Two years since she returned to Ryan. A couple of months since she stashed the wetsuit money in the nappy bag on some blind impulse. A flush of guilt, as if she's a smear on the perfect day, sullying the moment. She remembers that wartime painting she once saw in the Tate on a school trip to Liverpool. People on a merry-go-round. From a distance they looked happy. It was only when you looked closer that you could tell they were screaming.

The drive home to Glasnevin takes half an hour. Whenever she stops at a red light, she sneaks glances at Ryan. Her husband is on his phone, scrolling, brow furrowed, maintaining his aloof saint pose. *Like St. Peter,* she thinks, *standing on a knot of snakes.* She wouldn't have known about this before she met Ryan. Now she has an impressive knowledge of the gospels and the Old Testament—the burn-in-hell parts, and the parts related to women who disrespect their husbands.

Her attempts at conversation have become increasingly

desperate. She sounds like a radio talk-show host running out of ideas, prattling into the small hours with no one listening.

She's shrinking, during this late afternoon drive back into the city. She's fading, as she drives down the Clontarf Road, into that view over Dublin; the city clasped like a crab's claw around the bay. Beyond, the crooked wizard's hat shape of the Sugarloaf. The blink of the candy-striped Poolbeg chimneys.

"Grand day out wasn't it?" she tries.

Ryan says nothing. He won't even make eye contact, has barely spoken to her since the beach. It's as if he can't really see her, can't see past his anger for long enough. If only she could flip the switch back to how he was this morning, when his good mood stretched between them in a warm panel of sun.

She parks in the driveway of their pebble-dashed semi on Botanic Close. A boxy 1970s build, with a long narrow front garden, overgrown hedges. The landlord or a previous tenant planted pyracantha along the wall, and it has webbed out, ugly thorns reaching in all directions. A bloody graveyard plant, her mum called it, the last time she came to visit. Now at least Ciara's daffodils are brightening the place up, nodding their heads in the breeze.

Ryan gets out before she's even stopped the engine. He unbuckles the girls, brings them inside. She hears them screeching with laughter in the hallway.

Opening the boot, she's caught by a head rush. *Another one.* She waits for it to pass, then takes out the beach bag, the dripping wetsuits, the heavy, saturated towels, the plastic bag full of buckets and spades. She lowers the rear door using her elbow, shuts it with her backside. In the gloomy hallway, she stops and throws everything in a sandy heap on the lino by the coat stand.

Ella shouts, "AGAIN, DADDY!"

In the living room, Ryan is swinging the girls around, turning them into pendulums held by the ankles. A one-man version of Tayto Park.

She peeks round the door frame. "Looks like great craic."

Ryan looks at her as if she is something small and shit-caked, then goes back to swinging Ella and Sophie.

They love him. He's a good dad. Isn't he?

She shuts the kitchen door against their delighted squeals, boils a kettle, whips out a bag of penne, pops open a jar of tomato sauce and soon has some class of pasta concoction bubbling. Then without even thinking, she's in the bathroom wearing rubber gloves, armed with a spray bottle of Flash, and a pack of J-cloths.

It's a habit that started when she was pregnant with Sophie. She used to call it "nesting." That thing women do when they sense their baby is arriving soon. Grouting, hoovering, taking a mad notion to paint the backyard wall Azores Blue. Only, she didn't sense an arrival but an impending threat. Cleaning, painting, fixing every centimeter of that house felt like the only thing that was safe.

"Girls! Dinner's ready!"

Sophie clatters into the kitchen, moaning about being thirsty. Ella refuses to let anyone help her into her highchair.

Ryan looks at the pasta on his plate, moves it around with his fork and then stands abruptly.

"I'm going out."

She's in the kitchen scrubbing sauce off the Peppa Pig placemats when she hears the front door click. Wrung out, this is how she feels. Drained. After dinner, the girls' bubble bath, teeth brushing and bedtime stories. After emptying beach bags, shaking out towels, standing in the dark rinsing small wetsuits under the garden tap. The bright kitchen lights were giving her a headache, so she turned them off and plugged in the side lamp instead. Her eyes are hot, her body aches. And now it's that dreaded time of night, when the girls are asleep and she's no longer shielded by their scuffle and song.

Ryan walks into the kitchen. He boils the kettle, makes a mug of camomile tea for himself and sits down at the table. Ciara moves away, fills the sink and starts going at the saucepans with a Brillo pad and a generous squirt of Fairy liquid.

When she cannot take the silence any longer, she pulls the plug, drying her hands on her top and turns to him, tries to sound casual. "So, where did you disappear off to?"

"Out. I needed some space." He laces his hands on the table and looks at her. "I was totally humiliated today. All I wanted was to bring my children swimming, like any normal father."

"But we did go swimming! We were in the water for a while."

"Please," he scoffs. "We were in the water for about two minutes before you insisted we get out. You're always trying to control me. Just like your bloody mother, the way she orchestrates everything."

"Look this isn't fair, Ryan. I just... Don't bring my mum into this, please. I know you hate her, but—"

"What, are you kidding me? I've never said anything bad about your mother. Anyway,"—he's glaring at her now—"where is that money I gave you for the wetsuits? And the change from last week's shop?"

She can't seem to find the words.

It's that head-spinning feeling again. Becoming untethered. Grasping for memories that disappear as soon as she settles on them. Last time her mum came over from Sheffield, she had to stay in a B&B because Ryan wouldn't let her in the house. If only she could just press pause. If they could communicate through calm-voiced interpreters, like at a UN conference. Failing this, she needs to stop the conversation before it deteriorates further. *The wetsuit money is hidden, with the rest of my pilfered notes. My getaway fund.* Her heart quickens at that flicker of tension in his jawbone. She has very little time left to avert this.

"I have a headache, Ryan. I have to finish cleaning—"

"You have a headache? Ha! How the hell do you think I feel? I've had a headache for the last five years, dealing with this crap from you. Lying bitch. I want that money back tomorrow."

Please don't do this. Please.

Anything she says will be wrong. Words are useless. She has to step outside of language, away from it, into pure action. She reaches for a dishcloth.

"What the hell are you doing now?"

"Cleaning the sink." Her hands are shaking. "Look, I'm sorry for upsetting you, I didn't mean—"

"What, are you fucking kidding me? You're not sorry at all. What's wrong with you? You're crazy. No wonder you've no friends. I'm done with you."

"Ryan, please can we just—"

"I said I'm fucking done."

He stands up, chair legs shrieking against the tiles, and pushes the chair back so hard it clatters over. Her heart jumps.

He sidesteps past her, as if she's something diseased and festering, and fires his mug into the steel sink so hard the handle breaks, leaving flecks of china in the suds and on her hands. Leaving the kitchen, he slams the door with such force that the side lamp topples off the table and onto the tiles. The bulb shatters, plunging the room into darkness.

Hands shaking, still holding the checked J-cloth. Lemony Fairy liquid. Blood pounding in her ears, deafening. She has become the house. The toppled chair. The smashed bulb. The broken handle. Her bones and blood.

She waits and watches and listens.

One. Two. Three. Four.

A slit of light flickers around the kitchen door. His heavy steps reveal how far he is, how close.

Nights like this, she knows this is real, she's not imagining it. The fear is bright, animal, sure. Pure blue at the heart of a flame.

Afterward, it's always more difficult. There will be no apologies, and if she dares bring it up, he'll scoff. *What are you even talking about?* She will begin to wonder if it was all in her mind. Eventually his footsteps creak up the stairs. Their bedroom door slams. She's suddenly freezing. Shaking. She drops the greasy dishcloth, reaches for the blue hoodie on the back of her chair.

She swats on the light over the oven. The shocked kitchen stares back. A glitter of glass on the taupe floor tiles. She picks up plates, rights the chair, sweeps the shards—moving slowly, as if the house were made of ice.

2

Monday morning, she creeps barefoot to their bedroom window and inches the blind aside. His jeep has gone. He'll be on his way into town, parking near the Green and walking up to the Department of Public Expenditure on Merrion Square, gone until at least five thirty. She waits for the quick spill of relief, but it doesn't come. Instead, on loop, thoughts of what happened when she finally made it up to bed. *Enough,* something whispers in her mind. *No one should have to live like this. Enough.* Powered by the thought, she pulls out her bedside drawer, hands finding the smooth shapes of their passports—

"Mammy?" Sophie, standing in the bedroom doorway, one hand down the back of her unicorn pajamas, scratching her bum. "What's for breakfast?"

Red handed, she shoves the passports into her nearby shoulder bag and puts on a smile. "How about porridge?"

Of course she can't leave again, of course not. She has to keep busy, push these treacherous thoughts aside. Laundry, that's what she'll do. She carries the hamper downstairs, separates darks from lights, puts on a quick wash. Ella is awake now, calling to her.

Getting them dressed takes a while, with Ella insisting, "I do it my elf!" By the time she gets them downstairs, the cycle is almost finished. While the girls eat their porridge, she pulls the clothes from the cylinder. She can't eat yet, not until later on in the day. It's not nausea, just a complete lack of appetite. Deep down, she knows the reason. From her texts, her sister Sinéad has guessed it too.

When will you find out? Will you ring me? Xox

Ciara slides open the patio door into the garden, steps into the bright morning. There's something calming about pegging washing. Leggings upside down, dresses held by their hems. The fragrance of the fabric conditioner, the damp clothes heavy in her hands takes her back to childhood summers in Sheffield. She remembers chasing Sinéad around their small lawn, under the rippling square shadows of freshly laundered sheets. *Enough.* As she's pegging, that word still whispers in her mind, but it's fainter now, barely audible, as the tidal pull of the daily routine takes over. *Forget it. Just a stupid notion.*

After breakfast, she walks the girls up to playschool, pausing to say hello to the cat they've christened Mog, who threads herself between their ankles and then springs coquettishly onto the wall. When they make it to Happy Days, Mairéad is just opening the gate, saying good morning to the kids as they trundle in with their lunch bags. At the last minute, Ciara plucks Hoppy from under Ella's arm.

"Hang on love. Remember what Mairéad said. No Hoppy at playschool. Mammy will mind him."

Ella frowns, but Sophie pulls her sleeve and they follow

the others. This is only Ella's second week. She shouldn't even be at playschool until September, but Ella wants to do everything Sophie does.

Ciara walks home, gets into the Micra, and for some reason puts Hoppy in her bulging shoulder bag on the passenger seat beside her. *As if you're going to be any bloody help here.*

She could have gone to the local Hickey's Pharmacy, but Ryan knows too many people in Glasnevin. Sod's law, she'd bump into one of his colleagues from the department, their neighbors or someone from Mass. So she's driven up to Blanchardstown Shopping Centre, bought a pregnancy test in Boots, and ducked into the bathrooms.

Two purple lines.

Sitting on the closed toilet lid, she chokes on a sound that's somewhere between a laugh and a sob. She puts her head in her hands, digs her fingers into her hair and cries. Then she pulls some sheets of flimsy loo roll from the dispenser, wipes her face, blows her nose, and unlocks her phone.

Sinéad answers on the second ring. "It's positive?"

Ciara pauses.

"I knew it. Fuck, I knew it was. I said to Mum, I told her wait till you see, I bet you any money our Ciara's pregnant again. I knew from your texts, how you'd been so knackered and off your food."

"Hang on, Sinéad, you told Mum?"

"Ah come on, Ciara. Sure she finds out everything anyway. The woman's psychic. Where are you now?"

"In the third cubicle on the right."

"Fucksake Ciara." Her sister sighs, and she can imagine her standing hands on hips of her scrubs. No nonsense, as if her younger sister were one of her patients in the pediatric unit. "Okay, look. It's going to be fine. You've had a shock, you need some sugar. Grab yourself a cuppa and a bun, and phone me back."

It's such a comfort to be given instructions, relieved of the pressure of decisions. Feeling steadier, she walks out into the airy shopping center. Hoppy is still in her shoulder bag, and she finds herself taking him out and hugging him to her chest. Looking for distraction, she walks into Easons and picks out a new Mr. Men book for the girls. *Mr. Topsy-Turvy's house is the topsy turviest house you've ever seen!* She walks through H&M, picking up a couple of tops, frowning and then putting them back. *Who are you kidding?*

She buys a tea and a blueberry muffin. *I'm pregnant*. Surely it will be a girl. It seems she always makes girls, in the way Sinéad says, *I don't make sleepers. Not my forte.*

When Sinéad answers this time, one of Ciara's nephews is screaming in the background, "NO NO NO NO." Three-year-old Rory, presumably still off with the chickenpox. Joey and Nathan must be at school. She pictures them in their hilltop Sheffield terrace with the ladder-steep staircase, so similar to the house she grew up in.

Sinéad speaks over the din, "Bit better now, Ciara hun?"

"Yeah. I'm okay. Bit of a shock just."

"Always is, love. When will you tell that arsehole you're living with—RORY WOULD YOU STOP DOING THAT. WOULD YOU BLOODY—Just a second, Ciara."

She feels herself squirm at her sister's comment. The reflex to defend Ryan. To take back the things she texted Sinéad, when she was crouching sleepless against the door in the girls' room last night. Her skin prickles, embarrassed. He's her husband, still. Love: barnacle-stubborn.

"Sorry." Sinéad's back on the phone. "Rory's a little dick-head. How many times have I said don't eat the fucking playdough. Jesus." She sighs. "So when will you tell himself, about the new baby?"

The stoniness of his face. It wasn't that he reacted badly when she told him about her other pregnancies. It was more the absence of a reaction. That's what stung. Made her hug him and try to kiss his turned-away cheek. *Aren't you pleased? Aren't you?*

She won't go through one of those pregnancies again. A door has shut in her mind. A line, firm and concrete. In her bones, in her muscles, she's never relinquished the memory of those months, when carrying each child to term seemed so precarious. Smuggling them to safety, that's what it felt like. Shielding her belly. Begging. Pregnancy was the only time she's openly begged him to give her a break. That time on the drive home from the hospital with Ella, stopped at a red light—she can still see it now, the exact pelican crossing on the North Circular Road—when she considered jumping out of the car to escape his torrent.

For now, she's dodging Sinéad's question, reeling the topic back to playdough and its edibility.

"Sure doesn't it look like food?" Sinéad says. "I mean, it's awful tempting. Playdough pizza. Playdough buns. For the love of God, what eejit came up with that?"

Her sister's accent is a mixture of Sheffield and Derry, like hers. Soft Yorkshire vowels, with a smattering of their mum's Irish phrases.

Soon they're onto chokeable Lego, trippable Duplo, *Dancing with the Stars*, calories and toilet-training. But Sinéad is like their mother. She doesn't miss a beat. Ciara's evasion will have been noted, but Sinéad knows her well enough not to push it. She likes to think that perhaps her sister senses she's coming to a decision. Sediment settling, solidifying.

Driving to Happy Days, she felt certain she'd collect the girls, drive back to the house, gather their belongings, and go. But as soon as they get home, Ella and Sophie want to play on the slide in the garden. Helplessly, she follows them, scooping up lunch bags they've abandoned in the hall, emptying leftover sandwich corners into the compost caddy. Again, the rhythm of daily life sweeps her along.

Outside, there's the hum of lawnmowers. Next door's kids are on their trampoline, blowing bubbles. Sophie has carted out her shoebox full of dinosaurs, shooting them down the small plastic slide. Ciara spreads her mum's Donegal blanket on the grass for Ella, who flops onto the soft green tartan, and rolls over, chatting to Hoppy. Moments like this feel like a gift. *See,* she thinks, *there's no need to leave. You're just exaggerating -- like Ryan says. You don't have to leave. No need to put the girls through that. It's all okay.*

Lifted by a sudden energy, Ciara picks up the trowel she left on the kitchen windowsill last week. Time to tackle the thistles on this lawn. She's asked Ryan to dig them out, but he said she was treating him like hired help, didn't speak to her for days afterward. A satisfying crunch of roots as she slices into the earth.

Just after four o'clock, the patio door shudders open. Sitting on the blanket singing songs to Ella, she's lost track of time.

Ryan strides out, and the day turns on its head. As if jolted by an electric charge, she stands.

"You're home early?" she says.

He walks up to her, moves behind her, his breath in her ear, his hands roaming over her body. "Last night was great."

Sometime in the early hours, her mind blurry, the room pitch black, she had been woken by his hands, his weight on her. Her face burns, her voice falters, "Ryan, the kids."

"Stop. They're not even looking."

The girls have gone quiet. She's trying to struggle out of his grip without making a scene. *I cannot hear myself think.* Her own internal monologue, erased. Replaced by his voice. His words in her head. *Lazy, selfish, cruel, heartless.* He turns her around to face him with that look of mockery. "What's even wrong with you? Jesus. Lighten up." He lets go of her arms. "I'm going for a shower. You making dinner?"

The patio door slides shut behind him and she realizes she is shaking.

There it is, deep in her chest. Louder than before: *enough.* She should have left this morning, while he was at work. Why couldn't she listen to her own intuition? She should wait until tomorrow, but something has snapped now, broken. She cannot endure another night, has to seize this moment of clarity, before the fog descends again. Before he walks back out here smiling, and she convinces herself again that it's all in her mind.

Laundry flutters on the washing line. Plenty of T-shirts, leggings, pants and socks to last a good few days. Ryan won't be down for how long? Ten, fifteen minutes? Her car keys and purse are in her shoulder bag, left on the kitchen table. In it, their passports from this morning, along with the wetsuit money—that small roll of pilfered tens and twenties shoved inside a size 5 nappy, somewhere he would never think of looking. *Clothes, passports, money. I can do this.* The idea makes her head spin so quickly she has to reach out and touch the breeze-block wall for balance.

The hairs on her arms lift. From next door, bubbles spin in slow motion. Her daughters' voices reach her now. Sophie is blowing dandelion seeds in the golden slant of late afternoon sunlight, counting, "One . . . two . . . seventeen . . ." Ella is rolling on her tummy, swatting the floating seeds. It's almost dinner time. In the cold indigo shadows along the garden wall, daisies purse their pink lips for the night.

Slowly Ciara eases open the patio door, and listens. As soon as she hears the thrum of the shower from upstairs, she dashes to the kitchen, grabs her bag from the table.

Outside, she starts pulling clothes off the line. Her pajama bottoms. White lace top. The one she wore that afternoon in Galway. Their honeymoon. A sharp, sweet memory. Almost enough to make her stop.

Toddler T-shirts. Digger. Tractor. Unicorn. There's no time for the peg bag. Washing pegs fall, leaving a pink-and-purple trail, bright haphazard stitches across the uncut grass.

Arms full of clothes, she stalls. Surely she will fold these sun-starched T-shirts into a pile and carry them into the house? Surely she will walk into the kitchen and start the usual routine of setting the table, lighting the oven and make-believing everything is okay?

Ciara pulls the last item from the washing line. A purple hoodie, size 3–4 years. Sunlight is slipping from the garden, long shadows reaching.

She whispers, "Come on over to Mammy now loves, we've to head out."

Ella gets up bum first. She runs over, elbows going like pistons, dragging Hoppy by one ear. Sophie skips, flying her pterodactyl. "Where we going, Mammy?"

"On a secret adventure," Ciara whispers, forcing a smile. She lifts the Donegal blanket, uses it to wrap her bundle of starchy dry clothes. *My phone charger. No wait, there's a spare one in the car. Their lunch bags. No, there's no time.* She ushers the girls ahead of her. "Hurry, hurry, shush now, quiet." Down the side passage, out of the drive, across the road, to where her car is parked beside the crooked hawthorn. In the gnarled branches, knots of pink buds are almost ready to blossom.

"Into your seats now girlies. Quick."

Her hands tremble as she buckles first Sophie and then Ella into their car seats. Fumbling with the three-point clip on Ella's seat, she's keeping an eye on the house, as if she's waiting for it to explode.

3

Looking for somewhere safe, familiar, she drives over to the Phoenix Park. The lull of the park stretches out for miles around her, a vast green pause at the city's heart. The sycamores are coming into leaf, a fresh, lime-green haze. Beneath them, wide-eyed fallow deer are grazing, guarding their young. In the distance, the chalk-blue mountains are dappled with patches of ochre in the early evening sunlight. Along the footpaths, joggers in exercise gear, dog walkers and people pushing buggies. Surely if she sat down on one of the old wooden benches and explained her story to any of these people, they'd say she was doing the right thing. That she isn't losing her mind.

"Mammy! Hungry!"

"Mammy, I'm actually BURSTING!"

"Hold on, Sophie." She turns left, down the avenue toward the playground. She parks, unloads them from the car, and brings them down a winding path, where the wild grasses grow waist high. She says, "Right, Sophie, let's do your wee."

"No, don't want to."

"But you said you were bursting?"

"Don't want to."

"Jesus Christ. Right, look. If you do a wee, then you can have a box of raisins."

Finally Sophie allows her mother to scoop her up and hold her bare arse over the wild grasses. Her daughter is heavy. She's trying to angle her so she doesn't get sprayed. Ciara shouts, "WEE NOW! WEE RIGHT NOW!"

At the thin spray of piss, Sophie giggles. Ella joins in, shouting, "WEE RIGHT NOW!"

She scoops Ella up, against her protests, lays her on the front passenger seat to change her nappy. Then she brings them back across the car park, to the primary-colored climbing frames and slides. It's fairly empty, dinner time for most people. Three teenage boys are skateboarding up a slide, and a woman in a purple coat is trying to cajole her toddler out of the playhouse (NO, WON'T).

Sinéad isn't answering. Ciara can't phone her mum. She wouldn't be able to hide the fear in her voice, and she can't have Mum panicking.

She messages, *Sinéad I'm out.*

Out where? Hold on I'm in tescos—that GIF of the baby in the yellow dungarees propelling a loaded trolley down a shopping aisle.

No worries catch you later.

She hoists Ella into a baby swing. Sophie wriggles onto a big swing and instantly starts moaning, "I need help. I can't do it."

Ella asks, "Mammy, when's it Christmas?"

This is what your kids do. They push every thought from your head. They create their own universe.

If she can just find somewhere to stay tonight, talk to Mum and Sinéad and figure out what to do next. All she knows is, she can't go back to the house in Glasnevin. She has €70 cash in the nappy bag, €150 in her current account, all that's left from when she last worked, before she met Ryan. Pushing alternating swings with one hand, with the other she starts googling *B&Bs near me.*

Her head is throbbing. She's sweating so much she has to keep wiping her upper lip on the sleeve of her fleece. *Jesus Christ, are you doing this? Jesus Jesus Jesus.*

"HIGHER, HIGHER, MAM, HIGHER!"

Sophie's pigtails swing beneath her sequined baseball cap. Her small frame tense with concentration. Her brown eyes. The way they sparkle with intelligence, fun. Ryan has always said Sophie looks like him. But if anything, she looks like her granny, Rhona Devine. Her skinny legs are flailing in a completely uncoordinated effort at gaining momentum.

"PUSH ME, MAM. HIGHER HIGHER HIGHER!"

The cheapest B&B she can find is €97 per night.

She's filling in a form on booking.com. Holidays in Dublin. Three star? Four star? Number of guests? Age of children on arrival?

A WhatsApp from Ryan: Where did you guys go?

He's added a confused-face emoji. A kiss and three red love hearts.

Clouds are gathering. A cool wind ruffles the trees.

"HUNGRY!"

"When's dinner, Mammy?"

Iona Bed & Breakfast—Your Home from Home. One room available.

BOOK NOW.

The Iona is on a row of Georgian terraces, down a quiet side street in Phibsborough. A cabbage palm tree leans in the front garden, casting spiky shadows. Stained-glass panels on the front door glow pastille-bright in the dusk. At other houses along the street, people are coming home from work, opening their front doors, stepping into warmly lit hallways.

God. What have you just done?

In the dusty reception, vases of plastic dahlias and a German stag party checking in. Ciara waits, Ella heavy in her arms, Sophie flying her pterodactyl around her legs, while the men ask for directions to the Gravediggers pub and the Book of Kells. The receptionist, a woman with long auburn hair and glasses, spins the map upside down to show them, circles in red biro. A man in his fifties is passed out in one of the high-backed chairs, as if this trip is proving too much already.

Sophie tugs her sleeve, "Mammy, my pterodactyl wants its other dino friends."

Her box of dinosaurs, left in their garden. Ciara tries to keep her voice steady, strokes her daughter's hair. "You tell pterodactyl we'll see the other dinosaurs soon. The heating in our house is broken, so we're staying here in this nice place tonight."

Sophie frowns at this, then hides behind Ciara, rests her head in the small of her mum's back.

Exploring Dublin leaflets are fanned out on the parquet hall table. She can hear the purposeful laughter of people on their holidays. The Iona boasts the best Irish breakfast in Dublin, according to the leaflet she's been refolding so much, the backdrop of green mountains is coming off on her sweaty palms.

Ryan (5 missed calls)

Seriously—where did you guys go? Is everything okay? I'm freaking out a little here. Call me

A stab of guilt. She quickly types a reply.

Everything is okay. Girls are okay. I will call you in a little while.

Hugging Hoppy, Ella rubs her eyes and lays her head on Ciara's shoulder. It's almost seven. Naps and bottle times and the entire ritual of her evening—dinner at five, bath at six—have been abandoned.

"Just the one night?" the receptionist asks. "Breakfast is included. Cash or card?"

Ciara slots her card into the machine. Please God it still works. The receptionist hands her a key on a thick leather tag. They're in the family room, a loft conversion.

Sophie is pulling at her again, "When's dinner?"

The cold evening air feels raw on her skin. Sophie says, "Wow. Mammy, it's so dark. It's like we're in outer space."

A chink in the routine. She's never out after bedtime. Alien, the realization there are people out jogging, going to the pub or the shop, when she's normally locked in till morning.

Still, it's bloody freezing. *Why didn't she bring coats for the kids? What kind of mother is she?* She fastens Ella into her buggy and zips her into the liner. She takes off her fleece and puts it on Sophie, rolls up the sleeves. As they walk onto the main road, a double-decker bus thunders past. Sophie waves, the arms of the fleece dangling like a scarecrow's. A couple of passengers wave back.

In Macari's takeaway, Ciara buys a big bag of chips, and they sit at a small white table by the open door. FM104 is playing, a commercial break followed by a list of nineties hits. Using a napkin as a plate, she bends the chips to break them in half, then blows on them and hands them to Ella and Sophie. Her stomach growls. God, the kids must be so hungry.

"What's a dream bathroom?" Sophie asks. "The man said it. He said, *Are you thinking about your dream bathroom?*"

"It's just an ad on the radio, honey."

"What's it mean?"

"You know. Nice tiles. A nice big bath."

A net of bath toys, ducks and boats and mermaids so loved that their eyes have worn off. Like the bathroom they've left behind.

On the way back to the Iona, they stop at a SPAR and Ciara buys a strawberry yogurt and a small carton of milk for Ella's bottle. They climb three flights of stairs to the attic, a homey room with stained pine rafters on the sloped ceilings. Soft white lamps. A wicker chair by the bed. She can hear other guests moving around downstairs, doors opening and closing. There's something comforting about this sound, a reminder they're not alone. The three of them sit together on the double bed. Using a teaspoon from beside the mini kettle, they share the yogurt between them. Hunger sated, things feel a little more manageable.

She feels that muffling, early-pregnancy tiredness washing over her.

"See, isn't this nice?" she says, "Like a wee holiday."

"Like when we went to the caravan in Portrush with Granny, and Ella got sick, and we were too small for the rides, and everyone cried?" Sophie asks.

"Yes. Well. Kind of."

Tantrums on hold, the kids are being weirdly placid. Sophie's face is expectant, as if she's waiting for a cartoon to start and wondering which episode it will be. Clearly this calm won't last but for now, her daughters are watching her every move, curious to see what she'll do next.

"Can we watch some *Amazing Animals* on the tablet, Mammy?"

"We have the tablet?"

"In the nappy bag. Ella shoved it."

"MAZIN MAMMAMULS!"

She scrolls and finds an episode they haven't seen, leans the tablet on a pillow between them.

Did you know that some great white sharks can grow to be half the length of a bus? They can travel at up to sixty kilometers per hour! White sharks attack five to ten people every year! But scientists think they are not trying to eat them! They are just taking a sample bite! Yikes!

Feeling stronger now, she steps out into the hall, propping the door open with her foot. Her heart quickens at the thought of the call she has to make. She can't bring the girls out of the country to her mum's without telling Ryan. She can't. *No need to tell him my every thought, but she has to let him know where they're going. He's their dad.*

When Ryan answers, his voice is calm.

"We're staying in a B&B," she tells him. "I can't take this anymore. I'm sorry for leaving like that. I'm sorry. But I just couldn't."

"I know. These past few months have been incredibly hard on me too."

His reply throws her.

"I want to take the girls over to Mum's for a couple of days, Ryan. To have a breather. To clear my head."

I cannot hear myself think.

A pause. Sophie shouts, "THE SHARKS ARE FINISHED."

Ciara bites her lip. Fighting the urge to tell Ryan everything. Where they are staying. What they had for dinner. It's hard to justify her need to keep him informed of her every move. To keep herself under surveillance. Offering up information before he has even asked for it: returning from the shops, emptying her bags to show kids' leggings, toothpaste, face cloths, so she can't be accused of stealing his money, of lying. The swell of relief from being overly honest and therefore keeping herself in the clear. And now? *A bit of a bloody departure.*

"So that's okay? I can go ahead and book the flights?"

Ryan's voice is quiet, measured. "I understand. Go to your mother's for a few days. You're right, we need to look at doing things differently. We've both been suffering."

"MAMMY!"

"Okay, so I'll call you tomorrow when we get to Sheffield."

"Fine. That's fine. I love you."

He hangs up. She shakes her hair loose. Rubs her hands

over her face. A horrible, sick feeling in her stomach. *You shouldn't have told him. But you had to tell him. You had to.*

Her phone pings. Sinéad.

What was that you were saying earlier? You're out where?

She doesn't deserve her sister's help. How can she put her family through this again? Ryan gets annoyed if he even hears her talking to them on the phone. It's all her fault. If she'd been able to manage him better. If she hadn't annoyed him so much.

Typing and deleting. Reversing blank space over the words she's written. The things she wants to say. Spelled out, it all looks so stupid. After she has composed and erased several different messages, Sinéad sends a GIF of a fat tabby cat face-planting in a sofa. *So tired.* Six sleeping face emojis.

Relieved to have sidestepped the need for explanations, Ciara replies with the laughing face. *Talk to you tomorrow. Tired here too.*

Driving rain hits the skylight like handfuls of grit being thrown against the glass. A sharp, brutal sound, as if hurled with great spite. The fragile calm of the evening has worn off, replaced by sudden freefall. As if the ground has disappeared from beneath her feet. *What are you doing, what are you doing, what are you doing?* In the darkness, she sits up, checks her phone. 3:14 a.m.

Ella lies sprawled diagonally on the double bed, her feet across her mum's legs, hugging Hoppy. After asking around sixty quick-fire questions, ranging from "Why are we here?" to "Do sharks have chins?," Sophie has fallen asleep in a fold-out bed by the wardrobe. As soon as her daughters' breathing was steady with sleep, Ciara went online and booked the flights. From her calculations, she must be down to the last twenty euro on her card.

8:25 Dublin to Manchester. From there, a short train journey to Sheffield.

She has checked in already. In just a few hours, she will be home, talking with Mum and Sinéad. But why, when she revisits her reasons for leaving, does everything feel so shaky? Even last night feels blurry. When she tries to replay the memory, it crackles like a damaged film. Rising in her stomach like a churning seasickness, a feeling of horror. Has she just walked out of her marriage for no reason? What kind of person does that? Closing her eyes, she exhales slowly, makes herself remember. Hands forcing her. Blank stone stare. Inky darkness. That searing pain. Stop. She opens her eyes, shudders to shake the oily caul of the moment from her skin. She stands quickly from the bed, goes to the skylight and opens it a crack, letting in the smell of the rain.

She has to coax herself to a place where she won't buckle. She has to push through this and reach whatever's on the other side. Getting back into bed, she snuggles close to Ella. Her sleeping child mumbles something and flings an arm across her mother's face. They are stowaways in this attic bedroom, waiting for daylight to assess the wreckage.

4

Ciara pulls up the blinds on the Velux windows. Rectangles of sunlight slant across their crumpled beds. She dresses Sophie and Ella in clean tops and leggings. Sophie can't fasten her shoes, but won't let Ciara help her. She says, "It's only the magic in our own house makes me do it!"

Most of the clothes from the washing line belonged to the girls. Ciara's black leggings from yesterday are stained with yogurt. She washed them at the sink in the ensuite, using the tiny bar of lavender soap, but she hasn't been able to get them to dry. She pulls on her white lace vest top and a pair of leopard-print pajama bottoms. Hopefully they look like patterned trousers, the kind she's seen the other mums at playschool wearing.

Her denim jacket was in the car. She pulls that on, untangles her hair with her fingers and uses a baby wipe to remove the grainy under-eye shadows of yesterday's mascara. She folds the rest of the clothes into two red SuperValu shopping bags from the glove compartment.

Just as they are leaving the attic bedroom, her phone pings. Ryan. She reads it while helping Ella down the stairs, into the breakfast room.

I know what's happening. You're not coming back. Last night I lay in my children's room and wept

Sophie and Ella won't eat the B&B breakfast.

"Mammy," Sophie explains, "these Krispies are not the same as the ones at home."

Ella throws her spoon and shouts, "WANT PORRIDGE!"

She gives them each a banana from the buffet. Small tumblers of milk. Toast triangles. Mini pots of raspberry jam. Sticky hands reaching to wipe on her top. She sips a mug of weak tea, stomach turning at the smell of fried eggs and bacon.

I love you so much. I don't understand why you are doing this

Her head hurts.

After breakfast, she herds the girls out of the Iona, down another side street to double-check that the Micra is locked, then round the corner to the main road. The 16 will take them to the airport.

"Wow Mammy, look!"

An Aer Lingus plane glides over their heads. When Ciara steps through the double set of sliding doors into Departures, the noise rises up to meet her. So many people. Everyone seems intent, purposeful, gliding past with their wheeled suitcases toward the check-in area and departure gates. She stalls, causing an obstruction. Holding on to her two girls, their red plastic shopping bags of washing. People flow past to either side of them, looking at their phones or tilting their chins up to read the flight boards.

She used to love airports. All these strangers. The feeling of hope, excitement. All those autumns when she set off for a new country, a new English teaching job. They'd never had holidays abroad when she was a child, apart from the ferry trips over to Ireland each summer, when her mum could afford it. She was twenty-three when she first got on a plane—

"Mammy, me up!"

She lifts Ella and starts walking toward the departures gate, sidesteps a couple kissing, the woman standing on tiptoes to lock her arms around her boyfriend's neck.

They queue at security and take off their runners. Cringing, she loads their plastic bags into trays on the conveyor belt. Three or four pegs are still attached to leggings and skirt hems, their coiled metal springs setting off the scanner. The man and woman behind the desk laugh but are gentle with her. "Family emergency," she blushes.

"Not to worry, love."

You're so beautiful, I've never met anyone like you

"On the BIG plane! Going to see Granny!"

I've loved you since the moment I first saw you. I will love you my whole life. Please give us another chance

"Flight FR548 to Manchester is now boarding."

"Sorry love, if you could just wait here please."

Her face feels hot. The flight attendant has taken their passports and is leaning toward a colleague as they study them. The first man comes back, rubbing a hand over his face. Salt-and-pepper hair. Kind brown eyes. A Northside accent. "Sorry love, but do you have written permission from the children's other parent?"

"I'm sorry?"

He sighs, shuts the passports gently and passes them back to her. He lowers his voice. "There's been a hold placed on the children's passports, love. They can't leave the country without permission from their other parent. From their dad. It should have come up, whoever sold you the flights should have—"

"But he said it was okay. On the phone, he said..."

She feels the queue of people staring at them, but when she glances over nobody is looking. *So stupid.* She sees him now, stepping outside, fresh from the shower, finding the garden empty, pegs strewn across the lawn. How long did it take for him to reach for his phone and call the guards? That conversation last night. *He must have been laughing at me.*

"What do we do now? What do we...?"

"If you go with Jason here, he'll bring you back round to the front. Have you someone you can contact?"

The Departures Hall is too noisy to make a phone call. She brings the girls back through the double sliding doors, into the cold air.

Sophie and Ella sit on the bags of washing, against the glass wall by the Coffee Dock. While the girls are occupied eating a bag of mini rice cakes, Ciara takes a biro from the side pocket of her bag and scribbles a few words on the back of her hand, like prompt notes for a lesson. As the dial tone rings, she tries to read what she's written but her hands are so sweaty the ink has melted, blending into her freckles.

"Ryan, I thought you said it was okay for us to go over to Mum's for a few days. You said it was okay. Now I'm at the airport and—"

He laughs, "Great. After what you've put me through this past twenty-four hours. Now you're phoning up, making demands."

Her mind races. She's scanning the indecipherable mess of her inky hand. On the white church behind the bus terminal, gold lettering. GOD IS LOVE.

Sophie says, "Rice cakes all gone! You have any more snacks?"

"Come home and we'll talk," Ryan says.

Home. She swallows hard.

"No," she hears herself saying. "Can we not talk on the phone?"

"In person. We need to talk in person. This impacts my children, this is going to have a damaging impact on them for life and you can't even spare five minutes to meet me and discuss—"

"Okay, okay. I will meet you. I'll have to go and get the car, then I'll bring the girls to playschool. It's early enough. I can still get them there and then I'll meet you."

It's as if the efficient voice of Sinéad has taken over, filling the static.

"The Phoenix Park café at ten," he says.

"Okay," she says, "I'll see you there."

He hangs up and her head starts pounding.

Where will they sleep tonight? Will there still be a room at the Iona? Where will they go?

She could go to a refuge. These places exist, don't they? But what would she say? *My husband does not speak to me kindly. Things happen at night, things I can't even talk about. My body doesn't feel like my own. His jaw clicks when he is angry. I think he might hit me, but he hasn't.* All these things seem to vanish as soon as she tries to put them into words.

I cannot hear myself think. I do not know who I am anymore. I do not know if I exist. I feel like a ghost. Life energy drained. A bloodless, cowered feeling.

He has spun her around so that the earth no longer feels stable. She doesn't know which way is forward and which is back.

5

She's found a stick of eyeliner in a sandy corner of the glove compartment. She pulls down the sun visor and uses the tiny rectangular mirror to draw a thin black line along her upper lashes. *War paint*. She fixes her tangled ponytail, rubs a jam stain from her top, gets out of the car and walks along the walled garden to the Phoenix Café.

"Car trouble," she told Mairéad, to explain why they were an hour late for playschool. Why the girls had a SPAR sandwich and a pack of cheese-and-onion Taytos instead of their usual lunchboxes, their pots of sliced fruit. Sophie held back reluctantly at the gate. Ciara kissed their foreheads and dashed back to the car, before either of them had a chance to protest.

It's strange being in the park without Ella and Sophie. The girls love to play house here, under the dark yews on the lawns beside the café. Weekends, when she's forever inventing excuses to be out, they've spent hours here, stooping under dense leaf canopies, shady green caves. She can hear their laughter in the lagoons of swaying tree shadow, see them clambering along branches worn smooth as polished teak by centuries of children's palms. The warmth of the memory centers her, calms her. She's doing this for them. So they don't grow up thinking this is what relationships look like.

In the courtyard behind the café, she finds a seat at one of the wrought-iron tables and waits. This must have been a stable yard, long ago. On one side, the Phoenix Park Museum, high barred windows overlooking the whitewashed square.

She feels his presence before she sees him.

Ryan hands her a bunch of chrysanthemums in crinkly cellophane, leans over and kisses her cheek. Caught off balance, she stares at the white ooze of cut stems. She's not sure if she should thank him. He will be angry if she doesn't.

While she's deciding what to say, Ryan stands over her, frowning. "Why are you wearing pajamas? And where are the kids?"

"At playschool, remember? I told you..." Her voice trails off. She looks down at her legs, cold in the thin leopard-print fabric.

"No, you didn't tell me. You never tell me anything." He pulls a seat out, sits down opposite her, spreads his palms. "So?"

He's wearing a burgundy V-neck jumper over a cotton shirt, his fresh shaven cheeks ruddy in the cool morning air. This is how he must look at meetings in the Department of Public Expenditure, earnestly explaining his spreadsheets. Something catches in her, snags. There's a sincerity about him, that sweetness she first fell for. Now he's in front of her, she cannot remember a single reason why she wanted to leave him. Her body is recoiling from the conversation, as if from icy water. She's messing with the tarnished buttons on her jacket cuffs, avoiding his eyes. From a distance, perhaps, this looks like a first date.

Then the facade slips. He shakes his head once. There is a cruelty to the gesture, swift as a passing cloud shadow. He says, "I need coffee before I can deal with this bullshit. You want one?"

"Just water."

He goes into the café and she waits, watching gulls with hooked yellow beaks strut the cobblestones, pecking dropped crumbs. By the archway, a woman in a red bandanna is twirling her hair at a man in a flat cap. Two little boys are licking ice-cream cones while their drooling Dobermann watches with a sort of heartbreak.

What are you going to say what are you going to say what are you going to say?

Ryan places a glass of water in front of her, ice cubes clinking. He slides back into his seat, rips open a sugar sachet, pours it into his espresso and speaks without looking at her. "Tell me your mother isn't behind this. Because honestly, this has Rhona Devine all over it."

"Mum doesn't even know."

Why does he make her feel like she's lying, even when she's not?

He scoffs, stirring his coffee. "I find that hard to believe. You can tell Rhona to stop using my children. Just because she's messed up her own life, she doesn't need to take over yours as well. Just because she's lonely and depressed."

She wants to put her hands over her ears. Coldness trills through her again, a feeling of vulnerability. She's completely naked with Ryan. All those traded confidences when they first met, spilled in a flush of love. The things she shouldn't have told him. *My dad left when I was a only a baby, Sinéad just gone three... Mum should have moved home to Derry but she's way too stubborn.* Ciara cringes at the memory of saying all this while Ryan listened, stroking her hair. She wants to scream. *Stop. Just shut up. Don't you know how he'll seize this? How he'll bring it up over and over, until you don't know which insecurities were yours originally, which were planted and nurtured by him?* She tries to steady her voice. "This has nothing to do with my mum."

The place is bustling, but she and Ryan are in a silent, still space, outside of time. She's sitting on the bed in the house in Glasnevin, back to the headboard, holding newborn Ella to her chest, eyeing the doorway behind him.

"You know how bad things have been." Her voice is gravelly.

He doesn't respond, so she tries a different tack. "I just wanted to bring them to Mum's for a few days. I thought we could all use some space. But I wasn't able to."

"What could I do? I had to do that. I had to contact the guards. I knew if you left the country, I'd never see my children again."

"That's not true, Ryan. You know that's not true. I'm not like that."

He takes her hands, peers at her until she is forced to make eye contact. "What do you want? Did you not get my messages?"

The bitter aroma of Ryan's coffee is making Ciara want to heave. She loves coffee normally. She takes a gulp of water.

"I'd like a separation," she hears herself saying politely, as if she were asking for another glass of water. He drops her hands. It feels as if her throat is closing, trying to stop the words from getting out. Her voice sounds very far away. The high courtyard walls amplify every sound, filling the space with echoes. Like being trapped in a giant glass bowl.

She's looking away from Ryan, up at the barred courtyard windows. Down at the mossy cobblestones. She says, "I don't want to fight. I want to work together for the sake of the kids." He doesn't say anything, so she keeps talking. "You won't let me go home to Sheffield. So, I was thinking, if you could at least move out of the house and let me and the girls stay there for now, it would be easier. For them. Until I find somewhere else."

He is watching her face intently. "What's happening? Why are you doing this?"

"After the other night—"

"What? Nothing happened the other night. Babe. I love you so much. This is insane."

"Look, Ryan, if we can just agree on a plan with the house."

"You want me to leave my house? Okay, this is actually crazy. How do you think you're going to manage?"

"I'll manage. I'll get a job. I'll figure it out."

"A job?" He finishes his espresso, stands. "I love you so

much, babe. I love you to death. But I can't be around you when you're being crazy like this. And you're pregnant." His eyes are testing her. He nods in confirmation. "I knew it. That's why you're being so crazy. Listen, I have to get to work. I've already missed a department meeting. I'll see you at home later."

They stand and he pulls her into a firm hug. Her head is hot, tears threatening to rupture, and his hands are on her cheek and he's wiping her tears away with his thumbs and he's saying, "Come on. I love you. Don't do this."

6

"Left? As in left for good? Jesus Christ, Ciara. QUIET RORY MUM IS BUSY." She can hear Sinéad walking through her house. A door clicks shut. "Right, I've locked myself in the loo for a bit of quiet. Holy fuck though, Ciara. Where are you?"

"In the park. Heading now to get the girls from playschool."

She explains about the flights, what happened at the airport, and how Ryan is refusing to leave their house. She's already phoned the Iona. They are fully booked for tonight and nothing is coming up on booking.com. "There must be something on," she says.

"It's bloody Beyoncé," Sinéad says. "She's on at the 3Arena tonight. Sure it's all over Instagram, people giving out about the hotel prices. Booked out for months. Jesus, Ciara have you not heard?"

Surely Sinéad knows about the bubble she's been living in. She deleted her social media long ago. Stopped listening to the news. Stopped seeing friends.

"I have to go and pick Sophie and Ella up, I'll be late."

"Go, go. Phone me back."

The girls are standing on the driveway of Happy Days

looking forlorn. The last two kids to be collected. Mairéad is rubbing Sophie's back, holding Ella's hand. Sophie's tears have slowed to hiccupping sobs. Like evacuees on a railway platform, the long faces on them. You'd think she had abandoned them for weeks.

"There now, there's mum. I told you she'd be here, didn't I?" Mairéad smiles at Ciara.

"I am so, so sorry, Mairéad, something came up and I—"

"Not to worry. Sure these things happen. You've never been late before. Someone was just a wee bit upset about her lunchbox, weren't you love? But I told her I'm sure you'll have your lunchbox tomorrow."

On the car radio the time is 13:10. She needs to make phone calls, to find somewhere for tonight. But as soon as they get into the car, Sophie starts crying hysterically.

"My lunch bag and my box of grapes!"

Nothing for it, they will have to go back to the house.

The coconut shells she hung last winter are still tied to the holly bush by her old front door. The insides of the shells have been scraped clean, scoured by tiny beaks. Sophie and Ella run on ahead, up the drive of Botanic Close, batting the papery heads of her daffodils. Sophie asks, "Is the heating fixed yet?"

"Hungry," Ella says.

"No love, it's not fixed yet. We're just grabbing a few things."

"My lunchbox!"

"Yes, Sophie. We will get your lunchbox."

Ciara puts her key in the lock. Opening the door makes

her think of her mum's word heartsick, and it takes all her willpower not to phone Ryan and tell him they're moving back immediately. The smell hits her. Sunday night's pasta bake. Ryan's pine-scented deodorant. Those incense sticks he insists on lighting. She feels herself tensing. Ella and Sophie career past her into the living room and start pulling toys out of boxes. *This will only take a minute.* While they are here, they may as well bring a few other things. She needs some jeans or leggings. Something that's not pajamas.

The girls' Tupperware boxes are upside down on the draining board where she left them yesterday. The lunch bags, left open on the kitchen counter. Heart fast, she slides open the patio door, and crouches to lift Sophie's box of dinosaurs from the wet grass. The cardboard is sodden, soaked by last night's rain.

A heat flushes through her. A surge of early-pregnancy warmth she remembers from her other babies. She's sweating, takes off her denim jacket and leaves it on a kitchen chair. But now she's cold. Sweating and shivering.

The girls are hungry. Sophie says they didn't eat the big box sandwich. "It wasn't the right kind of cheese, Mammy," she explains.

In the kitchen, Ciara takes a half-finished wholegrain loaf from the bread bin, pulls out four slices and slathers them with Flora. She grates some cheese, quarters the sandwiches, saws off the crusts.

She has to get moving. She has to find a room for tonight.

"On the sofa, girls. Quickly."

She sets the plates on their knees, turns on Netflix. Once

they are settled, she takes the roll of black bin bags from under the sink and runs upstairs.

In the bedroom, it's suddenly harder to breathe. Ryan's clothes are everywhere. His dirty pants and socks surround the overflowing laundry basket. Tea-stained mugs are stacked on the nightstand. The duvet tousled, his pillow yellowed with night sweat. What will she do if he comes home early?

Her side of the bed is almost empty. A lone coaster on the nightstand. A stray hair bobbin. There are so few traces of her in this house. Why can she only see that now? All those boxes of books from her English degree, still buried somewhere in the garage. Ryan said no one had any need for *Shakespeare's Sonnets* to be on display. *Beloved*. *The Color Purple*. Books she once carried across continents. Her clothes occupy only a small corner of the wardrobe. She pulls two faded hoodies and a handful of cheap tops off their hangers. An old navy blazer, from her teaching days. A black maxi dress that probably wouldn't even fit her now. Black leggings. Torn jeans, hard with over-washing.

A flurry of starlings lands in the conifers behind the house, their speckled plumage a turquoise gleam. She thinks of her mum's backyard with its array of birdfeeders refilled daily. Paving stones, white with sesame shells and bird shit. Rhona loves birds, can identify any bird from its song. Her mum would know what to do, what to pack.

Like a signal, she spots the corner of her old suitcase under the bed. She yanks it out, coughing on dust. This will make life easier. She folds her clothes into the case, then goes into the girls' room and starts pulling out drawers. Grabbing only the most valuable, the most essential, she's feeling oddly calm. Some part of her brain is focused on the high flutter of birdsong. The certainty that she's doing the right thing. Packing all their worldly possessions into this same banjaxed wheelie suitcase she's lugged across so many airports. Pink camouflage pattern. The ugliest suitcase in the world. Easily spotted at baggage reclaim.

Soon the case is full. She shakes out a black bin bag, starts filling it. Soft toy animals. Spare runners. A full bag of nappies. She shakes out another bag for toiletries. Johnson's baby bath. Face wash. Moisturizer. Another bag she fills with kids' books. *The Gruffalo, Room on the Broom, That's Not My Puppy.* Book corners straining, ready to puncture the thin plastic.

Towels? No space. Maybe just one. Her Brazilian flag towel. She remembers buying it on the coast road at Caraguatatuba, from a shack almost hidden by a dense bank of acai palms.

Laptop.

Baby photos? Baby shoes! *Stop crying. Stop stop stop.*

Makeup bag.

Maternity leggings. *Where the hell are your maternity bras? Mog the Forgetful Cat.* Duplo blocks.

She checks her phone. 14:32.

Time to make a move.

She lugs the suitcase down to the car, shoves it into the boot, then goes back for the bin bags. Soon the car is packed to bursting. She jogs into the kitchen for her jacket. Bedtime bottles. Spare teats. From the press above the worktop, a six-pack of oatmeal bars. Rice cakes. Alphabet biscuits.

One last check around the living room. The listening beige

walls, the stairs, dust piled at their edges, the porcelain-white lampshades all hold the painful knowledge that they were sometimes happy here. Looking around, she sees traces of those fleeting moments. Piggybacks up the stairs. The girls' wobbling first steps across this maroon carpet. Sunday morning, maybe only once or twice, when the girls piled into their parents' bed, and it seemed, everything seemed—

Something catches her attention. A box slung by the window. A box full of picture frames.

At the top of the pile, a framed photo of her wedding day. The glass a fractured cobweb, the image refracted into tiny shards. Did he throw it? Punch it? It's as if the picture has absorbed the hate leveled at it. Her smile, slit.

"Right then girls. Time to go." She turns off the TV. "Ella, bring Hoppy."

Her heart is so loud she can barely hear herself speak. Sophie and Ella are ignoring her. She says, "Come on, we have to go."

Sophie huffs, "No I don't want to."

"Sophie, please. I'll buy you some chocolate."

"But I want to play here!"

"Here, we'll bring the dinosaurs with us, right? Look I've got the box of dinos. We'll bring all of these."

She picks up the wet shoebox again and it rips. Dinosaurs tumble out. She grabs a shopping bag from the drawer under the sink, hurling triceratops, brachiosaurus and T-rex into a Tesco carrier. Ella is helping, all sunny smiles. "There go!"

Sophie proudly carries the bag out of the house. "And they can play with my pterodactyl and I got my lunchbox and—"

She buckles them into the car, drives away. At the traffic lights, she sees Ryan's black jeep pulling in at the Circle K petrol station. He must have finished work early. Or maybe he didn't go to work at all. He gets out, straightens his belt and reaches for the pump. On his bumper, a pro-life sticker of an embryo with its umbilical cord knotted into a love heart.

An elderly man pulls in at the pump behind Ryan, leaning into the car for his walking stick. She watches her husband step over, gesturing to the man, asking if he needs help. From this distance, he's just a nice, well-dressed civil servant. Respectful to everyone. A regular Mass attender. Volunteer at the local GAA club. Monaghan accent only slightly diluted by years of living in Dublin. Devoted to his parents. Nothing to be scared of. His eyes are hidden behind sunglasses that reflect the sky. Clouds race.

7

Low-Low Town is a miniature city built for toddlers. In a high-ceilinged former industrial warehouse, children from crawling age upward careen around in Little Tikes cars and loot the mini supermarket with plastic trolleys, which they abandon in the mini jail. These places are torture. The bright walls. The headachy lights. But the play session costs only €8, and it will buy her some time.

Sophie and Ella hand over their runners at reception. Ciara sits at one of the round tables with all the other bored-looking adults. She watches the girls climb padded frames and slide into ball pits. From a ten-foot-high platform, they wave down at her through the mesh. She gives them a thumbs up. Then she takes out her phone, starts scrolling and dialing and praying. Searching booking sites. Listening to hold music. Vivaldi. Mozart.

Everywhere in Dublin is fully booked.

"Beyoncé," everyone tells her. "Are youse going to the gig?"

There's a room on Airbnb for €110 per night, but it turns out there is a minimum five-night stay. She keeps searching. Sinéad is on a twelve-hour shift at the hospital. After 5 p.m.

she messages: *Ciara, I know you don't want to hear this, but there must be somewhere you can call. A helpline? For people with nowhere to go x*

A beeper sounds. Their play session is up. The girls slither down from the slides, and she sits them at her circular table for chicken nuggets and chips, served on clown plates. Another €9. Boxes of blackberry-and-apple juice. Paper straws, a disaster. Purple juice dribbles down their chins. When they have finished eating, she brings them to the toilets. She changes Ella's nappy on the rickety fold-out changing table. Insists Sophie uses the loo. Tries not to let them see she's crying.

On their way out, they collect their battered runners from the cubbyhole behind the counter. The young man handing out the shoes says, "Thanks guys! Safe home!"

In her car, parked under an orange streetlamp, Ciara googles *emergency accommodation Dublin.*

Dublin City Centre Homeless Executive.

Homeless. She feels herself inhale sharply. *Jesus.*

She clears her throat, dials the number. "Hush, hush." She looks over her shoulder at the girls, puts a finger on her lips.

Voicemail. "This line operates between nine and five, Monday to Friday. Outside of these hours please contact the Emergency Homeless Helpline."

When she gets through to the emergency line, a woman tells her there will be a wait. People are being allocated accommodation on a case-by-case basis. It is extremely busy tonight. She takes Ciara's number, says they will phone back. She is number twenty-nine in the queue.

*

Feeling lightheaded, she drives around the Northside, waiting for the phone to ring. She tells herself, this is happening.

Sophie and Ella start squabbling, so she presses play on the CD player. *Ladybird Traditional Tales.* It's bloody Cinderella, she realizes too late. As if that's what she needs right now. *And they lived happily ever after.* Next up is Sleeping Beauty. The girls won't let her turn it off.

The time on the car radio says 20:34.

Both girls are bright-eyed and yawning. Ciara's neck hurts.

She pulls in at the Applegreen petrol station on the Navan Road, dashes in and fills Ella's nighttime bottle from the milk dispenser by the coffee machine, checking over her shoulder to make sure no one is watching. Back in the car, she phones the Emergency Homeless Helpline again. The same woman eventually answers and says sorry, they are at capacity. There's nothing for tonight. Their best bet is to register at the Central Placement Service on Parkgate Street in the morning. The office opens at nine. If she is stuck for tonight, she can present at the local garda station.

Dear God, you can't do that. You can't have the kids sleeping in a cell.

Ciara thanks the woman and hangs up.

A siren whoops somewhere nearby. The night feels somehow darker.

Sinéad is phoning now, but she can't answer. She could go back to the house. But look at how angry he was before she left. He will be even angrier now. Two years ago, when she first left him, she only stayed away for three weeks. When she returned, the feeling of punishment was palpable. The house was filthy. She had to scrub caked-in shit off the toilets, wipe congealed grease off the cooker. From that point on, he said his every mood, every outburst, was her fault, caused by the stress of her leaving. She had given him the perfect excuse.

She gets out of the car. Leans into the back seat and tucks the soft blanket around the girls. "Close your eyes now, have a wee rest."

Turning out of the Applegreen, she drives up toward Castleknock, checking the mirror. If she keeps driving, surely they will fall asleep. The girls' eyes keep closing, heads lolling, but they wake up each time she stops at a red light. If only she could just drive without stopping. Half a tank of petrol left, Ciara drives up the Navan Road, through the crossroads, onto the M50.

She's reminded of nights when Sophie was weeks old. The motion of the car was the only thing that would get her to sleep. She remembers buckling her baby girl into the car and driving off, at three or four in the morning, the roads empty, racing up to traffic lights, willing them to stay green. A getaway driver. If the car stopped at all, Sophie would wake and start crying. Ryan hated being woken at night, so it was just Ciara and her daughter speeding around the M50, in search of sleep.

It's a clear night. The circular motorway merges onto the southbound N11, out of Dublin. No more streetlights: she's driving into darkness, only able to see as far as the stretch of road caught in her headlights. The further they get from the city, the more stars emerge in the dark blanket of sky. A quarter-moon floats overhead. She remembers overnight car journeys from Sheffield to Derry. The five-hour drive up to Stranraer in Scotland, ready for the early morning crossing to Larne. *Mum, the moon's following us.*

The road snakes past mountainsides dark with jagged pines, through the valley of Devil's Glen, deeper into the Wicklow Mountains. On instinct, she turns off the N11 onto a narrower road that climbs higher, onto the moors. Ryan brought her up here one August night to watch the Perseids meteor shower. Their first summer together. She was in love and stupidly happy, brimming with that feeling of gratitude toward the universe. Lying back on the cold car bonnet, waiting for tiny spits of light to streak the sky. A bottle of sweet pear cider. His hand in hers. A tightness starts up under her ribcage.

"Mammy, where we going?"

"Soph. You're meant to be asleep."

"But where are we going?"

"We're going camping."

"But we don't have a tent."

"We're camping without a tent. It's even more fun."

She's been driving for over an hour and a half when a wave of tiredness floods her. Pregnancy tiredness. The watery quality of it reminds her of the weight of ocean waves. The feeling of being overwhelmed, pulled under by the current. Her eyelids are drooping. This isn't safe.

On a hillside, she pulls into a gravelly lay-by. Ella has been asleep since they left Dublin and finally Sophie has drifted off too. She keeps the engine running for a bit of heat, takes out her phone and messages Sinéad: *We are okay. We are staying with a friend tonight x*

What friend? Sure you don't have any friends

Thanks Sinéad

Stop. You know what I mean. ARE YOU SAFE? Xxx

There's no one about. Only the watchful sway of the pines, ruffling in the wind. She messages Sinéad a few more times, reassures her. She just has to get through tonight, then go to the housing office in the morning. They will surely help. Things will seem clearer in the light of day.

A message from Ryan.

I see you have emptied the place out. I do not understand what is happening. I'm so traumatized by all of this. If you are not coming back, then we need to talk about custody.

Her heart lurches in her chest. Sophie and Ella, asleep in the backseat. Children she has raised entirely by herself. Every late-night dose of Calpol or course of violent yellow antibiotics, every piss-wet sheet, or vomited-on towel, every tear, every pinstriped birthday candle. She has done all of it. Her life has shrunk down into a rock-hard kernel, and that kernel is her kids.

For a second, she's back in the garden again, fear and adrenaline soon replaced by her instinct to placate him. She types back. *Why don't we meet up again and talk about things properly?*

If you don't come back, I'm contacting a solicitor.

A molten heat is spreading across her chest bone. She turns

her phone off, drops it into her bag. The backs of her eyes feel hot. She is a twitching, eye-darting furred thing, backed into the thorny undergrowth. Hunger gnaws. A film of bile sits at the back of her throat. She should have pushed through the nausea, eaten something at the play center. Thoughts dart, hurtle, spin.

You should go back you should go back you should go back you should go back you should go back you should go back. What are you doing what are you doing what are you doing? You should go back you should go back you should go back you should go back you should go back you should go back. What are you doing what are you doing what are you doing?

"MAMMY!"

"Ella! How are you still awake?"

"Mazin mamamuls. Let's watch the mazin mamamuls, Mammy."

"It's too noisy, love. It'll wake Sophie."

"MAMAMULS!"

"Right, okay, okay. I'll tell you about them so. The Christmas crabs sometimes eat each other, and the ants shoot poison into their eyes."

"More!"

"And the secretary bird stomps its prey to death with its massive talons. A blue whale can do a fart so big, a horse could fit inside it. And an owl's feathers are basically soundless..."

Ella has drifted off, clutching Hoppy's ear in her chubby fist.

It feels like she has found a parking spot at the end of the universe. Hard to imagine that just round the next forest bend, she would see the light spill of the city. Memories fizz and blur. Moments caught in strobe light. Dancing with Ryan. His lips on her bare shoulders. Sophie's first cry from behind the blue surgical curtain. That splintered cup, rolling on its side in the sink. Flecks of china on her hands. Ryan's voice, overhead in conversation with his brother on the phone. *I really let her have it. Disrespecting me like that. Don't you worry, I really let her have it.* Pine needles. Forgotten beanie animals with glassy rainbow eyes.

8

She wakes into white mist. Overnight, a cloud has descended on the mountain, leaving the pines barely visible. Apocalyptic, as if the rest of the world has disappeared. When she moves, her neck and shoulders hurt like they have been held in a vice, and there's a sour taste in her mouth.

Tucked against the steering wheel, on her mum's knee, Ella is stirring. She woke several times during the night, crying out.

"Where are we, Mammy?" Sophie is pushing off the blanket, leaning over her mum's shoulder, yawning. "What's for breakfast?"

Ciara gets out of the car, into the cool damp whiteness. She tries to rub the ache from her neck, shakes her legs, stamping away the pins and needles. Ella and Sophie clamber out too. They jump around and kick at the gravel while she rummages in the packed boot for oatmeal bars, cartons of juice.

As the fog begins to thin, the world slides back into focus. Beside the lay-by, there's a field of honey-brown cows with wet noses, chewing cud and watching them intently. Wood pigeons coo in the firs. From further down the mountainside, the loud, indignant bleat of lambs. It sounds like they are shouting MAM! MAM!

Once the girls are fed, she drives slowly back into the city. She's almost out of petrol. What was she thinking, driving all the way out here? The girls are still hungry, so she has to stop and buy them more snacks. Now she's stuck in traffic. *Stupid, driving to Wicklow. Stupid, stupid*. She had a twenty in her purse this morning, but has already spent €7.50 on muffins and apple juice. *They'll need to eat again soon. Lunch. Dinner.*

Nothing for it, they'll have to abandon the car and walk. Driving through the Phoenix Park, she turns off Chesterfield Avenue and swings into the cricket club car park. A sign on a nearby lamp post says *Parking is Reserved for Members of the Cricket Club Only. Clamping in Operation*. But there's no one about. She will risk it. Glancing at the rear-view mirror, she catches Sophie watching her. "We going to the swings again?" her daughter asks.

"No, love. We're going ... for a meeting."

"Cool! We never did that before!"

All the things are happening today. All the things she never did before.

What came over her last night? She can't quite understand how she acted. Bloody stupid, driving off like that.

She turns her phone back on.

Ryan (15 missed calls)

Ella is tired, wants to go in her buggy. It's in the middle of the packed boot, under bulging bin bags, which she hefts onto the gravel. The wheels are caught on something. She wrestles to untangle it, and another of the bin bags rips. Ciara unfolds it, straps Ella in, jams everything back into the boot, and starts walking toward Parkgate Street.

What is she going to say?

A malty breeze is wafting from the Guinness brewery. At the rich, hoppy smell, her nausea stirs. Her mouth is dry. She feels herself slowing as they near the gate of the park, and their destination.

Starlings sweep between clouds. The birds break formation, scattered granules across a dove-gray sky. Sophie runs across the wide lawn around the Wellington memorial. *Try to be present,* isn't that what those parenting websites are always telling her? She exhales slowly, tries to focus on the calm expanse of the park. After five years of marriage, she's developed a love of open spaces. She's learnt to be wary of any contained situation, to avoid being cornered. Car journeys. The kitchen. Their bed.

What exactly is she going to say?

A young boy flies past on an electric scooter, followed by a girl who shouts "MOVE, YOUSE! MOVE!" A butterfly lands on a dandelion by Sophie's feet. She crouches to examine it, watching as it closes its wings. "Look, Mammy, it's camouflaging itself."

Her phone is ringing.

"Ciara?"

At her mum's voice, Ciara feels as if she's just fallen from a great height and been caught.

"Ciara, love. Sinéad told me. You must be awful scared."

How does Mum do this? How does she manage to intuit

everything before a word is said? She's part safety net, part tornado.

"I'm serious, Mum. I'm not going back this time. I'm just trying to figure something out. We'll be okay. Last night was rough, but we're walking now to this place where they will help us."

"Me and Sinéad will come and get you, so we will."

"No, Mum."

"We'll drive over to Holyhead. I'll book the ferry."

"No. Mum, you don't get it!" She lowers her voice. "Didn't Sinéad tell you? Ryan won't let me take them out of the country. I tried. We were stopped at the departures gate. Because of last time."

Two years ago. An icy January. Ella only three weeks old, Sophie not yet two. The night before she left, she sat on their bed with Ella asleep against her chest while Ryan towered over them, jabbing his finger, then putting his face inches from hers, saying something. Saying what? All she can remember is the way his jaw clicked, his pupils dilated, turning his eyes black. He was trying to get her to agree with something, that was it. "Say it. What's wrong with you? Why can't you just say it? Just say it."

When she said no, there was a moment when his rage seemed to flare and all the air was sucked from the room. He lurched toward her, the veins in his neck pulsing, muscles tensed, eyes bright with hate. She shielded Ella with both arms and braced herself. At the last minute, he backed down, storming from the room, leaving her with her heart in her throat.

Later, she carried Ella into Sophie's room and kept a vigil over both of them, sitting with her back to the locked bedroom door. After he'd gone to work the next day, she got the girls into the car and drove to the airport. She can still see Sophie, her pigtails bouncing as she danced over her reflection on the polished tiles of the departure gate, waving at the planes. *Flight FR102 to Manchester is now boarding.* The relief of home.

And yet within days of landing back at her mum's red-brick house on Bate Street, she felt as if she had stepped back into the raw days post-partum. Emotions fraying. Uncontained. A formless, shapeless darkness. Permanency shattered. Home, stability, gone. She couldn't stop crying, filled with the horror of it. The sense that this must be happening to someone else. *You've walked out of your house with a tiny baby and a toddler. What kind of mother does that?* The voice of her demons, which was now Ryan's voice as well, shouted so loudly she could barely remember to eat, sleep, or feed her children.

Rhona took over, putting on batches of laundry, hanging her granddaughters' dungarees and sleepsuits to dry on the radiators, sending ferns of condensation up the windows. In Ciara's childhood bedroom with its view over Sheffield city, her mother held her. Rhona cooked the steaming casseroles and Irish stews of her schooldays. Sinéad came over with Rory running round her knees, and sat at the kitchen table drinking endless mugs of tea, frowning while she listened to Ciara. Some nights Sinéad didn't leave. She stayed sitting on the sofa with her sister, legs tucked under them, talking in low voices like when they were teenagers. Ciara had a sense of everyone being careful with language, wary of causing greater hurt, of tipping her into a decision. She didn't tell her family everything that had happened. Neither did she speak about the emails from her mother-in-law, detailing the specific tortures of hell reserved for women who break their marriage vows.

They'd been gone three days when Ryan arrived at her mum's house, holding a bunch of yellow roses and a stuffed bear the size of a five-year-old child. He sat in Rhona's good room, on her brown corduroy sofa, its worn patches hidden by bright, cheap scatter cushions. He hugged one of the cushions, sobbed and used all the tissues. Her mum quietly replaced the box, throwing Ciara a quick, unreadable glance. Ryan smiled through his tears, "Thank you, Rhona. We are so grateful to you. For helping save this marriage."

He slept on the sofa without complaining. He got up early and cooked a full Irish breakfast for everyone. In the evenings, she sat with him on the sofa, watching old movies on the small TV, the door propped open so she could hear the chatter of Rhona's kitchen radio. Each afternoon, he took Ella and Sophie to the park so she could rest. Those afternoons in her childhood bed, she slept as if she might never wake, safe in the knowledge that leaving was just a mistake. After two nights, Ryan returned to Dublin, saying he would see her at home.

Still, she didn't leave Sheffield. Rhona didn't ask about her plans, but kept bringing breakfast to her room each morning, and sidestepped around her decision. "Whatever you think is best, love. I don't want him saying I've influenced you. Take your time."

Ryan's messages started. Hundreds of messages. A montage of photos, relentless. Their wedding day. The delivery ward at the Rotunda, holding newborn Sophie. Each image stung. She thought about reptiles shedding skin. Already it felt as if these memories had happened to somebody else. There was a truth she was trying to reach. She just needed more time.

"Three weeks is long enough," he said on the phone one night.

She tried to sweet-talk him. "Surely we should take whatever time we need to get back on track. This isn't a good note to start on. Ultimatums. Threats."

He laughed, "What, are you kidding? How could you think I'm threatening you? I'm being so patient. I've been so kind. If you aren't back by Friday, I'm hiring a solicitor and changing the locks."

Now, on the phone, her mum sighs. "Well, this is just—Hang on a minute, Sinéad's Peter is here doing a job for me. Peter! It's Ciara on the phone! She says she can't take the weans out of the country without that arsehole's consent! Is that right now? Would you ask—"

"Mum, just phone me back. Talk to Pete and call me back."

"What's that? Peter love, I can't hear you—"

"Phone me back, Mum, love you. Bye!"

Jesus. Why does everyone in her family always do that—talk to someone else when you're on the phone? She unbuttons her denim jacket, flustered. Annoyed, that's it. She's really bloody annoyed. One call and they're already diving in trying to save her. As if she can't—has never been capable of—saving herself. And that feeling of *Stop smothering me, stop, stop proving him right.* Ryan's voice in her head. *Bloody hell, babe. Growing up with your family up your arse like that. No wonder you're so negative about relationships, God help you!* That pang in her chest. What if he was right? Her family are maddening. Here's her mum phoning again now.

"Right Ciara, so our Peter's away off to talk to Pat McCormack down the road, you know the wee man whose wife died of the bowel cancer last year? God rest her. Well he's a nephew who's a solicitor so he is and Peter is going to talk to him. Now, Ciara, have you money for the next while?"

"Yes. Well, not much but... Mum, I have to get myself out of this mess."

Totally dependent on bloody Rhona! Thought you were meant to be independent but sure all you do is sponge off your mother. "Therefore a woman must leave her father and her mother and must cleave unto her husband: and they shall be one flesh." Genesis 2.24. If only you'd been half committed to this marriage. If you hadn't kept running home all the time.

"What? Without any help? Jesus, Ciara. Why in under God would you think you had to do that? We'll send you money."

She remembers the condensation on the inside of Mum's windows. Breaths fogging in the icy bedrooms. Her mother's worn-down shoes, separating from the sole. The cheerful clutter of Sinéad and Peter's house. Her sister laughs about the three boys eating them out of house and home, only half-joking.

"You can't do that, Mum. Please don't be doing that. We'll be okay. I just need to find us somewhere to stay."

"Sure get on to Louise and Auntie Sarah? Would you not go up to Derry?"

A gush of cold wind between the trees. The vast impossibility of all this.

"I don't know, Mum. I don't know them that well. I can't just turn up. It's such a bloody mess." She's wiping her eyes on the backs of her hands. Along the steps of the Wellington memorial, small black-headed gulls are pacing, heads cocked, as if they're waiting for something. The girls' cheeks pinched red by the cold morning. "I'm sorry, Mum. I'm so sorry for all this."

"Ah look, Ciara. Ah love, look it's okay. We'll find a way to get you home."

She's fighting the urge to cave. To text Ryan. To drive back out to Glasnevin and put the kettle on. The impulse is so strong, she's having to grip onto Ella's buggy and frogmarch herself across this junction. A granite-beaked rook lands on the ramp railings in front of her. *It isn't going to move.* The bird waits, daring her, until she's within milliseconds of walking into it, then takes off with a rasping cry, carrying the sky on its wings.

Bastard.

"What you say, Mammy?"

"Nothing hun."

At the entrance to the Central Placement Service, she pulls a ticket from the dispenser. The small waiting room is crowded, ripe with body heat. There's no space for the buggy, so she takes Ella out, leaves it by the door. People are sitting on black chairs clamped to metal bars, a handful of kids watching videos on phones, a baby crying. At the back of the room, a man is pacing as if he cannot bear to sit. He looks as if he hasn't slept either. A woman shoos her son off a chair, gestures to Ciara. She nods a thank you, sits down and lifts both girls onto her lap.

Tiredness hits her. She's still wearing the leopard-print pajama bottoms and the stained white top. She's past caring. Her face is full of the girls' wispy hair. The weight of them on her legs is the only thing keeping her tethered to this earth.

After a long wait, she hears their number called. "Come on girls, it's our turn. Up we get."

At Hatch 4, their faces are reflected on the scratched Perspex glass. Ella on her knee, head back against her chest. Sophie draped over her arm, sucking the end of her ponytail. From behind their reflections, a woman wearing a polka dot blouse leans forward. She looks to be in her fifties, her hair cut in a bob, lips painted coral. "How can I help?"

"We've nowhere to sleep tonight."

"Who's we?"

"Me, the two kids."

"Ages?"

"Two and four."

"And you've no family?"

"They're all in England. They're from Derry, but I mean. They're all in England. Still. They're trying to help, but..."

God, the tiredness. She could lay down on this Formica desk and never wake up.

The woman's fingers rattle over her keyboard. "And where were you living previously?"

"With their dad. We were renting, just. But we can't go back there. He was...It was a bit difficult."

"Are you okay?"

"Sorry?"

"Have you made contact with a refuge?"

"Sorry? What? No. I don't know. I mean, he hasn't...It's never been physical. I don't know. I'm just...Sorry."

The woman sighs. "The refuges are full anyway, love. I can tell you that much. So, I'm writing down here that you're homeless due to relationship breakdown. I'm adding you to the waiting list to see one of our housing officers. You'll need to complete these forms in order to be assessed as meeting the criteria for homelessness. If you fill in this other form, you can start the process of applying to be put on the social housing waiting list. Here you go. For tonight there's an emergency room at the Hotel Eden. You know it?"

Ciara shakes her head. Her mouth is too dry to speak.

"It's down on Custom House Quay. Near the port. That's just for a few days now, till we see if you meet the criteria. You'll need to phone back here tomorrow. And you'll need to call the Dublin City Council Homeless Executive every fortnight to confirm the room. Here's a letter for you to give to the hotel. Okay?"

By some miracle, the car has not been clamped.

A text from Sinéad. *Where are you now? Did those people help you?*

She imagines Sinéad on her break at the children's hospital, texting furiously. Wild curly hair slicked back, brow furrowed. She can see her sister now, huffing and puffing, inserting IV lines, tilting tiny chins to administer medicines, worrying and worrying, dashing back to check her phone.

It is going to be okay. We will help you. Hang on in there. A strong arm emoji. It hits Ciara how much she misses her sister's no-nonsense kindness.

"We going now?" Ella asks.

When Ciara starts the ignition, the petrol light blinks on, but she can't buy fuel. If she spends any more money, how will she feed the kids? She will just have to chance it. *Criteria. Homeless. Call back. Assessed. Forms. Confirm the room. Just for tonight. Housing officer. Waiting list.* Mind racing, she drives out of the Phoenix Park and turns left, past the Courts of Criminal Justice, over the Luas tram lines, along the quays toward town.

Two damp red sleeping bags are protruding between the columns of the Four Courts. Shapes of bodies inside. Seagulls are squalling in wheeling circles, high above the river. As her car crawls into town, the streets become busier. She grips the steering wheel, keeping a foot hovering over the brake. Mad cyclists. Pedestrians with a death wish. Rows of tourists in bright raincoats are waiting to cross by the Ha'penny Bridge. Irish fiddle music is straining from pubs along Bachelor's Walk. A man is strolling along, holding a placard advertising City Sightseeing Boat Tours.

Petrol light still blinking, she drives past the black frown of O'Connell's scowling iron angels. Along the quays and under the latticed railway bridge, where someone called DAMO has written his name repeatedly in white spray paint.

As they pass the marble pillars of Liberty Hall and continue down the quays, the river widens out and the pavements become emptier. Fewer tourists make it this far downstream, where the bright, quaint postcard-Dublin fades. On the opposite bank, six- and seven-story buildings with flat roofs, fronted by greenish glass. Offices mostly, she guesses, unfamiliar with this part of the city. The sea must be close. From the way the river widens, they must be near the estuary, but you can't see the bay from here. From this angle, it looks as if the city reaches a cliff edge and simply stops.

The docklands are built on reclaimed land, she remembers learning when she first moved to Dublin as an undergrad, and later, much later, when she returned here to marry Ryan. *All this used to be under water.* Out here, river and sky are the same pewter gray, and the Liffey flattens to a texture like concrete. As if she could walk across it, out into the bay, over the sea, across Wales and half of England, and home.

She turns into the underground car park for the Hotel Eden. Is she allowed to park here? Two men in overalls are kneeling by the automatic barrier, unscrewing its metal box. While the barrier is up, she drives past. *Smile. Confident wave.* One of the men absentmindedly smiles back.

The lift from the car park brings them up to the breakfast lounge. She's hit by the sweetness of watermelon, the smell of fresh-baked pastries. Her stomach rumbles. Late morning, guests are traipsing to the buffet table, filling small bowls with cereal, spooning grapefruit segments onto plates, to the soundtrack of Westlife's "You Raise Me Up."

At the reception desk, they are greeted by a woman in a crisp white shirt, whose silver nametag says LAUREN.

Ciara hands over the letter from the Central Placement Service. As Lauren unfolds it, her smile weakens. She purses her lips and reaches under the desk, takes out a gray folder, pulls out a sheet of paper and passes it to Ciara. It has been photocopied so many times, some of the words are fading. Ciara scans it quickly.

...temporarily housed through the Dublin City Council Homeless Executive...hotel facilities are out of bounds, including the gym, the lobby, the café...noise levels...reserves the right to evict...Use of the lift is prohibited. Access to these rooms is via the back staircase, which can be accessed either from the fire escape in the underground car park, or through the side door on Quay Street...

"No candles," Lauren is reading from another list. "Check-in time is before 8 p.m."

"But we've just checked in?"

Eyes to the ceiling. "Each. Evening."

Lauren underlines 8 p.m. on the sheet. She is maybe twenty-three or twenty-four. Choppy blonde haircut. Heavy eyeliner drawn unevenly, making one eye look slightly bigger than the other. A dark-haired man whose name tag says MARCO strides past with a pile of leather-bound menus. He and Lauren exchange hi-hellos and flirty smiles before she turns grimly back.

"These rooms are in high demand. We can't have empty rooms if youse are not here. So you have to sign in by 8 p.m. each night."

Lauren takes out a wad of laminated cards. "These coupons can be used in the carvery or the chipper down the street."

"It's okay," Ciara says. "I'm planning on working, so I don't think we'll need vouchers. We'll be okay, thanks."

For a moment, Lauren looks flummoxed.

"There's nowhere to cook in the room, so youse will need these."

She thrusts the cards at Ciara. Ticks off another point on her list. "Last thing. The room is dependent on availability. Busy times youse might be asked to vacate."

"Vacate as in leave?"

"Look it," she sighs. "It's all on the sheet. I don't know why they make me read you all this shite, to be honest with you. Just sign here. Phone number there." She points a shellacked nail. "No smoking in the bedrooms, okay? You're on floor five."

"Are we going home now?" Sophie tugs on her mum's jacket.

Lauren hoists herself up on her toes, leans over the reception desk. She grins down at the kids. "Oh hello. Cute. They want a lolly?"

Ciara steps into Room 124 and drops her shoulder bag at her feet.

Stuffy ironed polyester. Bleach and musty air. She goes to open the window, but it's on a safety catch and only opens a fraction. Outside, rusty fire escapes, barbed wire. Beyond that, the mountains. RTÉ disks blinking on the top of Three Rock.

Crimson, heavy-duty carpet. Double bed. Fake pine headboard. Gray bedside lamps. White duvet, tucked under mattress corners. Maroon curtains, the same heavy-duty corduroy as her mum's sofa at home. A rectangular stain, where a TV has been removed from the magnolia wall.

"Cool!" Sophie dives onto the bed.

Ella wants to join her, but can't get her nappy-padded bum up. Ciara has to lift her. The two of them bounce on their backs, rolling into each other.

Sophie says, "Try the bed with us, Mammy!"

White tiled bathroom. A bath, at least. The girls hate showers, they howl blue murder. Toilet, sink, bath, all fairly clean. Pacing the narrow gap between bed, wardrobe and window, she's swallowing quick calculations, telling herself, *It'll only be for a few weeks. You'll make it fun for them.* Still, this room is throwing her into a head spin. "Come on girls, let's get out of here. Get some food."

As they are leaving Room 124, a woman in a zebra-print dressing gown walks out of the room next door. Short red hair, dark at the roots. Bare feet. Toenails painted hot pink. She seems to sense Ciara's embarrassment and laughs. "Not to worry, hun. We're all in the same boat. They have us all here on floor five. Easier for them to manage."

Ciara tries to smile. Nearby, a child is blasting out "Amhrán na bhFiann" on the tin whistle. In the endless corridor there's a hot, salty cooking smell. Deodorant and nappy bags. Someone giving out to a child. A small voice wailing. It's a sound quite different from a normal hotel corridor. It reminds her of São Paulo. The year she spent teaching near Parque do Ibirapuera, living on floor thirty-five of a forty-floor block. That feeling of lives being lived in close proximity. Devices being plugged and unplugged. The low buzz of electric toothbrushes. You could even hear the flick of the neighbors' light switches.

"Hopefully it won't be too long," she hears herself telling this stranger in the zebra bathrobe. "Just till we get ourselves sorted with somewhere to rent. Probably just a couple of weeks."

God, the sound of herself. Prattling on, as if this were a city break.

"Ah yeah, hun." This woman smiles kindly. "Sure ye could get lucky."

She has €15.40 left. Two doors down from the hotel, opposite the famine memorial, a sandwich board advertises coffee and fresh muffins. But when they walk into the café, smartly-dressed office workers from the IFSC are lounging on comfy sofas to a backing track of quiet jazz. Sophie shouts, "I NEED A TOILET!"

Next door, there's a Papa John's pizza place, dance music pumping. They sidestep a Wet Floor cone. Floor-to-ceiling windows, industrial yellow plastic high chairs, a long list of pizzas. She says, "Can we just get a plain cheese pizza? And do you have a juice that's not fizzy?"

"Up my nose! Fizz up my nose!" Ella says.

"Sure, no problem, we have apple or orange. Both of those are still."

She wants to hug the cashier.

At Formica tables by the fire exit, her daughters eye the pizza box in total wonder. Sophie says, "What's gonna be in there?"

Again, the hysterical urge to laugh. They've never had pizza from a box before. *Ryan and his healthy eating regime.* She tips a punnet of chips into the pizza box so they can share. They're fed now. Another small victory. She leans forward. "Sophie? Are you thinking about your dream bathroom?"

Outside spring rain drizzles the puddles. Dublin, drenched in a briny mist. Lorries heave along the quays. When the adrenaline dissipates, she feels sick. Exhausted. Unfortunately this tiredness is not contagious. The kids skip along the quays, "Me first, me first, me first!"

She's forgotten about the side entrance. Has used the main revolving door, to the disapproving glare of a hotel manager standing behind reception. *Stupid*. That old impulse, to pull the curtains and tug the duvet over her head.

Resisting, she powers through the afternoon. Through cereal bars and coupon chips for dinner. Through *The Gruffalo's Child*, and an *Amazing Animals* video about Sea Lions. Their normal routines feel strange in this hotel room with its landscape prints and oversized lamps. There are light switches everywhere. *Which bloody switch operates which bloody light?* The kids think this is hilarious. She swats the switches, creating a flashing disco.

Once she's managed to turn all the lights out, the room is lit by the glow of her phone. *Homes to rent in Dublin*. She fills in a couple of inquiry forms, clicks send. Ella is asleep in her arms, but she can sense Sophie lying awake, feeling the strangeness of it all. A rumble of traffic rises from the quays, the pulse of music from another bedroom. Shielding the light of her phone with her hand, she replies to messages from Sinéad, Mum. *No it is okay, please don't be sending me money, you can't afford it*. She opens another page, searches. *Your baby is the size of an olive*.

An email. *Yes, the house is still available to view. Please bring one month's deposit and one month's rent, along with work references*.

A new search: *jobs in Dublin*.

II

SHELTER

SUMMER 2018

9

Ciara leaves the girls asleep in Room 124. Barefoot, in her cotton pajamas, she runs down the backstairs to the underground car park. Early May and the nights are stretching, a faint ray of daylight still visible in the gloom of the concrete garage. She opens the boot. Pushes her hair back from her face. *There is a black maternity bra somewhere in this Nissan Micra.*

A week since they first arrived at the Eden, the car is still packed with bags. She hasn't brought much up to the room, just the wheelie case and some toys. The rest wouldn't fit. And she's afraid to unpack, in case, the moment she settles in, they are told to leave.

She brought their completed forms back to Parkgate Street last Friday. Every day since, she has phoned the City Council Homeless Executive to find out the status of her application. As far as she can tell, they are on a waiting list, waiting to be put on a waiting list. All they say is phone back. Phone back each fortnight and confirm the room.

Well there's no point standing here. *As if you expect the bloody bra to come flying out by itself.* She has to be fast, in case one of the girls wakes up and finds her gone. Ciara lifts a black bin bag out of the boot, opens it up and feels around inside. Nothing but kids' clothes. She pulls out another bag.

Loud laughter. A group of women totter past, arms linked, wobbly in their heels. Quickly, quickly. She didn't want to leave the girls alone in the room, but when she took off her bra this evening there were red welts where the underwire had been digging into her.

Eventually her fingers find the soft elastic, the big felt cups. *Got it. In the book bag. Where else sure?*

She shoves the black bags back into the boot, slams the door and runs back up the backstairs, bra under one arm.

At Room 124, she slots her key card into the door.

It doesn't work.

She tries it again.

A red light. A sound like *uh-uh.*

What are you going to do? What are you going to do? What are you going to do? Your kids are in that room. Christ, Ciara.

She raps on the door of 125 and the woman with the red hair opens it, a little girl on her hip. "Oh heya. You all right?"

"My key card's not working."

"Oh fuck. Yeah that happens."

"I've left the kids asleep in there and I don't know what to do. What should I do? I don't even have my phone on me. Could you call someone?"

"You're okay, hun—what's your name?"

"Ciara."

"I'm Cathy. Listen, you run down to reception. I'll stay here at your door, make sure no one gets in. Or out."

She's halfway down the long corridor when Cathy hisses

in a shout-whisper. "Ciara! Go the other way. Take the fuckin lift!"

Adele's "Someone Like You" is playing in reception, where groups and couples are sitting in the leather bucket chairs. Waiting staff in long maroon aprons are circling, serving drinks from trays. Lights glimmer on the quays outside.

Ciara waits at the reception desk, folding her arms over her chest.

Two American couples are checking in. They must be about her mum's age, in their late sixties. One of the women is holding a leaflet for the hotel spa. On the cover, a photo of a beautiful woman with stones laid along her back. *Escape the pressures of everyday life at the Hotel Eden.*

Marco is on his own behind the desk tonight, his handsome, serious face lit by the computer screen. He takes Ciara's card, types something into the computer, and swiftly hands her a new card. "Have a good evening."

Back at the room, she jams the key card into the slot. A green light. The door clicks open. Thank Christ. The girls haven't stirred from where she left them. Sophie, asleep in the fold-out bed by the window. Ella sleeping horizontally across the double bed. She rushes in and kisses them all over their faces, not caring if she wakes them. *I love you, I love you, I love you.*

She props the heavy door open with her shoulder bag, steps back out into the corridor. Cathy is still leaning against the wall beside her room, watching her little girl wobble along behind a walker. Ciara whispers, "Thank you."

"Ah come here to me," Cathy pulls her into a hug. "You're okay, missus. It's happened me that many times. These fire doors are a pain in the fuckin hole. They slam shut so easily. Number of times I've been locked out."

They both watch the little girl tottering along. Her walker starts singing FOLLOW ME AND HAVE SOME FUN!

Cathy runs over to her, flicks a switch. "I've told you before, Lucy. We've to keep that turned off. Too noisy. You'll have us all kicked out."

Lucy protests but then goes back to pushing the walker, legs strutting cowboy-style.

Cathy sits down on the floor, sighing. "This one has me heart broke. Doesn't sleep. Eighteen months and she's not walking yet. But sure there's no space for her to walk in the fuckin room. I've two teenagers. Adam and Lyra. You've probably heard them."

"Have you been here long?"

"Six months. Family hub before that. This is better. The hub was like a fuckin prison camp, you couldn't leave your room hardly. They checked on you three times a day. At least you can use the halls here, long as you're quiet. The lobby too, long as you keep a low profile. Most of the staff are sound."

Cathy looks at her closely. "I hope you don't mind me asking, hun, but are you all right, like? Because you don't seem all right, in fairness. You seem fairly fuckin shook."

Ciara laughs, embarrassed to find her eyes filling. "No, I just...We just left. And I'm pregnant again. That's why I needed this bloody bra." She waves the thing she's still holding under her arm. "I left my marriage, and it's all been a bit... You know."

"One of those." Cathy nods. "Fair play to you. Takes some guts to leave."

"I just don't know, if I did the right thing."

She looks down the endless corridor. Mottled red carpet blotted with stains. Scratched walls. The stench of cheap industrial disinfectant. Sepia prints of colonial-era Dublin. Ryan's voice in her head. *For no reason. You are tearing this family apart for no reason at all.* She says, "I don't know if I should have left. He didn't cheat, or drink, or gamble. And it wasn't physical. He didn't hit me or anything."

"Your husband didn't hit you? Well that was very fuckin nice of him. Make sure you text and say thanks."

Lucy's walker has hit one of the fire extinguishers. Cathy picks her up, carries her back down the corridor, the toddler's arms flailing.

"You did the right thing. Look, you didn't bring your kids to live in a hotel for no reason. These fuckers fairly screw with your head. Sorry now for being so blunt. Just that I've seen one of my best pals go through this. My friend Alex. I'll give her a shout, and you should join us, next time I'm meeting her." Lucy starts wailing. "I've no experience of that shit myself, but Alex will chat to you. I've been on me own since before this one was born. Prick of a landlord sold the house. I can't find anywhere else to live."

10

Thursday morning, she's driving the girls across the city to Happy Days. This journey can take over an hour, bumper to bumper along the quays, criss-crossing the river, then crawling through the bottleneck of Phibsborough. Some days she has been tempted just to skip playschool, but she's clinging onto their last scraps of continuity. Lunchboxes, filled with sandwiches and sliced fruit she prepares, with difficulty, on the nightstand. Paper-plate art. Painted handprints. Anyway, what would she do, stuck with two little kids in a hotel room? How would she make any phone calls? Fill in any forms? Look for a job?

She drops the girls at the gate, waves to Mairéad. Then she drives down to the shops, parks and checks all around, making sure there's no one she knows. Quickly as she can, she hauls their bin bag full of dirty laundry out of the car. In Soaps 'n' Suds launderette, she bundles everything into a machine. Darks and lights all jumbled up. Feeding coins into the slot, she thinks of that Lucia Berlin story. *You can dye here anytime.* She sets a timer on her phone for forty minutes.

Her account is down to €14.40.

What will she do when it's gone?

Sinéad has sent her £100. The international payment will take 2–5 working days to clear.

Once her forms have been assessed, she will hopefully qualify for Homeless Housing Assistance Payment. It should cover part of her rent, and the deposit for a house. None of the people she has spoken to seem able to tell her how long the application process might take.

While the wash spins, she waits in Brambles Café on the corner, sitting by the open window, where the sweet baking smells don't make her feel sick.

BABIES BEING BORN HOMELESS is the headline in today's *Evening Herald*. She folds the paper, puts it aside and looks up at the small TV above the sugar stand. A man is interviewing people at Connolly Station. "Just weeks ahead of the referendum to repeal the ban on abortion, we've decided to take to the streets and find out what Dublin is saying..."

A young woman in a black REPEAL T-shirt becomes tearful, passionate. Her friend puts an arm around her shoulders, nodding intently. "It's a human-rights issue," the woman is saying. "Every day, hundreds of Irish women are having to travel to the UK for abortions. Most are on their own with no support. No aftercare. Not everyone can even afford to travel. They're getting these dodgy pills online—"

Another woman squares her jaw. "I'll tell you what it is. These women trying to abort their babies. It's pure selfish. That's all it is. Pure, utter selfishness."

Ciara's head swims with all this. She remembers an article she once read, about a man who had been deaf all his life and was fitted with a device that allowed him to hear for the first time. How he took great care planning what he wanted to listen to first, so as not to feel bombarded by sound. For years, she has been cut off from the world. Ryan is so confident in his opinions. Whenever she voiced any views different to his, he would laugh and then explain at great length why she was wrong. Her head floods with that uneasy feeling of having lost track of her own mind.

I cannot hear myself think.

Her phone rings. Sinéad, complaining about the boys, asking if she has heard from the housing office. After a while, Ciara tells her, "I have to go. I'm picking them up from playschool. Then we're going to see Ryan."

Sinéad's voice hardens. "Tell him to fuck off. He's put you through enough. Why does he need to see them? He never bothered with them before."

Ryan has been relentless all day, texting her non-stop. *This is extremely urgent. I need you to bring my children here.*

"Sinéad. He's their dad."

"You're not to tell Daddy where we're staying, okay Soph?"

They're standing outside the house, waiting for Ryan to get home from work. She could use her key, but she wants to make a point. This is just a visit. She's dropping the kids off and then leaving.

On the gnarled hawthorn tree, clusters of off-white blossoms have erupted in their absence. Fallen petals outline the verges and curbs. Her medley of daffodils are bowing their shriveled stems. It's one of those May days when all the seasons are showcased at once. Autumn gales, winter rain, and now quasi-summer warmth. The girls, dressed in wellies and sun hats. Ciara tries to adjust her jeans. They're getting tight already. A gust sends flurries of blossoms swirling.

"Did you hear me, girls? Don't tell Dad about—"

Ella sings out, "In the super fun hotel!"

"Yes. Just please don't say that to your dad."

"Why not?" Sophie frowns. "Why—"

Before she can answer, he's here. Ryan parks his black jeep across the street and gets out. Blossoms drift in a confetti as he crosses the road toward them, carrying an old paint bucket. He smiles and waves.

"DADDY!" Sophie shouts, stomping so the lights in her welly soles flicker. On Ciara's hip, Ella is chewing Hoppy, watching stoically.

As Ryan approaches, she finds herself checking his expression to figure out what mood he is in. A well-learned reflex.

Reaching them, he places the bucket on the garden wall beside her. He laughs. "Don't look so terrified, babe. You're hurting my feelings."

Smiling goofily, he turns to Ella and Sophie. "Girls, you are not going to believe this. Look what Daddy rescued."

He moves aside a torn sheet of cardboard. In the bucket there's a nest of matted brown grass, wood chips, loose asphalt. And in the middle of this mess, three tiny chicks clamber over each other and crane their sinewy necks. Featherless, their squirming bodies are tongue-pink.

So this is it. The thing that was so urgent. A bucketful of chicks.

"They were under the roof space," he says. "Some builders are in, doing renovations over the summer. They were about to throw them in the skip, but I happened to be passing."

Yellow beaks widen, emitting defenseless squeaks. The sight of these chicks reaches into her and moves her instinctively, in the way her daughters' first yells made her breasts hurt, made her cry. Her babies: Sophie in her bright red raincoat, wellies flashing wildly; Ella, staring down from her perch on her hip; the new baby, the size of a blueberry.

"Is it your mother who loves birds? That's right. Good old Rhona. She knows every birdsong, doesn't she?" Ryan is studying her face, smiling. "I wonder what Rhona would make of these fellas. She'd love them, right?"

She nods mutely. No one will ever know her like he does.

Sophie tugs on his sleeve. "Daddy, they don't have feathers?"

"That's right, honey. They're only babies. Your mammy will help me look after them. Your granny taught her all about birds. Isn't that right, Mammy? Let's take them into the kitchen."

"Ryan. I'm meant to be just dropping them off. I wasn't intending to—"

"Sure come in for a cup of tea, babe. The girls want you to help." He laughs, "Honestly, you've got to stop looking so terrified. It's only me."

The hall smells of their detergent. Ryan's thick black socks line the radiators. Their wedding photos line the walls. She looks around for the broken photo, but those boxes have been moved. There are hoover tracks on the carpet, the whiff of lavender furniture polish.

Everything she's read online advised her to meet Ryan in public, not to go back to the house. But he has been so contrite and apologetic. Did she get it wrong? Was it all in her head?

Now, Ella and Sophie run into the kitchen. "Daddy are you bringing the baby chicks into our house?" Sophie asks. "And are you going to feed them?"

Stepping into the house is like ducking her head underwater, but her daughters don't seem to have noticed the weirdness of being back here.

Ryan places the bucket of nestlings on the kitchen table. He loads a syringe full of cat food. "If we could just get these little fellas to eat."

Again, the squeaking, the open beaks. Looking closer, she sees tufts of gray fluff sprouting on their backs, and bruised-looking bulges where their eyes will be. They are more like dwarf hamsters than birds, the way they squirm and snuggle up to each other. Their heads look too heavy for their fragile necks, their skin is so translucent she can see the grizzly workings of organs underneath.

Ella stomps, her wellies flashing, "They're eating it! They're hungry, me too. I want a snack. You got some snacks?"

Ryan looks up, "You're staying for dinner, right?"

He looks back at the chicks. His hair has fallen out of place after a long workday, and the shadow of a beard softens his face. He's concentrating so intently, like a little boy building a toy airplane. Despite herself, she feels a wave of tenderness toward him, similar to how she feels when her kids fall and howl MAMMIEEEEE.

Come over any time, Sinéad used to say. *Day or night, get on a plane, get over here, and just ring the bell.* Ciara used to thank her, while thinking *there wouldn't be enough time.* If his anger ever spilled over to that point, there was no way they'd make it out alive. Lying awake in the girls' bedroom, she used to plot escape routes in her head. Stairs, hallway, landing turned into a labyrinth.

Hands trembling, she opens the fridge. Two organic children's yogurts, out of date. A microwave curry and four cans of Coke where the milk should be. A wave of sadness rises in her chest. She shuts the fridge door. "Spaghetti hoops?"

Once they've finished eating, she clears the plates and brings them over to the sink. She runs the taps, looks back and catches a cameo of Ryan laughing with the girls, Ella on his knee, Sophie coloring at the kitchen table. They love him so much. Can't she see how much they love him? What is she doing to her kids?

She turns back to the sink and hears Ryan say, "Hey, here's an idea. Why don't you guys stay and help me look after these chicks? You'd like that, right Soph? You wanna stay here at our house, and help Daddy mind the baby birdies?"

Sophie jumps up and bounces around. "Yes! The baby chicks! We'll mind them!"

Ella laughs and bangs her teaspoon on the table.

Ciara turns off the taps and steps away from the sink.

"No, no, no hang on a minute, Sophie. Ryan, we can't do that. We aren't staying. Sophie come on honey, we have to go."

"Not fair!" Sophie's cheeks redden.

"Oh sweetie, that's okay," Ryan kneels and pulls Sophie into a hug. He strokes her hair, looking up to watch Ciara's face. "I'm sure Mammy will let you come back home and see the baby birdies tomorrow. Isn't that right, Mammy?"

"Yay!" Sophie pulls away from him, wiping streaming snot on the back of her sleeve. "We come back tomorrow, Ella! Mammy, we see baby chicks in the morrow."

Hawthorn blossoms glow in the indigo dusk. She checks her watch. They have to be back to sign in before eight. Ryan carries Ella to the car, fastens her in and kisses her forehead. Ciara finishes buckling Sophie, shuts the car door. There's not a single person on the street. Ryan steps closer, hands in his pockets.

"Tonight was nice," he says.

She fidgets with her hair, tucking it behind her ears.

"So you're staying with Tania? She's the hippy one, the one who's always smoking pot, right?

"Yes, no. I mean, she's settled down a lot—"

"It's okay." He laughs. "I'm not mad at you. Look, babe. Things have got a bit out of hand here, haven't they? I mean, lord. You have the kids staying with some woman they barely know. I'm here bonding with a bucket of chicks. Honestly, you have me losing my mind."

He reaches for her hand, runs his fingers over her slim

gold wedding ring. "Look you know I love you. I'm not the monster you're making me out to be. Can't we at least meet up by ourselves and talk?"

11

Walking along the quays, Sophie keeps stopping to look at the tiny bronze sea creatures hidden in the metal spotlights. Starfish. Minnows. Oysters. The girls hop from one to the other, crouching to coo at these hidden treasures. At this pace, they will be late. "Come on girlies, we have to hurry up."

It's Saturday morning and they are meeting her cousin Louise off the Belfast train. Her mum has orchestrated this meeting. Sinéad texted *Good luck with her ladyship.*

She replied *Piss off, you're terrible.*

Under a bright blue sky, the river is ultramarine, streaked with swirling undercurrents. Sophie and Ella run along the cobblestone quays now, their summer dresses swirling. Ciara has made an effort this morning, cleaned their faces and pinned fake flowers at the side of Sophie's ponytail. Rummaging in the case, she found her black maxi dress, which just about fits. She brushed her hair, did her makeup properly. She hasn't seen Louise since her brother Darragh's wedding, almost five years ago. Louise has never met Sophie and Ella.

"There youse are!" At Connolly train station, Louise steps

out of the crowd and hugs her in a waft of delicate, expensive perfume. The always-unexpected tug of her Derry accent reminds Ciara of her mum. Something of Sinéad about her mouth, her jawline.

"Girls, this is Mammy's cousin Louise."

"Call me Auntie Louise. They can call me auntie, can't they? Now, I didn't have time to wrap these or anything..." Louise pulls two pink boxes out of her tote and hands them to Sophie and Ella.

Tropical Barbie and Surgeon Barbie.

"Look, Mammy!"

"Ah Louise. You didn't have to get them anything. Thank you." She reaches over the children's heads. Gives Louise an awkward air-kiss hug.

Louise had a treasure chest full of Barbies when they were kids. During those summer trips back to Derry, while their mothers talked and cried and drank tea in the kitchen, the cousins would tip all the Barbies onto the shaggy living-room rug. "Let's have a wedding," Louise would say. Ciara and Sinéad would be too busy linking the naked dolls into human chains and hanging them between sofas and door frames. She still remembers the time when Louise, who must have been eight or nine, threw Ken and Barbie on the rug, ran into the kitchen and bawled, "Them English ones aren't playing properly so they aren't! Is it time for them English ones to go on away home yet?"

She mentions this to Louise, and her cousin laughs. "I don't remember that. I only remember the time your Sinéad stole one."

"Oh God. I'd forgotten that."

"And Aunt Rhona had to post it back from England."

"And it was your favorite. The bride one. Lord. You were always asking when we were going home. Only our mum spent her life telling us Derry *was* home. We thought we *were* home."

"Must have been wild confusing for youse, right enough. Your mum was some woman, the way she raised the two of you by herself."

"Ah yeah, that's just Mum." She turns to her cousin. "Will we take a run out to the seaside?"

At the fishing village of Howth, they walk the promenade. Houses painted in bright colors, primrose, cerulean, salmon pink, nestle against the rugged cliff head, as if cowering from the prowling sea. A few tourists are queuing outside Beshoff's fish-and-chip shop and Maud's ice-cream parlor. Boat masts rattle in the gusty breeze. She tries to turn her attention to this cousin she barely knows, deployed by her mum and Aunt Sarah on a rescue mission, but she's out of the habit of conversation. It's difficult to know what to say.

Louise says, "Your wee mummy says you're in a hotel?"

She nods. White yachts bob on the dark water.

"So you're in a bit of a situation, sounds like. Any money?"

"Not much. He controlled all that."

"Controlled it?"

"Well, I'm not good with money. It was his money anyway, so it made more sense for him to manage it."

"Aye. Right. Well, mummy said to give you this." Louise

hands her a white envelope, slips it into her open handbag. How much? The hunger. The guilt. The urge to check.

"Louise, I can't—"

"Ah sure. It's only a wee bit of something. Would the girls like some ice cream? I'd love some honeycomb, so I would."

Later, on the DART train back into the city, Louise leans over the glow of her phone. "How about this one? Three-bed in Clontarf. That's a wild nice area, isn't it?"

How can she even begin to explain? She doesn't have a deposit. She doesn't have a job. She's waiting for a waiting list.

"Maybe a bit steep. Hang on now." She looks up. "You're working, Ciara? Teaching isn't it?"

"I haven't worked in a long time. I want to get a job though. I need to start looking. He didn't want me to work, and I just sort of..."

Drifted. Got through each day. Focused on the minutiae. First shoes. Vaccinations. Chesty coughs. Sweet-potato puree. Made a religion out of motherhood. A cult that blocked out everything else.

Their faces, opposite each other on the window. Their eyes are the same shape. Mum's eyes. Aunt Sarah's eyes. Their reflections brighten as the evening outside darkens. Sophie's doll, renamed Howth Barbie, is abseiling off the seat. Sticky ice-cream cheeks, flushed faces, happy-tired. Today was a good day. Perhaps the first good day they've had in weeks. A string of lights marks the outline of Dublin Bay. A ferry moves slowly out of the port. Louise keeps swiping, passing her phone to Ciara and then swiping again.

Ciara thinks of their mothers. Of growing up within the ache of Rhona's homesickness for Derry. Evenings when her mum phoned Aunt Sarah, the way she would stand in the hall, twisting the phone cord around her finger. "I'm phoning home, would youse lot keep it down." Sinéad used to laugh, "E.T. phone home!" The Ireland Mum talked about was a different place from the one Aunt Sarah lived in. Mum was forever reminiscing. "Remember this, Sarah, remember that!" Aunt Sarah only wanted to talk about the latest bomb scare, the latest shooting. Conversations between Mum and Aunt Sarah were like listening to actors with different scripts. Perhaps not even reading for the same film.

The train is pulling into Connolly when Louise looks up. "What about them? Those students. Who teaches them?"

A group of teenagers are blocking the width of Platform 3. Bright yellow rucksacks. White headphone wires trailing over vivid raingear. As they disembark and walk past the group, Ciara recognizes the sound of Italian. A handful of group leaders in hi-vis vests are attempting to corral the teens toward the exit. *"Oi! Ragazzi!"*

"There must be jobs for English-language teachers here," Louise says. "That's what you did before, right?"

That night, once the girls are asleep, Ciara takes out her laptop. The thing is ancient, takes a while to load. Her most recent CV is from 2013. She typed it during her last term of teacher training, intending to apply for jobs that autumn. But by then, she was living in Ireland, married to Ryan, pregnant with Sophie. Now her eyes run over the neat rows of print.

BA English Literature.

Certificate in Teaching English as an Additional Language.

The catalog of her travels. Aula Inglés, Catalonia. Accadamia Inglese, Bologna. English Academy, Saipan. Speak Easy English School, São Paulo. It's as if all this happened to someone else. Then there's her Postgraduate Certificate in Primary Education. Hard-earned. A scraped pass in the end, not the honors she wanted.

How can you explain a five-year gap in employment?

Raising two children without support. *Logistics management.*

Trying to keep Ryan in a good mood. *Strategic planning.*

De-escalating his rages. *Conflict resolution.*

She messes around with the document, changing the font. She summarizes the last half-decade in a single line. *2013–2018. Maternity leave.*

It's late now and her eyes are sore. There are several ads for English-language teachers on Gumtree.ie. She clicks on the first one. What has she to lose?

12

Daylight Animal Rescue occupies a patch of scrubland off Junction 3 on the M50. They're walking across the ramshackle farmyard, Ella on her hip, Sophie jumping puddles, Ryan in his wilting work shirt and loosened tie, carrying the old paint bucket. She picked him up from the house in Glasnevin earlier. He said it would be easier than taking two cars. She was too tired to say no.

Her forehead feels stretched too tight. Senses on high alert, she's trying not to gag at the manure and petrol tang. As they walk up the path to the animal sanctuary, Ryan puts his arm around her waist and kisses the side of her head. He smiles shyly. "Let's hope this works."

"Skye, Rocky and Chase!" Sophie peers into the bucket. She has named the chicks after the Paw Patrol pups. Maybe not a great idea, seeing as they are now the color of rotting chicken fillets, gray with a greenish sheen.

"Baby birdies!" Ella claps.

Ryan has the soft, sleep-deprived look of a parent at a hospital bedside. Memories reel. Their first date: meeting him at the Peace Gardens steps, light playing in the white foam of the fountains, his hand slipping into her hair at the base of her neck. The way he looked at her after they kissed. She'd never felt so desired. He was returning to Ireland a week later, and she spent the next seven nights in his single bed, dashing home each morning for clean clothes. Mum and Sinéad watched her comings and goings, puzzled and excited, as if they had caught this giddy love-fever too. Ryan came along to her lectures at university, watched her making notes, his arm protectively holding the back of her chair.

Stop. Stop. Stop. She is so used to preempting harsh words, looks of scorn and contempt, but she has to remember that his kindness is a choice. A decision he makes in order to achieve an end.

At the end of the farmyard, a man with a long ginger beard and a black beanie hat strides out of a Nissen hut. His face is serious; the sleeves of his army camouflage shirt rolled up, as if ready to deal with something messy. "Eoin," he shakes their hands. Ryan is quiet, so Ciara finds herself explaining about the chicks and where they found them.

Eoin peers into the bucket. "These lads are nestlings. Not chicks. They're too young to be even fledglings. They shouldn't be away from their nest." He folds his arms, shakes his head in disapproval. He mutters something, all Ciara catches are the words *fuckin eejits.*

Does he think they kidnapped these birds? Removed them from their nest by force? Eoin looks closer into the bucket, bending over with his big hands on his knees. "You'd need to be feeding these lads constantly. See the way the birds swoop, back and forth to feed their young every few minutes. No way you could replicate that." He stands up, sighs and scratches his head. He looks at their faces. "Tea?"

Ryan shakes his head.

Ciara says, "Sure, why not."

"Have a seat." Eoin gestures to a handful of deckchairs at the side of the yard. Five fluffy brown chickens and a mud-splattered goose are chasing each other between old car parts and computer debris. She sits in one of the chairs and watches Sophie running after a flurry of stressed-out ducks, with Ella teetering after her.

"Honeys," she hears herself calling rather pointlessly in their wake. Her legs feel so heavy she cannot summon the energy to run after them. In Ryan's presence, she feels a familiar exhaustion.

"The kids are grand, sure leave them." Eoin hands her a Styrofoam cup of scorching tea, which she takes in both hands, grateful for its heat. He sits down on the deckchair beside her and lights a cigarette in his cupped palm. There are other people at work around the place. A couple of teenagers brushing down a piebald pony.

She asks him, "Will they survive? The nestlings?"

Eoin squints and exhales a plume of smoke. "Hard to tell. Birds almost never fall from their nests. They're very young. Come on and I'll show you."

They stand and follow Eoin around the side of the building, to where a makeshift aviary has been created under a copse of slender saplings. At Eoin's voice, there's a flurry of black wings. Two birds land on the rusty wire.

"See this lad?" Eoin points to the smaller of the birds, "Hooded crow. That's what you're looking at with your fellas. See, if a crow has its head tucked under its wing, it's scared. Any captive crow will be mad unhappy if it's alone. Stressed. Imprinted on you, see? Unreleasable. And nestlings as small as your guys, keeping them warm would be the main thing. Keeping them warm, safe and fed."

"We were hoping you would take them," Ryan says. "You're obviously the expert. It's unbelievable what you're doing here."

Eoin shakes his head. "No space."

He doesn't like Ryan. Ciara can feel it. She has noticed over the years how some people are instantly wary of her husband.

Ryan smiles tensely. "Fair enough."

From across the courtyard, the piebald pony whinnies, stamps the dry earth. The teenage girl is stroking its neck, her voice coaxing, soothing.

"Tell you what," Eoin says, "I've an old infrared lamp I can give you. Stick your fellas under that each night for a bit of heat. You never know."

While Eoin goes into the hut to get the lamp, Ryan puts his arms around Ciara's waist, peering into her face. To her horror, she sees he's crying. "I love you so much," he says. "I am so sorry you were hurt in any way. I'll spend my life making it up to you. I can't live without you."

Ciara looks down at the bucket in his hand. The squirming nestlings are smaller than Ella's palm. Tiny. Defenseless. Now they're opening their pink beaks into diamond shapes, squeaking again. Calling for their mother. Their blind eyes tilted toward the fading daylight.

The car jolts and shudders as she reverses out of the potholed lane. She waves bye to Eoin, who is standing in the doorway of the hut. He salutes in reply. What must he think of her? Of them?

Ryan is in the passenger seat, holding his bucket of nestlings, with the infrared lamp wedged at his feet. He's blowing his nose, drying his eyes. He says, "Thanks for your help today, babe."

"It's okay," she mumbles.

In the backseat, Ella is talking to Hoppy. Sophie is spitting on her finger and drawing love hearts on the window.

Ciara feels Ryan watching her intently. As she's driving, he reaches and puts a hand on her thigh. Her muscles tense at his touch.

Crows use houses as surrogate cliff faces. Out of all the things Eoin told them, this is the sentence that's following her home, round the motorway, back to Glasnevin, trying to ignore her husband's hand on her thigh. "Crows prefer a fork in an oak's wide branches, or a rocky precipice," Eoin said. "But if neither are available, a house will do. Houses can be cliff faces."

Something else Eoin said, when she asked how long the chicks would normally stay in their nest. He frowned, saying, "Not as long as people would expect. I mean, think about it. If you're a bird, the nest is pretty much the most dangerous place you can be. Sure, predators know where to find you."

Traffic crawls. His hand is still on her thigh. After what feels like hours, she pulls in outside their old home. Ryan gets out with his bucket and lamp, leans in the open car door. "See you tomorrow, guys." He looks at Ciara. "Love you."

She nods, doesn't say anything. *Fuck the consequences.* She turns out of their street, onto the main road into the city, and accelerates hard.

Back at the hotel, she can't sleep. Hearing the TV from Cathy's room, she steps outside, props the door open with one of Sophie's sparkly purple runners. She taps on the door of 125. When Cathy opens, she whispers, "Do you have any chocolate?"

Cathy laughs, whispers, "Come in for a sec. Lucy's just gone down. Adam and Lyra are out gallivanting somewhere."

Room 125 looks more like a normal sitting room than a hotel room. It's disorientating, as if she has stepped through a hotel doorway into someone's home. Cathy has replaced the white bedding with flowery duvet covers. Seeing Ciara staring, she smiles. "Penney's best." On Lucy's cot, a Peppa Pig duvet and knitted blanket. Photos in frames have been placed along the windowsill. There's a rice cooker by the mini kettle. "A godsend," Cathy says. "You've to hide it though. Don't let the fuckers catch you with one."

The hotel's colonial-era prints have been taken down and replaced with a canvas of the Brooklyn Bridge at night. More photos are tacked along the wardrobe doors, pictures of birthdays and days at the beach. The lighting in here seems different, thanks to a string of wicker-heart fairy lights around the curtain rail.

Cathy says, "It looks better than the first day we landed in here, I can tell you that much. I was a fucking mess. Place was a kip. But look it, there are things you can do. Now where's them biscuits? I swear to Christ, if those fuckers have eaten them on me..."

A surge of affection makes Ciara smile. Funny, how friendships can be accelerated by circumstance.

Cathy produces a six-pack of KitKats from the wardrobe. "Come on and we'll sit outside."

They sit on the floor between their rooms, talking in low voices.

Further down the corridor, a door opens. The couple from 134. They can't be more than nineteen or twenty. They have a tiny baby who looks just days old. The dad nods to Ciara and Cathy as they pass. "How are you? How's it going?" He tips his baseball cap. An old man's gesture. He holds his chest out, deepens his voice. His partner puts up her hoodie. Her clumpy mascara makes her look even younger, like a child playing dress-up. She looks bewildered. Ciara wants to reach out, hug her and say, "I don't know how I got here either."

How can you bring a tiny baby like that home to a hotel room, Ciara? How?

As if reading her mind, Cathy asks, "How you feeling? Baby still making you sick?"

"It's getting a bit better. Nearly at the twelve weeks now."

They unwrap their KitKats. Ciara is trying to put into words a thought she hasn't fully formulated. She says, "I know some people would say it's selfish, me having the baby. Some people would say I shouldn't go through with it."

Cathy nods. "Is that what you want? There's places you can

go, in England like. Friends of mine have done it. Not easy, but. Expensive."

She shakes her head.

The thought of the airport, again. Walking into the terminal. Walking to the gate. Who would mind the girls? She couldn't bring them with her. If she's away for a night, their room at the Eden will be gone. *Their room.* As if they own it. They'd have to find somewhere else. The thought of all of it. The tiredness of it. The heaviness of it. *Who are you kidding? It's more than that. You know it's more than that.*

Not a decision. A lack of decision. As if leaving was the one radical act she was capable of, and now in the aftermath she is overcome by a sense of inertia, unable to see beyond the next meal for her children, the next phone call with the housing office, the next drop-off with Ryan. Her body continuing on its trajectory unfettered, breasts engorged, legs gripped by night cramps, quickening starting in her belly like trapped moths. She doesn't know Cathy well enough to explain this, and anyway, what words would she use?

"Bed time," she says, getting to her feet.

Cathy stands up, stretching. "Right. Time to hit the hay. I must give Alex a bell, arrange for us to meet up. Careful around that ex of yours though, yeah? Seriously, hun, there's too many horror stories."

Later, lying awake on her back, Ciara's fingers find the scars on her lower abdomen. She's had two C-sections within two years, both emergencies. Two white scar lines, converging like electricity pylons reaching the horizon. Twice, she's been sliced, split open and watched babies being lifted from behind a surgical curtain. And what is this, if not another splitting and breaking open?

Maybe she got it wrong. Maybe he's a loving husband and she was the problem all along. She could gather all the evidence, pin it on a corkboard, connect culprits and motives with red thread, and she still wouldn't have any answers. Her only witnesses, Sophie and Ella, are so young that they will never remember any of this.

The body is the last thing to grant forgiveness.

Even after Ryan has said sorry, and has cried openly in the animal rescue center, and after she's said *It's okay.* Even now he's rescuing crow chicks and texting her sweet love letters. Her body still remembers the precise feeling when she sat in bed, shielding Ella with her arms, while he ranted and jabbed the air, and his jaw clicked, his eyes bulged and she thought *Christ, he's going to hit me.*

Even now, when she's told him she forgives him, and when the thought of divorce makes her feel sick, and when she's desperate to save her fledgling family, part of her body (toe tips, ear lobes, the backs of her knees) is listening, tense, on high alert, ready to take flight.

13

On the video call, a wall of shipping containers corrugated with rust. The loud groan of a foghorn. Mum and Sinéad's faces crowd the screen. Behind them, the funnel of a P&O ferry, and a line of cars queuing up to board.

Sinéad smiles, "Surprise! Dr. Parkinson gave Mum the all clear for the boat! She's not to fly but he said the boat is grand. Ah, Ciara. Ciara love, don't cry."

They're staying in Clontarf, in a whitewashed B&B on the waterfront. On the driveway, Sophie and Ella dance around their granny. Rhona is wearing a fuchsia raincoat, jeans and a paisley headband over her gray bobbed hair. Sinéad, in her black leather jacket, curly hair tied up in a topknot, picks up her nieces and spins them, "The size of youse!"

She hugs Ciara, meets her eyes, "You okay?"

Rhona reaches up to embrace her daughter, her tears spilling openly. Ciara had forgotten how small her mum is. Rhona holds both her hands and looks at her face. Her mum's hands are trembling. "So great to see you, Ciara darlin. So brave what you're doing, so it is. And another wee baby. My God. You're some woman yourself."

Time races. She brings them to the beach at Bull Island. Spreads out her Brazilian flag beach towel. Her mum has brought a picnic. Tinfoil-wrapped sandwiches, and a chocolate cake from Tesco. Once they have eaten, Ciara rolls up Sophie and Ella's leggings and they run in and out of the waves, squealing.

There's a restaurant near the B&B called Bella Roma. As evening falls, they sit next to the window, at a table with a waxed red-checked tablecloth. She orders penne for the girls, and Sophie shouts, "Yes! Pasta! We didn't have pasta for ages!"

She's right. They've been living on takeaway chips, overboiled veg and rubbery meat from the hotel carvery, dry tortillas and greasy rotisserie chickens. They haven't had pasta since they left.

Sinéad catches the expression on her face. "Right. I want the biggest bloody pizza I can find. I've been on this blinking diet for six weeks. Six weeks!"

Ciara laughs. Her nausea seems to have died down, as if there's a lull in the storm. She eats like she hasn't eaten for weeks. Oozing mozzarella. Crunchy garlic bread. Sophie and Ella take turns to sit on their granny's knee. She sings to them. "Lavender's Blue," "Wind the Bobbin Up." Yes, this is what you're meant to do. You're meant to sing to your children. When did she last sing to them?

Rhona is sitting next to her, and keeps squeezing her hand, leaning against her. She's quieter than usual. Ever since she was diagnosed with the heart problem, it's as if some of her usual energy has faded. She used to always live life at full kilter, but now there's something fragile about her. Something careful, wary even. As they are walking back to the B&B, she mentions this to Sinéad. Her sister sighs. "Mum says the meds are making her tired, that's all."

"You think that's true? You don't think there's more to it?"

"Ah I don't know, hun. Fuck. Sure you could drive yourself crazy worrying."

Walking along in the dark, Sinéad links arms with her. Sophie and Ella are behind, holding hands with their granny. Lights across the bay are a thick glimmer in the sea fret. At the endpoint of the North Bull Wall, Our Lady Star of the Sea, on her seventy-foot-high concrete plinth, watches over Dublin Bay. Palms turned upward, eyes downcast. Floodlights pick out her starry halo.

"What time's your ferry?" Ciara asks.

"Sailing at nine." Sinéad sighs. "Wish we could stay longer. Bloody work. Bloody kids."

Now that it's almost time to say goodbye, Ciara feels close to tears. Nausea is rising in the back of her throat again. She remembers that stomach-sick feeling from being a child, not wanting to let go of her mum's hand.

Sinéad says, "Come in for a cuppa sure."

In the bedroom at the B&B, the girls sit on the bed next to their auntie. She's showing them photos of their cousins on her phone. "And here's our Rory dressed up as a Minion, no idea why. Yeah, that yellow paint took a while to come off..."

Ciara is on her phone when her sister nudges her elbow. "That's him, isn't it. You're messaging Ryan."

"Sinéad—"

"Here girls, you want some cartoons?" Her sister turns on the TV, puts up the volume and takes Ciara aside. She lowers her voice, folds her arms across her bust. "I knew it. I said to Mum. I said this is pointless, waste of a journey. She'll only end up going back."

"What's this?" Rhona walks out of the ensuite bathroom, fixing the buttons on her bobbled lilac cardigan.

Sinéad whispers, "She's texting Ryan again."

"You're not going back? Dear God." Her mother sits down heavily on the bed. "After putting the weans through all this? Would you not have an ounce of sense? What in under God is the point of all this, if you're only going back again?"

"Jesus, would youse give me a chance to breathe." Sophie is looking over, anxious. Ciara gives her a smile. "It's okay, love, just chatting. We're leaving soon." She lowers her voice again. "I'm texting him to organize bringing the girls over tomorrow."

"Bringing them over?" her mum asks. "Why's he want so much time with the kids when he never bothered his arse before? We saw you, when they were babies. How little he did to help. And he wouldn't let us help either."

"Mum! I've told you already, I can't stop him seeing them. He's entitled to see them."

Sinéad snorts. "Half an hour that's all I'd give him."

"Why can't you understand? We have to go." She turns to the girls, raises her voice again. "Come on loves, we'll turn that off now."

"Ciara—"

"We've to go or I'll be late checking into the hotel."

"Check in?" Rhona frowns. "Are ye not well and truly checked in, for the love of God?"

"Look, Mum, we have to go." A quick kiss on her mum's cheek.

"Here," Rhona says. "Take the rest of the cake with you. And this as well." A folded fifty euro. Ciara's eyes well.

"Kids, say bye to Granny and Auntie Sinéad." She hugs Sinéad. "Talk to you later."

Sinéad squeezes her tight, "We love you, Ciara. You know that."

Outside the bedroom door, she stops for a moment and listens. Sinéad's voice.

"She told you about this earlier, about having to check in… no, Mum, she did in fairness tell you about this earlier…I'm not getting at her, you're getting at her…I know, but this is how it started the last time. This is how he creeps back in…"

That rise in her. Teenage levels of aggravation. Telling her what to do all the time. Trying to run her life. Ryan's voice sneers in her head. *Your family love to control you, don't they.* Her feeble replies, easily scoffed at. *Come on, Ciara, it's so obvious. You'd be mad not to see that. Your family have been out to ruin this marriage from the beginning.*

As she's getting into the car, she hears her phone.

Remember this?

A photo. She has seen it before she can stop herself, and is thrown back in the moment. Baby Sophie on her dad's knee, screwing her face up at the taste of her first spoonful of rice, while Ryan makes an imitation of the same expression. He has put a filter on the image, giving it the rosy, saturated tones of a sixties polaroid. A summer day, Sophie in that smocked dress underneath her bib, Ryan in his shirt sleeves, laughing. The image burns. The closeness of them. The love.

Signing in at reception just before eight, Marco hands her an envelope. "Room 124? This came for you today."

It's her application for social housing. The hurried biro scrawl. *RETURNED DUE TO INCOMPLETE SECTIONS AND MISSING DOCUMENTS.*

Incomplete? How was it incomplete? What does this mean—back to the bottom of the waiting list again?

All these jobs she's applied for, not a single response.

On the screen in the hotel bar, news footage of a packed lifeboat on a teal-blue sea. The images flick to footage of the post-referendum celebrations. Women crying and hugging each other, waving flags high. *MY BODY, MY CHOICE.* A tearful reporter smiling over her microphone. "This is an historic day for all Irish women."

It was today. How did she not even remember that the vote was today?

Back in the hotel bedroom, the girls are hungry again. They've already eaten through her stash of fruit and rice cakes, so she unwraps her mum's leftover cake, slices it using a teaspoon handle, gives them each a generous chunk. Cake at bedtime—what is she doing? The sugar will have them hyper, sure they'll never sleep. *Fuck it.* She shakes crumbs off the duvet, tries to lift the endlessly accumulating tide of grime. Another message.

Why don't you just come home to me. I love you so much. What are you doing to us, to our daughters?

No space.

No space to think.

Thoughts tangled up in each other, a chain of reasoning, never reaching a conclusion. It's difficult to make good decisions when your head is loud with sirens.

14

Cathy has won a Facebook competition: a family pass for Dublin Zoo worth €68. "Lyra and Adam won't come," she says, "Miserable bastards. And under-threes are free anyway, so Lucy and Ella won't need a ticket. It's for two adults, two kids. Come with us? We'll make a day of it. Alex is coming down with her little fella. All we'd have to do is split the cost of one extra adult ticket. Seven euro each."

Early the following Saturday morning they set off. Alex is living out in Newbridge, so they catch the Luas over to Heuston Station to meet her off the train. On the tram, Ella sits on Ciara's knee, hugging Hoppy. Sophie bounces up and down on the seat beside them, "We there yet? We there yet?"

Sitting opposite them, Cathy leans forward, "C'mere to me Ciara, I meant to say to you earlier. Basically, don't mind Alex. We grew up together, so she's grand with me, but she can be a bit... Well, it just depends what day you catch her on."

"Okay..."

"She's been through a lot. But she means well, honestly. And she's been in and out of court that many times. Might be a good person for you to talk to. She knows the ropes."

"When did she leave?"

"About a year ago, I think. I lose track. I shouldn't really be telling you this, but she's left a few times. He has his ways of luring her back." A shadow crosses Cathy's face. They've reached Heuston now, and the tram doors hiss open to let them off. Ciara tells the girls to hold hands, and helps Cathy with Lucy's buggy.

"He's a musician," Cathy is saying, walking close to her and speaking quietly so the kids can't hear. "Pubs, night-clubs, weddings sometimes. But his family have some sort of business too—bathrooms? Kitchens? Something like that. So they're loaded. Alex was only eighteen when she met him. We all thought he was the bee's knees. Sex on legs, so he was. Drop-dead gorgeous. They got married a few years later, then she had her little boy, Damien, and she was doing all the raising of him. Garry would be sleeping half the day, after his gigs. He'd murder Alex and Damien if they so much as made a sound. She only told me this years later, like.

"We lost touch there for ages. They'd moved out to Kildare, somewhere outside Kilcullen where Garry's family's from. Middle of nowhere really. I visited her one time, massive place so it was, like something out of a magazine. Huge garden with a treehouse and all. But I was never back again—Garry didn't like her having pals in the house. I used to try to meet up with her, but she'd always have some excuse. I thought she'd gone all snobby, too good for the likes of me! Too cool for school with her rockstar husband and her big fancy house. It was only later I found out."

They've stopped at the front of the station. Cathy peers

around the sides of the columns, "She's meeting us somewhere around here."

Sophie has her arms outstretched, trying to balance on the cracks between the flagstones. Ella and Lucy are munching rice cakes.

"You know what Garry used to do?" Cathy lowers her voice to a whisper, "He used to hit Alex on the back of her head, so there wouldn't be a mark on her face. Choked her a few times too, but he was always careful not to leave a bruise."

"God." Ciara feels hot tears spring to her eyes.

"I know. He put her in hospital this one time, and I think there were social services involved or something, I'm not sure exactly...She left him then anyway and came back to her mam's with Damien. That's when we got back in touch—my mam used to live next door to them, God rest her." Cathy checks her phone. "Ah here, she's been waiting for us in the bar."

They cross the station concourse to the Railway Bar, where staff are serving tea and coffee, and passengers with bags and cases are sitting at the long sofas by the picture window. Alex stands up when she sees them. She's a petite, pretty woman, younger than Ciara expected, perhaps only in her late twenties. Behind her, a little boy of around seven or eight is sitting on the leather sofa, watching something on a mobile. Cathy hugs Alex and introduces them. "This is Ciara, the one I was saying to you about. My next-door neighbor. Ha."

Alex nods, "How are ya." She doesn't meet Ciara's eyes, and a jolt passes through her—the distinct feeling that Alex doesn't like her, or she's annoyed with her, which is stupid because they've only just met. Maybe Alex senses that Cathy has told her more than she should have. Ciara thinks of the way her mum used to gossip with the huddle of Irish mums at the school gates. Even as a child, she hated the way these other mums looked at her, smug with knowledge. Sinéad never seemed bothered by this. "The Irish mammies mafia," she used to call them. "Sure let them gossip about us, if they've nothing better to do," she'd add. But Ciara used to feel so angry with Rhona for talking about her. Guilt courses through her now, for having trespassed on Alex's story.

"Will we make a move?" Alex says.

"Drink your coffee," Cathy says, "there's no rush."

Alex has a half-finished Americano in front of her, and a Fruit Shoot for Damien. On a big sports screen above the bar, the news is playing. A journalist wearing a smart red blazer is standing outside a semi-detached house cordoned off by yellow tape. Ciara can't hear the TV over the din of the bar, but she reads the captions running along the bottom of the screen, white letters on a red banner. "*Woman found dead at her home in Cabra named. Eileen O'Sullivan, 39-year-old mother of four. Husband Michael O'Sullivan remanded in custody…*"

Ciara looks away, glances at Alex. Was she watching the screen too? Her expression gives nothing away, but there's a briskness in the way she stands up, flicks her hair out from under her jacket, zips Damien's hoodie.

"Will we get the show on the road? Where's this zoo?"

The girls jump around giddily when they near the entrance, where tropical jungle sounds are being played from speakers.

Behind the ticket desk, a large man with a goatee squints at Cathy's phone and shakes his head, "I dunno now..."

"It's bleedin genuine!" she's protesting. "I won it off the Dublin Mums' Facebook page! Look it up!"

"Yeah..." he says, "It's just that... Well, this is a family pass. Two adults and two kids. It's for a family, like."

"This. Is. Our. Family." Cathy's face is deadpan. She nods to Ciara and the kids behind her, "Unless youse are discriminating against same-sex couples now, are yis? In which case I'll need to speak to a manager—"

"No, no..." The man's face flushes, and he hands Cathy's phone back. "No that's grand, I was just... Just checking, that's all... Here you go, here's a map. The zoo closes at six."

Away from the ticket desk, Cathy starts laughing so hard she has to stop and catch her breath. "Daft eejit," Alex says, but she's smiling. Damien has been sulking beside her, still transfixed by the phone. He looks up now and tugs her hand. Alex bends to hear what he's saying, and her dark hair brushes his face.

In the South America House, golden lion tamarins dart through the branches. Spider monkeys with stripy tails peep down at them with their sweet, melancholy little faces. Next, they follow the trail down through a bamboo tunnel to the elephants.

Around midday they find a wooden picnic bench by the Reptile House, and Ciara unpacks the jam sandwiches she made in the bathroom at the Eden. Cathy has brought a big bag of popcorn and some boxes of Ribena, which she hands out to the kids. While they're eating, a peacock struts past, trailing its dazzling tail feathers.

"Look, it's got eyes on its tail!" Sophie says. "Like the one we saw on the *Amazing Animals*!"

After lunch, they stroll on: down the hill, past the gentoo penguins, under the tunnel to watch the Californian sea lions diving through flues of bubbles, then up the steps to the African plains. It's getting busier as the day goes on. Young couples on dates, holding hands. Packs of youth groups with matching hoodies. Mums and dads with backpacks, following their kids from one enclosure to another, taking pictures. These families, do they feel her stare? Look at them, navigating the zoo in a wordless two-step, manifesting her deepest longing. *You should go back, you should go back.* She stares as if they are a different species.

Late afternoon, when they make it back to the entrance, the girls pull her into the zoo shop, but everything is too expensive. Ciara suggests ice cream, but Sophie doesn't want one. She doesn't want a €2 keyring, or a Dublin Zoo pencil either. She wants a stuffed golden lion tamarin, which costs €28. In the middle of the shop, Ciara tries to explain in a quiet voice that she can't have the toy right now, but maybe for her birthday after Christmas. "But that's AGES away." Sophie starts crying: "And I want it now!"

Eventually, Ciara has to drag Sophie out of the shop and through the turnstiles with everyone watching them. She must be the worst mother on the planet. "It's not fair!" Sophie sobs.

Damien starts moaning too, wanting the phone, which Alex is refusing to give him. Lucy has fallen asleep in her buggy. Ella tugs at Ciara's sleeve, "Tired."

"Here," Cathy wheels Lucy's buggy over to Ciara, "mind this one for a minute." She turns to Sophie, Damien and Ella. "Right gang, follow me."

Behind the tea rooms there's a grassy hill with a bandstand at the bottom. Cathy turns to the three kids, who have stopped moaning and are watching her with wary curiosity. "Okay gang," she says, "I bet all of youse are far too chicken to do THIS."

The kids watch wide-eyed as Cathy lies down on the grass and starts rolling down the hill, bumping along and cursing wildly, her red hair flying. Sophie squeals with laughter, putting her hands over her mouth. Ella is already getting down on the grass to copy Cathy. Damien checks his mum's face, as if looking for reassurance that this is safe, before laughing, lying down and rolling after her.

"She's some woman," Ciara says. Cathy is at the bottom of the hill now, dusting herself off and standing, arms outstretched, ready to catch the children as they roll.

"She's brilliant," Alex says. "She's a good friend. One of the only ones who's stuck around." There's a pause, before she says, "So, Cathy tells me you've just left?"

"Yes, just a couple of months ago."

"You were lucky. Getting a room that fast. I've been out a year now, but when we first left, me and Damien had to sleep on my mam's sofa. We couldn't get anywhere. I've three sisters living at my mam's, with their kids. Ten of us in that house, one bathroom, and we lived there six months. But I guess some people land on their feet. You working?"

"Not yet. I've been trying to find something. I've applied for loads of jobs, but I can't even get an interview."

Alex nods. "Keep trying. Something will turn up. Once you can start earning your own money, you feel more independent. But let me tell you something—stay out of those courts, and if you do end up in court don't expect anyone to believe you. Keep him onside. Don't withhold access. Keep things as friendly as you can. You've got to be smart, yeah? He'll try to use the kids to control you. These fuckers always use the kids. They know . . . That's our kryptonite."

"LOOK AT US, MAMMY!" Ella shouts.

"I'm watching you, love."

"Me too, Mum!" Damien shouts.

Alex gives him a thumbs up and he grins.

"He's gorgeous," Ciara says. "A wee dote."

Alex gives a soft smile. "He's my world," she says. "It's mad, you know. Garry never even looked at him before. Now he's talking about fifty–fifty custody. If I'd known he'd do that . . ." She stops for a minute, watching Damien rolling down the hill for the third or fourth time after Sophie and Ella, then getting up and chasing them to the top again, dry twigs stuck to his hair. Alex's face as she watches her son carries a mix of love and nostalgia.

"But look it," she says, "even if I'd known, about the courts and everything, I still would've left. Or I'd have ended up like one of them women you see on the news. Famous."

Ciara doesn't know what to say. "You've done really well," she finally manages. "Last time I only stayed away for a month." Her voice sounds patronizing, condescending—she didn't mean it like that.

Alex turns and looks at her. Her eyes are dark brown, her lashes long like a child's. It's the first time she's made eye contact properly all day, and Ciara gets the feeling she's sizing her up.

"It's early days for you," she finally says. "Leaving is one thing, but staying away is another."

That next day, after playschool, Ciara brings the girls up to St. Stephen's Green. It's changed since her college days. Where are the ducks? Replaced by hostile seagulls. She takes a photo of them on the little stone bridge leading into the central quadrangle, sends the photo to Mum and Sinéad. They both send love hearts back. *Gorgeous wee dotes.*

Ella clings to her hand. Sophie looks restless, trying to balance on the side of the pond. Ciara leads them to the lawn near the bandstand, where a few couples are sunbathing and a boy is learning to ride a bike, wobbling across the daisied grass. The girls are used to being swung around by their six-foot-something father. She needs to show them that she's fun too. "Run to me," she tells them. "Go on, run and I'll lift you."

Sophie looks skeptical, but Ella charges at her mother and jumps. Ciara swings her daughter old-fashioned carousel style, Ella's skinny legs diagonal.

"Let me have a turn," Sophie says.

Ella shouts, "AGAIN, AGAIN!"

They love being swirled around and toppling back onto the wet grass. Damp knees, muddy bums and a trek back down Grafton Street. Landing into Room 124, adding mud-splattered runners and grass-stained leggings into the mix of general clutter. She goes into the ensuite, turns on the bath taps and throws a quick splash of baby bath under the running water. Not much left, she has to make it last. Just as she's emptying the lunch boxes at the bathroom sink, Ryan texts:

Why don't you guys come by the house to see the chicks tonight?

He's added a coffee cup emoji, a love heart and a yellow chick. The temptation. Thoughts of the clothes horse, dishwasher, burnt crumbs in the bottom of the toaster, drawers full of clean folded socks. Of stepping away from this stress.

Euphoric recall. Nights when she sits in the bathroom, scrolling to distract herself, wary of sleep, she's been reading about how the brain clings onto good memories—the highs. This is why her mind keeps replaying their wedding night when he struggled with the buttons on her white fishtail dress, and they fell into bed laughing together and—

She replies: *No we are busy*

Water thunders from the taps, steam rising. Ciara turns off her phone, and her heart quickens. There will be a consequence for this. She tries to push the fear aside, to get back to the joy she felt in the Green this afternoon, calls the girls, "Right, in here you two! Bath time!"

Ella flops down and pulls off her socks. Sophie struggles with the heart-shaped buttons on her cardigan, brow furrowed. "You need help there, Soph?"

"No, I can do it!"

After a couple more minutes, Sophie sighs, "Ugh. You do it, Mammy."

As Ciara is working each button out of its loop, she looks up to find her daughter quietly studying her face. Has she spotted that her mum is upset? It's so hard to hide her emotions from her daughters within the confines of this room. Finally, Sophie kisses her nose. "I like the green bits in your blue eyes."

"Thanks, sweetheart."

"Why are they there?"

"Stuck!" Ella has her vest over her face. Ciara yanks it over her head. When they are undressed, she lifts them both into the warm soapy bath.

Ella is refusing to sit down in the tub. She stands, arms stretched for balance, chubby legs wavering. Sophie says, "Look at Ella. She's surfing!"

15

Early June, the heat is rising. In the waiting room at the Rotunda Hospital, a video is playing on loop. Causes of nappy rash. Colic. Healthy meals for the family. A smiling woman throws celery, mustard and spinach into a pot, but she hardly has time to stir her Healthy Midweek Stew before the next snapshot begins to play. The best setup for your baby's nursery. Ciara has been holding onto a full bladder for two hours and feels about ready to burst, when finally a small blonde nurse steps into the waiting room. "Ciara Fay? Into the midwife please."

Age. Height. Weight. The usual.

"Are you afraid of your husband?" The young nurse continues typing, as if she's asked the most mundane question in the world.

Why is she asking that? An uncomfortable feeling creeps over Ciara, and she shifts in her seat. Is there something about her expression? The wary, tired, tense feeling—does it show?

"Sorry," the nurse says, "we just have to ask. It's on the form. We ask everyone. Statistically, domestic abuse increases during pregnancy."

"They didn't ask me that, the last couple of times."

"Maybe a new thing. New computer system." The nurse gives a tired half-smile, her fingers on the keyboard ready to click.

What will happen if she says yes? What would that trigger? That catch in her throat.

"No," Ciara answers with a nervous laugh, hand on her belly. *Ask me again.* She watches the nurse, her tidy hair, her relaxed mouth. *Go on. Ask me again. See what I say next time. Ask.*

"Hop up onto the bed for me," the nurse says.

Cold, clear gel on her skin. At the press of the probe, a dart of fear flickers through her. The first time she had a scan like this, she was barely twenty-four and living in Barcelona, dating a Catalan boy who lived down the street. She hadn't known anything about babies or what to expect from her hospital appointments, but at her twelve-week scan, the screen showed only an empty sack. A black space inside her womb. The loneliness of it.

"A missed miscarriage," the doctor was finally able to translate. Her boyfriend's grandmother, who lived in San Sebastian, had already given her a tiny white knitted cardigan. Even after they broke up, Ciara carried that cardigan around with her for years, knitted arms folded gently, pressed between clothes in the middle of her suitcase. *These things happen,* she tells herself. *That's life. Things don't always work out.* Two healthy children. She should be grateful.

Tears are sliding down her cheeks, onto the white paper sheet.

The nurse is looking at the screen. "There we go," she says. "There's baby."

And there it is. On the screen above the bed, a white comma shifts in and out of focus. A tiny gray bean in the middle of a black speech bubble. The fast chug of a heart.

"They died," Ryan says as soon as he opens the door. "All except one."

"I'm sorry," she mumbles, inwardly shuddering at the thought of their tiny bodies, their sightless eyes.

Sophie peers into the bucket. "Where's all the other ones?"

Before Ryan can introduce the girls to the concept of death, Ciara smiles and says, "Great news! Two of the chicks flew away to see their mammy!"

Luckily they seem to accept this. Sophie says this lone survivor is Chase. Now grown to fist size, the crow chick is covered in dark gray fleece that doesn't yet resemble feathers. Ryan is showing her how to feed it.

"It's easy," he's saying, "Just pick up a lump of cat food like this"—he demonstrates with a pair of eyebrow tweezers she must have left behind—"and drop it into his beak."

There it is again, a high-pitched squeaking that doesn't seem to be coming from the chick at all. At what point will this chick realize his mother isn't returning? The crow's bright crimson beak stretches impossibly wide. He swallows the food, then immediately opens his beak, looking for more.

What would happen if she left Chase in the woods behind the playground in the Phoenix Park? Would other crows, like the ones on the telephone wires along Botanic Close, swoop down and feed him? Probably not. The way they glower down, wings hunched, they'd probably kill him. Chase can't hold his neck up for long. He stretches, then falls back against the makeshift nest. The baby flutters in her belly. Early December, the nurse said. A Christmas baby.

"Here," Ryan hands her the tweezers, "why don't you give it a try?"

He smiles, puts a hand on her back. He's trying to get her to move back in. And he wants her to look after this chick while he goes on a golfing weekend. But something has shifted in her since talking to Alex, and seeing her baby on the scan today.

Outside the window, a pair of swifts are diving across the white stretch of evening sky. Rhona's favorites. In proportion to their body weight, they have the widest wingspan of any bird on earth. They migrate between South Africa and Ireland each summer, sleeping on the wing.

Ryan's hand on the small of her back. Firm, warm, intoxicatingly familiar. It would be so easy to think she could lean into him and step back into those early days, when everything felt so—

No. Shaking her head, she breaks the trance. A discordant ringing in her head. A microphone, dropped. For a split second, his hand remains, before he allows her to step away.

She says, "We'd better get back." She hesitates before adding, "We can't keep doing this, Ryan. In future I will drop the girls off to see you and then pick them up later."

"So you'll bring them over and leave them with me?"

"Yes."

"A few times a week?"

"Sure." *How many days is "a few"?* She's annoyed with herself for being vague, placating as always.

Ryan shakes his head. "What's the plan here? Do you even know what you're doing? I'm worried about you, honestly."

She's trying to keep her voice steady. "The nurse asked me this question today. She asked if I'm afraid of you. And the answer is yes, Ryan. The answer is yes. You're only being nice to me because you want something."

Did she say that? Did she actually say that to him? *Jesus Jesus Jesus, Ciara. Are you really doing this?*

"Excuse me?"

"This won't last," she says. She puts down the tweezers, wipes her hands on her leggings and stands up straighter. "You'll flip right back into berating me, criticizing me. The minute I say no."

Ryan looks aghast. "Are you kidding me? I love you so much. I've been going to therapy every week. My therapist thinks you really need help. She says it's learned behavior—"

"Come on, girls." She hoists Ella onto her hip, takes Sophie's hand and leads her out of the house.

At the doorway, Ryan grabs her upper arm. "Is this what you want? A court case, a custody battle? You think I'm going to be your friend?" He scoffs, his face contorted with contempt. All kindness, all gentleness has evaporated. "I'm not going to be your friend. You did this. You caused this. I'll get what I'm entitled to. I'm their father."

"Let go of me please. It's over, Ryan. This time it's really over."

"Oh so we're doing this are we?" His face is furious. His pupils dilated. A vein pulses in his forehead. Her heart is pounding. He tightens his grip on her arm, puts his face close to hers, hisses, "You have no fucking idea what you're getting into."

She feels Sophie's hand slip into hers and squeezes it tight.

Ryan lets go, turns back into the house.

Tears blurring her vision, she looks down. "Mammy," Sophie says, "what was your best bit of today?"

In the hotel room that night, she applies shea butter lotion to her palms, massages her hands and wriggles her gold wedding band off her finger. She puts it into the zip-up part at the back of her purse. Her breathing is slow. This doesn't feel real. She goes to the window and looks out over the rooftops. A flutter startles her. A bird? Not at this time of night.

A bat. A small shadow flits across the arc of streetlight.

She boils the small kettle, stirs a milky tea. She carries the mug to bed, climbs in next to Ella. *It's going to be all right, it's going to be all right. Just breathe.*

"Mammy?"

"Ella. It's sleepy time. Come on."

She snuggles down, face close to her daughter's face. Her brown eyes, soft cheeks. "What you thinking, Mammy?"

A pause.

"I'm thinking about my dream bathroom."

16

"Housekeeping!"

In her doorway, a man in his early thirties. Tanned skin. Shaved head. Dark brown eyes. He smiles at her. "Good morning. We here for change your towels, sheets. We gotta check the room." He glances to the ceiling, a swift gesture of disapproval. He adds in a whisper, "No worries, I don't take down your photos or take your rice cooker or nothing."

She recognizes his Brazilian accent in the rhythm of his words. A pulse of music is threading into the room from the phone in his pocket. A samba rhythm, a song she remembers from São Paulo bars and clubs, Eu Só Quero É Ser Feliz.

It's just after 7 a.m. Down the corridor, other doors are also being opened, shouts echoing. Like a dawn raid. Like an eviction. *Housekeeping!*

The young couple with the baby are standing outside their room. Their child's mewing cry reaches into her chest. The old man from 150 is walking in and out of his doorway, looking at the carpet. The four little girls from 143 are being herded out of the room by their mum, still in her dressing gown, shouting at the housekeeping staff. "Absolutely no fucking need...keep the room bloody pristine...fucking privacy...Homework, Eabha, you've left your homework!"

Cathy slams out of her room wearing a bright yellow bomber jacket, Lucy in her arms, her teenagers slouching behind. "Bloody joke," she hisses at Ciara. "Catch you later, missus."

The man in her doorway says, "Look, I sorry. Maybe we can leave it, yeah?"

"Diego!" Behind him, a small woman with cropped black hair and an earlobe lined with silver studs is holding a clip-board. "I need Room 124 done. Now."

"Okay, boss!" He gives her a tired smile.

Ciara looks at her watch. "I have to leave in the next five minutes or I'll be late." She looks at the man. "This has to be fast. Girls, you stand there by the window."

Ella is chewing Hoppy's faded blue ear. Sophie skips around, excited by this drama. "Who's that man? What's he doing in our room?"

He smiles, "I'm Diego. And you?"

"Sophie, Ella and the mammy is Ciara! We're on holidays in this BIG HOTEL. Because the heating in our house is broke."

Ciara grabs the damp white towels from the bathroom, embarrassed by their sour reek. Diego throws them into the laundry sack at the door. Together they tackle the duvet. She stands on the bed, rips apart the studs, while he pulls the cover down, untucks the fitted sheet. What must Diego think of this place? She sees the room through his eyes, the casual squalor of it. Breakfast dishes in the bathroom sink. Her old black bra, hanging on the corner of the radiator. A bulging bin bag of dirty laundry by the bed. A split pack of nappies on the windowsill.

"I have to go," she tells him. "I should be in the car already. I'm an English teacher. I've a new job, it's my first day." She can't keep the pride from her voice. The thrill when she got the email the other day.

Diego nods, pulling the sheets off Sophie's fold-out bed, his tanned hands fast. "No way. First day? You can't be late."

He throws a folded pack of clean sheets onto the bed. "Done."

"Come on, let's go." She grabs the girls' hands and they run down the corridor.

As they're nearing the back staircase, Diego shouts, "Good luck with first day!"

Her job is at the English-language school in the university down the road from Happy Days. The free Early Years play-school session lasts only three hours, but Mairéad offers extra hours in the afternoon, €30 for the two girls for the week. This seems far too cheap. *Does Mairéad somehow know about their situation?*

On the central university plaza, students mill around outside the campus café. At the language school, a woman in a cobalt jumpsuit and silver jacket introduces herself as Veronica, the director of studies. She hands Ciara a clip-board and holds the door for her as they leave the language office. "We've had a massive intake of students over the past fortnight," she says. "More Italian teenagers than we know what to do with. I've had to move teachers around, reallocate classrooms. Your CV was a godsend."

"I haven't taught for a few years." Although Veronica is wearing stilettos, Ciara's having to scurry to keep up.

Veronica opens the door to another building.

"Well, you'll soon get back into it. Probation for the first three months, okay? We'll look at your contract after that. Now then, this is you." Veronica leads her into a first-floor classroom in the old part of campus. Ivy tendrils lace the tall sash windows. Desks have been arranged in a U-shape, familiar from her teaching days in Italy, Barcelona, São Paulo. She finds herself smiling. This feels like coming home.

Veronica says, "I'll leave you to it."

As students start to filter in, Ciara can't stop smiling. She tucks her hair behind her ears, straightens her navy blazer. It's been years since she has stood in front of a class. Since she has inhabited a persona other than that of mother, wife. She'd intended on working when she moved to Ireland and got married, but Ryan always had a reason for her not to. When she was pregnant he said it wasn't good for the baby. Then he said childcare was too expensive. So much of her energy has been focused on getting through each day. On trying to hear herself think.

The students sit down, chatting quietly, and take out their books and pens. Fifteen young men and women, mostly in their early twenties, seated around the whiteboard looking up at her in hopeful expectation. Sunlight filters through the ivy leaves, sluicing the room in dappled, greenish light. Now that the seats are full, she goes round the room, asking them to introduce themselves. Then she walks to the board, picks up a marker and starts writing.

I am 36 years old.

I have a dog and two cats.

I used to live in Brazil.

She says, "Which one of those sentences is false?"

The students laugh. Buoyed, the tightness in her chest begins to melt. A tingling feeling, like blood returning to a limb. Two months since they left. And yet here she is. Here she is. Things are going to be okay.

She's smiling so much she might cry. Now she's pointing to her sloping cursive on the grubby board. "Seriously, folks. This is a game. Which one is false?"

A young man near the back raises a hand. "I think you not thirty-six, teacher. I think you twenty-one, no?"

"Ah, I see you're going to be my favorite student."

More laughter now. But already, the more competitive students are attempting to guess. She's trying to remember all their names from their introductions. Bianca from Sardinia, Chan from Hangzhou and Yuki from Osaka.

"I think you don't live in Brazil, teacher." Elisa from São Paulo leans back on her chair, chewing the end of her biro, her eyes teasing. "You don't cope in Brazil. Too hot for you. You melt. Like barbecue. Oof."

More laughter. Ciara folds her arms across her chest. "Nice try, Elisa. But they are all true, apart from this one. I don't have a dog and two cats. I have two kids instead. Now it's your turn. Write down three sentences, two true and one false. See if you can fool your classmates."

She circles, reading over their shoulders. Most of them write two ordinary-sounding statements, and one that's blatant fiction. *I stay in Dublin for three months. I have two siblings. My sister is Madonna.* The ones who succeed in baffling their classmates are those who recognize the best way to hide a lie is to make it sound ordinary.

At eleven-o'clock break, she checks her phone. Ryan has been messaging, telling her which days suit him this week—Tuesday and Thursday, and half a day on Sunday. She's been trying to organize set days, so they don't have to keep texting, but he says he won't be tied down, cannot be expected to conform to her schedule.

She can feel her mind getting drawn back into the maelstrom of worry, but when she steps out of her classroom, two other teachers along the corridor beckon her to join them for coffee. They buy cheap lattes from the shop and sit on benches outside the student union, under trellises of flowering honeysuckle. The other teachers introduce themselves as Olivia and Maggie. They ask where she's from, which countries she's taught in. Soon Ciara finds herself swapping stories, laughing at jokes, worry eclipsed by a feeling of camaraderie she hasn't experienced for so long.

Sitting in their usual spot in the corridor, Cathy laughs when she tells her about Diego, and how they changed the bed together.

"Pure gorgeous, he sounds like," Cathy says.

"Just his accent. His music. It brought back happy memories, that's all. I was in Brazil when I was twenty-eight. Loved it. The last time I felt really free."

"You were banging some lad out there were ye?"

"No! I was on my own. But I was happy. Independent. Then I came home to Sheffield. I was ready to come back. Started my teacher training. I'd nearly finished it. That's when I met Ryan."

"Swept you off your feet, yeah?"

"Ah yeah. You know. He was doing a course over there, but it was almost finished when I met him. It was my thirtieth and there was a ceilidh at the Irish club. Old ones sitting around with pints reminiscing. A few of us young ones went to the Leadmill afterward."

"The Leadmill?"

"It's a nightclub. That's where I got chatting to him. Well, it was too loud to talk, but we danced. I was fairly well oiled like, and Sinéad had bought the most ridiculous balloons. Anyway, I went back to his place then. Turned out he was northern. From Monaghan, where my granny was from. He wasn't drinking, he doesn't drink, but he was great craic, had me in stitches. He just seemed so genuine. Is that daft to say?"

Cathy nods, listening.

"He just took over. Other lads I'd dated, it would be like getting blood from a stone. Trying to get them to commit to anything. But with Ryan, we were seeing each other every day. It was as if he filled up all my thoughts. We'd only a week together, then he was due to move back to Ireland. He'd passed his civil service exams, had a job lined up in Dublin. He wanted me to go with him. I couldn't think of a reason not to. Or maybe I was scared not to. I really felt like this was the biggest love of my life. And he kept telling me how special this was, how I was nothing like his ex who treated him so badly. I felt like I needed to mind him. He told me he'd had such a tough life. He needed someone to love him. He said no one understood him like me."

"So you're a schoolteacher? Would you not go back to doing that? Class holidays—and a bit more stable for youse."

"Well, I didn't get that great a result. Made a mess of my final placement, too distracted by Ryan I guess. My own stupid fault. Scraped a pass. And anyway, I can't teach here. I don't speak Irish."

Cathy is studying her face. She says, "And who told you that?"

Tuesday evening has come around too fast. "Mammy's not staying this time, girls," she tells them as she's driving toward their old house.

Sophie frowns. "Why not?"

"I have to do some shopping, love. Sure you'll be grand on your own with Daddy. You'll have great fun."

He opens the door instantly, as if he'd been waiting behind it. Ciara hears herself babbling as she hands him the nappy bag, explaining about snacks and the spare changes of clothes. Ryan says nothing. She can feel his anger. "I'll pick them up at six?" she says.

"Fine." He shuts the door in her face. She fights the urge to hammer on it.

He will give them back, won't he? He won't do anything stupid? Drive off with them? Change the locks? She forces herself to turn and walk away.

17

Forty-three Italian teenagers are gathered in emperor penguin-style huddles outside the language school. Black hoods up, hands in pockets, scowling at their phones. From the slouch of them, these kids hold her personally responsible for the Irish climate.

"The main thing," Veronica smiles as she hands over the clipboard and first-aid kit, "is to show them all the main sights. Oh, and not to lose any of them. Of course."

The four Italian group leaders have slunk away, leaving Ciara to herd the teenagers out of the concourse, toward the main avenue.

"But it rains in Italy, doesn't it?" she makes the mistake of asking one of them as they're walking toward the bus stop.

"No," a girl with white UGGs and aggressive eyeliner replies. "In Italy we do not 'ave this rain."

Oh yes you do, you little fecker. She remembers the rain in Bologna. Sheltering under the porticos. Riding her flatmate's motorino out of the city. Teaching in an archaic converted castillo off the Piazza Maggiore.

The Italians dawdle down the avenue, under the dripping

canopy of summer leaves, boots and runners squelching through puddles. Thank Christ the bus is just pulling in as they reach the stop, but getting all forty-three teenagers onto the upstairs deck of the 13A at the same time is some task. Locals put their shopping bags on their knees to make more space for this invasion of perfume, hairspray and complaining.

"English! Let's speak English!" Ciara soon tires of saying.

Reaching town, the rain stops. Down Gardiner Street, sunlight reflects off car windows, sending watery patterns up the dusty Georgian facades. Shoals of people are surging across pelican crossings.

The Italians have no interest in O'Connell Street, the GPO, or her potted history of the Easter Rising. It starts raining again, and they shelter under the entrance to the GPO while a torrential downpour turns the pavements white. An old man in a sleeping bag holds a cardboard sign. *Homeless please help God bless.* A Jack Russell is asleep on his lap, ears twitching. One of the Italians drops a coin into the man's McDonald's paper cup.

When the rain eases up a little, she brings them over O'Connell Bridge and along D'Olier Street to Trinity College. Each time they cross over a road, half the group get left behind, and they have to wait for them to catch up. At Trinity, she tries to explain that the small wooden entrance signals the narrow path into knowledge, but none of the teenagers are listening, and it has started raining again with a vengeance.

She leads them back over O'Connell Bridge. Swans rise

off the Liffey, their wings beating an angry pulse against the water.

As they are about to cross the road at the Spire, one of the girls shouts something and whistles. The group noticeably rally. Excitement spreads through them. A glimmer of enthusiasm for the first time that day. As a collective forty-three-person wave, they tug her toward Henry Street. Amidst the flurry of excited Italian, she catches a triumphant word: "Shopping!"

Back at the language school half drenched, she is just on time for her afternoon classes. There's an unread text from Ryan.

5pm today. Do not be late

He's angry. It's hard not to react. For the past two weeks, she's been dropping the girls off and leaving, careful not to get drawn into conversation with Ryan. Proud of herself each time she drives away. Waiting in Brambles Café. Or putting on a load of washing at Soap 'n' Suds and watching it spin.

A magpie struts past her classroom window. *One for sorrow.* Her mum used to have a pair of magpies who visited her garden every day, leaving tokens of shiny things, Bottle caps, hair clips. Rhona used to collect their gifts in an old tin can. *Two for joy. Three for a girl.*

Her head reels. Standing in her classroom, she is trying to think, but her students keep asking questions.

"How to conjugate the present participle?"

"How I can catch train for Belfast for see Titanic museum?"

"What's the difference between present simple and present continuous?"

"Look." She's writing on the board. *At least this is an easy question.*

WE LIVE IN A HOTEL. "That would mean it's permanent."

WE ARE LIVING IN A HOTEL. "That means it's temporary. Just for now."

Her class look at her, blank faced. Finally Chan raises his hand, "Teacher. I not understand this example."

Bianca says, "I not understand neither. Why anyone would *live* in a hotel?"

Today they are meeting Ryan at the coffee shop in Marks & Spencer's on Henry Street, close to closing time. She is meant to be dropping the children with him and leaving, but when they get to the café he has already ordered her a coffee. He slides the latte over to her. "Mammy's going to hang out with us, isn't that right girls?"

"Mammy stay!" Ella hugs her mum's knees.

Sophie is holding her hand and doesn't let go.

"Okay. Maybe just for a few minutes."

Eating prepacked sandwiches, it's as if they are pretending to have a normal family dinner in the empty café, with the staff wiping down counters and cleaning the coffee machine. Ryan has bought the girls a small cheese sandwich, and *oh dear God* they're taking forever, eating every last crumb. Ryan hunches his shoulders. She smiles tensely over her lukewarm coffee.

"So how's the chick?" she asks.

"Not good," he says.

She's not sure why she has the hysterical urge to laugh. Instead she says, "Oh really?"

"Yeah. Not good at all. I think he'll die like the others."

"Oh... so not that great at all then."

"No."

He looks terrible. His eyes are red rimmed and he's wearing an old gray jogging top and paint-smeared jeans. Her reflex of guilt is automatic, before she catches herself. *This is deliberate, you know he's trying to make you feel bad.* Ella sits on his knee, and Sophie chatters.

"Why don't you guys come by the house tomorrow to see Chase?" Ryan says. "You'd like that, wouldn't you, Soph? You'd like to come home to your nice house?"

"Let's go see Chase!" Ella says. Then she starts complaining, rubbing her eyes with her fists.

"Right, time to go." Ciara starts clearing up, putting their dishes onto the tray. "Someone's tired. Time for beddy-byes, isn't it hun?"

"Mammy, I'm actually not even tired!" Sophie moans.

Ryan walks them through the store, past children's wear, men's wear, groceries. He says, "I'll give you a lift."

"It's grand, we'll get the bus."

"The bus to Terenure? That will take ages. It is Terenure, right? Isn't that where Tania lives?"

She still can't understand how Ryan has believed this lie. She hasn't seen Tania or any of her Trinity friends in years. Sure, she doesn't have any friends. Once she moved in with Ryan, her friendships gradually began to recede. Ryan used to smirk at Tania and her other college friends—*bloody liberal hippies.* Whenever he saw her texting, smiling at her phone, he would sink into a sullen mood that could linger for days.

Even when the girls were babies and she had her hands full, he messaged her constantly. A stream of texts, punctuating her day, until her friends' voices were drowned out, erased.

"Babe, please. I'm not going to hurt you. Come on, don't be ridiculous."

"My shoe!" near the exit of the store, Sophie stops walking, her left runner askew.

He sighs. Crouches down to help Sophie refasten the Velcro. His hands bent to a more gentle shape, his voice softening as he talks to his daughter.

"Here, let Daddy carry that." He stands, tucking Sophie's lunchbox under one arm. Before she can do anything, he takes each of the girls by one hand and walks ahead, leading the way. Her children are laughing—they think this is a game. Ciara follows, as if enchanted by the Pied Piper from Sophie's picture book. She follows him out of Marks and she follows him across the shopping center and she follows him up the escalator to the car park and she follows and she follows and she follows, all while thinking—*stop*. Hurrying behind him, she is trying to protest, We really don't need a lift, it's fine, honestly, but he will not engage, will not answer, and she's trapped in a place of irrational, dreamlike logic—her body automated, her vocal chords cut.

Do not get into the car with him do not get into the car with him do not get into the car with him do not get into the car do not

"You don't have child seats in the jeep!" Saved by this realization.

Ryan doesn't look at her. "They'll be fine."

He buckles the girls in. They're giddy with the thrill of

being so low down. "It's like a cave!" Sophie says. "We can't see out!"

"In the bear cave!" Ella joins in.

Ciara ducks into the front passenger seat, dread swelling under her rib cage, making it harder to breathe.

Driving out of the multistory, he speaks without turning toward her. "You know what you're doing is illegal, taking my children away from me and bringing them to sleep on someone's sofa?"

Like flipping a switch. The way his moods catch her off guard.

"We going back?" Sophie asks. She's craning her neck, trying to see out.

Ciara holds her breath, waiting for her daughter to say the word *hotel*.

"Everyone has been telling me to fight you," he says. "Everyone is disgusted by what you're doing. My friends keep telling me to take you to court. You've no intentions of coming back. Which way am I even fucking going?"

"Left... Next right... Over the bridge..."

They've been driving for ten, fifteen, twenty minutes, across the river, past Christchurch and St. Patrick's Cathedral, his voice getting angrier, words battering into her. Ciara is trying to focus on directions. She just needs to convince him to drop them off somewhere, anywhere, out of this car. Terenure—that's where Tania used to live—better go there, in case Ryan remembers. Who knows if Tania still lives there. It's been years. And what if she does—what then?

What will she say when they land on her doorstep? *How will I explain this?*

"You dumped me. Took my kids from me. Threw me aside like fucking garbage. Your children's father! Your husband! All I ever did was love you, care for you, provide for you, but oh no it wasn't enough."

"Straight on. Next left."

Without realizing, she's following the bus route she used to take when she was at college, living out here in this South Dublin suburb with a few pals. That's where Tania lived, yes. Near the house where Ciara lived in third year. Stumbling home tipsy late at night, walking these streets with linked arms, past this strip of shops, Brady's pub on the corner.

"Here we are!" Tania's old home is on a street of semi-detached houses. White guttering. Wet slate. Pebble-dash, shingle gray. Windows like watching eyes.

Ryan stops the jeep. Ciara unbuckles her belt, moves to get out, but he grabs her arm, leaning closer and speaking under his breath. "Are you even listening? This is insane. You're fucking pregnant, for God's sake. You can't just trample all over my rights as a father. Are you moving back or not? Because if not, I want full custody. I've been talking to a solicitor. The way you're acting... reckless, putting them in danger... he says I'd win full custody easily."

Her body is a damp twisted knot, her heart making it hard to breathe, hard to concentrate, to speak. She's shivering now, surely he can see that. She thinks of that term *thermal shock,* of glass heated to the point where it's about to shatter. She remembers that night when she was at the Christmas party.

Your fucking child won't stop screaming. As soon as she opened the front door, Ella's hands reaching for her. The hot tremble of her tiny body. She cannot leave them alone with him overnight. She cannot.

In the backseat now, Ella is chewing Hoppy's ear, while Sophie has fallen asleep with her head on one side, mouth open. *They think we're going to the hotel, or home.*

"Yes we're moving back." The words trip out before she can think. "I just need to pack and get organized. Another week at most."

He's eyeing her warily. "Fine. If you're coming back, then fine." He loosens his grip a little, leans across the handbrake, forces her chin up and kisses her firmly. "I'll see you at the house tomorrow."

He lets go of her arm and she scrambles out of the jeep, flings open the back door, lifts Ella out and onto her hip, unbuckles Sophie and half-heaves her out of the car, landing her onto the pavement. Sophie stretches, rubbing her eyes, still half-asleep. Before her daughter has time to start asking questions, Ciara slams the door.

"Where are we?" Sophie asks.

"Wave bye-bye to your dad," she says. They walk up the nearest driveway and stand beside a potted fern, while she pretends to rummage in her bag for keys. Ryan's jeep is still behind them, engine running. *Don't let anyone open the front door. Please, Jesus, don't let Tania, or worse, some nice polite stranger, open the door of this lovely suburban home. Please please please.* But Ryan hates waiting, has clearly given up. He sounds his horn, salutes as he drives away.

As soon as his tail lights have rounded the corner, out of sight, she hurries the kids back down the drive. Further along the road, the yellow lollipop of a bus stop makes her want to cry with relief. All routes lead into the city. All she has to do is wait for a bus to bring them back to the Eden. At the bus shelter, Ella sits on her knee, not even protesting. Ciara buries her face in her toddler's hair, inhales sweat and baby shampoo, and feels her heart rate slowly settle. Sophie is climbing on the plastic seats, still asking a flurry of *why* questions. Street lamps flicker on, cherry red in the dusk.

High season, families are queuing in the lobby. Men in football shirts with sunglasses on their heads. Women with tanned legs, in three-quarter linen trousers or maxi skirts. Kids with mini ride-on cases shaped like cows, trains, dragons. Outside the revolving doors, Lauren is perching on a stepladder, tipping a watering can over the hanging baskets. Wilting begonias drip, baptizing the heads of another group of tourists as they disembark the *Beautiful Erin Coach Tour.*

Ciara is waiting at reception, tapping her feet nervously and messing with her hair. A hen party with glitzy wings and haloes are checking in. Sophie and Ella are hugging one of the pillars in the lobby. Sophie asks, "What's this for?"

"I don't know, love. It's to hold up the ceiling."

"So the ceiling doesn't fall on anyone? Cool. We don't have them at home."

Behind the desk, a woman with a dark ponytail and glasses smiles up at Ciara. Her nametag says ISABEL. "How can I help?"

"I was asked to report to reception? Ciara Fay. We're on floor five."

"Just one second please."

That gray folder again. Isabel leafs through it, taking out pages, frowning and putting them back. *Don't throw us out don't throw us out don't throw us out don't throw us out don't.*

"Ah here. It seems there was a signature missing the other night, and I just have a note to remind you to sign in."

"That's it?"

"Yes, that's all for now."

"There's no letter for me? Nothing from the housing office?"

Isabel peers around the desk. She looks flustered in her heavy white shirt and black tie. A mini fan behind reception is only stirring the heat. "No sorry. Nothing here for you yet."

"Thanks." Ciara turns away.

Sophie wraps her arms around her mum's waist. "Mammy? When we were birds, what birds were we?"

"What? Sophie, sorry I just can't. Ella, off that table! No climbing! We are not at home."

Sophie sighs. "Yeah when are we going home? Daddy says the heating is fixed. And Chase the birdie is getting big, with real feathers!"

"Ah great. That's lovely, hun."

She nods politely at other holiday-making mothers who catch her eye and smile toward the kids. Surely there are two judgments reached by people who see a pregnant woman with a clatter of scruffy kids in a hotel. Either she's been evicted, or her scruffiness means she's too rich to care, and she probably owns this place.

It's still another fortnight until she gets paid. There's no point even searching for a place yet. She'll need €2,000 for the first month's rent, and another €2,000 for a deposit.

Housekeeping haven't been back to floor five. She's often thought of that morning with Diego, their hands working together, wrestling the white sheets.

She can't take any more of these messages from Ryan. He was livid when she confessed they are not moving back after all, and that she only said that to get away from him. *Liar. Ruining your children's lives. For no reason. Leaving for no reason. We could have been so happy.*

On floor five, Cathy has propped her door open with one of the fire extinguishers. A hot wind is funneling through the cracks of her open windows. Lucy is sitting on her knee in the corridor, sweaty, narky, tired.

A skinny young man is leaning by the fire escape, talking on the phone. She often sees him there, talking in a language she doesn't recognize. Close up, he is older than he first seems. It's his narrow frame, baggy hoodies and baseball caps, his vulnerability, that makes him seem like someone's teenage son trying to hitch a late-night lift home.

The woman in Room 141 has left her door jammed open too, the baby in its buggy in the hall. She has a handheld vacuum and is always cleaning. About once a week, she throws everything out into the corridor and slams the door. You can hear her shouting and crying at her husband. Sometimes she leaves her children outside in the corridor too, where they sit on the piles of towels, crockery and books.

Then she spends the day reassembling the room, piecing it all back together. "Fuckers will only wreck it again," Cathy said to her once. The woman didn't reply.

"Driving me mad," Cathy says, fanning herself with a rolled-up *Riverdance* leaflet, "driving me absolutely bananas. Wait till you hear the latest."

They're leaning against the cool walls of the corridor, talking between their doorways. "Look at this," Cathy hands over her phone. Cobweb smash in one corner. A video of a man in a black hoodie scaling concrete walls, to a soundtrack of pulse-racing techno. He leaps between railings. Backflips over flights of steps. Office plazas transformed into theme parks. Dull concrete bridges turned into helter-skelters. Ciara winces at the near-misses. The almost-grazings of his skull against concrete slabs.

"Tracers conquer fear," says the voice-over. "Parkour is about owning your environment, reimagining its potential."

"Parkour. This is what my two have been at. Little bollixes. *Water parkour* they're calling it. Which means lobbing themselves into the Liffey. You'd want to have eyes in the back of your bleedin' head."

Ciara frowns. "Can they swim, Cathy?"

"Can they fuck."

One morning, she answers an unknown number, thinking it might be the Central Placement Service. She regrets picking up as soon as she hears her mother-in-law's voice. "Ciara, what is going on?" Assumpta says, "Ryan-Patrick has been on the phone. His heart is broken. It seemed for a while there you were patching things up, but he tells me that hope has now been dashed. Surely you're not doing this again. To the girls."

Ryan-Patrick. She often forgets that's his full name. The slagging she got from Sinéad when she first met him. *"You'll be in Mum's good books for eternity now you're marrying a genuine Irish man with the most Irish name in history. Nice move, Ciara. Game over. I fold, Ciara, honestly it's too good. Well and truly outplayed."*

"Ryan tells me you seem quite unwell? I wonder have you seen a doctor? It's quite worrying for the children. I was at Mass only this morning and I said to Father Boyle, I said there's a family in need of extra prayers. Did you want to end up in hell, Ciara? Because it's a real genuine worry."

Hell. She thinks of Vic Cathedral, the hellscape fresco spread over pillars, walls, ceilings. Twisted limbs and bloodshot pleading eyes, the horror in those faces. She had nightmares after first visiting that place, and woke in the shuttered shadows of her apartment to visions of naked forms turned monochrome.

"I don't think this is fair," Ciara finally manages. "You've only heard his side of the story. You've admitted yourself, Ryan can be very—"

"We've heard enough," a male voice interjects. Ryan's father, Graham. Of course, they always make phone calls together. "What would you know about marriage?" her father-in-law says, "Raised by a single mother, across the water, in poverty. We warned Ryan-Patrick to stay clear. To find a nice Irish girl with a decent sense of faith."

"Now dear," Assumpta says, "the thing we need to know is

this. Are you returning Ryan's children to him? Or shall we give him money for a solicitor?"

A solicitor. She's known this is what he's planning, why he's been strangely quiet for the past few weeks. On access days, while she unbuckles Sophie and Ella and unloads their bag of toys and snacks, he stands in the doorway, arms folded. Then he makes a fuss of the girls, picking them up and swinging them round, ignoring her.

She's not sure which is worse. Hearing from him or not hearing from him. During silences like this, her hackles are raised, her back to the wall. It was always like this. Those times when she knew she had aggravated him, waiting for his reaction was the worst part. Deep in her stomach, that feeling of dread.

She has looked at the information on the Teaching Council site a few times. Now, as soon as she phones Sinéad and explains what she has discovered, it becomes true.

"I could have been teaching here all along," she tells her sister on the phone one night, "primary teaching. They give you three years to learn Irish, and you can work during that time."

"Shit." Her sister tuts. "And he said you couldn't do that?"

"He was adamant it couldn't be done. He said it wasn't permitted. He said it would be impossible anyway, for someone who wasn't Irish."

"You are bloody Irish!"

"Well, you know. Not fully. I wasn't born or raised here."

"Ciara! You were raised by an Irish mammy. Our whole

family is Irish. You have an Irish passport! That fucking dick-head. He always goes for your weak spots. He knows how to hurt you. Can't you see that?"

"Sinéad. How is this helpful?"

"Sorry. Jesus. Well, look, at least you know now. You can teach like you always wanted to."

"Well, not always. I wanted to be a performance poet, re-member me dragging you to all those spoken word nights?"

"Yeah well, that was just a blip." Sinéad laughs. "And how has he been? Since you told him that it's definitely over. Does he hassle you at drop off?"

"His mum phoned. She says he's hiring a solicitor."

"Jesus, Ciara. Then you'd want to get one too."

18

Twenty-seven, 28 degrees. Fires in the mountains. Heather blazing. The beaches are packed during the day. After dusk, she drives over the port bridge to Sandymount, where the girls run along the shingle. They collect shells and splash in the shallow waves.

Her bump swells until it can no longer be disguised by flowing blouses. A happily oblivious mound, straining against her €7 Penney's sundress. Ella traces the freckles on her shoulders, "Mammy's got DOT-TO-DOT!"

A hosepipe ban has been enforced. Shannon Airport registers 32 degrees, a new record. There has been a run on paddling pools across Dublin. On FM104, Jim and Jackie are hosting a call-in for reported paddling-pool sightings. A man phones to say there's about a dozen pools after being unloaded on a pallet at the front of Woodie's DIY Store in Finglas. By the time she nears Happy Days, a woman has called to say the Woodie's pools are all gone and she's raging.

After work, on days when Ciara doesn't have to bring the girls to see Ryan, she takes them to the Phoenix Park. The grass is parched. "It's hay!" Sophie runs around the lawns. Ella follows, dragging Hoppy, clad only in her sunhat, factor 50 and a saggy nappy. Ciara has been trying to toilet-train her, with limited success. Little pants line the side of the bath. The hotel carpet has become blotched with dark patches where she's tried to clean up accidents. All the websites tell her to keep her daughter in pants, not to revert to nappies, and to stay at home for a week until she is fully trained. But they can't stay in the room in this heat.

Unrealistic, unbelievable, this summer.

The Eden is getting busier each day. Whenever they pass the front entrance, yet another white coach is parked in the lay-by. Tourists disembarking under the dripping hanging baskets.

Where are all these people sleeping? Surely the hotel must be nearing capacity?

Each time she phones the Homeless Executive to confirm their room, her heart races. She's trying to grasp onto the happy, sunny feeling of when she first started teaching again, but it's like trying to hold water in her hands. Worry keeps her awake at night. What will Ryan do next? What if her application for homeless status is rejected? What if she doesn't qualify for the housing list? And even if she does, how will she find a home?

In this heat, the girls are sweaty, grumpy. Sometimes hyper, other times dazed, their small bodies sprawled across the white hotel duvet. The staff in the Eden restaurant give out butterballs of vanilla ice cream, tumblers of ice cubes. Sophie and Ella melt the cubes on their fingers, "Look Mammy, look at my ice ring!"

Each night she wakes with cramps in her legs and has to stand on the bathroom tiles, stamping away the pain, trying to cool down. Safety catches on the windows only allow them to open a crack. To stop any of us from taking a leap for it, Cathy says. Each morning, the sun rises bright, defiant.

It's too hot to think.

Late July, her first paycheck from the university hits her bank account at midnight, and she dances. This is her first salary in more than half a decade. Her girls are asleep, so she jumps up and down in their bathroom.

This is how she'll do it. This is how she'll survive and move on to the next place. Work and money, her own money, was always her means of charting a course out of trouble. Now with her salary in her own hands, and with that money from Louise, she'll have her deposit saved within a couple of months. Maybe she could even pay to register with the Teaching Council, look for a job in a school, start learning Irish. Her desire to squirrel this money away, matched by her urge to spend it.

She settles for a trip to Bray Aquarium that weekend. In the inky, undulating dark, Sophie and Ella press their noses against the glass tanks. Watching manta rays glide past as if flying underwater.

A sweltering night in late July, she leaves Ella and Sophie sleeping in Room 124. She brings two key cards, in case one of them malfunctions. In maternity PJs and a vest top, she walks down the corridor, feeling every step on the soles of her hot, swollen feet. She knows it's against the rules, but she waits at the lift and steps into the gasp of metal doors, presses the button for ground.

She tries the frosted-glass-paneled door into the Eden restaurant. To her surprise, it gives. Tables are set for breakfast. Silver cutlery. Heavy linen that refuses to bend at table corners, stuck out in stiff skirts.

Ciara waits at the stainless-steel counter until one of the kitchen porters walks past, carrying a stack of clean white plates. His name badge says DERMOT. "Have you any orange juice?" she asks.

"Kitchen's closed." Dermot looks at her again. "Sure, hang on there. I'll ask Chef and see."

This is what she always craves when she's pregnant. Strong tastes. Bitter. Salty. Last week she dragged the kids the whole way up Capel Street to a Vietnamese takeaway she remembered from college days. Fresh pineapple juice. Chicken fried rice, salty and strong.

Dermot returns with a tumbler of freshly pressed orange juice. She thanks him, embarrassed by her craving. The thirst with which she gulps the icy juice.

She carries her half-full glass out to the lobby, where it's cool and quiet, lit by soft lights under the reception desk. Electric candles in oversized storm lanterns flicker by the pillars. Small disks of white light run along the ceiling, a runway leading nowhere. She spots Marco's head behind the counter, bent over a book. Housekeeping staff are hoovering and wiping down surfaces.

A woman Ciara recognizes from floor five is sitting at a table by the window, rocking a baby on her lap. She's singing softly, her voice fluting gently across the empty space. An old Irish lullaby Ciara knows but cannot name, one her mum used to sing when they were children.

Ciara reaches for the sugar pot, tips out all the sachets and spreads them over the table. Each Gem sugar sachet has an old Irish saying printed on the back, with the English translation underneath. Words of wisdom. Confusing riddles. What is she looking for? A sign? Some guidance?

She looks up and sees Diego. He's wiping tables nearby, humming and nodding his head to a beat. His hair has grown, and he has a short beard flecked with gray. Baggy black trousers and a black T-shirt. Herringbone tattoos on his forearms. When he looks up and sees Ciara, he takes his earphones out and walks over, cloth in hand. "How's it going?"

"I'm making a mess," she looks at the sugar sachets. "Sorry, I'll tidy up."

"Is okay," he says. "But you think you need more sugar? You sure you have enough?"

"I need to learn Irish," she says. "But look at this. I don't even know how to pronounce any of this." She hands him a sachet. The inscription reads, *Ar scáth a chéile a mhaireann na daoine.*

Diego reads the English translation aloud. "*Under the shelter of each other, people survive.* Hang on." He takes out his phone, pulls out a pair of thin reading glasses, the kind you get from a vending machine.

"DIEGO!" the manager shouts from across the foyer.

He calls back, "One moment, Katya! Shelter . . . shelter . . ." He frowns. Screen light plays on his glasses. "Yes. Shelter.

Home. It means like *people are home for each other.* Yes. I like this very much."

"It's not really true through, is it?"

Diego takes off his glasses. He looks about to say something, but the manager shouts at him again. He sighs. "I gotta go. See you around?"

When she rings the bell one Thursday evening, Ryan stands blocking the doorway with his arms folded, no sign of the girls. Ciara tries to peer past him, expecting to see Ella and Sophie trundling down the hall with the backpacks she fills with toys and snacks whenever they come to visit. "Are they ready?" she asks.

"No. They're not coming." Ryan steps closer. "Sophie tells me you're living in a hotel?"

A flash of fear charges through her and she tries again to see past him into the house. Where are they? Why can't she hear them?

"I didn't want to tell you," she says, "I knew you'd be livid."

"So you just thought you'd lie to me?"

"I was going to tell you, I just—"

"Lies," he raises a finger toward her, pointing at her face, "that's all this relationship has been from the very beginning. You never loved me, and you don't give a shit about those children. All you care about is yourself." From the edge in his voice, she knows he's struggling to control himself. "The girls are staying here," he says. "You're not bringing them back to some grotty hotel. They can stay here, where they belong—"

"Mammy!" Ella pushes past her dad's legs. "This bag too heavy!"

"I've lost my cardigan, Mammy," Sophie follows, wiping her nose on the sleeve of her butterfly top, "the purple one with love-heart buttons."

"It's in the car, love." Ciara stands her ground. Oblivious, her daughters meander past her toward the Micra. She just needs to get them away from here. "See you on Thursday then," she says to Ryan.

He gives a hard, jeering laugh. "So that's it then? You're just going to drive off again? You think you can get away with this?" He pulls something out of the back pocket of his jeans, hands her a white envelope.

19

Ciara clicks Ella into her buggy and tells Sophie to hold on to the handle. A bright August evening, they walk past College Green, up Dame Street, and onto Camden Street. Some pubs have their windows and patio doors flung open, crowds of people spilling out onto the pavements. Pushing the buggy, Sophie's clammy hand in hers, she sees her daughter's eyes tracking faces as they weave through the throng of the bars. Ella tilts her head back, studying the gargoyles leering over balustrades. She thinks, *Please don't tell your dad you were out this late. He's claiming I'm a bad parent, has enough ammunition as it is.*

Past the George, the Long Hall and the Cosmo Bar. She hasn't been here at night since college days. Walking down this street is like stepping into the knee-high boots and ponytail of her student self. Impossible that this same body, which carried her along this street between sweaty bars and dancefloor mist, is now clad in maternity leggings, holding one child, pushing another in a banjaxed buggy, walking past the bus shelter and turning into—

The wrong building. This is the wrong building. This is Whitefriar Street Church, where Ryan used to bring her to Sunday evening Mass, one of their weekly rituals when they were newly wed. She'd daydream during the service, and they'd go for Chinese food afterward, at one of the restaurants further up Aungier Street. She tries to summon the emotion of this memory, but it's like watching a video of someone else's life. All she feels is numbness, coldly aware of the envelope in her handbag.

Sophie, curious as always, has dragged them up the entrance hall, through the double doors. "Look, Mammy. Cool!"

The church is almost empty. A folksy band are rehearsing by the vestibule, singing something about God's love, but they keep stumbling and restarting. Sophie and Ella gawk up at the marble saints. Near the altar, a blaze of tiered nightlights. A few tourists clink coins into the cash box at St. Valentine's feet. Beside the shrine, there's a heavy lined book propped open, where couples write notes of love and gratitude. Ryan wrote something when he first brought her here. Something about soulmates.

"They buried St. Valentine's heart in here," she finds herself telling the kids. "You know, like Valentine's Day? When we say m-wah, I love you!"

"Why only his heart?" Sophie asks. "Where they put the other bits like arms. Leg. Tummy. BUM! Ha ha. Where they put his bum, Mammy?"

"Jesus Christ. Shhhh we have to be quiet. We're in a bloody church."

"Mammy? What would happen if they put his heart somewhere else? Like on the roof going BOOM BOOM BOOM and everybody heard it? What would happen? What about if your heart was on the roof, Mammy? What would happen then?"

Next door, in the community hall, the parquet floor is marked out in squares and rectangles. *NO SMOKING. CAUTION WET FLOOR. Tickets now on sale for Show Boat by the Musical Society. Raffle Tickets 3.50.* Various notices are stuck with yellowing tape to the metal-edged door. High sports-hall ceiling. Curtained stage. Everything slightly chipped, slightly faded. Her chances of shiny concrete solutions seem to slip with each step, buggy wheels squealing.

A couple are sitting on plastic stackable chairs by the wall, both staring at their phones, and another woman is pacing with a baby in her arms. By the stage, a man in his fifties sits with a laptop balanced on a camping table.

He looks as if he might be in charge, so Ciara approaches him. "Sorry. I'm looking for the Free Legal Advice Centre?"

"You're in the right spot then so," he says. "I'll take your details here. Then the solicitor will see you when she's ready." He puts on a pair of reading glasses and peers at something on the laptop screen. "Can I get a name?"

He types with one finger, spelling aloud. "C-I-A-R... Now, how can we help you?"

"I've just left my marriage." Her cheeks are so hot, they must be bordering on the color of the brick-red walls. Sweat is seeping through her hoodie. "I'm looking for advice." *And I'm pregnant, and we're living in a hotel, and he's just handed me this letter, and...*

He clicks a couple of boxes.

"And what was the reason for the marriage breakdown?"

"I don't know. It was. It was just difficult. Will I get to speak to a solicitor this evening?"

"Difficult? There's no box for that. Physical abuse... infidelity... sexual abuse... ?"

Her heart quickens and she feels herself avoiding his eyes. With one hand, she pushes Ella's buggy back and forth, while with the other she messes with her hair. "Could you not just tick 'other reason'?"

"Fair play. I have it there now. Other reason." He spells aloud again, "O-T-H-E-R... If you want to take a seat there. Our solicitor will see you shortly."

In a small office above the Carmelite Hall, a slender woman shakes her hand, introduces herself as Grace. Eyes flitting, Ciara spots headed paper on the desk. *Grace O'Reilly, Solicitor. Specializing in Family Law and Custody Disputes.* Ciara hands her the white envelope. "My husband gave me this. It's a court summons."

While the solicitor opens the envelope and takes out the A4 page, Ciara unbuckles Ella and lifts her out of the buggy. She takes the tablet, presses play on another *Amazing Animals* video. "Just a few wee minutes, okay?"

She sits down opposite the solicitor. Tries to steady herself.

Grace refolds the letter, sets it down carefully beside her on the desk. "Well as you know, I'm sure, you can't begin divorce proceedings for two years post-separation. But before we look at that, let's go over the background to start off with. Tell me about the marriage. When did you meet?"

"2013." She stalls, remembering seeing him for the first time, when he walked into the Irish club in Sheffield with his friends. Her birthday. Those stupid balloons. Later that night, in the sweaty seventies room in the Leadmill, his body close to hers, his fingers on her neck.

"And you started dating?"

"Yes. He was starting a new job in Ireland, so we only had a short time together in Sheffield. After he went back to Ireland, he called every day. Wanted me to move over as soon as I could. I'd been planning on finding a houseshare in Dublin, but he didn't like that idea. He said if we really wanted to be together, we should just go for it."

Grace is transcribing Ciara's story into looping scroll across a yellow legal notepad. Strip lighting catches the solicitor's soft gray hair, her opal earrings.

"And how did things go, when you moved in?"

Ciara feels herself pause. It's still hard to explain. They had just moved in together. This should have been the start of a big adventure, but he always seemed dissatisfied, distant. He didn't even kiss her the way he had at first. Already, she wanted him to return to the person she'd met. She missed him, although she laughed at herself for thinking this. *How can you miss someone when they're right there beside you?*

She says, "Well we got married then. In September 2013."

Grace looks back at her notes, "So you'd known each other how long? Three months?"

"I know... It was all such a hurry. He really wanted to get married. I thought it would make him happy. And then within about a month, I was pregnant with Sophie. I thought that might make him happy too." She explains the history of her two pregnancies. The way that things unraveled. Her first attempt at leaving. Her current attempt. The hotel.

Once Ciara's finished speaking, Grace looks back at what she has written. Her pen taps her scrawled words. What pieces of the story are her eyes lighting on? *Came storming down the hall...eyes dilated, face white...called the guards but hung up...silent treatment, mood swings...walking on eggshells...threatening...nightmare...*

Ciara sees too clearly the gap between these careful sentences, and the reality of that night sitting on the bed cradling Ella, when, he came at her like—like what? Like something possessed. Not a breath of human warmth or compassion left. Instinct took over, her heart making it hard to hear. Out of so many nights like this, she's not sure why she keeps remembering this one.

Grace lifts the envelope, "And now he's served you with this."

"He gave it to me when I was dropping the kids off the other day."

Grace unfolds the letter and her eyes scan the page.

Sophie has figured out how to turn up the volume on the tablet to max. *"Tigers each have their own distinct print, like a human thumb print! There are only a small number of them left in the wild!"* Ciara steps over and turns it down.

"So he is filing for custody. He is claiming your accommodation at the hotel is unsuitable. He wants the children to live with him."

Hearing Grace say the words, Ciara starts to shake.

"It's okay. It's okay," Grace passes the box of tissues. Ciara takes one and blows her nose, balls the tissue into her fist and squeezes it to stop herself from screaming.

"Just try to keep calm, Ciara. We are going to fight this. Has he ever had the kids on his own?"

"I've been leaving them with him for a couple of hours here and there. Never overnight, even when we were together. The only time he's ever had them for a whole evening was last year. Once."

A Christmas get-together organized by the Happy Days mums, so she didn't hear his first three calls. *Your kid won't fucking shut up.* Jittery apologies, dashing from the restaurant. Running red lights. She could hear Ella crying from the road. Ryan, shaking and shaking her. She couldn't reach him when he was like this. It was if he couldn't see or hear her. Ella almost diving from his arms—MAMAMAMA.

Grace is silent, listening. "And did you report this to anyone?"

She shakes her head. "I know. It sounds so stupid."

"Not stupid at all."

The solicitor is looking at her notes again, tapping her pen. "The house in Glasnevin is rented. So you have no legal right to it. Look, what we are going to do is file a counter motion. We will negotiate with his solicitor and try to reach an agreement."

"But a friend advised me to stay out of court."

"Well, yes. You probably want to stay out of court if you possibly can. Once you're in front of a judge, it can go either way. Some judges will recognize emotional abuse. Others are all for the father's rights, no matter what. They will award every-other-weekend, or fifty–fifty custody, or even full custody. At that point, it's out of your hands."

Grace is still frowning at her notes. "The thing that concerns me here is your housing situation, Ciara. That could be difficult. The fact that you don't currently have anywhere stable for the children to live. He will use that to his advantage. I would get on to the housing authority again, first thing tomorrow morning. Really put pressure on them."

"Tigers can spot their prey from three football pitches way! They use their massive teeth—"

"WANT TO GO HOME."

"Mammy," Sophie's tugging her sleeve, "is she going to give us a sticker?"

"No, she's not a doctor, love."

III

MOON-SKULLED

AUTUMN 2018

20

Room 124 appears to be shrinking. Barely autumn, it's cold at night now. The heating isn't on yet. "Mid-October," Marco tells her in a bored voice. "At the earliest."

Already the girls' noses drip strings of snot, their hoodies stained with pink drips of misfired Calpol. Wads of toilet paper for their pockets. *Use these tissues, not your sleeve.* Ciara is hoping Mairéad doesn't phone her to come and collect them. If she doesn't work, she doesn't get paid. The car windows steam up. Ella cries so hard, tears sprout from her eyes like that pissing, crying bath doll they used to have, which would squirt tears when she squeezed its hard orange tummy.

"Amazing animals," Ciara says, "Mammy will tell you about some amazing Irish animals. How about the swallows? You know they're flying back to Africa—a long, long way, Ella? And they won't be back here till next summer."

"MORE!"

Sophie says, "Mam, why are the swallows taking summer with them?"

"What's that, love?"

It's early, and she's had maybe three hours' sleep. In this waking-sleeping state, it's easy to imagine the swallows pulling the gossamer curtain of summer away from the sky. *Where will we be when the swallows return?*

Later that afternoon, when they arrive home from work and playschool, it's bucketing outside, so she brings them for a walk around the hotel. They've been trailing the corridors, when she bumps into Diego on the third floor. He's carrying piles of dirty white towels out of rooms, shoving them into a canvas bag, while being shouted at by the crew of women. "Diego, would you fuck off," they laugh at him affectionately. Reggaeton music pulses from his phone.

"You speak Spanish?" Ciara asks him, hearing the lyrics.

"Oh, hey there." He smiles. "Yeah, my mama, she's from Bolivia. Actually I was hoping I see you." He rummages in his pocket and produces a Gem sugar sachet. "This one. Is good, no?"

She looks up at him. "You chose this one deliberately?"

"Deliberately? *Deliberadamente.* No, honest God I don't."

"*Dá fhada an lá tagann an tráthnona.* No matter how long the day, evening comes."

"Pretty good huh."

She looks up to say something to him, but he's away off down the corridor.

Along the quays, the tops of the lime trees are beginning to yellow, while dark September rainclouds gather overhead. A squally wind is ruffling the surface of the river into a rough gray hide. Ciara drives out of the city, up Glasnevin Avenue, where chestnuts hang amidst dark leaves, ready to drop.

Leaving her daughters off at Happy Days, Ciara kisses their foreheads and hugs them tight. All these messages from Ryan. Late-night texts, dozens of them, one after the other. *You better brace yourself. Wait till we get to court. You're going to lose everything. Shame on you. It serves you right for treating your husband like dirt. The children belong with me.* She tries to block the words out, to swallow the shame. She needs to cry, to schedule a regular crying time, in the way she used to plan to dye her hair.

Grace phoned yesterday to say that Ryan has rejected their proposals. After weeks of back-and-forth negotiations between solicitors, they have reached stalemate. Now they have applied for a court date.

Waiting for Mairéad to open the gate, Ciara is holding back tears. Not wanting the other parents to see, she bends to zip up the girls' hoodies. Ella wriggles away from her.

"Please, please Ella, you have to zip up nice and cozy. Or else you will get sick and Mammy will cry."

Sophie, trying to do a handstand in the driveway, looks over with a perked-up expression of interest. "We've never seen Mammy cry," she says, as if this might be something worth trying. Like prodding a snail or dropping a woodlouse into the paddling pool.

According to the housing office, she is still on a waiting list. She explained her situation, and the custody case, but a man with a bored voice told her she has to wait. She needs to phone to confirm the room again today.

"NO HOODIE, NO!"

She feels Ella's forehead. Hot—too hot. She should keep

her off school, but she has to work. She tells herself Ella is just warm from the car journey, tries not to notice how pale she is.

Mairéad opens the gate, "Morning everyone, come on in."

Teaching is difficult today. She loves this class: Xi from Shenzhen, Arthur from Milan, Nikita, Akeyo and Yuri from Kyoto, Chan, Nikki and Han from Seoul, Laura and Philippe from Paris, Marcello and Tadeu from São Paulo, Muhammad from Jeddah. Some classes are quiet, tense, but this group have gelled really well. She wants to give them her best, but it's hard to focus when she's worrying about Ella, checking her phone every few minutes in case there's a message from Mairéad.

She's reaching for her favorite icebreaker. *Find Someone Who!*

"Okay everybody, let's mingle." She makes circular motions with her hands. Chairs screech, students sidle up to each other. *Find someone who has the same favorite food as you. Find someone who watched a film last night*. She imagines alternative questions. *Find someone who is heavily pregnant. Find someone who lives in a hotel.*

Once the activity is finished, she puts the students into groups and asks them to tell each other about a festival from their home town.

"The Star Festival in Tanabata," Yuri is explaining to Bianca, Akeyo and Arthur. "We celebrate *Orihime* and *Hikoboshi* meeting in the Milky Way. We write our dreams on—how you say? Silk? And we put—hang—like this, in the bamboo."

At the end of the lesson, she hands out the monthly feedback forms.

Yuri, Niki and the Italian cohort fly a row of ticks down the "strongly agree" column. *Teacher is well prepared* (Strongly agree? Agree? Strongly disagree?) *Teacher is friendly and enthusiastic. Her lessons are useful.* She watches the students ticking, rubbing out, reassigning ticks further toward the Strongly disagree column, arms hooked around the page, hiding their answers.

Ella's cough worsens during the night. A thick rattle in her chest. Ciara is woken from a dream in which she's on a white beach, trying to walk to a sea that keeps inching further away. She turns on the bedside lamp and checks Ella's forehead. She's on fire. There are no extra pillows, so Ciara rolls up some towels from the bathroom, uses these to prop her daughter up. It doesn't make much difference. Ella coughs and splutters, choking on phlegm. Ciara lifts her and paces the narrow space between bed and window, rocking and hushing and willing away the hours until morning.

At the first strain of daylight, she pulls the blind gently, careful not to wake Sophie. Along the rooftops, the sky glows luminous pink, as if someone has taken a highlighter pen to the clouds. The walls of Room 124 turn coral, fuchsia.

Time is shrinking. Her future is blank, impossible to imagine, her past with Ryan a quagmire. She can't see any further than this hotel bedroom, this burning child in her arms. Trapped within the confines of her worry. Ella starts fussing again. Ciara rummages and finds a thermometer at the bottom of her washbag. She puts it into Ella's ear. Within seconds, it beeps. The easy-read screen turns red.

Ciara gives her syringes of Calpol and Nurofen, and she cools down for half an hour.

She sends a message to Veronica, explaining why she won't be in work today. Then she calls Sinéad. Regrets it instantly. Her sister knows too much about all the things that can go wrong with small bodies. "Are you getting any fluids into her?" her sister asks. "Any rash?"

"She's a bit red-looking. On her tummy."

"What kind of red? Bumpy red? Is it blanching? Fuck, I wish I was there. You need to get her seen, Ciara. There's meningitis going round over here at the moment. You can't risk it."

It's too early for the normal GP, so she phones the out-of-hours doc. She speaks to a registrar, a nurse and then a doctor who runs through lists of symptoms. His voice is calm, and she thinks he's about to tell her to continue with the Calpol. Instead, he says, "Child that young? Temp that high? You'd need to bring her to the emergency room."

Sophie is awake now, looking for breakfast. Supplies are running low again. She has to make do with an oat bar and a bruised banana. Half an hour later Ciara turns out of the hotel car park into rush-hour traffic. At Temple Street Children's Hospital, she checks in at the desk, and they wait in a room with Disney animals leaping across the walls. Winnie the Pooh. Elsa and Anna from *Frozen*. Plastic fish float up and down in a tube of bubbles, the water changing color hypnotically. A Minions movie is playing on a small flat-screen TV. A little girl is lying with her head on her dad's knee. A baby of maybe six months is crying ceaselessly, passed from one parent to the other. A teenage boy has his arm wrapped in a bag of frozen peas. "Bunk beds," his mum tells Ciara, "bleeding curse."

Ella's temperature is still too high. The doctor suspects pneumonia. She'll have to be admitted. Her daughter's eyes are scared. "MAMMY WANT MAMMY WANT MAMMY."

Ciara's heart breaks at the sight of the cannula in her daughter's tiny hand. A nurse brings them upstairs to the children's ward. They have a family room available, she says. A box room with a high cot, a camp bed and alphabet curtains. Hours melt and morph into each other. They sit on the small bed together, watching *Frozen* on her phone. Every few hours, nurses come and check Ella's temperature.

Ella won't sleep in the cot bed, and neither will Sophie. "There's probably monsters in there," Sophie howls. Ella clings to her mum, arms reaching around her bump. So they sleep together in the narrow fold-out cot, to the bubble of IV fluids. Night nurses come to check on Ella. "Would you not put her in the cot?" they ask.

By morning, Ella has reanimated after twelve hours on fluids, and is now trying to climb the cot and abseil off it. "We can't discharge you until the doctor does his rounds," the nurse says. "Would they like some ice cream?"

It comes in tiny tubs, with separate compartments of strawberry jelly, which the girls devour. Both high on sugar, she tries to keep them from braining themselves in the tiny room. "No cartwheels," she is saying, "absolutely no handstands, do you hear me Sophie—"

"Excuse me?" A doctor has stepped into the room. He has blondish hair and ruddy cheeks. "This must be Ella? Well the good news is, her bloods have come back, and we can rule out pneumonia. She is responding to antibiotics, so it seems to be mild bronchitis, which can be treated at home. I'll give you a prescription for antibiotics, but I can also give you a small bottle to keep you going for today. These will need to be popped in the fridge."

"The fridge? Sure," she lies. "No problem."

Back at the Eden, the girls clamber into her double bed. The windowsill seems like the coldest place, so she puts the medicine there. The hotel shuffles and creaks around them. In her belly, the baby somersaults and elbow-butts as if jostling for space. According to Google, her baby's eyes are opening this week and it's learning to blink. Its ears are fully developed. Sounds are watery and muffled by the placenta, like a conversation from behind closed doors. Tones and pitches are apparent, but actual words are lost. Deeper sounds reach the baby more easily. Drumbeat from next door, when Cathy is out and Adam and Lyra turn their music up loud. The groans of traffic on the quays. The low whir of the housekeeping staff's industrial hoover. At these noises, she feels little heels joyfully pummeling.

"Make a house, Mammy!" Sophie says. She bends her knees to hold up the duvet, and her daughters climb into the makeshift tent, cuddling and squabbling. "How about we be unicorns?" This room is all that exists.

Above the rooftops, satellite dishes blink on the black shoulder of Three Rock Mountain. *We're safe,* she tells herself.

Ella and Sophie are okay. And the baby can hear her voice, clearer than any other sound. What was it she read online earlier? Studies have shown that a fetus's heartbeat quickens at their mother's voice. She turns off her phone. Closes her eyes. She can feel it now. The peace.

21

Her students are leaving and Ciara is wiping the board when Veronica, in a tiger-print blazer, walks into her classroom and leans against one of the desks. Just over a week since Ella's stint in the children's hospital, life has settled back into its routine of desperate waiting. Veronica chit-chats for a few minutes, then folds her arms. "Your feedback forms have been fairly mixed lately, Ciara. Do you have your weekly plan there?"

Oh God, why did she spill orange juice on it in the room this morning? And why did she then shove it into her shoulder bag along with the spilt pack of raisins, now congealed onto the edges of the dog-eared paper, like sheep shits?

If only she could tell Veronica. About the hotel, the hospital and the housing office. About the upcoming court date in November. About the colossal earth-shifting effort it has taken just to get her into this classroom for the past few weeks. Just to be able to stand in front of these students. To be able to speak.

She's wringing her hands, twisting her fingers. "I really need this job, Veronica, if you could just...please. I'll improve my plans. I'll work harder."

"Okay, Ciara." Veronica scans through her plan and purses her lips. "I might just pop in and observe one of your lessons though. These feedback forms. The managers get themselves in a twist over them."

Veronica teeters out the door in her stilettos. When Ciara steps out of the classroom a few minutes later, she's not sure if her legs will carry her across the campus to the car park. A cold day, mackerel sky. Sunlight glints off the immaculate lawns, skittle bright in the sun. Along the edges of the paths, drifts of fallen leaves, tawny, apricot, russet. A bird flies across her path and lands in front of her. Once she starts noticing them, crows are everywhere. Sharp beaks, watchful eyes. She thinks of Chase, who she sometimes sees fluttering around the hallway when she drops the girls off.

Maggie catches up with her outside the SPAR. "Ciara! It's been ages. Where've you been hiding?"

"Ah. You know, just. Busy with the kids and stuff. Oh, and Veronica is coming in to observe me."

"Christ's sake. Would she ever give over." Maggie takes her arm. "Come on. I'm buying you coffee."

Later in the afternoon it lashes, as if it had forgotten to rain for months and is now making up for lost time. In the waiting room at the Rotunda, footage is playing across two TV screens of people walking along barbed-wire fences at the border into Europe. Now the reporter is speaking about those who don't make it across the Mediterranean. There's a place in Lampedusa called the Boat Graveyard, littered with scraps of broken boats and children's shoes.

The report from Lampedusa ends. A photo of a hotel room appears on screen. White bed sheets. Mini kettle. Ciara's heart jolts. "Record numbers of people entered emergency accommodation in September 2018. Pressure is now mounting on the government to provide an alternative to hotel accommodation, which housing action groups have described as unfit for purpose. In Dublin, a group of activists have—"

"Ciara Fay? In to the doctor."

In the consultation room, Ciara takes off her leggings. She climbs onto the high bed and lies back while a doctor with ash-brown hair and warm hands presses a probe onto her abdomen. On screen, the baby jumps as if startled, and wriggles around, turning over like a person bothered from a deep sleep, trying to rearrange itself back into its dream. As the doctor presses circles across her taut skin, the baby flutters into focus from every angle. Fingers, toes, shadows for eyes, and the silhouette of a button nose. Its heartbeat, which once took up its whole body, has migrated to its proper place, gilled within its chest.

Examination finished, the doctor hands her a roll of white paper towels. Ciara mops the gel and struggles back into her maternity leggings.

"This pregnancy," the doctor says, "it's your third?"

"Fourth."

The doctor looks at her notes on the computer screen. Frowns.

"Third baby," Ciara adds. "One loss."

"Ah, I see." The doctor writes something down. "Two

Cesarean births? Emergency ones? In this case, we will need to schedule a planned section at thirty-six weeks."

"Thirty-six? That early?"

"Ms. Fay. Your pregnancy is high risk. You're carrying a lot of fluid, and your blood pressure is higher than we would like it to be. We need to avoid you going into spontaneous labor. It wouldn't be safe."

"But is everything okay? With the baby?" Ciara feels as if her ribcage is tightening. She's known something isn't right. This pregnancy hasn't felt like the others.

"Baby is okay at the moment," the doctor says, "but we just need to keep an eye on both of you."

Later, she shows Sophie and Ella the strip of ultrasound photos. The baby spooled up in a suspended roly-poly. Head outlined by a halo of light. She thinks of that line from Plath. *Feet to the stars, and moon-skulled.* "Look," she tells them, "That's our new baby."

Sophie squints at the photos, chewing the end of her plait, "Why's she black and white? Where's her toys?"

Autumn sun hangs low in the sky, catching the windows along the Liffey, turning them into flickering furnaces. Puddles marble the pavements with threads of light. Early evening, she's out walking with Ella and Sophie, their shadows long-legged, as if on stilts, like the Catalan giants she saw in Barcelona.

Looking over her shoulder, she sees Diego strolling along the quays in the direction of the hotel, head bent over his phone. Nearby, the *Jeanie Johnston* is listing gently, and a scrawny heron poses on the Liffey wall. At office windows, people are sitting at their desks, looking at screens. What if the Eden was glass-walled like that? Floor five, a vivid seam running through the bland exterior. Teddies on windowsills. Birthday photos tacked to wardrobes. School uniforms hung behind doors. Rice cookers hidden under beds. A thick, bright ore.

Reaching her, Diego smiles. "*Tudo bem?* I don't see you for long time. You are okay?"

"All good," she says. "Off to work?

"Yeah," he groans, falling into step with her. He's wearing a soft oatmeal jumper, the neck turned up. "Too much work."

"And are you studying here too?"

"Oh yeah, all the time I study. Every minute everyone tell me, Diego, stop, you study too much! Put away the books, Diego, please." When he smiles, she sees his chipped tooth, slightly off-center.

"Seriously though," she says. "What are you doing here? You didn't come to Ireland to hoover the Eden."

"Ah." He rubs a hand over his face, groans. "Physiotherapy I was gonna do, work in a hospital. There's this master's, in New York... Yeah. Don't look me like that. I need learn more English, I know. It's just so fucking difficult this language. I was in classes this morning. Waste of time. My teacher was like, pretend be a shopkeeper." He shakes his head. "I try to get a grade seven IELTS, you know."

She feels herself cringing. "I think I have actually taught that exact same lesson. The shopkeeper one."

They've reached the famine sculptures. Haunting skeletal

faces, bony frames keening toward the docks, leaning as if walking against a gale. Stick legs stumbling forward. Ella pats the mangy bronze dog. "Nice doggy."

"What part of Brazil are you from?" Ciara asks him.

"From São Paulo, but not the city. The city is too crazy. I'm from a really small town. Caraguatatuba."

"No way," she laughs. "You're from Caragua? The beautiful beach. Down the road from Ubatuba?"

"You know it? Oh my God."

It's hard to describe the vulnerability of his expression. He looks surprised, and also caught out. She thinks of her mum in her kitchen in Sheffield, angling her radio on the windowsill, bending the antennae to a precise angle to catch the Irish stations. She remembers her own years living abroad. The way she felt when she heard a Sheffield accent on the Barcelona metro. A Derry lilt on a São Paulo bus, just out of reach. She remembers spotting a Discover Ireland billboard at the top of an escalator in a shopping center somewhere outside Santos and stopping still. Homesickness: like having the world tilted under you. The baby rolls over in her belly.

"I taught in Ubatuba," she says, "I'll dig out some photos, give you a laugh. I was generally very sunburnt."

"I don't imagine you there," Diego says. "My God. I must tell my friend Rodrigo. Sorry. I don't mean embarrassing you."

All those years she spent continent-hopping. Slipping between lives, between languages. The beautiful blurriness that comes from living life in translation. Equator cities where her pale skin and freckles became a badge of Irishness, uncomplicated by her English birthplace. The freedom she felt. More truly herself than she'd ever been. But still, the isolation. Her Portuguese was poor, so she found herself trapped outside language, hungry for talk, connection. Not until deep in her marriage would she feel as lonely.

"Listen," she says. "Maybe I could help. With your exams?"

He's stopped, arms folded. "You gonna make me pretend to be a shopkeeper?"

"No." She smiles. "No, I promise I won't."

22

"Help, Granny. I've been captured by two little witches." She holds the phone back so her mum can see the Halloween costumes she sent.

"Ah look at them. Are those sizes okay?"

"Hello, Granny! We're bad witches!"

"Bless." Sinéad's face appears on screen. "Don't they look cute."

Sophie and Ella are somersaulting on the bed now, pointy hats and black mesh dresses flying over their heads.

When they signed in at reception earlier, Lauren and Marco were sticking foil spiders along the pillars. Isabel was stringing wooly cobwebs over the storm lanterns and tacking paper skeletons to the windows. An inflatable vampire wobbled by the main door. She overheard an Australian tourist telling his son that zombies are an ancient Irish tradition.

On the video call, her mum's face is creased with worry. "You're looking very thin, love," she says.

"Mum! The size of me!" She holds the phone back again, so they can see her bump.

"Your face, I mean. You look drawn. And you look shattered. Are you getting any sleep?"

"A bit. It's hard to get comfy. Hard to turn my brain off."

She phones each week to confirm the room at the Eden. Sometimes she's put on hold, and while she waits, her mind races. If they are kicked out of here, where will they end up? Grace keeps saying she really has to find more suitable accommodation. At drop-offs Ryan is curt, dismissive, as if he's already won.

The upcoming court appearance is filling her every thought. Most evenings, once the girls are asleep, she sits in the bathroom on the closed toilet lid and reads her statements over and over. Grace advised her to try and back herself up with evidence, so she's spent hours trawling through old messages from Ryan. Losing herself in the quicksand of them.

I have been utterly devastated by this, I have no idea what's going on. You are destroying our family for no reason at all.

I love you so much, you are the best thing that's ever happened to me.

There have been thousands of messages over the last few months, a torrent. She scrolls, takes screenshots, scrolls again until her head is sore. His behavior will be so difficult to prove. Some of these messages would seem nice to anyone who didn't know the context.

Sometimes she phones Sinéad, who plays devil's advocate, asking, "What will you do if he says this? What will you do if he says that?"

Grace's last email was short. *Ciara I know it's hard, but we need to show that you are at least in the process of transitioning to suitable accommodation. I'm worried it will be too easy for him to make a case against you otherwise. Is there anything else we can do to help make this happen?*

"You need to mind yourself," Sinéad says. "Have you thought about what I said the other night? Would you not think of seeing a therapist, Ciara?"

"I can't have that on the records. He'll use that against me. I'm okay. I'm just tired, that's all."

"Are you sure that's right, though?" Sinéad asks. "I think you're overthinking things a bit here, Ciara. I don't think they can criticize you for going to therapy, can they?"

"I don't know," she says. The court is a big unknown, this is what frightens her. Having her life laid bare. Being at the mercy of a stranger's judgment.

Halloween night, Cathy's teenagers are dead schoolkids, and little Lucy is the snowman from *Frozen*. "Sure don't youse look class!" Cathy says when she sees Sophie and Ella, but her voice is less enthusiastic than normal, and her smile doesn't reach her eyes. Ciara has plaited the girls' hair and drawn spiders on their cheeks with her black eyeliner. Stripy tights under their witch dresses, their pink castle-shaped beach buckets as Halloween bags.

"Ah sure they're as cute," Cathy says. "Come on and I'll show you where we went last year. There's no houses on this street. And the ones up by Trinity are only stingy students. They wouldn't give you the steam off their piss. Sure you'd be wasting your time."

The kids clatter down the backstairs, but the alley is

flooded. Clogged with a putrid soup of murky water. A dead rat is floating by the bins. "Jesus Christ. We can't bring them that way," Cathy opens the door into reception, and they trot across the lobby like a procession.

Outside, the night sky pops and fizzes with fireworks. Groups of teenagers scuttle past, all dressed up. There's the sweet smell of rotting leaves.

Cathy brings them up past Pearse Street Station, toward the Grand Canal Dock. Down Barrow Street. Hope Street. Joy Street, kicking through leaf piles. They ring doorbells along rows of red-brick terraces, streets of squat bungalows painted gray, blue, cream. In open doorways, she catches glimpses of other families' lives. Houses with cotton-wool spider webs draped over banisters, bowls of mini Haribo packets by the door, shoe racks of runners and wellies. Houses where dinner is cooking. Fish fingers. Pasta. Smoke alarms sounding. Mums shouting up the stairs to their kids, "Trick-or-treaters, come and see!"

The girls stand shell-shocked on strangers' doorsteps. *Bless.*

An elderly woman with a basket full of Tayto crisps and Mars bars dotes over the kids. "Don't youse just look bleeding brilliant? Let's get a look at you. Holy moley. Scared the bejesus out of me, you're deadly."

Cathy says, "They're having fun." Her voice is subdued and her smile looks somehow sad.

A thought charges across Ciara's mind, and she asks, "How's Alex?"

"Ah. Don't ask," Cathy looks at the ground. "Sure she went

back, didn't she. I called round to her mam's the other week, and she says Alex is away back with Garry. I was so fucking livid with her, when I first heard—"

"Cathy, I'm sorry."

"No. You know what, I get why she did it. He wouldn't give her a bleeding break. Sure she probably thought it was easier. A way to make it stop."

Two weeks before her scheduled section, November crashes in. Last week, the leaves on O'Connell Street had been barely ochre-singed. Now, bare branches web the white sky.

Ella's third birthday. Her daughter blows out pinstripe candles on an Aldi chocolate roll in the cluttered bedroom. Cathy and her kids have joined them. Everyone sings and admires Ella's present, a second-hand scooter Ciara found on Adverts.ie.

An icy wind whips away the last flitting leaves from the spindly rowans outside the Eden, leaving the branches skeletal. The first frost in the city center is a fugitive, glancing thing, unlike the satisfying whitening of their old suburban garden. Bird-feeder mesh. Crunching grass. White fronds etched on windows. Here, the frost melts within half an hour, as if the pavements are geothermal, the buildings sweating their own metallic heat.

From the window of Room 124, the Dublin Mountains have been powdered white. Ground level, two hotel porters are shoveling puke-colored grit across the Eden's main entrance. Sophie kicks it, skids, lands on her bum, howls. Ten minutes later they're back upstairs, searching for dry clothes.

A new family has moved into 126. They have a baby who cries a lot, while the young mum walks the corridors, cooing and shushing. Ciara can hear the baby's crying seeping through the walls. The sound cores her.

Savings: €743.

I have to get us out of here. Holy fuck. How did this happen?

Halloween decorations barely removed, Lauren and Marco are striding about the place with Christmas trees. Each time Ciara spots a spangled fir sticking out of a shop window in the city center, dread lurches through her like a kind of vertigo.

Her baby is the size of a honeydew melon. Its movements more solid now, the rising humps of a subaquatic creature pressing up against the surface of her skin.

Cathy is on her second Christmas in the Eden. "It's all right," she says, "they've Santie and all for the kids."

Ciara feels clumsy, elephantine, uncoordinated as a toddler, bumping into door frames, bashing into the bathroom sink each time she underestimates her girth. In the classroom, she's always dropping papers and books. As yet another worksheet flutters from her swollen hands onto the pencil-gray carpet, her students dash over to help. Trying to boil noodles in Room 124 one evening, she spills a kettle of boiling water all over the locker. The bedside light flickers out. She barks at Ella and Sophie to stand back, "Careful, careful, careful!"

Anger catches her one midweek breakfast time. Silver bells. Curling ribbon. *Fucking Christmas trees.* She didn't see it coming. Didn't think she had such anger in her, that such rage was on her palette. Now fury has her in its stranglehold. Ground molars. Tight jaw. That feeling, like a helium balloon pressing against her ribcage. Trying to contain the fizzling spite that wants to leap out of her skin. At night, she can't sleep. She lies on her side in the grainy dark listening to the hotel recalibrating around her.

Her days are the same.

"Morning everyone, turn to page twenty-six please."

"Shoe goes on the other foot, honey."

"Yes, baby is kicking regularly."

"Hi, I'm just phoning to confirm the room?"

But the cracks are beginning to show.

She didn't want to be the kind of mum who yells, bribes, threatens. The two girls are at each other again in Room 124, slapping and tugging ("MINE NO MINE") and she didn't mean to shout. She can feel the listening walls shirking. Her breath shallow, the baby taking up every inch. The pain in her groin and her thighs is spreading, a molten creep, gripping stronger. At her last hospital appointment, the nurse said it was Braxton Hicks. Nothing to worry about. Her court date is getting closer.

"Sorry for the late!" Diego arrives at her table in reception, out of breath.

"You're an hour late," Ciara says, standing to leave.

Cathy has been minding the girls, and she has been waiting in the lobby, sitting in one of the bucket chairs, sipping a glass of tap water and keeping an eye out for the managers. She isn't supposed to be here, is risking a lot just to meet him for a lesson, for a little extra cash.

"I know, my bad, I so sorry. Three floors I had to paint today." *Paint. This is why he is flecked with paint.* "Maybe we can catch up? You like coffee?"

"Diego. The lesson was only meant to last an hour. You've missed it. I can't stay. My babysitter's done, she has to go to work. Do you have that essay for me to look at?"

"Ah." He scratches the back of his head. "I leave on my bed. I so sorry. My bad."

She stands up. "Your first lesson. You'd think you could have been on time. This is pointless. Completely pointless, Diego. This isn't going to work. I need some air before I go back up to that bloody room."

She's just stepped into the revolving door when he catches up, his backpack jogging on his shoulder.

"Ciara. Come on, we can talk about this?" He's saying something in Portuguese, and they are going round and round this bloody door, between the hotel lobby and the hot exhaust-fume blast of the quays. Her eyes smart as Ryan's voice enters her head. *I'm trying to save our family. Why won't you let me do that?*

She's stepped out onto the quays now, crossed over to the Liffey wall. She just needs space to breathe. The inky spill of the river, lights dancing on its surface.

Diego is beside her now. "Sorry I such a horrible student."

"You're the worst."

"I know. I know. Fucking disaster but look. I make something. See. Here you go." From his backpack, Diego hands her a plastic tub.

She prizes open the tub. "Misto quente?"

"You know this?"

"Yeah. Misto quente. The best food on earth."

She remembers arriving in Brazil, the plane charting a path between skyscrapers. That first morning in São Paulo stopping for breakfast in a roadside café. Misto quente, the hot cheese ooze of it.

"Okay, you look like you start crying. Let's go, Ciara—these fucking phrasal verbs, you see this list? I must learn this. Two minutes. Outdoor English lessons. Hit me with it." He squints his eyes as if bracing for impact. Despite herself, she laughs.

She takes the sheet of phrasal verbs, tests him on a few. He gets them all wrong. "Oh fuck," he says, "is too fucking difficult. Look," he leans back, taking a cigarette out of his packet. Hands her a sugar sachet. "I find this one today."

"*Is ait an mac an saol.* Life is strange."

He nods, blowing his smoke away from her. "I can keep this one?"

"You're worse than me."

As she's walking through Temple Bar, light catches the darkened bulbs on unlit Christmas trees, giving them a soft, dusty glow, like dandelion clocks. She stops outside Dolphin House, East Essex Street. No dolphins on the building. *God, the things you think about, when you spend most of your time with small children.* She must have passed this building hundreds of times. Student pub crawls. Walks with Ryan, back in the days when he still held her hand. All the times she has walked these cobbled streets, she has never paid any attention to Dolphin House. A red-bricked corner building, next to the Project

Arts Centre. A small gold plaque beside the heavy mahogany door. District Court.

Heart fast, she walks up the steps and pushes open the glass door. A dated reception area. That fuggy smell of old paper. Rows of orange cushioned chairs. A security man in a black shirt directs her to take a ticket from the dispenser. His radio crackles.

She takes a seat at the end of one of the rows. Checks her phone. Mairéad has sent some photos to the Happy Days WhatsApp group. The kids are making Christmas baubles out of paper doilies and glitter glue.

Grace walks into the waiting room, unbuttoning her long black coat, taking off her cashmere scarf, nodding hello to the security guard. She is comfortable in this space, knows how to navigate it.

"How are you holding up?" Grace sits down beside her. "We should be called this morning, hopefully. No sign of himself?"

"Not yet."

"Hold tight. I'll see if I can talk to the registrar. See how full the list is today."

Grace walks up to the desk. She's soon deep in conversation.

On a pillar beside Ciara, a poster of a woman crouched in the fetal position, her arms crossed over her head. *Need someone to talk to about domestic violence?* On the wall, a poster of a woman's face. Unmarked, defiant. *Not all bruises are visible.* There are other posters too. Helplines for Women's Aid and the Free Legal Advice Centre. She's trying not to stare at the people sitting around her. A handful of men. Solicitors in suits. Beside her, a young woman who can't be more than about eighteen is trying to pretend she's not crying. She has a tissue in her hand, keeps ducking her head to wipe her nose. There's something fragile about her, thinness emphasized by a Lycra tank top and fitted jacket. In front of her, two women who look like mother and daughter. Their faces have the same contours, and they are both holding their handbags in their laps. The younger woman has her hand on the older woman's arm.

In her head, Ciara keeps on revising her statements. *I am a good mother. I have been the children's sole carer for the past four years. I am working hard to secure a home for them.*

The hand on the white plastic clock above the desk inches slowly forward. Almost eleven o'clock. Grace returns to sit beside her. For the first time ever, she looks flustered. "He's not here. We've passed the cut-off time. The list is full."

"So what happens now?"

"What happens is we're back to the bottom of the list for another court date."

"I don't understand. Why would he do this?"

Grace leans closer. "Because he is messing with your head, my dear. He knows this is stressing you out. He is playing mind games."

At Happy Days, Sophie is waving a furry yellow toy over her head. Ella is hugging a scrapbook and beaming. "Look what we got, Mammy!"

Mairéad smiles at Ciara. "Look at you! You're glowing! Not long now?"

She tries to smile, pats her bump, "Just a few weeks."

"Bless. The girls are so excited. You know the story with our friend Billy Bear, right Ciara? Just a few nice photos with the bear in them. Anything fun you do this weekend, just stick a photo in the scrapbook."

"Okay, no worries. Girls, say bye to Mairéad!"

It's Ryan's day. Dropping Sophie and Ella off at their old house, she heaves herself out of the car, walks up the driveway. When he opens the door, she says, "What happened? We were meant to be in court today?"

He ignores her, stooping to hug the girls.

"We got the Billy Bear, Dad!"

"Ryan? Where were you today?"

"Oh yeah. Something came up at work." He stands back to let the girls into the house. Over his shoulder, a black shape flutters. Chase. Why does he have the bird in the house? It has grown to the size of an oddly proportioned blackbird, its black beak and gray talons too big for its small bulk. Tufts of fluff amongst its chest feathers. It squawks, fluttering around again. She flinches.

Ryan is watching her. "You really need to calm down," he says. "We can get another court date. It's no big deal."

She turns, gets back into the car and drives away. She parks outside Soaps 'n' Suds, under dripping sycamores, and unloads the bin bag of dirty laundry from the boot. Slamming the door shut, she catches sight of her reflection on the car window. The cut of her. Faded gray hoodie, belly protruding over her maternity jeans. Close to tears. This is why he's dragging this out. The longer this continues, the more worn down she will become. The more the fear will devour her. By the time she gets to court, she will barely be able to speak, let alone defend herself.

In the launderette, she bundles everything into a washer, feeds a handful of coins into the slot, and collapses on one of the wooden benches. She's brought the Billy Bear scrapbook, flicks through it for a few ideas. It would rival the Book of Kells. The stickers. The illustrations. The detailed diary entries explaining Billy's weekends, each more wonderful than the last. Photos of happy kids, happy families. Baking cakes. Building a pillow fort in the living room. Planting seedlings in the garden. Kids cuddling Billy in their bedrooms.

What are you doing? What are you doing? What are you doing?

She puts her head in her hands, lets the tears spill. Luckily this launderette is the type of place where you can quietly fall apart without anyone paying much heed. All cried out, her breath steadies. Washers and dryers rumble, like the low chug of a fetal heartbeat. Darkness at the steamed-up windows.

Ciara shuts the scrapbook, dries her eyes on the back of her sleeves and turns her attention to the posters on chipboards beside the machines. Ads for second-hand laptops and housekeeping services. *SINGLES NIGHT.* Two odd socks dancing under a mirror ball. Beside this, a smaller sign: *STAFF MAINTAIN THE RIGHT TO WORK IN A SUPPORTIVE, NON-ABUSIVE ENVIRONMENT. ANYONE ENGAGING IN THREATENING OR INTIMIDATING BEHAVIOR WILL BE ASKED TO LEAVE.*

Her eyes keep returning to this metal placard. *Threatening or intimidating. Not kicking or punching. Threatening or intimidating.* The words repeat in her head until they become a mantra. Like words from the books she used to love. Toni Morrison. Maya Angelou. *You may trod me in the very dirt / But still, like dust, I'll rise.* Feeling stronger, she's hefting damp clothes out of the machine, folding them into plastic bags, carrying the bags back to the car. To save money, she doesn't bother with the dryers. Later, she will drape everything over the side of the bath and the bathroom door to dry. She turns on the car radio, drives to collect her children.

This time Diego is early. He's waiting for her, sitting by the window in the hotel lobby, looking out at the rain. All week her students have been disgusted with the weather, but Diego seems merely amused. He gestures to the window. "Winter in Ireland, it's always like that? It don't get—how to say—flood?"

This was Cathy's doing. Ciara had been reluctant to meet up with him again after he was so late. Cathy said she should give him another chance, insisting she'd mind the girls and almost shoving Ciara out the door.

In speech, Diego's English is warm, easy, with a spattering of carefully curated idioms. On paper, it's as if his words have been wrung through a mangle. From what she can tell, he's translating from Portuguese word for word, so the syntax is completely upside down. Along with a dose of Google translate.

"Look Diego, you can't start a sentence with the word 'and.'"

He's a terrible student. But he's great company. He listens. It's easy to make him laugh. He seems to find her quite funny, and she loves that. She used to make people laugh all the time. Sitting at long tables in the basement college bar, sipping vodka and blackcurrant that would leave her tongue thick the next morning. She'd be one of the quieter ones at the table, but she'd tell the odd story that would have her friends in stitches. She wonders where they are now, her Trinity classmates. Doubtless few of them are sitting on a threadbare sofa in a hotel lobby, listing irregular verbs for a rough-shaven, wild-haired Brazilian, then running up the back staircase of the Eden, to where her girls are sleeping.

23

Ciara tacks three cards onto the whiteboard: SHOULD HAVE—COULD HAVE—WOULD HAVE. Veronica is sitting in the corner, biro poised.

"Right folks," Ciara says, "here it is. The lesson on regret."

A few of the students laugh. Ali shakes his head. "Oh God."

"I'm giving each group a scenario," she says. "I want you to tell me three things they should have done and shouldn't have done."

She writes the construction on the board: *Subject + should + have + infinitive without to + object*

When they read the scenarios, there's more laughter. Veronica circulates too, reading over their shoulders.

Scenario One: *A couple decided to go camping in a forest. They forgot their torch and their map. As night fell…*

Scenario Two: *A man arrived in London to meet his long-lost relations, but he had no idea what they looked like so…*

Scenario Three: *A woman fell in love with a man who seemed to be her soulmate, so at first she didn't notice…*

While the students are talking to each other, Veronica

comes up to stand beside her. "Well, this is very good, Ciara. Punchy. Funny. Engaging. You're a good teacher."

"You sound surprised?"

"No, no . . . Just, you never know . . . What to expect. I see on your CV you have a primary teaching qualification? Well for the love of God would you not apply to a few decent schools? Teaching English is grand, but you know what it's like."

She nods. Hours for English-language teachers are unreliable, dependent on student numbers. No sickness benefit. No maternity pay, just the state benefit. No pension.

"I'm on it," she says. "I have to pay to register with the Teaching Council. And I'll have to learn Irish."

Veronica scribbles something on her page. "Right, well you've passed your observation. You're very competent. We're happy to keep you on. Not that you'll be with us much longer?"

"Another week."

Hot pains grip her thighs. A creeping soreness in her lower back. The baby is so still. She downs glasses of icy-cold water, lies on her left side and waits for movement.

A dusting of snow, the roofs opposite a dizzying tessellation.

Her phone. Ryan. *I love you so much. I'm in bits. I'm seeing the GP this evening. I nearly phoned the emergency room last night. This is killing me. How can you do this to me?*

Those pains, stretching across her thighs again. A new pain in her groin now, sharp and deep. She remembers when she was pregnant with Ella, sitting in the forecourt of the Dublin

Road Texaco, clutching the globe of her belly as the warm surge of another contraction pain cramped through her tail bone. As the pains intensified, she sat staring at the front of the shop, watching Ryan stride from window to window through the bright-lit shop, toward the till where he stood to pay for the petrol. She'd begged him to fill the car in advance. He'd scoffed at her, "You sound like your mum. Always fussing and worrying over nothing. Sure there'll be plenty of time."

I'm just trying to save our family Ryan messages. *That's all I'm trying to do.*

Diego is attempting to quit smoking and take up drinking tea instead. In the lobby of the Eden, he pours from a small white pot. He's told her this is part of his Irish cultural adaptation. "If I keep trying, maybe I will like." He takes a sip, grimaces. Lifts the white teapot lid, stirs it again, and presses the teabag hard. He checks her face and says, "You are in bad form?"

"Where did you learn that one?"

"Is correct say—you are in bad form?"

"Yeah."

"You are broken tonight, no?"

"What?"

"Tired? You say God almighty I'm so broken, no?"

"Wrecked. You can say wrecked. Not broken. That's something else. And broke means I've no money."

"Yeah. So you say God almighty I'm in bad form coz I'm wrecked and totally broke."

She nods. He seems pleased by this, writes it down in his notebook. Ciara takes a sip of the tea and shudders. "Jesus, that's rotten. You know pulverizing the tea bag won't turn it into coffee, right?"

They both drink, grim. There's an awkwardness between them now. He's right, she is in bad form. Stressed, tired.

"My marriage ended, Diego," she blurts out.

He looks up, "Now? This happen today?"

"No, no. Months ago. That's why we're here."

"Ciara, I'm sorry."

She puts her head in her hands, and now Diego is beside her, his arm around her, and she can't focus on the individual words he's saying. He's talking about how he was raised by a single mother, a Bolivian immigrant, in a forty-floor block in central Santos before they moved to Caragua. "My mum, she's an incredible woman," he says. The warm closeness of him is having a soporific effect. Closing her eyes, she remembers the suddenness of nightfall in an equator city, São Paulo skyscrapers lit up like lanterns. It feels like the moment will last for eternity, but now he's moving away and she's drying her eyes, hiding her embarrassment by opening another textbook.

He's putting on his glasses, frowning at his IELTS papers, clicking his biros, scribbling to find a pen that works.

Every part of her feels swollen. Her hips, a constant ache.

At break, she can't see Olivia or Maggie, and her feet will not permit her to walk any further. Rooks scatter before her as she crosses the campus back to her classroom. Ragged wings, sharp beaks. Even her brain feels heavy, waterlogged. Each step requires colossal effort. *You should call the emergency room again, these pains aren't normal.*

She begins a reading lesson, tells the students they're going to read a text and then answer questions on it.

"Martin Luther King gave this speech..." Chan reads aloud.

In front of the class, she leans against her desk, dizzy. She hasn't even read the page. She has no lesson plan, just a "Who's Like Me" snatched from the recycling tray, and this text about "I Have a Dream." Looking at it now, it's too easy for them. Her skin feels clammy. The baby is still. The pain in her groin is getting stronger, spreading to her lower back and down her thighs.

Chan keeps reading: "the most important word in the text has been all but erased from history. He did not say, *I have a dream*. He said, *I still have a dream*. Despite everything, he said he *still* had a dream. Question one..." Chan stops reading. "Teacher?"

She wakes surrounded by her students' knees. Baggy jeans. Scuffed runners. Ali is down on his knees, shouting, "Alive! She is alive!"

Bianca on her phone. *"La professoressa!"*

How long was she out for? Long enough for the young French lad Philippe to run over to reception. He dashes back into the classroom now, followed by Veronica. She's wearing runners. This is what Ciara will always remember about this moment. Veronica has taken off her heels and is wearing a pair of scruffy-looking Reeboks under her pencil dress.

"Have a seat, everyone," Veronica says. "Stay calm and sit down. Your lesson will resume shortly. Stay there, Ciara."

Veronica crouches down and thrusts a bottle of water at her. "Drink this. Stay calm. It's all going to be absolutely fine. The ambulance is on its way."

"I'm not going in an ambulance, Veronica. I'll be grand, honestly."

"Ciara . . ."

Then she notices the warm wetness underneath her. Before she even heaves herself around to look, she knows it's blood.

It's then the pain really starts. Warm, firm, steady, deeper than with her other two.

It's all happening so fast. She's in an ambulance, with a paramedic holding her hand, being jolted around under the siren whoop, and she must have blacked out at some point because the next thing she recognizes is the narrow room of the pre-labor ward. A soundtrack of deep breathing, like being in a room full of scuba divers. Heartbeats thud from fetal monitors round the room. Unborn babies' hearts beat fast, like galloping hooves on a dusty road.

Everything is hitting her in a quick montage. The pain in her belly, stronger, stronger. The seismograph of her baby's heartbeat scribbling wildly. As if magically teleported from another dimension, a cast of medical personnel pop up around her bed and mutter at their clipboards. There are two or three doctors, several midwives. Everyone is checking machines and charts. Why is nobody looking at her? A nurse holds up a pair of long white pressure socks. Another nurse removes her earrings. She's aware of her whole body juddering now, her teeth chattering, and at some point someone says, "Ciara, do you understand what's happening?"

24

Play of light on her eyelids. Struggling toward consciousness, she is swimming toward the surface of a deep red pool. Eventually she manages to get her eyes to open. There's no curtain drawn around her bed. Darkness at the window. *How is it evening already?* An IV line is feeding into her left arm, the bandage bloodied as if it had been attached in great haste.

Nobody else in the room.

Her hands move to her belly. Deflated.

Where's my baby?

The glass bassinet by her bedside is empty. Her ears ring. Her heart pounds. She's made a sound. Not a word. A pure animal noise. She's trying to get out of bed, but she can't move her legs, they are numb.

"Oh now, there now." A midwife is heading toward her through the blur of tears. What is she saying? "There now, there now." And now she realizes, with a gush of sobs, that the nurse's cooing is intended for the bundle in her arms, swaddled in standard hospital-blue towels. While Ciara's mind is in shock, her body takes over. Her arms bend into a cradle, just as the nurse says, "Here's your baby boy."

Ciara buries her face in her child's cheek. Blood still pounding in her ears, her face wet, snot streaming. And there it is—the high-pitched, bleating, newborn cry. An indignant chirp at having been plunged into light, noise, cold. The nurse withdraws with a gentle smile, as if the patient were not having a minor meltdown. "I'll give you two a moment to say hello."

"Thank you," she says, "Oh God, thank you... But my other two. Ella. Sophie. Where are they?"

"Other children?" The nurse looks at her clipboard, flips the page. Ciara thinks of Sinéad in her hospital scrubs, hair tied back with bobby pins, quick, efficient hands. The nurse frowns. "I've only just come on for the night shift. I'll check if there was a message left by whoever was on this afternoon."

Imagine the pair of them still sitting on their lunchboxes outside Happy Days. Their big eyes in the gloom. Mairéad would mind them, wouldn't she? They wouldn't wander off, would they?

Minutes later, the nurse returns. "They are with your husband." She smiles as if she has just given good news.

"What?"

The nurse's expression changes. "Oh. Is that not what was supposed to... ? Hang on, there's a note here. *Patient requested friend Cathy to collect the children from playschool... confirmed...* Then there's another note made here at three fifteen. *Cathy phoned—children not at playschool, had already been taken home by dad, please contact.* Then they've written the name of a hotel. I'm not sure if that was a mistake or... Does that clear things up?"

"No. No, they can't. They're not supposed to be. This all

happened too soon. My mum is coming over to mind them, she's arriving next week. Please could I have my phone?"

"Your bags have been brought down to the ward. We'll have you down there in the next hour. Try not to worry, love." The nurse straps the blood-pressure monitor to her arm and holds it in place while studying her slim silver watch. "All good."

When the nurse leaves again, Ciara has an urge to shout after her. *Don't leave me on my own.* She can see Ryan towering over the girls, shouting at them until they cry. The sickening feeling of having been proven right. This image of his rage then merges into an opposite scenario. Ryan on his hunkers, helping them build a Duplo tower. Ella standing with her hands on her little belly, laughing as he picks her up. Sophie hugging him around the knees. *See, I'm a great dad, why can't you see that?*

This new bundle—Noah, she'll call him Noah, after her granddad—latches on. There's the lip-biting tug, familiar from her other two.

Babies can freeze time.

The sounds of Dublin city are floating in distant waves of traffic thrum and siren song. Like an ocean they're suspended above. *Just me and this dark-haired stranger.* His fingers bluish and still wrinkly from the womb, as if he's been left in the bath too long. He's so much smaller than his sisters were.

Babies also speed time up.

Two porters finally wheel her down to the ward and banana-board her onto the bed, her legs still leaden in the knee-high white pressure socks. They draw the blue pleated curtains around her metal bed, and a nurse says, "Make yourself comfy. You'll be in here at least five nights."

Five nights? She can't stay here for five nights. They'll lose the room if she doesn't sign in.

"Where is my phone, please?"

The time on her phone is 19:37. Ryan's voice doesn't hold the rage or the performative joy she'd been expecting. Instead, within a couple of words, she's picked up on his barely suppressed resentment. "You could have told me you were going into hospital," he says.

"I collapsed. Did they not tell you? I had an emergency section. A general anesthetic. I lost a lot of blood."

"How come you didn't tell me that?"

"What? Ryan, look, are the girls okay? Are they still awake? Can I say night-night to them?"

"Fine." he sighs heavily. "I'll get them. They're watching TV."

"Ella? Soph?"

Two sets of quiet breaths. She can feel her daughters listening down the phone, pictures them sitting on the old leather sofa, their runners sticking out over the edge. Ella hugging Hoppy. Sophie balancing on the armrest. "Girls, listen. Mammy's going to be home soon. You be great girls for Daddy, okay? And I'll be home soon, I—"

"Yeah they're just kind of busy watching their show right now, sorry."

There's a real smirk of enjoyment in Ryan's voice. "By the way, I can't believe you had some batshit-crazy woman try to pick them up. *Cathy?* Who the fuck is she? Thank God I was able to get over there and rescue them. Mairéad was very understanding. You didn't leave any spare clothes for them or anything."

Breathe. Just breathe. Do not get drawn into an argument laced with emotional landmines.

"Will you give them some supper before bedtime, Ryan? Sophie will have an apple, but she only likes it—"

"Right, I've to go. Talk to you tomorrow."

"Wait, Ryan!" He's hung up. Noah stirs and starts to cry. She's speaking into the silence of the empty dial tone. "We had a baby boy."

When she video-calls Sinéad, her sister squeals and cries and shouts over her shoulder, "Peter, come and see this beautiful baby!"

Her brother-in-law appears behind her sister's shoulder, smiling and drying his hands on a dishcloth, "Ah bless," he says, "look at the size of him, little mite. Congratulations, Ciara." There's a racket and then her nephews' faces crowd the screen.

Sinéad is crying, "Oh he is beautiful, beautiful! And you're there all on your own. Oh my God."

She phones her mum. Her mother's voice trembles. "I'll come over now," she says. "I'll get on to the ferry company, see if I can change my ticket."

Morning sunlight falls through the long blue curtains. On the end of the cot, there's a Sellotaped sheet containing her son's details. A border of teddy bears. *Name. Date of birth. Time of birth. Delivery method. Mother's name. Address.*

Her eyes keep moving back to the word *Address*. For the

last eight and a half months, this baby has been the only one who had their housing situation sorted.

Don't panic, don't panic. For the next few days, their home is here in this cubicle with its steady supply of toast and tea – and opiates. The pain from her surgery is strangely absent, but she knows it's only hidden. *How will she manage those backstairs at the Eden?*

Cathy has messaged. *We're signing in for you. We're keeping your room. DON'T WORRY. Secret mission.* She's added an emoji with sunglasses.

But of course she's worried. What if they get caught? What if they all get kicked out because of her?

Noah is stirring. It's a relief to focus on the baby, and step out of her thoughts. In his sleep, Noah looks so wise, as if he's been here before. He opens his eyes, and before he can start crying, she lifts him, pulls her nightgown aside and brings him to her. He latches onto her breast, sucking slowly while fixing his mother with a steady, deeply trusting gaze. The surge of love in her chest. As if her heart might burst.

Fed and happy, she lays him down in the bassinet. Noah's tiny fronds of fingers stir, strumming invisible airflows, as if he's conducting an orchestra.

Earlier this morning, a nurse took out her catheter and got her to try standing up. Sensation has returned to her legs. She tests them out now, stepping gingerly across the ward to the bathroom. In the mirror above the sink, her face has returned to normal. The person of the last few months has gone, and she looks like herself again. The deflation of her bump makes her feel lighter, but also less substantial.

Without the cannonball of Noah weighing her down, she might just float out of the hospital window, never to be seen again.

Back in the cubicle, Noah is crying. Standing over him is Ryan.

Jesus Christ.

His face is flushed, his black work coat unbuttoned. "I carried this crap all the way from Merrion Square," he says, "It weighs a ton." He's holding Ella's old car seat and a bag stuffed with baby clothes. He throws both down beside the bed and peers into the cot. "She looks very small," he says, "Why's she giving out like that? What does she want?"

Sleep? Milk? What else is there? The list can't be that long. When she speaks, her voice sounds small, raspy. "He's probably tired."

"He?"

She edges past him, picks up Noah.

"Hang on, did you say *he*?"

She doesn't want to breastfeed in front of Ryan, doesn't want his eyes on her.

Ryan takes off his coat, sits down by the locker and says, "I only have half an hour. Very important meeting in the department, and then I've to collect the children. I've had to take half the afternoon off." He shakes his head, incredulous. "Why does that playschool finish so early? I can't keep taking time off like this. I presume you're coming home once you get out of here." He's watching her closely. "Obviously you cannot bring my son home to a hotel." She stares at him. Can't find the words fast enough. Maybe the anesthetic hasn't worn off yet. Her brain is still numb. "The girls are settling in back at home," he says. "They're pretty happy, actually."

"They are?"

As soon as Ryan leaves, she takes out her phone. With one hand she cradles Noah, while with the other hand she googles "cracked nipples" and "fast loans" and "homes to rent in Dublin." The nipple advice centers on cabbage leaves. The houses are the same ones that have been advertised for weeks, all of them rented out already.

Noah needs his nappy changed. He's a little knot of arms and legs, his natural inclination to curl up like a newly-opened scroll.

"There he is!" Seeing them out of context, it takes her a minute to place the couple who have appeared at her bedside. He's wearing a tweed suit, while she's in a mauve dress coat with a sparkling spider brooch. Assumpta. Graham. Her in-laws. Ryan behind them.

"Our first grandson. God bless him. The image of his father. Look at him, Ryan, doesn't he look like you? Pick him up there till we see you together."

Ryan holds the baby awkwardly, his head flopping. Noah starts to bawl. Assumpta is smiling in her general direction. "He's a grand baby, Ciara. Thanks be to God. Ryan tells me you'll all be reunited at home, isn't that just lovely."

"Girls?"

Two small faces peer behind their dad's legs. Her whole body hurts. She's used to being so close to them. Seeing them from this distance, they hardly look like her daughters at all.

They're wearing the same clothes she dressed them in two days ago. Ella is hugging Hoppy, who seems to have got even scruffier, his red heart stained and torn. The girls are shy around her, edging closer.

"Go on," Ryan nudges, "say hi to Mum and your new baby brother."

Shuffling against each other. Chins tucked against their chests. Sophie fretting her hands. "Come on to Mammy, come up here. Come on up on the big high bed. Best girls in the world."

Within half a second, they are on top of her. They smell of wee and sweat and playdough. Ella hurls herself into Ciara's arms and starts to cry. "Where were you?" Sophie says, stroking her mum's hair, "we were looking for you. Where were you?"

"Mammy coming home?"

For the next two days, she does what she's become expert at doing. She pretends everything's fine. It's something between hopelessness and a survival instinct. She texts Mum and Sinéad. Sends photos, videos. They reply with hearts and hug emojis. Her mum has been trying to get over, but crossings from Holyhead have been cancelled because of the storms. Ciara has never felt so far from home. Sleep is fleeting. As soon as she wakes she turns to Noah's cot, as if to check that she didn't dream him.

You sleep, you wake, you sleep. The drugs keep coming, as does the tea, and so it continues until the fifth morning, when her favorite nurse, Yetunde, pulls open the curtain and says, "Well, Ciara my dear, you can go home today."

A tug at her chest. *Ella and Sophie.* "Can I get ready now?"

"Sure." Yetunde smiles again, lifting blankets from the bed. "I'm sure you're dying to get out of here. You'll be glad to get home to your own place."

There are forms to be signed and yet more forms. A different nurse, impossibly young with freckles on her nose, sits by Ciara's bed and tells her to be careful when having sex, as women are extremely fertile in the weeks following childbirth. "We'd recommend you wait at least six weeks before having intercourse," she says.

"Six weeks," Ciara mumbles. "Okay."

A horrible memory surges through her. After Sophie was born, Ryan must have calculated the six-week wait down to the exact day. On the sofa, he kissed her hard. She told him she was still hurting. She should have asked him to stop. Did she worry what would happen if he didn't? What that would mean?

The nurse is watching her closely, "You're day five postpartum," she says, "this is when your hormones tend to crash. You might find yourself quite weepy. You might remember from your other babies?"

"Yes."

"It's perfectly normal. But if it's going on for more than a couple of weeks, you might need to talk to someone, okay?"

Crash is the right word. It happens as she's kneeling by the bed, strapping Noah into the car seat. She doesn't have a snowsuit for him, so she wraps him in a cellular blanket—soft white cotton, dotted with holes, like a fisherman's net. Tucking the blankets around his feet, careful of the foot where he had his heel-prick test, she's caught by a sudden wave of raw, hot emotion. She wants to sit here and cry. Blinking back tears, she says goodbye to Yetunde and the other nurses, then takes the lift to the ground floor. Past the pre-labor ward, the reception and the café, past pregnant women entering the hospital, and women leaving with small car seats in tow.

Nearing the exit, she's braced for voices. For someone calling her back. Surely someone will stop her? Surely they will sense she's walking out of this hospital into the December cold with no one to pick her up, and no home to go to? Didn't they know she was lying, when she said her husband would meet her at the entrance?

Stepping out into the traffic-rush of Parnell Square, the cold air catches her breath. She tucks the blanket tighter around Noah, who is wide awake now, going cross-eyed looking at the yellow airbag sticker on the side of his seat, and making shapes with his mouth. He'll need feeding soon. She has to get him out of this cold.

When she starts to walk, a pain shoots across her abdomen. She stops, half bent over. *Slowly, slowly. Just take it slowly.* She inches down the pavement and ducks into the first café she sees.

A text from Ryan. *What time do you need collecting? It will be good to be reunited in our home as a proper family with our new son.*

Cathy isn't answering. Olivia and Maggie will be teaching.

Her mum won't be here until tomorrow night. She looks at Sinéad's number, trying to find the words. No, she can't be worrying them like that. She calls the only other person she can think of.

Diego's English school is just around the corner. He arrives within ten minutes, wild-haired and disheveled, wearing a black Santos FC hoodie and smelling of cigarettes. She explains to him about the car she left in the university car park, gives him directions and hands him her car keys. She waits, nursing Noah, drinking tepid tea, imagining Diego walking rows of cars, looking for a silver Micra with Finding Nemo window blinds. She pictures him unlocking the car, navigating road-works and one-way systems, finding a way back to her.

Just after 10:30, he walks back into the café.

Thank you barely seems adequate.

A thought occurs to her. "Was the car clamped, Diego? Had you to pay? Because I'll have to give you—"

"No, no. Not clamped! Well, actually yes. Was clamped. But I explain to the security guy. All was okay. Thanks God he's a guy that likes babies."

He's pulled in outside the café on the double yellow lines. He fastens Noah's car seat into the back with surprising ease. Catching Ciara watching, he smiles. "My two sisters have babies. I have lots of practice with these things."

Ciara eases into the passenger seat. She directs him out of the city center, and Diego crawls along Glasnevin Avenue at twenty kilometers per hour. "I not drive on left side before," he says, "So I must to go slow." Horns blare. Cars overtake, skimming past. Diego's hands grip the wheel in a ten-to-two formation. She has the heating turned up full blast for Noah. Diego's curly hair is sticking to his forehead under a black bandanna. He's chewing gum, his jaw working furiously. She's not sure if she wants to laugh or cry.

At Happy Days, Sophie and Ella throw themselves at her. She brings them to the car, where Diego is waiting with Noah. "Say hello again to new baby brother." They stare in horrified fascination.

Sophie asks, "Why's Day-go driving our car?"

"He's helping us, honey. Mammy can't drive at the moment. Granny is coming to help but she's not here yet. We're going home to our room now, okay?"

"NO."

Ella is suddenly bawling. A single word.

"NO! HOPPY!"

Under her direction, Diego parks horizontally, blocking the drive. She says, "I'll just be a few minutes. Phone me if Noah wakes up. Or if anyone else arrives. Okay? Girls, wait here. It'll be quicker if I do this by myself."

The front garden has become overgrown, making the place look derelict. Couch grass chokes the flowerbeds. Her heart thumps as she fumbles for the keys. The door screeches on its hinges.

In the silent hallway, she can almost hear her children's laughter. The suck and slip of little feet on the tacky lino. Stir-fry sizzling in the pan. Birthday candles dribbling wax.

Something flies at her. She screams, shields her eyes.

The pulse of wings. Chase squawks and lands on the banister, regarding her with his head on one side. This is the first time she's been up close to him since he was a nestling. Black wings, tattered. Granite beak, lethal. Looking closer, she sees he is tethered by a length of garden twine just long enough for him to fly around the hall and landing. Why the hell is Ryan keeping him in the house? The place reeks, the lino streaked with bird shit.

Chase takes off again. His wings, a furious beat, creating a whirlwind in the hall. Dust and dry leaves rattling.

Shielding her head, she manages to grab the rope and pull it toward the downstairs bathroom. The weight of him. *Don't kill him, don't kill him.* She wrenches the rope, hard. A scatter of wings, claws, squawking. She slams the bathroom door shut and hears Chase scratching on the other side. A furious flutter.

She's ready to run back out, but steels herself.

Ella won't sleep without Hoppy. Where the hell could he be?

She creeps up the stairs, heart still thumping. Stepping over the stair that creaks. An ingrained habit.

Walking into the girls' room, she wells up instantly. Kicked-off duvets, the shapes on the sheets where her daughters have slept for the past few nights. Their little grubby socks and twisted knickers on the floor. A half-drunk cup of milk on the nightstand. She lifts Ella's duvet cover, looks under pillows.

She kneels to search under the bed. From downstairs, the crow is still. She catches sight of the door, the fairy chart laddered by pencil markings of her children's heights. All those nights she half-slept leaning against the back of that bedroom door, praying for morning. It's hard to imagine what happened here. But isn't that always the way? A crime scene yields no emotional evidence. We stand on the battlefields waiting for the voices of history to hit us, and all we hear is birdsong.

This house is a mirage. Get too close and it will dissolve into sand.

She is bleeding. Her scar is tugging and smarting. Her cheek stings from where Chase's talons must have caught her.

"Ciara? Hello?"

Diego. His voice at the door.

Noah. That fresh newborn bleat. A trilling, rising, searching cry. A stabbing pain shoots across her breasts.

"I think we have problem here! We have somebody need Mamma very fucking quickly!"

Where where where where?

Hoppy's ear, trailing from under the side of the mattress. She pulls it. Gets to her feet. Before leaving, she grabs a couple of baby items from the hot press. A hooded towel. Her breast pump. The gray wrap she used for carrying Ella and Sophie.

A text from Ryan: *At the Rotunda. They said you discharged already? You should have called me. I will collect the children from playschool. See you at home.*

Diego carries their bags upstairs, and at her insistence leaves them alone in the mess of the room. She nurses Noah to sleep and lays him in the cradle of his car seat. In the bathroom of Room 124, she peels off the girls' clothes. Hard, sweaty socks. Hoodies with filth-blackened cuffs. The jut of Ella's ribs. Has he fed them at all? She's letting the tears fall now, wiping them roughly with her palms. The messages from Ryan start.

What the hell is going on? I just got home. Why is Chase locked in the downstairs loo???? Where are my children? Where is my son?

[Ryan is typing...]

You are completely out of your mind. I am calling my solicitor first thing in the morning. You better

[Ryan is typing...]

She turns off her phone, lifts her two girls into the bath. "Whoosh! Here we go!" She uses one of the white hotel facecloths to wipe thick, caked-in snot from Ella's upper lip. The skin underneath is red raw.

Ella cries. "No, Mammy. Me hurt me, no."

Using strawberry conditioner and a wide-toothed comb, she painstakingly teases the knotted clumps from Sophie's hair.

"Are you hungry?"

Outside, Dublin is drenched in a fine veil of mist. Noah tied to her chest in the sling, they walk along the quays to the Papa John's, where they ate on their first night. For a minute, she's buoyed by the girls' excitement, but when the adrenaline dissipates, she feels sick with exhaustion. She could collapse right here and sleep on the Formica table. Unfortunately this tiredness is not contagious. The kids race each other along the quays.

Going down the backstairs was easier than getting up them. Each step causes a twinge of pain across her belly, so she takes the stairs one at a time, like a toddler. In the room she takes out a half-finished packet of digestive biscuits, gives the girls one each. They eat sitting on the carpet by the window, pillows against the radiator. The girls in their pajamas, Noah at her breast. Sophie pretends to gobble her biscuit like a squirrel. Ella laughs and copies. Relief in their laughter, in its slightly frantic edge.

They all climb into the double bed and watch *Amazing Animals* on her phone. The girls fall asleep like that, watching secretary birds stomp their prey to death and piranhas whizz into a frenzy at the scent of blood.

IV

WHEN WE WERE BIRDS

WINTER 2018

25

Forging a path through the Christmas crowds, they've made it to the underground Tesco in the Jervis Centre. Ella in her buggy, Sophie holding onto the handle, Noah tied to her chest in a sling, his downy head close enough to kiss. Already in the three weeks since his birth, Noah has changed. His vision is becoming more focused. When Ciara lays him on the bed and leans close to him, his eyes follow the movement of light in her hair.

Since Noah arrived, she's become a little more immune to the Christmas trees. They no longer instill instant dread, but rather a low-level horror. A level of horror she can deal with. In Tesco, walls of selection boxes, towers of Roses and Quality Street, barricade the shelves of normal food.

They've made it up and down the food aisles, and they're queuing at the till. Is that Diego up ahead? It's been three weeks since he met her at that café near the Rotunda. She hasn't seen him about the hotel much. But then, they've hardly left their room, apart from signing in each evening. Cathy has offered to sign in for her, but Ciara has refused to let her—Cathy has already risked enough, signing in while she was in hospital. Ciara still feels guilty, shouldn't have let her do that.

At the till, Diego is unpacking mangetout, cantaloupe melon and chorizo onto the conveyor belt. He's wearing a white T-shirt with a Brazilian flag. *Ordem e Progresso. Blue for the sky and rivers, yellow and gold for the riches of Brazil, green for the forests and white for peace.* Why is he wearing short sleeves? Isn't he freezing?

He looks up. "Ciara! Here," he's unloading a net of satsumas and a pack of sweet potatoes, "Two second. You wait, I can to help."

"Don't worry. It's okay!"

"Two seconds." He's smiling now, handing the cashier his card, talking to her while he packs his shopping. The cashier, a woman with silver hair and peacock-blue glasses, laughs at something he's saying to her.

Diego lifts a net of garlic bulbs and a bottle of red wine into his shopping bags. He must be cooking dinner for someone. Someone young. She thinks of her students. Yuri or Akeyo with their flawless skin and gleaming hair. Or Bianca from Sardinia with her smoky eyeliner and knee-high boots. She looks down at her dowdy maternity leggings, baggy now around the waist.

"You got bags, Ciara?"

She hands over her wad of folded plastic reusables.

"Buttons, Mammy?" Ella tugs at her coat.

She's half-dazed, half-mortified, watching their parade of processed crap trundling down the till to Diego's hands. Noodles. More bloody noodles. Fresh food in tiny quantities. Two strawberry fromage frais, one small carton of milk.

She couldn't begin to explain to Diego, or even to herself, what has happened to them over the last three weeks. Her mum arrived the day after they got home from hospital. She got a taxi from the port, and Ciara smuggled her up the back-stairs, explaining that she wasn't allowed any visitors. Rhona stayed with them for seven nights. She bought them a rice cooker. She found a local library, got them all registered with library cards, discovered a free Irish class who meet every Thursday evening in the Ferryman across the quays, booked Ciara and Noah into a baby-massage class starting in April, and drove Ciara back to the GP for more pain relief. Stronger pain relief. "Discharging her with a packet of Nurofen," her mum told the doctor. "Absolute joke."

Before her mum went back to England, she told Ciara, "You need to keep busy, love. Keep your routine. Get the girls to playschool, get yourself out of this room. Could you not teach a few private students, bring Noah with you? And phone us, keep phoning us. Don't let him get you down."

The library has been a godsend. A sanctuary. They've been there almost every day after playschool, hiding from the winter cold. She sits at the bright little tables with Noah, while the girls root around in the low bookcases, returning to her with discovered treasures. "Mammy, read this one." In the adult fiction section, she has found the books she loves. Like reconnecting with old friends. She's borrowed a beginner's Irish book called *Buntús Cainte*. It's a series of mini lessons, with an accompanying CD. The library were able to give her an old CD Walkman to use, insisted that she keeps it—sure nobody uses those any more. Each night when the children are asleep, or sometimes in the early hours when she's sitting up, nursing Noah, she puts her earphones in, listens to Nóra and Pádraig talking. *Tá an lá go maith. Níl sé go dona inniu.*

"How are you managing?" Sinéad says. "All on your own with the three of them. Fucksake, Ciara. How are you coping?"

She tells her sister, "It's easier, honestly. Doing this on my own is much easier than when I lived with him."

The way he watched her struggle alone, then refused to let her sleep. He took personal offense when she tried to go to bed early. Late at night used to be his favorite time for picking fights. Delirious with tiredness, listening to him listing all the things she was. Lazy, selfish, materialistic. Then later at night, his hands pushing her, forcing her. He wouldn't let her sleep.

"Honest to God," she tells Sinéad, "now it's easier. I've people helping me." Cathy, tapping on her door with another delivery of nappies, takeaway chips, buns for the kids. Lauren rushing over in reception, bending over Noah's buggy, smiling and cooing. The librarians, the way they fuss.

Diego hands her the last of the loaded bags, which she's jamming into the bottom of the buggy. "That's it? You don't need more food, no?"

"That's us for now."

Stepping onto the escalator, Ella screeches. As Ciara reaches for her daughter's hand, Noah's buggy swerves back, nearly knocking her over. Diego touches her back lightly, grabs the buggy handle and steadies it. At the top of the escalator, back in the light-filled igloo of the shopping center, giant polar bears sway on trapeze swings hanging from the ceiling. "Last Christmas" is blasting from the speakers. Diego steers the buggy out of the rush of shoppers. "I am a good driver?" he asks Sophie.

"No, no you're not!" Sophie says, laughing up at him. The music has changed to "Silver Bells," and in a shop window, two mechanical penguins are bending their beaks to kiss amidst the cotton-wool snow.

He asks, "The kids, they excited for Christmas?"

"Well, we're living in a hotel, so..."

"Ah yeah, but kids is kids. It's Christmas. They don't mind where they living. They with they mama. Ciara, they with you."

December twenty-second she leaves the kids with Cathy and drives toward her old house, inching out of the city, part of a slow-moving snake of tail lights. Tapping the steering wheel, eyeing the clock.

At her old home she hauls open the metal shutter on the garage and pauses. It's already late in the afternoon. Ryan will be finishing work soon. She's cutting it fine. From nowhere, a sudden defiance rises. Ignoring the pain in her scar, she starts lifting boxes. Anything labeled CHRISTMAS gets shoved into the boot to be driven back to the Eden. Raiding the place, as if there won't be any consequences. As if she's not afraid and keeping one eye on the driveway the entire time, heart about to detonate.

Back in the underground car park of the Eden, she calls Cathy, who sends Adam and Lyra down to help carry the boxes up to the fifth floor.

"Cool, Mammy!" Sophie pulls out a light-up snowman.

Ella sits smiling, surrounded by tinsel. Noah, in Cathy's arms, wide-eyed looking at the lights, legs jolting with excitement.

"Mammy, where we gonna put all this stuff?"

It doesn't matter. She is feeling reckless, high on Christmas spirit, giddy with the knowledge of her own daring. She turns up the radio, FM104 blasting "All I Want For Christmas" and stations her old outdoor decorations along the corridor. Adam and Lyra help out, spacing the snowmen and reindeers between doors. Lyra has a Bluetooth speaker, turns the music up louder.

Ciara sets her tree up in the corner of the hotel room and lets the girls load each bendy plastic branch with baubles. Adam and Lyra help her with fairy lights, window stickers, stockings. It's too much. It's way too much, but the effect is appallingly beautiful. This much light and glitter in such a small space feels like a physical manifestation of a long-suppressed feeling she can't quite name. Something like hope. The room felt cramped before. Now it feels ready to burst with nervous energy. In the tacky glitter of 124, Sophie holds her cheeks in her sticky palms. "You know Mammy, I seed Santa."

She hugs her daughter close, kisses the top of her head. Surely something happens to the love in these situations. Like fired sand, she thinks, love strengthens, brightens.

Cathy sticks her head in the door. She sees the lopsided tree, the kids basking in its glow. She looks at Ciara's hands, covered in gold glitter, and Adam and Lyra sticking silver snowflakes along the windowsill and Santa climbing the curtains. She can tell by the way Cathy smiles that she gets it. This quiet, tinsel-fueled rebellion. And she doesn't say *wait till the housekeeping staff see this,* or *are you off your bleeding rocker.* She pulls out her phone and says, "That's bleeding gorgeous. Come here till I take a picture."

Christmas Eve, Ciara kneels on the white tiled bathroom floor, wrapping dolls and plastic horses she bought in the middle aisle of Lidl. A net of gold chocolate coins each. An orange and an apple from the hotel breakfast buffet. She video-calls Sinéad, who is doing the same thing. Strips of Sellotape on the legs of her jeans. Stockings wedged with tiny parcels.

Christmas morning, the noise starts early. A little boy of around six years old who she's never seen before is racing a remote-control tank up and down the corridor. The girls from 140 are running in and out of their room, the eldest playing One Direction full volume on her new phone. The young couple with the baby pass her door, nodding to Noah, "Congratulations love." Their baby is now crawling, dressed in a mini Santa suit.

Her mum has sent new jumpers and leggings for the girls, and a pack of Peter Rabbit sleepsuits for Noah. Sinéad has sent them each a toy Puppycorn. A plastic egg containing a soft toy dog with wings and a glittery horn. She messages her. *Cheers for the dogs with glittery dicks on their heads, WTF?*

Sinéad replies, *Rory got a robot but Santa forgot to leave him any fucking batteries is it too early to start on the wine love you x*

A scarf from her mum. A €50 voucher from Sinéad and Peter, with a note *Spend this on YOU, okay? Seriously Ciara if we find out you spent this on kids clothes or bloody nappies we will murder you. Happy Christmas sis xox*

Lunch is a cold rotisserie chicken she bought yesterday, along with diced cucumbers and cherry tomatoes, Ella's favorite. Chocolate coins for dessert. Afterward, she drives the children out to their old home. They have agreed over text to split the day. At the door, Ryan greets Ella and Sophie with presents almost as tall as them. Frozen in the doorway, heartsick, she watches them tear off red and gold wrapping paper. "Look, Mammy! A Paw Patroller and a Mission Cruiser!" Bright red and blue plastic trucks, with sound effects and missile-launchers. Sophie and Ella jump around the living room as if there were springs in their soles, not sure where to put their small bodies.

Ryan watches, his laughter deep with pride. "That's what you wanted now, isn't it?"

Noah is tucked into the sling, his head resting on Ciara's chest. Her scar is sore. Where's their child support? Ryan has yet to give her a cent. She thinks of the cheap dolls she gave the girls this morning, already stripped bare and missing clumps of hair and limbs, discarded on the carpet of Room 124.

Glancing outside to the back garden, she sees Chase tethered to the wall by a length of twine. The bird is pacing, scratching at the frozen earth. He's almost the size of a fully grown adult crow, but his feathers are still soft, dull. Looking closer, his eyes are navy.

"Mince pie, Ciara?" Assumpta, down from Monaghan for Christmas, is hovering beside her.

"No thanks," she says.

Assumpta stands looking at Ryan and the girls, nodding approvingly. "Such a great dad. Haven't you the best dad in the world, girls?" She turns to Ciara. "Here, let me take the wee man, if you want to head off. Give Ryan his time with his children."

Ciara's stomach twists. "Noah needs to be fed," she says. "I can't leave him with you, he's too young. I'll be back for the girls this evening."

A look is exchanged between Ryan and his mother. He stands, steps closer to Ciara and lowers his voice.

"Yeah, about that," he says. "I spoke to my solicitor. We are back in court in January to sort out the custody arrangements. I presume your solicitor told you?"

She begins to speak, but finds her voice is gone. For the past few weeks, her children have felt like the only thing that's real. The housing office, the court date, all of it has fallen away.

"Two evenings and one weekend day isn't enough," he is saying, "Not that you even stick to that agreement anyway, since Noah was born. I need time with my son, and the children need to be living in their own home. A judge will have to settle this."

"Will you turn up this time?"

He gives her a scathing look.

She kisses the girls, tells them she'll be back soon.

Outside, it's starting to snow. Big soft flakes swirl across the empty street, melting as soon as they touch the wet pavements. Trees glimmer in bay windows. She hurries to the car, pulling down the fleecy ear flaps on Noah's trapper hat.

26

The waiting room of the district court at Dolphin House is warm, but Ciara can't stop shivering. When Ryan walked in, wearing his long black overcoat, for a minute he stood looking around, taking in the shabby seats and posters. Ciara knew that look—sneering contempt mixed with indignation. Immediately she felt herself tense, become hyper-alert. Now Ryan and his solicitor are sitting a few rows behind her. She feels his stare on the back of her neck, a dark sonar. When she sneaks a look over her shoulder, he has his head bowed, scrolling on his phone.

So today their court appearance will go ahead, unless the list is too full. Part of her hopes it will be, so she doesn't have to face this.

Last night, running through her testimony on the phone with Sinéad, everything seemed clear. But now she's jittery, full of foreboding. What is it her mum says? *I can't get the cold out of my bones.* God, what she wouldn't give to have her mum or Sinéad with her right now. She's been waiting here since just after 9 a.m., and now it's well after lunchtime. Grace has been over to the desk a few times, talking to the clerks. She had emailed to remind Ciara there are no catering facilities at the courthouse, but still she forgot to bring food, or water, and now her mouth is dry.

When their initials and case number are called, Ciara's heart lurches. *CF and RF. Case 14R5, Courtroom 4.*

"That's us." Grace stands and leads her out of the waiting room, along a corridor, into a room on the right. She follows her solicitor down the red carpet, into the first pew. It's almost like a church, rows of seats and an altar at the front. Her eyes lock onto the judge, sitting behind a bench elevated above them by several steps, the gold harp of the Irish state on the wall behind his head. He's a man in his sixties, gray hair visible beneath his off-white wig. Cuffs of a navy jumper are protruding at the edges of his black robes. His small frameless glasses reflect the strip lighting, so it's impossible to see his eyes.

Ryan walks in, followed by his solicitor—a woman in her forties who struts confidently, flicking her hair. She's wearing a fitted black suit and a taupe silk shirt, her look completed by a slash of lipstick, pillar-box red.

Ciara tries to stuff her scarf, gloves, handbag and black winter coat under the seat but there's not enough space, so she leaves them in a jumble on the pew beside her. Trying to steady her breathing, she straightens her blazer and smooths the cheap white shirt she bought in Penney's last week. The makeup she applied this morning has melted away. When she checked her reflection in the loo earlier, she had looked ashen.

Her breasts are hurting, milk hardened. This is the longest

she's ever been away from Noah. She should have brought the buggy up from the car boot, in case Cathy wanted to take him for a stroll. Nappies—had she left enough nappies? Hopefully the girls settled for Cathy eventually. This morning, Sophie and Ella had been moany, clingy, as if they'd picked up on her stress. She sometimes thinks they are symbiotic, the three of them like trees in a forest, linked through their roots. Despite her constant efforts to pretend everything was fine, her raging cortisol had flooded the small hotel room, setting them all off. Tantrums always happen when she's least able to cope.

Ryan slides into the row opposite, unbuttoning the jacket of his expensive suit. He looks calm and well rested, hair combed neatly in place. She catches a faint note of his aftershave—pine and tea-tree, acrid and strong. His charcoal suit is the one she helped him pick out last summer, for his friend Paul's wedding in Westport. That sky-blue tie. They were in the shop for ages, while she plied the kids with snacks, distracting them with cartoons on her mobile. She remembers the way he struck up a rapport with the sales staff, charming them, while she thought about the night she'd just had.

Grace stands to speak first. "Your honor," she says, "My client, Ms. Ciara Fay, is a dedicated mother, who has her children's very best interests at heart. As you can see from the screenshots of messages here, Ms. Fay has been subjected to ongoing emotional and psychological abuse, which has impacted her well-being and that of her children. Mr. Fay controlled the finances and tried to cut his wife off from her support network—friends and family were not allowed in their home. He has never taken an active role in parenting the children. His frequent outbursts and rages…"

Ciara knows her solicitor is not telling them everything. But how can Grace tell the judge things she doesn't even know? Parts of the story Ciara has been unable to articulate, has never properly acknowledged. Things she has put away, thinking she will deal with them when she is ready.

Too soon, Grace's speech is over. Ciara's life with her children compressed into a couple of paragraphs. The judge is writing some notes. A handful of words. Which words? How has he interpreted what Grace has said? Was it enough?

Ryan stands. "Your honor," he smiles in that gentle way he uses with people he's trying to win over. "I have been in pieces since my wife left home so unexpectedly, taking my children without my consent…" He's speaking calmly, patiently about his active, hands-on parenting style. His words float above her head, but all she can concentrate on is his face. His mouth. She must be losing her mind.

Ryan ducks his head, adjusts the knot of his silk tie, embarrassed and apologetic as he confesses the stress caused by his wife's unstable moods and frequent abandonment. "It's been really hard," he says. "Thank you for listening, your honor." He sits down again and—no, surely not—wipes tears from his eyes. His solicitor rubs his arm, mouthing, "Are you okay?"

This cannot be happening, this cannot be happening, no, no, no, no, no.

It's like she's fighting against gravity. Trying to stop herself from falling off a cliff, when she's already jumped. She can hear how convincing he sounds, knows in what direction this is heading.

When it's Ciara's turn to speak, anxiety makes her voice sound hoarse. The judge is looking at her, but she still can't see his eyes, only the band of white light on the lenses of his glasses. His lips are set in an impassive line, his fingers linked on the bench in front of him. All her late-night rehearsing with Sinéad seems to vanish. She hears herself saying "it was very difficult" like a child moaning over a complicated sum. She tries to explain how much she loves her children, and how she's trying her best. How she could no longer cope with the difficulties in her marriage. She feels as if all eyes are on her scruffy blazer, her cheap, milk-stained blouse. Her words sound desperate, as if she's lying. Beside her, Grace pats her arm, whispers something reassuring.

Her allotted time is over, and the judge is listening to Ryan's solicitor.

"Model father... fifteen years in the civil service... hard working, reliable, law abiding... Mrs. Fay's erratic behavior... Removed the children from the country without their father's consent... attempted to remove them again in April 2018... stopped at the gate at Dublin Airport... unsuitable accommodation at the Hotel Eden... sub-standard, cheap hotel... inappropriate... lack of space, and stimulation... poor nutrition... complete disregard for the children's well-being... child hospitalized due to bronchitis as a result of living conditions... failed to inform the child's father that she had been in hospital."

"Is that right?"

At first Ciara doesn't realize that the question is directed at her. The judge is staring at her. "Is that right? You failed to inform Mr. Fay that his child had been hospitalized?"

Grace stands. "If I may. Ms. Fay has been put under conditions of extreme stress due to Mr. Fay's refusal to vacate their family home, made worse by his failure to pay maintenance. As you know, we are in the middle of a severe housing crisis, which has made things even more difficult. My client is trying her best to secure a home, in almost impossible circumstances."

For the first time, Ryan looks uncomfortable. His solicitor swoops in, explaining that Mr. Fay has been left to manage a house on his own. "His wife left for no reason at all, and he has been forced to take unpaid leave on several occasions as a result of this trauma. He has pledged to pay means-tested maintenance as soon as he can feasibly do so."

The judge writes something down.

A few minutes later, when he starts giving his judgment, Ciara's heart is banging so loudly in her ears that she can barely make sense of what he is saying.

"Primary custody... mother... sole care-giver... father must be informed of children's residential address... cannot be removed from the state without father's consent... importance of the role of the father... every other weekend... one overnight... age of children... reviewed in due course... maintenance order... direct debit..."

And then it's all over.

The judge gathers his papers, stands and leaves the courtroom. Grace shuts her laptop, and Ciara bends to gather her bundle of garments. One of her woolen gloves has fallen under the bench. She can't reach it. She'll have to leave it. What does it matter anyway?

Outside the courtroom, Grace holds her back. "Wait and we'll let them go ahead, unless you want to get into a conversation?"

She watches Ryan stride on ahead of her and push through the double doors with both hands. Before the doors swing shut, she sees him loosen his tie and turn to say something to his solicitor. His hand cuts the air. A scathing, angry gesture.

Only now, the relief hits her. She turns to Grace. "He didn't win? I still have custody, right?"

"You certainly do." Grace is fixing her scarf. "The judge could have awarded him custody, but he didn't. Believe it or not, Ciara, this is actually a good outcome. Ryan was only awarded access."

Now Ciara is speaking fast, too fast, rambling, her voice high-pitched with stress. "I didn't tell him which hotel, Grace. Sophie wouldn't have known the name of the hotel, she couldn't have told him, his solicitor knew all about the Eden, the hospital, the exact dates we were there, and he knew everything. How did he know that, Grace? How did he know that? How?"

Grace links arms with her firmly. "Let's get you out of here. Come on."

In the Porterhouse, on the corner nearest the court, Grace finds seats by the window and disappears to the bar. Their table is an upturned barrel. Tricolor bunting loops across the windows, and the Dubliners are playing on the sound system. Ciara still can't get the cold out of her bones. Images of the courtroom keep flashing across her mind. Ryan's mouth. The judge peering down from the distance of his bench.

"Here." Grace returns to the table with two shots of Baileys and instructs Ciara to drink. Sugary alcohol scalds a trail down her throat. The kick is strong.

"Believe it or not, you got off lightly," Grace is saying. "The judge wasn't happy about your hotel situation, but he wasn't happy about Ryan's failure to pay maintenance either. One overnight per fortnight. Two evening visits per week. That's not too bad, Ciara."

The room is spinning now. The music on the speakers seems to have become louder, faster. A reel, or is it a jig? A painted leprechaun on the window is leering at her. There's a peal of loud laughter from a group of men at the bar. Grace is speaking, but she can't concentrate on what she's saying.

After a short while, Grace checks her slim silver watch and says something about leaving. As she's buttoning her coat, she says, "Ryan didn't get what he wanted, so he is likely to appeal this, Ciara. We have to be prepared to go back to court again. No word from the housing office?"

"Nothing."

"I'll walk you out," Grace says.

Outside, on Parliament Street, Grace says she will be in touch, then turns and walks in the direction of City Hall. Late afternoon, the winter sky is brightening to a crisp arctic blue. Ciara pulls her scarf up to her chin and shoves her hands into her pockets. As she walks hurriedly along the quays, back toward the Eden, all the things she should have said to the solicitor flash through her head.

If he has them overnight he'll never give them back. Grace, he'll do something. To get back at me. I feel it instinctively. Grace, they've never been away from their mum. They're only little. Noah's only six weeks old. Grace. What about Noah?

In the Baltic January gloom she is sitting in the corridor, curled up in a ball at her doorway. She has the door of 124 propped open with a towel, in case her children wake. For once, the corridor is empty. She's not sure how long she's been sitting like this, when a hand touches her shoulder. Cathy, in her black bar-tending shirt, must have just finished her shift. "What's up, Ciara hun? How did it go today?"

"The judge gave him an overnight."

"Ciara." Cathy pulls her into a hug.

"Noah is so young. I told them I'm breastfeeding him. I told them."

"Hang on. Noah too?" Cathy sits back on her hunkers. Her voice has changed, taken on a note of defiance. "That's a load of bullshit, that is. A six-week-old baby? What a load of shit."

"I told them. I tried to tell them . . ."

"Don't bring them," Cathy says. "What can they do? Just ignore it."

She holds Cathy's eyes, a silent conversation passing between them.

A text pings. She reads it and looks at Cathy. "You wouldn't stay here and mind the kids for ten minutes? I've asked a friend to help me with something."

"Go for it." Cathy puts out a hand, helps her to her feet.

Downstairs in the lobby, Diego has left his hoover by one of the pillars. Lauren is behind reception, painting her nails.

Ciara sits on the edge of one of the bucket chairs. "He always knows where I am," she tells Diego. "What I'm thinking."

"So you want me check your phone for spyware? I see your text. I'm not good with these technologies, honest God, Ciara. But I have my friend here, he can help." Diego turns, shouts across the lobby: "OY PUTA!" A short man in navy housekeeping scrubs gives him the finger, yells back. "This guy he come from Moldova. Portuguese we teach him."

"Not English?"

The Moldovan man is over at their table now. He smiles, nods to her, "Hello how's it going?"

"This phone, Stefan. You can check for spyware?"

Stefan takes her Nokia, slips it out of its grubby case. Holds it close to his face, squinting, thumbs fast. His expression is so intense that she has an image of him standing back, smashing her phone on the polished tiles. Pieces of her life scattering. Photos. Messages. Late-night searches.

Diego is watching him too. "This guy so fucking smart, honest God. He have like degree in IT, PhD."

"Why are you teaching him Portuguese?"

"Ah." Stefan beckons Diego. The two men stare at her phone, scrolling.

"Puta que pariu," Diego mutters.

"What?" She's scrambling up, having to turn sideways in order to stand, pain shooting across her scar. "What is it?"

Diego looks at her. "Ciara," he says in a low whisper, "Someone have installed an app here. You know you have share messages with your husband?"

"RAT," Stefan says. "Remote Administration Technology. Everything you have share. GPS tracked. Screen-sharing. Probably he installed a long time ago. He take your phone?"

"He gave it to me. For my birthday."

"Ciara..." Diego looks as if he is trying to find the right words.

"Turn it off." She snatches the phone. Bile at the back of her throat. He has known where she is all along. The games he played, driving her out to the suburbs that night, pretending he believed she was staying with Tania. His outrage when Sophie told him they were staying in a hotel. It was all a performance, none of it real.

"Tudo bem, Ciara. Easy, easy. Sit, sit. You want some water?" Diego looks flustered, as if he's worried she might break down in front of him. "I get for you new phone. Stefan! New phone, yeah? You sort out something? Tudo bem. Come on. Is okay. Vai ficar tudo bem Ciara, vai ficar tudo bem."

27

The Social Housing Allocations office has a different feel to the Central Placement Service. The CPS was full of panic. Blue railings. Courts of Criminal Justice standing opposite. But the SHA just feels desperate. Tired love ballads. Dirt-trodden carpet. Sitting in the waiting room, she looks out of the window.

In the distance, the Dublin Mountains look as if someone has dusted icing sugar over them. She thinks of her mum, chatting in the kitchen while she tapped the sieve over a batch of fresh-baked fairy cakes. Not that Rhona baked very often, maybe only once a year, but somehow the memory has stuck.

Her number is called and she readjusts Noah's sling, coaxes Ella and Sophie to their feet.

"Well," the man behind the desk says. "I'd say you've been through the mill?"

He pauses, opening up a space for her story, but she can't think of anything to say. Her head hurts with the effort of trying to make-believe everything is going to be okay. She's negotiated the heavy maze of Christmas, and the steely grayness of New Year. But since the court appearance, her strength is fraying. She wants to talk to someone, but she can't tell her mum about this. Her heart couldn't take it. Sinéad is working nights this week, texts with sleeping-face emojis.

"How old are the kids?" The man tries again to make eye contact.

"The girls are three and almost five. My baby is seven weeks."

"Bless," he says. Sophie is currently peeling the *Crisis Housing* poster off the door and licking the Sellotape. Ella, teething again, sucks a Liga biscuit, her chin caked in sand-colored mush. Tied to Ciara's chest, Noah's downy head brushes her chin. He's more alert now, moving his head around, watching everyone with the seriousness of newborns. His eyes are somewhere between the brown of fresh-turned earth and the dark blue of an ocean storm.

"We're in a hotel," she's telling the man behind the desk. "I've been phoning every week to check on my application for the housing list. But I thought maybe if I came in here, it might help. If I spoke to someone in person."

He frowns at his computer screen, "Yeah, you should have been assigned a housing officer? Someone to help?"

"No one's been near us."

"Sorry about that now." His fingers rattle at the keyboard. "Second time today that's happened actually. A woman was in earlier, very same thing. System's overwhelmed. People are falling through the cracks, you know? An average of 232 more people in Ireland are finding themselves in this situation every month?"

What's the meaning of his supportive smile, his upward

intonation? Is he trying to be helpful? In certain cases, there's comfort to be had in such numbers, in the reassurance that you're not alone. This isn't one of these cases. Sometimes the idea that other people are going through similar shit is not helpful at all.

He looks up from his screen. "Right then. Ciara, isn't it? Okay, Ciara so I have inputted your details again. A housing officer should definitely call you this time. Listen, I know you're waiting to hear about the housing list, but you know you can actually start house-hunting? If you get somewhere, you can apply for HAP—Housing Assistance Payment—retrospectively?"

"Really?" She sits up in the chair. "So I can start looking?"

"I guess so? If you'd have enough for the first month's rent? I don't see why not?" He smiles. "Good luck?"

When Ryan answers the door on Tuesday evening, his demeanor is bright, triumphant. This is how he always looks when he feels he's winning. His slightly manic energy reminds her of when she agreed to marry him. His hard smile, and the way his eyes seem to glow with self-satisfaction. She's come to recognize these flares in his energy, and to anticipate the dark side of their ebb.

She's been tussling with her thoughts all day, worried about bringing the kids for access. Now that he has been legally granted an overnight stay, will he just try to keep them? She's counting on the fact that Ryan has work the next morning, and is unlikely to want to put himself out.

"Girls!" He makes a fuss of Sophie and Ella, kissing their

cheeks. They squirm away, dancing into the kitchen, where Chase is at the window, beak tapping on the glass. "And how's my little man?" Noah is tied to her chest in the wrap, and Ryan pulls back the material, leaning so close that she can smell the stale coffee on his breath. Unwittingly, Ciara takes a step back. Noah whimpers and she kisses his forehead, rocking him.

"He's tired," she says, "he's due for a nap. I'll just take him for a walk, while the girls play. I'll collect them at six?"

Ryan's expression has changed. "The judge said I'm entitled to time with all three children. That includes my son."

"Well, he's about to go to sleep." Her mind is pedaling fast. "I could take him out of the wrap, but he'll cry. It can be hard to settle him. Quite often he won't really take a bottle. Sometimes he will. It depends. If he's very upset, then he won't. And he'll need a nappy change if he wakes up. Definitely."

Ryan's face contorts before he can hide it. Recomposing himself, he says, "Fine. For today, that's fine. But you need to schedule his naps so that it doesn't interfere with my parenting time. I need my time with him. Oh, and Ciara. One more thing." She knew he wouldn't let her get away this easily. "Abuse? In court the other day, your solicitor—what was her name? The batty one with the fucking carpet coat—she said I was abusing you? Emotional abuse—what the fuck does that even mean? Bloody joke."

The carpet coat. She can't even remember what Grace was wearing in court that day. She only remembers the way her coral lipstick had worn into the creases of her lips. *"You got off lightly, Ciara, it could have been worse."*

She jogs Noah up and down, shushing him. "Ryan, I don't know why you're asking me this. And anyway,"—something snags in her mind, giving her a jolt of courage—"why were you tracking my phone?"

"Sorry?"

"There was spyware on my phone. You've been tracking my location. When you pretended you'd just found out about the hotel, you were lying."

"I don't know what you're talking about. We need to speak later, Ciara. To arrange my first overnight with them."

Daft, the Dublin Accommodation Finder Terminal, a website she first used to search for student houseshares over a decade ago. She remembers reading somewhere that it was started by two brothers while they were still at secondary school. They knew they'd hit on a good idea when they started getting phone calls from estate agents while riding to school on their bikes. The logo, a small orange arrow that is also the shape of a house. A banner image of a cozy living room. *Find Your Way Home.*

She searches *homes to rent, Dublin.*

Two nights later, she is standing outside a house in Terenure, the South Dublin suburb where she lived in her third year at college. A black Georgian door with semicircle window. Clean, crunching gravel path. In the doorway a dark-haired man in his mid-forties, wearing a Dublin GAA top. "Here let me help you with that." He steps out to guide Noah's buggy into the hall. "Ciara? Lovely to meet you. I'll show you the flat if you'd like to follow me. You might need to leave the buggy up here." *A flicker of hope. He seems nice.*

Today she feels close to fainting. The dizziness that's been building over the last week has reached a whole other level. She should not be in charge of two small children and a baby, but what else is she supposed to do?

She traipses down the stairs after the landlord. "Here's the kitchen." He opens a door to the right of the hall. "And here's the bedroom-living room."

It takes her a minute to realize what's happening. Sawn in half, the flat is divided by the communal hallway. "There's locks," he says, "both doors are lockable."

"It's not really going to work though, is it? With three young kids."

"No." He frowns at the dissecting hallway, as if seeing it for the first time. "No, I suppose not."

Almost every evening for the rest of January, they queue, breath steaming, outside Stoneybatter terraces, Blanchardstown apartments and tall red-brick Phibsborough houses split into flats. In every overpriced living space, all she can see is Sophie, Ella and Noah. Their eyes, their pink-tipped fingers.

Mold flowering up bathroom ceilings: Ella.

Lightbulb swinging gaily from frayed electric cables: Sophie.

"There was a bit of an issue with rats with the last tenant, but sure they were probably leaving food around and if you'd a cat sure you'd be grand": Noah.

Even when she's able to convince herself that she'll get rid of the mold, she'll fix the bloody light fitting, she'll get a bloody cat to kill the bloody rats, and she reels off enthusiastic emails, *I'd love to take the house*, there's never any reply.

Low-Low Town seems more brightly lit than normal. *Keep busy,* her mum has been saying. So, Ciara has driven up to Blanchardstown after playschool, not anticipating how the sight of the Low-Low Town entrance would take her back. She sees herself parked under the streetlight that night last April, tucking the girls in with the Donegal blanket and driving into the mountains. She wants to reverse out of here. There are other play centers with less painful memories. But the girls are already unbuckling themselves, and Noah is due a feed.

They pay at the desk, and deposit their shoes. The girls make a beeline for the mini-supermarket and are soon catapulting along behind small trolleys full of cardboard food. Ciara takes a seat, lingering at the fringe of the group of parents. She wonders if they have all brought their children here for the social interaction. Pointless, because all the kids in Low-Low Town ignore each other, still at the age when they view humans of the same size with abject suspicion.

"How are you doing?" A stocky man with a gold earring leans over and introduces himself as Oliver. He has dark blond, disheveled hair and he's wearing a black Edinburgh Fringe Fest shirt. Soon, he's telling her about his wife. He says, "It's incredible how she can do it. How she can fit into a box."

"A box?" Ciara realizes she hasn't been listening at all.

"Aye. About so high, and so wide," Oliver gestures with

confident hands. "It's her main act. Her signature performance." His accent—Scottish maybe? His cheeks are smile-creased although his face is young. "Whoops!" He steps out of the way just before Ella goes careening past on a tiny fire engine. "She does a few other bits," he says. "Tightrope. Stuff with kites and a metal frying pan."

"Okay." She really needs to eat something. What is this man talking about? Some sort of theater act? Hedging a bet, she asks, "And do you perform too?"

"Ah just bit of flame-eating, knife-throwing, you know yourself. That sort of thing. Ah, there's my wee woman now." His daughter, ethereal with her white-blonde hair swept over her eyes, dressed in paisley-print cargo pants and a furry gilet, wanders over and leans on his knee. She's studying a talking teddy, clearly trying to figure out its mechanics. "This one's three and she's visited twenty-seven countries already." Oliver laughs. "Three months in Paris, Edinburgh before that, then we got work on the Dublin Fringe, thought it was a cool spot to base ourselves while we're gigging in Europe. Lots of parks. Ruby likes it."

She nods and smiles, trying to concentrate on what he is saying. Grace phoned this morning, to see how the new access arrangements are going. When Ciara told her she hasn't left them overnight with Ryan yet, her solicitor's voice became serious. *"Ciara, that is court mandated. Breach of court order, you will get yourself into big trouble..."*

In her arms, baby Noah squirms and nuzzles her shirt.

"Uh-oh, he's hungry." Oliver smiles, tactfully backs away. She sits on one of the plastic stackable chairs and begins to unbutton. Noah latches on, the familiar tug at her nipple, only with this baby it hurts like hell. *Why was it so much easier with the other two?* As she holds her scarf over her breast, she's trying not to watch Oliver standing against the floor-to-ceiling window chatting to another mum, nodding attentively as he listens, gesturing with open palms.

How has a flame thrower with an acrobat-contortionist wife ended up here, in Low-Low Town?

Mum texts her. *Any more houses love? Any joy?*

Monday, a terrace in Inchicore, down the road from the Irish Museum of Modern Art. A brackish stream meanders through a stone-walled gorge behind the back garden wall. Again, that surge of hope. The place is quirky, ivy-spattered. "There's no central heating," the landlady in the red anorak leads them up the creaking staircase, "but we've these storage heaters, which are class and very cost-efficient."

Swallowing her doubts, Ciara says, "Sure, we'd love to take it."

The woman nods, "I'll add your name to the list."

Tuesday, a terrace in Stoneybatter, round the corner from the Glimmerman pub and the Saturday farmers' market. They wait in the eye-watering February cold, along with a sullen-looking couple in their twenties, two women with jet-black bangs and Mary Quant dresses, three men in corduroy jackets, smoking rollies.

This terrace with fleur-de-lis net curtains seems to have been lifted from several decades past, but isn't quite clean enough to be retro. A man in his fifties, sweat patches darkening his business shirt, takes one look at the two sticky kids and baby Noah and glances away, but he proceeds with the ritual of showing her around the house. "The toilet is beside the kitchen," he says, with the tired voice of someone who has explained this twenty times in the last five minutes.

"It's unusual," she says.

They all stand staring at the toilet, cordoned off from the cooker by a tinkling beaded curtain, before she adds "Is it legal?"

"Ah yeah. It's not a bother."

"Right. And just one more thing. Do you take HAP?"

The man folds his arms across his belly. "Now, that was clearly stated on the phone."

"Oh was it?" She's reaching for Sophie and plays with her braids. "I'm just in a tight spot, with the three kids. It's very hard to find somewhere. I just thought you might consider."

"The house is for rent at market value. HAP does not provide the market value." His voice sounds like a recording. The hurried terms and conditions at the end of a radio insurance AD.

"Right, okay, I just thought I'd check."

"It was very clearly stated now, in fairness."

Something has changed. Her voice sounds high and over-friendly. References and deposit. Yes, he'll add her name to the list. They go back down the creaking stairs, through the small hallway with the naked bulb blazing. "Thanks very much," she says at the door.

The man nods but doesn't smile. He shuts the door behind them.

Outside, the street lamps are making everything grainy, like a black-and-white film. A handful of stars. Orion's belt, and the W of Cassiopeia.

Sophie tilts her head up at the sky. "Mammy, you know that star beside the moon is Jupiter and the one there is Mars? Mairéad told us, when we were learning about space."

28

Days have fallen into their strange routine. Mornings, she brings the girls to Happy Days, then meets students for lessons at Brambles Café. This was Diego's doing. His suggestion, that he could move his language school classes to the afternoons, meet her in the mornings for lessons, whenever he's not working at the Eden. His books are now covered with detailed notes, pages highlighted and dog-eared. She can feel his nerves. He really wants this.

She has started teaching some other students too, friends of Diego, and people who responded to the ad she placed on Gumtree.ie: *Professional English teacher available for private lessons.* She didn't mention there would be a baby in attendance, but Noah is generally happy enough in her arms, and none of the students seem to mind. Wednesdays, she teaches Maria, who wants to be an accountant and insists Ciara calls out lists of numbers, which she transcribes. Fridays, Ciara teaches Abdul, who wants to study medicine but cannot understand the past participle.

After her Brambles lessons, she picks up the girls and brings them to either the park, the library or Low-Low Town, depending on the weather. Dinners are concoctions she boils in the rice cooker. In the evenings, when she doesn't have to bring the kids to Ryan's, they queue outside houses and walk through potential homes. After the kids' bedtime, she phones her mum and Sinéad, listens to another lesson from *Buntús Cainte*, trawls through Daft. She's been searching seriously for almost three months now. The number of places available to rent in Dublin dwindles every day.

At night, she dreams of houses. She thinks of that story by Ray Bradbury. Of the house continuing to function long after its occupants have gone. *Tick-tock, seven o'clock*. She searches for images of houses reclaimed by nature.

What will happen if you don't find a home?

From talking to people on floor five, she knows that some have been in emergency accommodation for years. At what point—raising three children in a single room where they don't have space to play or even learn how to walk—at what point will she lose parts of herself that are irretrievable? At what point, even if she gets a home, will it be too late?

One night, Cathy knocks on her door and hands her a plastic bag full of baby clothes. "From Alex."

"Alex? Is she okay?" Ciara pulls the door over behind her.

"I texted her, told her you'd had a baby boy. She left this bag off with her mam." Cathy's eyes are filling. "Sure she knew you'd need them."

Ciara kneels in the corridor and gently unfolds garments from the bag. Powder blue cardigans, little navy dungarees, rabbit sleepsuits, all so beautifully cleaned and ironed they look like new.

"God love her," Cathy says, blowing her nose.

"Is she still . . . ?"

"Yeah."

"But do you think she'll . . . ?

"She's thinking about it."

Today Low-Low Town is louder than normal, bordering on collective hysteria. Parents are having to shout to hear each other. Leaving here will be like stepping out of a nightclub with a scratchy throat and ears ringing, without the advantage of being drunk.

The kids are tired, people keep saying. *After the long weekend. All the Patrick's Day fun. They are overtired.* It makes sense. Tired adults collapse. Tired toddlers wind themselves up into a fury.

In her arms, Noah tilts his head to watch all the action. He's getting chubbier now. Michelin Man legs, round cheeks and a tide of fair hair that gathers in a tuft on his crown. He's started giving his first gummy smiles. Is he sleeping? mums at Low-Low Town ask her. Does he sleep?

"A silent disco walking tour," Oliver is saying. "People wear these headphones and we play a soundtrack while we bring them on a tour of Temple Bar. Oh and we're performing in the Meeting House Square in a couple of weeks' time, myself and the missus. You should come!"

"Will she be doing the box trick?"

"Oh aye. Sure that's her signature. In fact if you wouldn't mind, maybe Ruby could sit with you during the show? Let me show you these pictures. Look here, that's when we were in the Burren. Gorgeous." Oliver is showing her photos on his phone. "That's my wife there."

The woman is fairly broad in the shoulders. *How does she fit into a box?*

Thursday night, she leaves the car running to keep Noah warm and brings the girls up the driveway. At the door, Ryan looks over her shoulder. "Where is he?"

"He's asleep." She tries to avoid eye contact. "He'll wake up if I try to move him. He's happy there in his car seat."

Ryan folds his arms. His jaw sets into a thin, angry line, "You expect me to believe that every single night at this time, my son is either shitting, hysterical or asleep?" She looks away, down at the mossy path. "And every single weekend when I'm meant to have an overnight, the children are sick?"

"It's true! They've all had tummy bugs, you know that. I didn't think you'd want to deal with all the vomiting and diarrhea."

That look of distaste. He recovers. "Right, that's it. If you don't let me have the three children, including my son, overnight, I'm going back to court. My solicitor says I can file a complaint. You could be looking at a serious fine—or even a prison sentence."

She tries to laugh. "A prison sentence? I don't think—"

"That's what my solicitor said. Look it up."

"I better see to Noah—"

"I was awarded an overnight. That is a legally binding order."

"Right, okay..."

"I am getting my overnight, that's final."

Friday evening, a rush-hour crawl to Rathmines to view a cottage in the middle of a Georgian quadrangle. An old park keeper's lodge, the house squats low, as if to hide from the onlooking eyes of the houses on all four sides. Still, it has a homey feel. A flagstone kitchen, big bay window. *This could be the place.*

A woman in her twenties with a pixie haircut and dangly earrings points out the herb garden at the back, trailing her fingers through mint, thyme, lavender. She shows them the four-legged bath, and the open fire with peat briquettes staked in a wicker basket by the hearth.

Scented candles flicker on every sill. Flames quiver in the drafts, light notes of manufactured cinnamon, along with the mold and damp-clothes reek. "I'll be in touch." The woman smiles as they step back into the dusk.

Then Ciara sees the queue. An impossibly long line of people, shuffling quietly forward under the whispering sycamores.

Back in the Social Housing Office, Ciara is aware that her voice sounds slightly hysterical. "I was told that a housing officer would call me. Nobody has called me. Nobody. Has. Called. And I just...I've been all over. Called every house on Daft. I need somewhere. For them."

And for court, if we end up back in front of a judge.

"Hang on now, till I have a wee look." The woman behind the glass has a Derry accent. Ciara finds herself thinking of walks in St. Columb's park, that view across the Foyle between yellow wind bushes. She's taken by a thirst for conversation, wants to conjure her mum and Sinéad through the swapping of beach names, street names and surnames, right here on this desk. But a manager paces behind the Derry woman, and the waiting room is full.

"You should qualify for HAP right enough, once you get on the social housing list," the woman says. "Just fill in this wee form here. Processing time is about three months, so it is."

"Three months? All right. Okay. And then I look for a place to rent, with my HAP? And landlords are okay about taking that?"

"They can't legally refuse. It's all in the leaflet here. Good luck with it. Next!"

Leaving the building takes a while. Ella needs to wee but then refuses to get onto the toilet ("Too high! I fall in!"). Then Noah shits and it's one of those day-destroying nappy changes. Then everyone is hungry and needs rice cakes, and she doesn't have any left. They are finally crossing the road when a hand touches her arm, and the flushed face of the Derry woman from the housing office says, "Can I talk to youse for a wee second?" She tilts her head toward the diner on the corner. "Are the girls allowed a wee scoop?"

Her name is Lorraine. She only has twenty minutes, and they've spent ten of those talking about Derry. She knows Aunt Sarah's old neighbors, the Hegartys. Went to school with the eldest lad.

They watch Noah gurgling in her arms, saying aya-aya-aya-ah. His eyes have turned very blue now, gorgeous. His hair sits in a swirl about the soft spot of his fontanelle. The girls are quiet, spooning their ice cream. Lorraine leans forward and her face becomes serious. "There are things we aren't supposed to say in the housing office, you get me? So, what I said about HAP? Not strictly bullshit. But not how it works in real life."

"So the landlords don't take HAP?" That sinking feeling, although she's not disappointed. Not even surprised.

"Yes—they do. They have to. But a lot of them prefer not to—not if they have a choice. Which is bullshit if you ask me, because HAP is stable income, government guaranteed. But they have to meet certain standards, have the place inspected, and fill out a few forms." She throws her hands in the air. "See? They don't want to be arsed with it. So, picture this. You're rocking on up to some semi-d with your HAP form and your wee gang here in tow. Next viewer is one of those dicks from the Grand Canal Basin. Google or whatever the fuck. Maybe two or three of them, cheap bastards looking to share the gaff, even though they're on salaries that would make your head spin. Or maybe some couple, newly married, renting while they build their own house in Ballythefuck, whatever. Nurses, doctors, teachers. Two incomes, all the references. Get what I'm saying?"

Ciara sees herself standing outside one of these closed front doors. She's so busy wiping noses, holding hands, doing mental arithmetic, she's barely aware of the suits and skirts around them. The newish cars. The whitened teeth. The white-gold wedding bands.

"They'll rent to someone else if they have a choice."

Lorraine nods, takes a gulp of the coffee and winces. "And you know what it's like at the moment. The rental market is nuts. Not enough houses being built. People can't get mortgages. Everyone is renting."

Sophie is licking drips of ice cream from the glass bowl. Ella's drooling raspberry-ripple onto her cat-patterned bib.

"So what do I do?"

Go back, says that voice. You should go back. Look what you're doing to your children. Game's up. It's an impossible situation. Just go back. It wasn't that bad. Go back, go back, go back.

Lorraine sits up straight now, her voice urgent, listing points off on her fingers with their chipped navy nails and chunky rings. "Turn up in your sexiest fucking suit—I'm not joking here. Invent a husband if you have to. Leave the weans with someone for an hour. Don't mention the HAP. Just turn up with your deposit, work references. Pay the first three months as normal. Then just say you've qualified for HAP a few months later."

"Isn't that illegal?"

"It's not illegal. A wee bit of fabrication. Sure what do they know? Relationships end. Circumstances change, so they do."

"All right. You think that could work?" The fizzle of hope is so small she could almost miss it. Like the first quickening of her babies in her belly. That first flutter of *maybe.*

Speaking Exam, Part Two. *Describe a place that is very important to you. You should say: where this place is, what it looks like and why it is important to you.*

Diego is looking out of the window of Brambles Café, talking about the apartment where he grew up, in the shadow of St. Augustine's chapel. The church spire was the first thing he saw when he stepped out of the hot, metal-tasting gloom of the São Paulo metro. He's telling her about the closeness of living in such tight spaces. Apartments turned into little palaces. And she wonders, do we carry echoes of the homes we grew up in? It seems the warm kitchen, constant TV chatter, summer evenings on tiled streets and dusty plazas, night-shuttered coziness of his childhood apartment sits on Diego's skin. He carries that warmth with him. That subtle respect of people living in proximity—the averting of eyes, ignoring of noises—ensuring each person has their corner.

Is there something about her which is also a terraced house, in a city built on seven hills, with distant lights at every window? And what about her daughters? Will the hotel stay with them for life? Even when they're finally settled, will they ever fully unpack? These are the types of things she talks about with Diego.

Somehow clock hands leap.

It's ten o'clock and then it's twelve o'clock five seconds later, and she has to go and collect the girls, and he's gathering up his books.

Sometimes he talks about the other families in the Eden. The mess of daily life he encounters when cleaning out rooms. He listens to her talking about the houses she's visited, and one morning he hands her his phone. "Ciara, this house. You see?"

A sunlit living room. Pine floorboards. A good stretch of

lawn. This is the house. She knows, and by his expression he knows it too. The area, Coolmine, would be handy enough. "Will I phone them now?"

"Phone, phone," he says, and he gives her arms a gentle squeeze.

"Best behavior, right?"

She's standing with Sophie on a doormat made of rough straw, FÁILTE with flowers round it. Late March, the days are stretching. The air is cool and crisp, the evening sky above the rooftops still draining of blue. The street lamps have just come on and glow like hot red lozenges. Ciara is wearing a pencil skirt she's barely managed to squeeze into. Lipstick. Heels. Polo-necked sweater. Her navy blazer that doesn't quite button. Under her arm, a folder with deposit and work reference at the ready. A dog barks and there's the whoop of a siren somewhere close. She feels her daughter shiver in her thin pink hoodie. She should have put her in a warmer coat. Ella and Noah are with Cathy, but Sophie insisted she wanted to come.

Her phone. Ryan, replying to a message she sent earlier.

Saturday night is fine with me, but if this does not go ahead, I am going to court and filing for breach of access.

The front door opens and a man in a suit the same gravel gray as his hair says, "For the viewing? Come on in."

Voices from inside the house. Loud laughter and the sound of feet on floorboards. The other viewers, of course. It's weirdly bright, every light in the house blazing as if it's some kind of late-night emergency. The hall smells of damp towels and cold air, sprayed over with a spritz of cheap air freshener.

The agent holds a biro, which he clicks sometimes as he says things like *excellently maintained* and *ideal location.*

There's a painting above the sofa of a woman on a beach, paddling and looking down so the hair falls over her eyes. Below this, a piece of orange wood has been nailed over the place where a fire should be. Sophie tugs her sleeve. "Mammy, is that to stop people climbing up the chimney?"

The man laughs. "You've a great helper here now. I've two at home meself. They'd keep you busy."

"Busy is right."

"Sure come on upstairs."

The bedrooms are brightly lit by naked bulbs. Their shadows stretch up empty walls. The man is talking about the bedrooms, using words like *spacious* and *ideally situated.* Ciara feels a little disorientated. The rooms look much bigger than they did on the advertisement. Why?

She can feel her smile becoming smaller. "And will you be providing any furniture? Beds, maybe?"

The rooms, she realizes now, are completely empty. Bleached rectangles and squares on the walls, where furniture must have been.

"Ah right, well we didn't know if people would be needing beds," the man says, rubbing the back of his neck and then folding his arms. "We thought we'd wait and see how people were set." He meets her eyes, sighs. "Look, we can get some beds. It's no big deal. But we'd just have to have another look at the rent, if we were furnishing the place, now wouldn't we."

*

Is fada an bóthar nach mbíonn casadh ann. It's a long road that has no turning.

She crumples up the sugar sachet. Shoves it back into the bowl.

FIND YOUR WAY HOME. Waiting for Diego to arrive, she's sitting by the window in Brambles Café, scrolling through Daft again. Rathmines studio. Cabra terrace with the yellow front door. Semi-d in Dolphin's Barn with a dusty monkey puzzle tree in the front yard. She has viewed all these already and had no response. A new ad has just been posted. She types into the inquiry box: *would it be possible to arrange a viewing?*

She keeps thinking about the last house she viewed. In her head, she has the entire place redecorated. On the cheap of course. Ikea curtains. *Beds. I could somehow buy the beds.* Photos on the fridge. This house has been keeping her awake at night, in the way love used to. Like how she used to lie awake thinking about Ryan, not able to sleep, in the days before she moved to Ireland to be with him. Hot-eyed with tiredness and longing.

"What's the story?" Just as Diego arrives, her phone pings. Her eyes well. He touches her back. "You are okay. Ciara?"

"I didn't get that house." She wipes her eyes. The swell of emotion has caught her off guard. She hadn't realized just how much she wanted that house. Or how high she'd got her hopes up.

"Ciara," he is saying, "I am so sorry. Those fucking *puta* landlords. You will find other house—"

"Diego? I was wondering. Could you do something for me?

To help me." She's blowing her nose now. Wiping mascara from under her eyes.

"Sure, what's up?"

She sits up, fixes her hair. "There's another house. I really need this. Well. Would you pretend to be my husband, just for half an hour?"

"Your husband?"

His presence is a lightning rod. All the noise in her head. The clamor of worries and predicted calamities. She finds herself seeking out his eyes, for the pure feeling of being anchored, steadied, held. There are moments when she's teaching him a new word, and he studies her face, copies the shapes of her lips and she thinks about stepping closer to him, touching his mouth. Her week has started to tilt toward his lessons. Now she's ruining everything. "Diego, it will be really quick, I promise. Just for the landlord, so they'll give me the house?"

He pulls back, laughing. "And when I don't move in?"

"I'll say we split up."

"Very short marriage. So tragedy."

"Look Diego I'm really sorry, but I just need this house so badly. It'll be fine. We'll say you work for Google. Or Facebook. One of those kind of places. You can choose."

"I can choose if I want work for Google or Facebook? Is a hard choose. They both excellent companies. They hire many Brazilian guys with terrible English?" He shakes his head, smiling. "Ciara... Ciara. I not pretend to be your husband. You can find a home. *Vai tudo bem.*"

29

The first night of overnight access, she sits in the car outside her old home, watching the windows until Ryan pulls the curtains. Early April: her medley of daffodils are dancing along the driveway again. She spent the afternoon nursing Noah on one breast while she pumped the other, the girls playing with their dolls on the bed to the whirring hum of the apparatus. One bottle of thin white milk was all she managed to express. She tucked it into the cool section of the baby bag, recounted the number of nappies, refolded the sets of extra leggings and pajamas for the girls, tears threatening at every minute.

"You have to do this, Ciara." Grace had been firm with her on the phone. "The letter from his solicitor made it clear. If you don't, he'll file for breach of access, and you'll end up back in court. He could go for full-time custody. You could lose them."

How many times did she sit in her car in this driveway, trying to stretch out the last few minutes before she had to go inside? She waits until the lights go out, and the cold starts into her bones, then she turns on the ignition and drives away.

Tonight feels like being underwater. She's spent so many

years either ignoring her emotions or talking herself out of them. To face her feelings, to come up against the frightening swell of her fear feels overwhelming. A low mist hangs across the river. She thinks of Anna Livia, skin like water, hair made of rotten seaweed, trailing the dark currents. A raw yell in the night. The feeling of standing at the Atlantic's edge as a child, holding Rhona's hand and having the sand sucked from under her feet, her mum's firm grasp keeping her standing. She wants to run from these thoughts. To escape the noise in her head. *What have you done what have you done what have you done?*

Diego lives in Smithfield, near the tramlines.

He answers on the second ring, meets her in the lobby and brings her up to his apartment, apologizing the whole way up to the third floor for the state of the place. He's sharing the two-bedroom flat with six Brazilian friends. Wearing baggy jeans and a blue T-shirt, he rubs her arm, frowning. "You are okay?"

She spots his black hotel uniform on a hanger behind the kitchen door. At the sight of the uniform—the whisper of 124, of her children—Ciara's heart lurches and she thinks she might faint.

"You like a beer?" In his kitchen, Diego is eyeing her dubiously.

She accepts a bottle of ice-cold Brahma, remembering its sweet lemony taste from São Paulo. Diego and his friends are deep in conversation. Portuguese flies over Ciara's head. She's in a bubble, not even trying to translate, thoughts pounding.

Somehow the bottle is empty and she's being handed another one.

Around midnight, everyone gets to their feet, the women pulling on biker jackets, reapplying eyeliner, the men downing their beers.

"We go dancing," Diego says. "I can walk with you home first Ciara, okay?"

"I'll come too." She catches his look. "What, you don't want me to come?"

"No. I don't say that."

Outside, the temperature has dropped. A keen, knife-edge cold is coming off the Liffey. Despite the glare of streetlights, the black sky is pierced with stars. "Shit, is freezing." Diego takes out his box of Lucky Strikes, puts a cigarette to his lips and cups his hand around the lighter, his face caught in the glow. He inhales deeply, as if it's been a long wait. "I still try quit," he says, exhaling slowly, "but this fucking cold. Always I want smoke. Disaster."

"Here let me have that." She takes a quick drag and hands it back. She hasn't smoked since college, and the combination of alcohol and nicotine makes her swoon. Steadying herself, she links her arm through Diego's and he pulls her closer. A brotherly gesture. Ciara knows he is minding her, in the way she grips her daughters' hands and holds her son tight to her chest, and in the way Sinéad will instinctively reach for her arm when they are crossing the street, even now.

They step into the Workman's Club on Wellington Quay. She's swallowed by music loud enough to drown out her thoughts, a deep bass that pulses through her skin. She's aware suddenly of her frumpy gray jumper, and pulls it off, shaking her hair loose. She's wearing an old black vest top underneath, scruffy and faded, but it's too dark for anyone to tell. She catches Diego looking at her, his worry a heavy pause between them. He's following his friends to the bar, but she takes his hand. "Come on and we'll dance."

At the back of the bar, a darkened room where bodies move to the deep, deep pulse. Ciara puts her arms around Diego's shoulders, pulls him closer until their hips pick up the rhythm. Her skin feels slick with sweat, her body reaching, leaning into the desire to close out this pain, stem it with physical sensation. In the strobe light, the images of her children's faces, and then Ryan's face, contorted with hate. All these things she knows happened, things he's told her she didn't see. All her invented memories. Diego puts his hand on her hips, dances with her gently in the way you might with a young cousin at a wedding, but she's pulling him toward her. There's a moment when something changes between them, their faces are so close, she can feel the shudder of his breath.

"Ciara?" He has stopped dancing. "You look like gonna pass out. We get you some air." He takes her hand. Back on the quays, pubs are starting to spill their revelers onto the streets. A traffic jam of taxis and night busses grumbles along the road.

She stops with the night wind in her face, eyes smarting in the cold. "I don't want to go back to that hotel room."

Without my kids. If she says the words, she will break. Ciara bites her lip. The icy, briny Liffey wind stings her eyes.

Diego says, "Okay." He lights a cigarette.

Back in his apartment, soft with the absence of voices and bodies, he leads her into one of the bedrooms and shakes out the duvet. He scratches his head, and stands looking at the room as if seeing it for the first time, "I sorry for the mess. You can sleep here. My roommates are not here. Tonight they stay in the girlfriend houses. I sleep on the sofa. You are okay?"

She nods, reaches up to hug him and leans her head on his chest, looking at the Brazilian flag partitioning the room in two. His friends signed it for him as a leaving gift when he came to Ireland, he explains. Their names and messages of love and support, written in Sharpie, have bled into the fabric. As he's telling her about this, translating some of the messages, Diego strokes her back gently, and then before she knows what she's doing, she's tilting her chin back and kissing him. He pulls her closer, onto the bed. Straddling him, she pulls back.

"What is it?" he says.

"My top is wet." There's thin milk draining down her shirt. "Oh shit, Diego, I'm mortified."

And he's suggesting all kinds of laughable solutions that make her ache with gratitude (*a towel? What am I meant to do with a towel, Diego? Kitchen roll? Are you serious?*).

Finally, they sit side by side on his bed. She's holding one of his towels wrapped around her. "I'm sorry about that," she says, not entirely sure what she's apologizing for—the kiss, the milk, ruining the moment?

"Don't be sorry." He pushes her loose hair back from her face and kisses her cheek. "You know I want...but I know is difficult."

"I've just never been away from my kids overnight before. And I'm really worried. About my baby." She leans her head against his shoulder and he hugs her until her tears subside.

"We need something," he says. "Something keep your mind busy."

"How about wild passionate sex?" She watches his face. "Joking. I'm joking."

He laughs, then starts opening drawers, looking for something. Over his shoulder he says, "You like movies?"

There's a TV at the end of his bed, with a DVD player. He messes with it for a while and then clambers back onto the bed beside her. "You see this? Ah, it is so good. You will love it."

The film starts playing. It's a documentary about an artist who goes to live with a group of *catadores*—garbage pickers—in Rio's biggest rubbish dump. Over time, he gets to know them and makes portraits of each of them. A mother and her two babies, a sheet draped around them—only when the camera pans closer, you can see the portrait has been made from old broken bottles, crumpled wrappers, tires. The artist wants to elevate these people's lives, he says, to show them something of beauty, but his wife is angry with him: *"What about when they must return to their real life? When you and the cameras are gone?"*

Ciara checks her phone. No messages. It's after three a.m. If she can just make it through until morning. How many nights has she willed the hours of darkness away? Nights of fevers. Nights of newborn hunger. Other nights, tense by her husband's side, resisting the vulnerability of sleep.

The film finishes. Diego has drifted off. She lifts the duvet over both of them, turns her back to him, pulls his arm around her. His hand rests gently on her belly, and she slips into a light, fretful sleep.

Her phone trills at six. She sits up in bed beside Diego. Ryan doesn't say much, but she can hear the barely contained anger in his voice. He says, "Can you come get them?"

Her mother-in-law greets her at her old front door. Over her shoulder, she can see the floor strewn with toys, the kitchen a mess, and outside the window, a glimpse of the slide, Chase sitting on one of the handles, preening his wings. "Your children are feral. Out of control. So used to being passed from pillar to post. Sure they don't know how to sleep in their own home. Howling the place down. That baby is completely untrained. And poor Ryan-Patrick is shattered, the poor man."

He had his mother come the whole way from Monaghan to mind them?

Ryan appears at the front door now, scowling. "Completely unacceptable. Hooligans. Utter mayhem."

I will never be more proud. She holds Noah tight, and wrestles Ella and Sophie into a cuddle, smothers their soft cheeks with kisses. "Love you, love you, love you." Nothing quiet about this love. Boisterous, shouty, exuberant love.

Around two dozen people are gathered in Meeting House Square, where there's a smell of burgers, sizzling onions and kerosene. Tourists mostly, identified easily by their lurid, appropriate raingear, backpacks and walking shoes. Most of them are looking fairly dubious. Oliver bounds over to her wearing a black leather bodysuit. His face has been painted into a red and black war mask, his hair spiked. Little Ruby is holding his hand, dressed in her furry gilet and a pair of psychedelic flares. "Ciara!" Oliver gushes, "Thanks for coming! You're sure you're okay minding my wee queen?"

"Sure. We'll have great craic, won't we Ruby?"

The child nods, hugging her dad's leg.

"First, we're doing the silent disco walking tour," Oliver says, "then, it's circus time! Headphones! I'll get you some headphones!" he pauses. "Oh your three wee ones! They didn't want to come?"

"Head colds again, my friend Cathy is minding them."

"You've a night off! Enjoy!"

It's the strangest feeling, walking around Temple Bar with headphones on. Music, punctuated by Oliver's mostly inaccurate historical commentary and ambitious dance instructions: "Hands in the air everybody! Now let's do the conga!" They are in one dimension, everyone else is in another.

Ruby holds Ciara's hand passively, well used to these shenanigans it seems. Along the cobblestones of Essex Street outside the Temple Bar ("YMCA"!), around the corner past the Project Arts Centre ("Hey Macarena"!).

"Hungry."

Ciara has taken her headphones off and stooped to the small blonde child. "Hungry."

Oliver is far ahead, somewhere past the Abrakebabra where the mob of increasingly enthusiastic tourists are now dancing to something involving salsa steps and hip thrusting. Customers are trying to sidestep past them, some getting pulled into the dance.

Ciara searches in her bag. Surely to God there's something edible in here. Fingers closing around a tiny box, she tries to brighten her voice into the cartoon-style chirpiness she uses with her daughters. "Raisins! Here you go, Ruby! These look yummy! You eat these while we wait for Daddy."

As they walk on, Ruby looks up and catches her swiping her phone. "What you looking at?"

"Houses."

"Why?"

"Ah, so you're in the why phase too?"

The Silent Disco Tour is crossing over the Ha'penny Bridge, to the sound of "Don't Rock the Boat." Ciara follows, and Ruby reaches up to touch the padlocks.

"Lovers started this craic a few years ago," Oliver explains through the headphones, "locking ornamental padlocks onto the white wrought-iron railings of the bridge, throwing the keys into the Liffey. Now there must be hundreds of padlocks. Some lovely, decorative. Others industrial-style stainless steel. Make what you will of each relationship they represent!"

She remembers taking part in this ritual with Ryan. The lock he'd used had been a fairly unremarkable brass padlock from Woodie's. As he'd tossed the key into the gulp of the river, she'd imagined the riverbed calcified with slowly rusting mountains of metal.

"No point coming back later to check on your padlock of eternal love," Oliver says. "Dublin being the romantic city that it is, City Council workers take plyers and blowtorches to the bridge every fortnight or so. After all folks, this isn't Venice."

The Disco Tour exits the bridge, flows back under the archway into Temple Bar, waving their arms to "Karma Chameleon."

Back at Meeting House Square, Oliver takes off his headphones. He's sweaty and out of breath. The Silent Disco Tour participants look exhausted, drinking from water bottles, peeling off raingear. "That was so awesome." Oliver hugs Ruby and gives her a kiss on the forehead. "How are you my angel? Ciara thank you so, so much for minding her. You're an absolute star. Before you shoot off—we're moving to Puerto Rico! Next Monday! This gig came up, I'll tell you about it, but anyway. You're not still looking for a place to rent, are you?"

"What? Oliver, are you serious?"

"Rent is €1,800. Steep but not the worst you know, and the agent is..."

His voice fades as she concentrates on calculations. €1,800. HAP won't cover that much. But it will cover part of it, if her application is acceptable. It should be doable, just about. A sudden head rush. Good fortune doesn't happen to her. Luck happens to other people, not her. And yet she knows, on some deeper instinctual level, this is the only way anyone finds a house now. Chance. Fate. Unlikely alignment of stars. *Say something, say something, say something.*

"Yes, definitely," she hears herself say.

Oliver smiles. "Oh excellent. That is great news. We haven't told our letting agent yet! He's not going to be happy. But look, if I tell him I have another tenant lined up. The house is class.

Will I give him your number? Come and take a ringside seat over here, the show's about to start. Quick, quick."

The first act is a woman spinning hula hoops around her legs, arms and hands. There's a note of worry in her face. What if she drops one? Next, a trapeze artist in a red leotard swings over their heads, her hair trailing. There's a moment when she genuinely seems to slip, and dangles suspended by one foot. Ciara holds Ruby's hand tightly. She remembers a short story about a woman who follows a troupe of acrobats through the streets of Rome. Now she's not sure if the story was a piece of magical realism, or something a person might realistically do when their marriage has just ended.

Between acts, a clown amuses people. Oliver and his wife are the last act of the night. He's changed into a sleeveless tuxedo, and cycles into the rink on a unicycle. His wife follows in a black leotard and fishnet tights. There's a defiance about her. Her eyes scan the watching crowd, and when she catches sight of Ruby, she gives her a wink. Then she throws a length of rope across the floor. With a flick of her wrist, it ignites. She poses and then cartwheels over the flames, her back arching, hands splayed. The crowd applauds wildly. And now she produces the box.

After the show, Oliver bounds over to them. Ruby jumps into his arms. He grins. "How was that? Did you like it?"

"Yes," Ciara says. "Well, no actually. I was terrified. It seemed dangerous."

"Dangerous? Ah no. Sure we wouldn't let anyone get hurt in front of all these people. It's safe."

"Safe danger."

"Yeah." He laughs. "Come on for a pint with me and the missus, and I'll tell you more about the house? I texted the letting agent there and he says that's grand."

"Oliver, I don't know what to say. I've been looking for months, I thought I'd never—"

"Don't worry about it, sure we're helping each other out. It's all good."

She wants to hug this man. To run away with the circus with him. She could cry with gratitude, but instead she says, "I'd better get back to the kids. But the house, definitely. We'll talk more tomorrow?"

She starts walking back toward the Eden, but then finds her legs can't quite carry her. Stopping on Bachelor's Quay, she sits on a bench and takes out her phone to message her mum and Sinéad.

I think I've found a house.

Sinéad replies instantly. *OMFG!!!*

She stands and starts walking now, picking up speed. Lights on the Liffey blurring and glittering like spilled sequins. Car horns blare. Sirens whoop. Pedestrian crossings sound. She wants to laugh. Wants to shout. Wants to back-flip into the Liffey like Cathy's parkour-obsessed teenagers.

Images flicker across her mind of Ruby's mother, the hypnotic way she folded herself smaller and smaller. Watching her, Ciara's breath had tightened. She realizes now she'd never really been interested in how the woman gets into the box. She only ever wanted to know how she'd get herself out.

V

LEARNING IN BRAILLE

SPRING 2019

30

After chatting for a while, Oliver hands Ciara the keys and says, "Well good luck with it missus," and leaves her alone in the house. She turns and catches her reflection in the full-length mirror by the front door. There are no full-length mirrors in Room 124. She cannot remember the last time she saw her full body. Small face. Blue eyes, dark-ringed. Pink fleece, well past its best. She looks completely terrified.

She steps into the empty living room as if the floor were a sheet of melting ice, and stands in the middle of the space, waiting. She has no idea what she's waiting for until she feels it: the stillness. Peace.

Breathing steadier now, she walks down the hall, into the kitchen, where she stops and listens to the hum of the fridge. She looks at the washing machine, the drawn blinds, the red kitchen tiles. Right now, the house surrounds her in its still, calm, magnolia hold. The small round, white table in the dining room carries the promise of laughter, chat, cups of tea.

She feels a desire to mammy the fuck out of this house. A need to draw the curtains against the night; to sweep dust from the lintels, wipe tables, throw rugs across the floorboards. An urge, like fixing tumbled-down ponytails and tucking vests into elasticated jogger waists, keeping her children's pale bellies from the cold.

Back in the living room, she imagines placing a peat briquette on the empty grate, watching it spark. Each image flits across her mind, into the darkness of the rain-splattered garden. She cannot believe they are allowed to live here. She cannot believe she's allowed to do this.

This is another life. It doesn't feel real.

There's no point staying much longer. She needs to get back to the kids, to start packing. Ciara opens the front door and stands looking out at the rainy night, the sparkle of a spindly rowan tree wrapped unseasonably in fairy lights someone must have forgotten to take down. Standing under the wooden porch, she feels, tangible as a hand on her shoulder, the soft, sheltering presence of the house behind her.

She turns out the hall light, shuts the door behind her and locks it. In her palm, the key feels solid, cold, real. She slips it into her pocket.

"So?" Cathy leans in the doorway of Room 124, arms folded in an oversized Dublin hoodie. "You got everything?"

Lucy is hugging her mum's legs. Lyra is sitting on the bed behind them, bent over her phone.

The young couple from 134 pass by Ciara's open door, saying hello. Their baby girl is almost walking now, holding onto her mum's fingers. Ciara feels her face flush. It's not fair. Why is she allowed to leave? She thinks of that book she bought for Sophie and Ella, *Christmas in Exeter Street*. In the picture book, guests begin arriving, filling up all the beds and eventually sleeping on windowsills, in the bath, the press, the fridge, until the final page, a double-spread of the house, crammed with bodies. Head swimming, she thinks of houses as matryoshka dolls, with other houses hidden inside.

Cathy tuts, as if she's read her thoughts. "We'll all be out of here soon. We'll tip up and visit you, sure. You on a bus line?"

"I think so."

She's barely on a road. Their new house is in a half-finished estate, narrowly held within the confines of the city limits.

As they're leaving the Eden for the last time, Ciara sees a woman with three young sons walk into the lobby. Plastic bags of clothes. A letter in her hand.

Daffodils nod on grass verges. Birds are carrying sticks to and fro. A quiet estate in Clonee, lulled by the surf-like swish of traffic from the M3 motorway. "Our new house!" Sophie skips in. "I'm so excited! I love it! Why are we moving here?" Ella more cautious, big brown eyes. Noah in her arms.

This unfinished estate is built on the edge of a wood. Trees tower, murmuring over the semi-detached homes. Glossy-leaved rhododendrons hold caves of shadow. Behind their house, a bank of leylandii gives way to oak and pines. If you stand in the garden, you can listen to the creak of branches in the wind.

She unloads bin bags from the car boot and carries them into the house. As she unpacks toys onto the living-room carpet, Sophie and Ella jump around with excitement. These things have been packed in the car all this time. Some of their toys they haven't seen since leaving home last spring. Now she watches Ella toddle over and reach for her farm. Her chubby hands are lifting sheep and cows, dunking them down the chute that lets out electronic farm jingles. *What a lovely day to care for the animals!*

Oh her hip, Noah kicks his legs and arms in excitement. He's recently discovered his feet, keeps grabbing them and pulling his socks off.

Upstairs, she shows the girls the room they will share. They bound from room to room, opening and closing doors, looking in every cupboard. Then they lay on her double bed, Noah on his belly. Tummy time. He can already hold up his head. His big eyes, taking everything in. Sophie and Ella clambering over her legs like walrus and pups. They lay cuddled still for perhaps two minutes. They are safe and they are here, about to begin, and it doesn't seem real. She feels like they're on holiday. Like summer self-catering, sand lisping the hallway, beach towels on the banister, admiring someone else's house. She can't afford this. She's paying full rent and didn't mention HAP. How many months can she manage?

Does she dare to do this? Dare she do this? Does she?

Happy ever after takes different shapes. For her, happy ever after looks like this: her three children cuddled up in bed, sunlight spilling through rented curtains. This is happy. This is ever after. This is peace.

Sophie wants to go back downstairs. She pulls open the patio door, and they charge out into the fresh air. In their new garden, sun catches starlings' wings, a flicker of light. Clouds part. Afternoon sun casts long shadows. Fir branches tilt and sway. She thinks of the clearing in *Beloved*. A sacred, reclaimed space where people danced. Pulling away a choke of weeds, in the far corner of the garden, she finds an overgrown rockery. Cheery gnomes. Fairies with chipped wings. In another overgrown corner, she finds strawberry plants with jagged, heart-shaped leaves.

A rickety plastic playhouse stands by the fence, but the girls run out of it squealing. It's been taken over by earwigs, crawling from each bolt, each window. By the patio, a sandpit Oliver and his wife left behind, woodlice scuttling from the lid.

Carrying Noah, she makes a cup of tea, then sits by the sandpit while the children play. Tea tastes so much better outside. Starlings in the branches.

According to the court agreement, she has to tell Ryan where they are living. She messages him her new address, but he doesn't reply, and when she brings the children to his house for their Tuesday evening visit, he sneers at her. "Social housing, is it?"

"No." She remembers the comments he used to make about single mothers on the dole, living off social welfare.

"Probably some dive you have them in."

"It's not. How can you say that when you haven't even—"

"I'm having them this weekend, yeah?"

The week has turned into a slippery slope leading to the next overnight. She can't see past this point, can't see round it. If she doesn't let him have them overnight, he will take her back to court. And yet she can't shake the memory of Noah crying, inconsolable, too upset to even nurse. And the way Ella clung to her, digging her fingers into Ciara's hair until her scalp stung, holding so tight that she later had to prize strands of her hair from Ella's fingers. For days afterward, they followed her around, not even letting her use the loo in peace. She's had to keep them off playschool a few times because they've both become distraught when she's tried to leave. How can she put them through that again?

You'd think she was still pregnant, the way she's going at this place. Blitzing the bathtub with Flash. Mopping the laminate floors into a muted glow. Stringing lights round the mantel. Wiping down the surfaces. *Nesting like crazy.*

Back in Botanic Close, she had wanted to make it homely for her daughters. Last time she moved back, she bought a set of jungle-animal bunting and looped it across Sophie's curtains. She wanted to make it a real little girls' room. The bunting was as far as she got. A few sad, yellowing posters tacked to the wardrobe. Somehow all motivation drained away once she'd been back a couple of weeks. Imagine trying to pick up a Skittle with chopsticks when drunk. That's what it was like. Trying to concentrate on choosing wall stickers while constantly putting out fires.

Now it's different. She has no money, but her head is clear.

She fills the house with cheap, bright things. She thinks of Rhona's scatter cushions on her worn corduroy sofa, and the ways her mum tried to brighten their home. She wants to make this house a proper home for the girls, so they will forget the past year in the hotel. So they won't notice what's missing.

She Blu-Tacks Sophie and Ella's playschool offerings to the doors and fridge. Handprints. Collages. Paper fish dangling from the light fittings. She gathers cheap furnishings wherever she can. In Oxfam she finds a five-euro print of an upturned boat on a beach. She hangs this over the fireplace. Two-euro photo frames. She arranges pictures along the windowsills.

Mairéad is giving Happy Days a makeover, throwing out a load of old furniture. The red plastic coloring desk makes a perfect coffee table. Old duck-print beanbags, scrubbed clean and sprayed with Febreze, make two extra armchairs. "These will be grand for our living room," she tells Mairéad, who looks a bit bemused. Ciara knows the beanbags and coloring desk are more suited to a playroom, but she doesn't have one. The spill of her daughters' laughter and noise is everywhere. Each room in her house is a playroom, brightened by a scatter of ponies, dinosaurs, blocks and rattles.

She's met a few of the neighbors. A family called the Crinions live next door. She's yet to work out how many kids they have, or which kids belong to which house on the estate.

Cathy comes out to visit one evening with Lucy, bringing a box of Victoria biscuits. Lucy doesn't mind the earwig playhouse, or the woodlice in the sandpit. She teeters around the lawn, chortling with delight. Cathy watches her, wincing as if in pain. Ciara feels it too, the way longing can manifest as a physical hurt. Cathy doesn't talk much. She seems nervous, on edge.

They leave before they've finished their plates of pasta, Cathy muttering about the bus, the sign-in sheet, the viewing she has in the morning, the appointment with the housing office. Ciara feels embarrassed to notice the smell of the hotel on her friend's hair. Back in the Eden, Cathy seemed much more defiant than Ciara was, much less constrained. Now she sees the smallness of it all. The way Cathy's life is being governed by the hotel schedule, her vision so intensely focused on the search for a home.

Holding Noah's new nappy on Ella's head. "Does this go here?" The girls, freshly pink out of the gurgling tub. "How about here?" She flattens the nappy across Ella's belly. "Oh I know, it goes here," and she claps the open nappy across her left boob.

Propped up on a bed of towels, Noah kicks his bare legs. Ella and Sophie are squealing, "Do it again, do it to me, Mammy!"

"Where does it go? Where?"

"On Noah's wees!" Ella sings. "Nappy goes on baby Noah's wees!"

She'd forgotten the feeling of laughter in her belly. And how it feels, putting a house to bed at night. Stretching to pull the kitchen blind. Locking up. Flicking off lights. Ryan never used to bother doing this. He'd leave the curtains open, lights crudely glaring. He was forever mocking her for taking such care. For rinsing the milk cartons before throwing them away. For drying the dripping bottoms of cups out of the dishwasher. Now, without him sneering, she can do things her own way.

*

"Beautiful house!" Diego crosses the threshold carefully, ducking his head although there's no need, and hands her a Tupperware box, *"Misto quente."*

"Obrigada." It's early evening and the children are asleep. Alone with Diego this close, the hall seems smaller, hotter. She's remembering that night in his apartment, the way it felt when she turned and kissed him. "Come on in," she says, hoping he hasn't noticed her blushing. "I'll give you the grand tour."

She shows him the garden, the open-plan living-kitchen-dining room.

He's looking around, smiling, admiring everything. "I not believe it, when you tell me. I swear God I was dancing."

"Coffee?"

She brings the pot and two mugs to the kitchen table, and talks him through Part Two IELTS essay questions. Together they fashion his rambling answers into a coherent response. She does a mock speaking exam with him. He scores less than 30 percent, defaulting to the Portuguese for most things. He seems nervous, or maybe tired.

"Total disaster," he says. "I don't know. All this words. I always confuse."

He pulls a box of Lucky Strikes from his pocket, takes out a cigarette, then seems to reconsider, puts it back.

Shoulders slumped, he looks like a downcast school kid. She softens, feels a newly awakened mischievousness take hold. For a minute neither of them says anything. Reading each other's eyes, like poker players, waiting for the other to make a move. When neither of them do, she closes the folder. "Right, class over. Ten out of ten."

"Ten out of ten for what?"

"I don't know. It's just something my daughters keep saying."

It's getting dark but she hasn't pulled the kitchen blind yet. She likes seeing the darkening sky, and the lighted windows on the houses behind theirs, the coziness of them. She's messing with her cup, running her fingers round the rim. She says, "I was worried it might be weird between us, after last time."

"Weird?"

"Strange?" She glances up, catches his eye and looks back at her cup again. "I tried to kiss you, yeah. Or I think I did kiss you. God." She covers her face with her hands.

"Ciara, it's okay." He takes her hands from her face, holds them. "Come on, look at me. It's not weird."

"No?"

"No, I mean. We are friends, yes? Sure, I would like to be more, I have to be honest. Oh fuck, what am I saying." He looks to the ceiling as if the right words were written there, runs a hand over his face. "I understand for you is difficult time right now, yes? And for me, I don't know even where I'm gonna be living in a few months. I don't want to..."

"I know. We're in the same boat."

"Yes." He brings one of her hands to his lips, kisses her fingers. She laughs and he lets her hand go.

"You hungry?" she asks.

"Always."

She's standing, looking in the bread bin for a pack of cookies.

"In the same boat," Diego says to himself. "I like this one." She looks over her shoulder to see him writing it down in his notebook, amongst his carefully curated list of Irishisms.

What's the story = tudo bem

PRESS = CUPBOARD

Later, when he's gone, she can still feel the warmth of his company. She's not sure which she appreciates more—this, or the feeling of peace.

31

There it is again. This time Ciara knows she heard Sophie.

Ella is in bed beside her as usual, Noah in his cot. She slips out of bed, tiptoes across the landing and steps over the floorboards that creak. Sophie's bedroom is softly lit by her nightlight. *YOU ARE PAWSOME* says the poster above Sophie's bed. The team of Paw Patrol pups grin crescent-moon smiles in the ultraviolet glow of the manic-looking sheep light. Her daughter is asleep, breathing rhythmically.

It gives Ciara almost unbearable pleasure to see this small box room filled with Sophie's things. A shelf full of conch shells, sticks, pebbles, the bobbins and clips her child seems to shed daily, always reaching bath time with her dark, unruly hair completely loose, leaving a trail of these glittery tokens throughout her day. Mismatched farm animals litter the rug, beside a bookcase of plastic-eyed beanie sloths, teddies, frogs, two zebras and a massive pink monkey.

Unspeakably happy.

Stupidly happy.

She now finds great satisfaction in things that should be unnoticeable. Like folding Sophie's socks into soft pastel-colored pairs, a drawer full of readiness for mornings of fresh filter coffee and steaming porridge with a swirl of honey. Like a toddler, she can sit in dumb excitement at the thrum of the washing machine. A line of fluttering, fresh-washed bedsheets produces a giddy heart rush of *happy*.

But there's still the tug of worry. The state maternity benefit is only €274 per week. A handful of private classes with Diego's friends, the money trickling in. Late at night, tapping numbers into her phone's calculator, subtracting and dividing. She never realized mathematics could make you feel sick. She could go back to work at the language school, but who would mind Noah? Childcare would cost more than she'd earn. She could ask Ryan again about maintenance, but she doesn't want to go back to court. Any money he gives her will come at a price. At least the money she's earning is her own. She feels sick when she thinks of the envelopes Ryan used to hand her, containing a few twenties *for the weekly shop*. All the years she simply subsisted.

Sometimes she worries the children will never forget their old home. That it will remain etched in their bones; a place they yearn for without being able to picture it. Ciara carries memories of all the places she's ever lived, and sometimes wakes disorientated by the montage of kitchens, bathrooms, living rooms. In sleep she'll open the door of her old home, onto a different street. A cliff face. A forest.

She hasn't told anyone about Sophie's nightmares. The shouts that send her running to her daughter's bedroom, where Sophie is curled up under her jungle-print duvet. Sophie never had bad dreams during all those nights in the hotel. Or even that night in the Wicklow hills in her car, all breathing in each other's breath. Her daughter's night terrors started just after they moved into the new house. Nights when Ciara has lain staring at the ceiling, her mind unable to rest, she's heard Sophie shout out in her sleep. Each time, she runs to her daughter's bedside and then stops, not knowing what to do. Should she wake her? Rescue her from whatever nightmare she's having?

If Ryan finds out, he'll go to town over this.

He knocks at her door. When she opens it, Ryan steps into her house before she can stop him. He's meant to be taking the kids for an overnight but he messaged to say it didn't suit. *I'll call over to your house. I will explain then.*

Wary of what he might be about to say, she sidesteps around him. He's carrying a crudely fashioned plywood box, leaves it by the door and walks past her into the living room, frowning at everything. She wants to hide the house under her skirt so he can't judge it. "Some previous tenants must have had a dog," he says finally, "look at all the scratches on the patio glass."

She'd never noticed before. The fine lattice of white scratches on the panes. Noah is whimpering in her arms, teething maybe. "So you're not having them overnight? That's fine with me, but... Did you want to take them to the park or something?"

"Yeah," he says. "Change of plan. Can we talk?"

He stands over her and she hovers, holding Noah. She's rocking him, trying to hide her fear. Ryan's presence in her small house is making her nervous. She stands near the doorway, ready to bolt.

"So, I've moved out of the old house," he says. "I didn't want to worry you. But the landlord was selling up. I had to move out."

"You've left our house?"

Our house. The feeling of loss is blinding.

"I know, I know." He is watching her closely. "It's upsetting. I was heartbroken too, believe me. I loved that place."

"But what...So soon? Didn't he have to give you some notice? That doesn't make sense–"

"Are you saying I'm lying?" He folds his arms. Raises his eyebrows at her.

"No...no...I'm not saying that." Her head is swimming. "But what about all our stuff? The stuff in the garage?" Her boxes of books. The girls' old clothes. Boxed memories, photos and birthday cards.

"Everything had to go, I'm afraid. I know. It's really heartbreaking. I even had to bring this fella." He kneels by the box and slides open the lid. Chase, cowered with his wings tucked back. His feathers gleam, his eyes jet black. Ryan is saying, "Now I'm sharing a house with a couple of colleagues over in Glasnevin. You remember my friend Cian, well it's his gaff. Nice house, but not suitable for the kids I'm afraid, so I'll have to spend time with them here."

"At my house?"

"Unless you want me to bring them over to Cian's? To the house share? Okay then. It's a bit of a bachelor pad though. You don't know some of the other guys..."

"No, no it's fine. You can come here."

"And as for overnights—well, I'm guessing you wouldn't want the kids overnight with some guys they don't know. And they were upset last time anyway. Maybe it's better if I have my overnight here?"

While he's talking, she thinks of all the things she should say. Each comes with its own worry. *What if he takes her back to court? What if they award fifty–fifty this time?* Anyway, he's not asking her permission. He's telling her what's happening.

"WHERE IS MY WOMB?" Ella shouts. "I WANNA MY WOMB!"

My room. Not that she will sleep in her room. Ella is so used to sharing a bed they still sleep together in the king-size, under blackout curtains and cheap flower print. It's cold these nights. Ella has taken to rolling over and sleeping curled against her mum, her face buried in her hair.

Later that night, Noah lulled into a milky stupor at her chest, she's laying him into his cot and tucking the blanket round his feet when the sound of muffled sobbing reaches her. This time it's definitely Sophie.

She's curled up under her duvet, crying.

"Sophie, honey," Ciara's kneeling, hugging her, "What's wrong? Tell Mammy?" But the sobs wracking her daughter's little body grab her voice, scrambling it into incomprehensible wails.

"Honey can you blow out like this, like blowing out a candle?" Sophie copies, blowing warm air juddering onto her cheeks. Her eyes wet, scared. Eventually she's able to gather this is about a hairband. A hairband Sophie has lost. Maybe in the house. Maybe at playschool. A red hairband, the one from this morning. The one with the bow.

Sobs are taking hold again, and she gathers her daughter to her chest and kisses her wet hair, heartsore with the helpless longing to protect her—to make it all better. *Isn't that what mothers are meant to do?* She hears herself telling stories, even while a voice in her head mocks—*distraction? Is that your only playing card?* Still, relief floods through her body when she's finally rewarded with a small smile and Sophie's breathing lulls. As her daughter begins to drift off, Ciara strokes her forehead. The tiny infant she first held against her breast on that dark morning four years ago still lingers in Sophie's face. Newborn days were easy, meeting the demands of breastfeeds and nappy changes. Tonight, for the first time, she saw a strange beast edging around her daughter. *Just think about what Sophie has witnessed.*

Sitting on the floor by her daughter's bedside, she pulls out her phone. *Be your child's emotion coach with these powerful tips,* says the internet. *Switch validation of tears into constructive conversation. Teach emotional resilience. Call for a free initial consultation.*

She soon feels the start of a white-screen headache. She can't see Sophie in any of these trite, neatly packaged explanations. Is this about a hairband? Or is it about having moved so many times? Sophie has never cried about leaving home, but now this? *What have you done?*

Standing in Ciara's kitchen chopping tomatoes, Sinéad listens as she talks about Sophie's nightmares. "She's probably just processing everything that happened," she's saying. "Give her time."

Sinéad has come over for Sophie's birthday, and is staying for three nights. Ciara has told her about Ryan's access visits at her house, but hasn't mentioned his threat of staying overnight here. For now, she wants to push these thoughts from her head. Today is Sophie's birthday party. It will brighten the place up. It will help Sophie to see that everything is okay. A house feels more like home once you've cooked a meal in it, and once you have invited friends over the threshold, it feels more home-like still.

Yesterday she caught Sinéad studying her scruffy black leggings and gray hoodie with the hole under one arm. "What did you spend that Christmas voucher on?"

Ciara shrugged.

"Fucksake, Ciara." Sinéad sighed. Later, she brought them up to Penney's. She bought flouncy dresses for the girls, with gauze skirts and glittery waistbands, along with sequin-studded pumps. The type of utterly impractical outfit Ciara can never afford to buy. She then led them across to womens-wear and insisted Ciara pick out something. She chose a shirt dress, a deep turquoise that falls to her knees. Sinéad nods approvingly now. "Matches your eyes, so it does."

The girls are running up and down the landing in their dresses. Noah is wearing one of the pairs of dungarees from Alex. Sophie and Ella's pumps are sending meteor showers whizzing across the ceiling. "We're being velociraptors!" Sophie shouts.

For her birthday, Sophie asked for a Peppa Pig house. Ciara borrowed money from her mum to pay for it, and sat up late slotting the walls together. Sophie has already evicted all the pigs and filled the house with dinosaurs.

"Five minutes, okay girls? Then everyone will be here."

"And the dragons came and moved our house to a nicer place." Ella has been talking to Hoppy, telling him a story. Last week Ciara handwashed him, mended his heart and dried him with a hairdryer while Ella sat watching.

"Move our house where, babs? Where is the nicer place?"

Ella keeps playing, chatting to herself.

"And the dinosaur picked up our house and ATE—"

"There's cars!" Sophie shouts from her bedroom a few minutes later. "Look out the window, Mammy!"

She stands, too quickly—that scar. Sinéad says she should go back to the hospital to have it checked, but it's fine. It will be fine. Catching a slice of her reflection on the wardrobe mirror, Ciara pauses. Caught in this birthday excitement, she looks more like her old self. Hoop earrings. Silvery eye shadow. Like seeing an old photograph looking back at her.

The doorbell rings. Cathy's teenagers burst a balloon on their way in the door. Sophie howls. Just when it seems the day might break, Cathy produces a small purple package and hands it to her. "Happy birthday, honey!"

It's the golden lion tamarin from the zoo.

Ciara whispers, "Cathy. That's too much."

"Stop, they had them cheap on Done Deal." Cathy takes Noah from her. "Come here to me, bubs. Ah look. I remember Damien wearing that."

More guests are arriving now. Maggie and Olivia from work, in dresses and runners, with bottles of red. Sam and Eva from Happy Days, and their mums in jeans and ponytails. Louise and Simon, down from Belfast for the day. The Crinions from next door.

Diego and his friends Rodrigo and Luana, with a six-pack of Brahma and a multipack of Tayto. Diego kisses her cheek. She whispers to him, asks him to please sort out the music. She's forgotten. Would he please stick something on? When his back is turned, Cathy nods toward him and gives her a wink.

It doesn't take many people to fill a home from which guests have been barred for half a decade.

Sophie is wired to the moon. Watching her daughter, Ciara's heart lifts. All the little kids are catching balloons and chasing each other in and out of the living room and up the garden, where she's strung colored lanterns and paper bunting between the trees. Diego's reggaeton and salsa music pulses from the stereo to the percussion of clinking glasses, laughter, chatter. The press of lips and hugs of congratulations. All these months of searching and scheming, it's only now that she really feels the benefit of this. The goodness of it. As if she's been guided by some deeper, more instinctual part, and it's only now the rest of her has caught up. And the joy. The joy is almost terrifying.

32

As Ciara reaches home, there's that gentle swell of pride in her chest. First hint of warmth in the spring sunshine. Blossoms in the trees. The scrape of her key in the lock. *Our house.* "Right girls, lunch bags in the kitchen. Come on, we'll go outside. Another snack? Really?"

Sinéad is still with them, heading back this evening, her wheelie bag sitting ready by the door. Sinéad puts the kettle on, tips a carton of strawberries into a sieve and starts rinsing, chopping.

The girls throw off their primrose jackets and charge into the garden. "ME FIRST, ME FIRST!" Flying down the plastic slide, sparrows scattering from the feeder.

When Ciara follows them into the garden, Ella runs at her, followed by Sophie, bowling her over nearly, and she laughs. She forgets the time and what day it is, and she laughs. Sun in her hair, birds in the cherry blossoms. She glances up, through the open patio door, the living room and the wide bay window. Ryan is watching. He's early for his access visit. He taps on the glass. Points to the door.

There will be a price to pay for her laughter.

This is how it is.

Laughter has a price.

Talk has a price.

Silence has a price.

He's never happy.

She wants to make herself as small as possible. To become a small gray stone and blend in with the pebble-dash on the house that holds her. The house that promises better days.

As she's walking through the kitchen toward the door, Sinéad gives her a look. "He's early. Let him wait."

Ryan steps into the house and every ounce of energy leaves her body. She wants to cry like an overtired baby. What would Ryan do, if she suddenly started crying like Noah?

Casual as sin, he walks into her kitchen. "Sinéad." He nods. "How are things. Lovely day."

His tone is bright and condescending, his eyes smirking at her sister, daring her to challenge him, knowing that she won't. Sinéad puts down the knife she'd been using, lifts a cloth and wipes the red strawberry juice from her hands. She folds her arms. "Ryan. Would you ever think of backing off and giving her some space?"

"Sorry?" He looks genuinely taken aback.

"You heard me." Sinéad's voice is cool and leveled. "Give Ciara some space. There's no need for you to be here in her house. This is just another form of control."

"Sorry," he scoffs, incredulous, "but this is what Ciara and I have agreed—"

"Ryan? Would you ever just fuck off."

Ciara takes her sister's arm, tries to steer her out of the

kitchen, into the garden. Ryan is livid, shouting something. She shuts the kitchen door behind them.

"Sinéad!" Her heart is barely contained within the cage of her chest. Every muscle, every bone, tensing to the pitch glass makes when you run a finger around its rim. The half-built estate, deathly quiet. Gaping empty window frames. The dark furze of the encroaching woods. "Please, Sinéad. You can't speak to him like that. You're making things worse."

"Jesus Ciara, would you catch yourself on. Can't you see what that man is doing?"

"Sinéad, please."

"Grand. You know what, I'll get myself to the airport. I can't watch this happening again. I can't watch you going back to him. I can't sleep for worrying about you. I said to Peter—"

"Oh, sorry you're losing sleep."

"Don't be so nasty, Ciara."

"I'm not."

"You have no idea what you put us through."

After Sinéad has gone, Ciara doesn't know where to put herself. Turned inside out, the wrong way round. Ryan is laughing with the girls, and she makes an excuse about Noah needing a nap, then pushes the buggy in pointless circles around the estate just to avoid the house. Impending punishment hangs over her all evening, but when Ryan is leaving, he is surprisingly gentle. "It's okay." He laughs. "Don't worry about Sinéad. I'm well used to her talking to me like that."

She finds herself apologizing for her sister's outburst.

Skirting round him, careful not to annoy him. Relieved that the fallout from this hasn't been any worse.

Her mum phones later that evening. "Our Sinéad is very upset, Ciara. She's been biting her tongue all this time. You can hardly blame her for letting rip."

"I know that, Mum. She was right, I know that... But now I'm having to deal with— with... I don't know." *With the consequences.* Why is that so difficult to say? Why can't she tell her mother about the shame she feels for placating him, the fear of what will happen if she doesn't?

Ryan sends a photo he took in the garden, of Noah on Sophie's knee, Ella peering over her shoulder. Strawberry chins. Giddy smiles. Innocent, trusting eyes. Then there's a message.

Thank you for your patience in allowing me to access your home to spend time with my children. I am eternally grateful. I know you don't want to hear this, but I'm still praying we can find a way to be together. Also, I am so sorry to have to ask, but could I possibly stay with you for a few days? I thought it would just be one overnight, but the houseshare situation isn't working out. I've moved out of there and don't have anywhere else to stay. I've actually been sleeping in my car but I didn't want to worry you. Even if I could just sleep on your sofa for a few days, that would be great.

She sits on her bed, staring at the message. It feels like the walls are closing in. If she doesn't agree, he will say she is cruel, heartless. She tries to sidestep. She messages: *Sorry but I don't think that would really work. It would be confusing for the kids.*

Great, talk about kicking me when I'm already down. I thought you're meant to be a teacher. I thought teachers are meant to have a bit of kindness, a bit of empathy for people. I should have known better than to even ask.

She's sweating now, her head loud. *Make it stop make it stop make it stop make it stop.*

She used to think she knew who she was. That she was kind, that she tried her best. With him, she feels a stranger to herself. Typing a message, she cannot hear herself think. *Okay that's fine. You can stay for a few days.*

He brings the crow, tethers him in the back garden. He shows her photos on his Instagram account, documenting how Chase developed over the months. Beautiful photos. Close-ups of the bird's wings. The way Ryan's chatting, relaxed and animated, it's as if nothing bad had ever happened between them.

He cooks Irish stew for dinner. Gives the girls their bath while she's seeing to Noah. After the girls have gone to bed, he says he wants to show her something on Netflix. It will only take ten minutes, he says. It's a comedy they used to watch when they first started dating. A new series has been released. They sit on opposite ends of the sofa to watch it. The next night, Ryan edges a little closer. By Friday, when he has been there for three nights, he puts his hand on her thigh and leans in to kiss her. She pulls back.

On the dark living-room window, her face is a blur, her arms folded to hide her cleavage in the old blue top which now feels too low-cut.

"Come here," he says. He starts kissing her aggressively and grabbing her breasts. "I'm so lucky you're my wife. I'm so glad we worked things out."

There's a siren sounding inside her.

It is too loud to act. Too loud to think.

Her body has tensed and knotted. She's fighting the impulse to get up and run. Don't piss him off, she tells herself. She knows how quickly things could escalate. Black night at the windows. Heavy rain, like fingers drumming the glass. Nobody knows Ryan is still here. Everyone thinks she's safe. Her children, asleep upstairs. Sophie in her fluffy pajamas with the llama hologram, Ella in a duck-print sleepsuit, both probably snoring, on their backs, hands flung, unsuspecting. Noah in his cot.

She pulls away. "Listen. The bird."

Ryan is trying to unbutton her jeans.

"The crow," she says again. "Does he normally make that noise?"

From outside, Chase is squawking wildly. Ryan sighs, stands and opens the back door. His back is turned.

"Just going to the loo."

Why is this happening? Why is this happening?

He catches her on the stairs. "You said I could stay."

"I was just being helpful."

His face is furious. "Messing with my head. Cruel, heartless bitch."

There's an edge to him now. From years of careful watching, she knows when a mood is bubbling below his skin. When his eyes are surveying, waiting for a mistake he can pounce on.

She asked him if he has viewed any apartments to rent. It was obviously the wrong thing to say. He sits on her sofa, watching her hanging laundry on the radiators. She's turned on the radio to avoid the silence and whatever he intends to pour into it.

FM104 are having a phone-in. "Things your family does that drive you mental." A man is talking about how his mum leaves the teabags in the sink. A girl says her sister keeps putting cotton buds in the loo. The fond, irritated love in their voices makes her think of her mum and Sinéad, of their silence for the last few days. She turns the radio off. Keeping busy, hanging damp leggings and toddler pants, prattling on about the weather. She's stupidly pacing about, dashing into the kitchen before she realizes he's followed her in there.

She turns at the sink and he's millimeters from her face. He takes the pair of star-print leggings from her hands, throws them down on the counter. His arms lock around her waist.

And now she sees it. Far from being a safe haven this house is a deathtrap.

The thing about the hotel, she was never alone. The estate outside carries a deathly quiet. Right now, she'd give anything to be sandwiched between seven floors of watermelon buffet, hen-party banners, lopsided halos, midweek specials. She's longing for Lauren, Marco or Isabel to breeze in and start berating her about the sign-in sheet. Over Ryan's shoulder, she sees the closed, impassive faces of the houses opposite, their windows black with reflected sky, their closed doors and shut letterboxes like tight-lipped mouths.

The last flowering cherry blossom tree glows in the

half-dusk. The street is completely deserted. This is how she used to feel in Botanic Close, those nights with her heart in her throat.

Each house is an island, oceans away from the other.

No one will hear her, even if she screams.

There's something wild in his eyes tonight. They dart madly across her face, scanning as if in a frenzied search for something lost. His jaw clicks. His hands roam over her body, clenching, grabbing. "Why don't you give us another chance?"

Again, her words catch. "I just—"

"The way you lie to me, abandon me, subject me to verbal abuse from your sister. How would you feel if someone treated one of the kids the way you've treated me?" Now his face is close against hers. His big hand strokes her neck. "I'd want to kill that person." His black eyes bore into hers. From somewhere outside in the darkening garden, the crow screeches. "I'd want to fucking kill them."

Backed against the sink, jammed between the kettle and the knife drawer, she has nowhere to go. "I'm not a monster," he's saying, "I've said it before. I'm not a bad person. I just want my wife and kids back."

His dark gray hair, grown out longer than normal, stands in sweaty tufts, his white scalp visible in patches. Pressed up against him, she smells the acrid tang of his sweat. She feels his racing heart. Sees the bluish veins pulsing on his forehead. His hands, rough, firm on her neck. She has reached the end of a tunnel only to find that it's sealed. What made her think she could escape? What made her think she was any luckier than the women who end up as statistics? He leans to kiss her. When she turns her face away, he grabs her chin in his hand and forces her toward him. Her head races. If she kisses him just once, will he leave her alone?

Because the doorbell's banjaxed, it's a knock at the door that interrupts.

"Let me get that," she hears herself say.

It's only when she opens her front door to the cool of the spring evening that she remembers it's Wednesday. *Of course it's Wednesday.* And didn't Diego tell her he was off work this Wednesday, and didn't she say—sure come on over and we'll do another run through your speaking test. The magnitude of this mistake causes time to stall. Everything becomes hyper-real. The cool green evening. The crisp air, fresh after the rain. The man standing in front of her, smiling and removing his headphones. Diego. The relief of his face. As soon as he sees her, he says, "Ciara? What's wrong?"

She closes the door over behind her, whispers, "You need to leave."

"What?"

"Please, Diego. Please, just go."

33

Next morning, she pushes Noah's buggy through the sliding doors of the Parnell Street Hotel. She asks the receptionist where to go, and follows her directions across the lobby, down a ramp, toward the Musgrove Suite where a sign is tacked to the door: *BABY MASSAGE WITH MIRANDA.*

Her mum messaged this morning to remind her about the class. Hearts and hugs emojis. *Thinking about you love x*

Ciara hasn't slept. Last night she sat with her back against Sophie and Ella's door, Noah in her arms, flooded by that sickening sense of déjà vu. Ella woke during the night, crying, "Want to go to Mammy's bed." She had to soothe her, whispering, "No love, Mammy's not sleeping in her bed tonight."

Because he was in there. Ryan was in her room. After hours of berating her to the point where she agreed—yes, we will get back together, yes okay—anything to make it stop—yes you were right—anything, anything—and he said right, fine, well things are going to have to change around here, we need to have regular sex, you can't expect me to go without sex just because you're so fucking uptight—and she said yes of course, she'd be up to the bedroom shortly—and then tiptoed upstairs, picked Noah up, went into the girls' room and locked the door behind her, head spinning. How was this happening again, how? How many tunnels of nights has she crawled through? Nights just like this.

In the function room, red velvet chairs are stacked in corners, and heavy gold curtains are tied back, letting in the bright spring morning. Around the space, half-a-dozen women are laying their babies onto towels, spaced like a sundial. She finds a spot in the semicircle and lifts Noah out of his hand-me-down yellow pram, dusty with rice-cracker crumbs. He is so beautiful. She lays his head on her shoulder, closes her eyes, feeling his warm weight.

Still cradling him with one hand, with the other she folds her Brazilian beach towel in half, spreading it on the carpet. She thinks of the flag pinned across Diego's ceiling, his friends' loving messages of *boa sorte* and *saudade* seeping into the fabric, and sees his face at her door last night, when she told him to leave. His expression was one she's seen before, on Sinéad, on her mum, when she's rejected their help, protecting them by pushing them away. Or was she only protecting herself?

The pause after Diego had gone. Standing in her hallway, hugging her sides, knowing what was coming.

There's a tremor in her hands as she smooths the towel, lays Noah down. His eyes are on her, so she forces a smile. "There you go, love. There's my little lion. Isn't this fun? This is going to be fun."

But there is no bullshitting this child. He knows she's

upset. What is it Sinéad says? Some babies are human stress detectors.

Noah's bottom lip quivers and before she can do anything to distract him, he launches into a loud, heartbroken cry. A one-man protest, inconsolable. Another baby joins in, followed by another, until most of the babies in the room seem to be crying, their sobbing reaching toward crescendo.

"Now then everyone," a woman in lilac yoga gear steps calmly into the circle and casts a gracious smile around the room, as if addressing a holistic conference. "Let's get into the mood with a little relaxation. Just close your eyes, use this moment to bond with your babies, and imagine all the tension leaving your body through your fingertips. Breathe in... Breathe out... Breathe in..."

As mums' hands find bottles, bra clips, soothers, the communal crying gradually resides into a hiccupping grumble. Relaxing music begins to play. A piano concerto. Blackbird song.

Ciara picks Noah up, holds him to her chest and closes her eyes. *Breathe in.*

The familiar hotel smell. Hoovering, fried breakfast and industrial air freshener. *Breathe out.* Muffled sounds from behind the walls, a pulse of pop music, footsteps and closing doors. *Breathe in.* Eyes shut, she's remembering the day they brought Noah home from hospital. Diego, carrying their bags up the back staircase at the Eden. Sitting on the hotel bed, nursing her tiny newborn, trying to quell the steadily rising panic. *Breathe out.* Scrolling through Daft, checking and rechecking the banking app, flinching at each door slam, each siren. Mum and Sinéad's voices soothing her, keeping her afloat. *Breathe in.* Dear God, what did she put her kids through? *Breathe.* And what now? She can't take them away from their home—again. *Breathe. Breathe.*

"Are you okay, dear?"

The teacher, Miranda, is leaning close, squatting with one hand placed on Ciara's upper arm, her lips moving. "Okay—are you—if you need—take a minute—really quite okay?" Behind her, other mums are giving sympathetic smiles. Ciara's face is wet, and she's holding Noah a little too tightly. She lays her son down on the towel, and he makes a grab for his toes.

There are so many things she could say.

I walked out of my marriage and lived in a hotel.

I'm afraid of my ex-husband and I don't know what to do.

I've pushed everyone away. My sister. My mum. My friend.

My ex seems to be somehow living in my house now, and I don't know. I just don't know.

She wipes her eyes on the backs of her sleeves. "The hormones!"

There are murmurs of support. One woman passes her a packet of Kleenex, and the woman beside her says, "I bawled into my cornflakes this morning, love. So you're grand."

Another woman beside her says, "My husband knows not to even try watching movies with me at the moment! I cry at everything."

Miranda stands. She looks relieved. From somewhere at the front of the room, she produces a life-size doll baby, and lays it in front of her. "Okay mums," she says. "Lay your babies on their backs like this and take their left foot. We'll start with some Swedish milking."

*

Once class is over, Miranda packs her demo baby into a holdall. She leaves the relaxing ocean music playing while everyone starts rolling their towels into nappy bags. Noah is fast asleep on the towel now, lost in the type of baby sleep that will surely last an hour or more. He doesn't even stir when Ciara lifts him and settles him, beanbag heavy, into his buggy.

"You coming for coffee?" the woman beside her asks.

She looks at this stranger's smiling face—this woman who confessed to crying into her cornflakes this morning—and there's an ache in her body. She wants to say yes, but there's a clock ticking in her head, counting down the hours. It's eleven o'clock now. Another couple of hours and she will need to pick the girls up from playschool, and then the afternoon will become a tangle of slides and footballs and Velcro runners and wiped noses and songs, and time will hurtle into evening when Ryan will arrive home, then into night.

"I'm sorry," she hears herself saying in a surprisingly calm voice, "I need to do something. I have to call into the Rotunda."

"Oh? All okay?"

"Yeah it's just my scar. My sister, she's a nurse. She's been on at me to get it looked at. It still hurts..."

She hears herself prattling on about the emergency section, the two sections before that. Before saying these words, she had no intentions of getting her scar checked, but the lie has suddenly become truth.

Ciara says bye to her classmates. Then she pushes Noah's buggy back through the lobby and out of the hotel, crossing Parnell Street and turning up toward the Rotunda. The waiting room is quiet today. Ciara checks in at the desk and sits on an empty row of seats, rocking the buggy, although there's no need. Noah is still comatose, a whiff of lavender oil off him. Watching him, she's drinking in the curve of his cheeks, the dimples in his chubby thighs.

Much quicker than she expected, she hears her name being called. The nurse looks to be fiftyish, with her black hair cut in a short fringe, and small gold seahorse earrings. Ciara follows her through the double doors and into one of the cubicles. "You've a great sleeper there," the nurse smiles. "Out for the count."

Ciara parks Noah's buggy by the long pleated curtain, and explains to the nurse about the pains that still shoot across her lower abdomen. Not all the time, but if she stands too quickly, stretches.

"Sure hop up onto the bed and we'll take a look," the nurse says.

Almost twelve o'clock now, an hour until pick-up time.

Where can they go tonight?

They can't stay in that house.

The anger in his face. Worse than before. Much worse.

The nurse presses gently around the bumpy red incision with the tips of her blue latex gloves. Ciara bites her lip and stares at the strip lighting. If time could somehow freeze, just to give her a chance to think. The nurse asks, "Where does it hurt most?"

From other cubicles, the gallop of babies' heart beats.

"All along that side is sore. It's been nearly six months now. Should it still be hurting?"

The nurse moves her fingers again, taking great care. "There is a lot of old blood trapped under your wound," she says. "The pain is most likely caused by this old blood breaking down." She straightens up, removes her gloves. "I wouldn't see anything to worry about at the moment. Give it another couple of months. If you're not happy after that, then come back in. Is that okay?"

Ciara nods. Lost for words. Lost from words. She's spinning. Back in the Rotunda, under the sonogram, sitting on the high white-tissue paper table, the words take shape and they are a presence now, clear and pushing up, wanting to be spoken: *I left the marriage because of my girls, to try and give them a better future. I left so they wouldn't think my life was normal. I needed to break normal. To smash it and reconfigure it, and what have I achieved? What kind of a new normal is this?*

"Can I ask you something?"

The nurse smiles. "Sure."

"Early in my pregnancy, a nurse asked if I was afraid of my partner. And I said no." The nurse nods. From the pity in her eyes, she clearly knows what's coming. "Things have just been difficult. If I did want to talk to someone, who would you recommend?"

"Have you contacted Women's Aid? Or what about your local refuge?"

"I don't need a bed in a refuge. I have a house, a whole house of my own, never mind a bed. But I can't seem to . . . I don't know."

"But why don't you just phone and explain?" the nurse says. "My sister is going through something like this. Anna

Livia refuge, that's the one she goes to. Will you give them a buzz?"

Ciara begins to re-button her jacket but her fingers fumble, and Noah has startled awake and begun wailing, and as she rushes to lift him and soothe him, she hears herself saying to the nurse, "I'm so sorry about this. I'm sorry, I'm sorry. I'm sorry."

"Here we are." She pulls in, turns off the ignition. It's late afternoon now. They spent the last few hours in the park, while Ciara gathered the courage to make the phone call. She's not sure what she was expecting, but the refuge looks like any of the other houses along this road. A white bungalow with planters of dahlias at the door and a stack of old tires filled with marigolds.

Sophie has unbuckled herself and leans her elbows on the front seats. "Why we sitting here, Mammy? Where are we going?"

Ciara doesn't know what to say.

At the front door, a woman with long black hair holds out her hand. "Saoirse. And you're Ciara, right? We spoke on the phone. Come on in."

One of the rooms at the front of the bungalow has been converted into a playroom. The girls dive toward a painted wooden doll's house. Ciara props Noah up with some pillows and he grabs the teddy nearest to him, bringing it to his mouth and chewing its ear.

"Sure take a seat." Saoirse gestures to the sofa, sits down beside her and speaks to her quietly, "So, you said on the phone that he's living in your house?"

"He says he has nowhere else to go. I don't want to turn him out and leave him homeless, but I just can't have him in my house, when he's behaving like this. Last night was... It was just really bad."

Saoirse nods. "I know it's not easy to hear this, Ciara, but he is taking advantage of your kindness. Pure and simple."

Ciara nods. For a moment, they both watch the children playing. Sophie, rearranging the doll's house, setting up furniture in each room. Ella, pressing all the keys on a toy keyboard, singing something, Noah gurgling at her.

Saoirse says, "People often talk about targets of domestic abuse as weak. What they don't see is our strength. We're not targeted for our weaknesses, you get me, Ciara? We're targeted for our strengths. Your kindness is your strength, and he is taking full advantage. I know it's a lot, what I'm saying, but just think about it."

Again, Ciara nods, somehow numb.

How did I even get to this point?

"Will you stay here tonight?" Saoirse says. "Tomorrow we can go to court, look at getting you an emergency barring order, to get him out of your house."

"God, I don't know." Ciara runs her hands over her face, presses her fingers together. "A barring order? I mean, he'll go mad. He'll say he's never hurt me physically, that I'm over-reacting. I don't know. If it's bad enough?"

"You don't have to wait for it to be bad enough, love. Women have died waiting. More and more, this is what we are seeing. It's emotional abuse, it's psychological, it's sexual. Doesn't make it any less frightening. And it can be just as hard to heal from. Harder in fact. Why don't you stay with us just one night? Look, I know it's not going to fix everything. Beds aren't a solution. But there are lots of other ways we can help. Group therapy. Counseling. Court accompaniment. And sometimes a bed can be a start. What do you think?"

That evening, once the children are asleep, Ciara steps into a room beside the playroom, where the walls are dotted with framed quotes. *When someone shows you who they are, believe them.* A woman, perhaps in her fifties, with blondish hair and a beaded necklace, stands to greet her, introducing herself as Maeve. She explains this is just an introductory therapy session, to help Ciara process her current situation. She doesn't ask about her childhood, or root around for scars. Instead, she says, "Tell me what's happening."

Ciara talks about how they met. Moves forward, explaining the ways things began to come undone. "He makes me feel like it's my fault," she says. "Things were grand to start with. Things were really good. But I just didn't get him, I wasn't able to keep him happy. And then he has this temper. He had a tough childhood. Lots of difficult relationships. He just loses it."

"That's his story," Maeve says. "His words. Not yours. His version of the story. His voice in your head. What would it feel like to listen to yourself for a change?"

Maeve is looking at her intently. It's reassuring to be listened to like this, and she can feel herself unknotting, but it's vulnerable too, raw.

"I'm sorry," Ciara says, wiping her eyes. "I'm just really tired."

"Look," Maeve says, "you've been letting him into your home for access, and now you're letting him stay there. Because he scares you, and you're worried what would happen if you stand up to him?"

She nods. Her throat, dry.

"So, you're letting him use your home, so you're there for the kids all the time. But Ciara, the thing is, the kids don't just need you to be there for them all the time. Believe it or not, they actually need you to be okay. You might think they're so little they don't notice. But they do. I'm not saying this to freak you out. They do notice, and the things they cop are not what you'd think. They know if you're okay or not. They know if you're stressed. Having him in your house all the time, what is that doing to you?"

"I feel like it's just me. I should be able to put up with it."

"And spend your entire life acting as a human shield? Ah now. It does matter though, doesn't it, Ciara? It does matter. You matter."

The enormity of it. The task she's still facing.

"You've left," Maeve is saying, "and I absolutely applaud you for that. But leaving is only the first step. We need to look at getting your life back."

The therapist studies her for another second. "Is there something else you need to tell me?"

How does she know?

"I've never told anyone about this," Ciara hears herself saying. "When we were sleeping together…" How can she explain this? How can she put this into words? "It's going to sound so stupid. But just sometimes I'd be asleep and he'd wake me up, trying to have sex with me. I know it's just..."

"And did you say no?"

"Sometimes... yeah sometimes I used to ask him to stop."

"And did he?"

"Sometimes. Not always. And then he'd be giving out to me the next day, saying I was cold, frigid, that I didn't love him. There'd be hell, for days and days sometimes. So it was easier just to..."

"Just to go along with it?"

"Yes."

Maeve's face has taken on a new seriousness. "You realize, Ciara, what happened. That is coercion. And more to the point, you were asleep. You couldn't give consent."

When she thinks of it now, it is like someone else's story. Like she's seeing it from outside. She thinks about the women with their black *REPEAL* T-shirts. *MY BODY, MY CHOICE.* Is that what happened—she ceded her right to choose? She allowed her body to become just another pawn in Ryan's mind games. How can she tell Maeve that what happened at night wasn't even the worst of it, or that it was just another part of the endless cycle of punishment?

She remembers one morning when she confronted him, standing in the kitchen with her back against the worktop, dressing gown knotted tight. She told him she wasn't okay with what had happened the night before, but he just scowled. "How do you think that makes me feel, you not wanting sex with me? Can you imagine how hurt I feel?

How depressed? For God's sake, you're my wife. This was never an issue with my ex-girlfriend. In fact, it was favorably received."

The memory makes her shudder. She messes with her necklace, bites her lower lip. "I've never spoken about this to anyone. I'm sorry."

Maeve studies her for a minute, then says, "You have nothing to be sorry about. It's brave of you to tell me this, Ciara. To tell yourself this."

"I used to think it was just me."

"This is what happens. Things get minimized. I mean, think about it. If it was any other context. If you weren't married, that would be considered rape." Again, she watches Ciara's face. "And you're still afraid of him."

Is that a question?

Maeve nods. "You're terrified of him."

34

Ciara is straightening cushions, throwing soft toys into boxes, lighting the lamps, when there's a knock at the door. She opens it with one finger to her lips. As she ushers Diego into the house, she looks out over his shoulder. The street is empty, and the velvety dark is streaked with soft white clouds, as if a child has smudged a chalky handprint across the sky. She stands back to let Diego in, careful to double-lock and bolt the door behind him. In her hallway, he looks at her cautiously. "You are okay?"

"Yes." She wants to say more, but for now this is enough.

When Ciara and the children came home yesterday afternoon, the house was dark, the air stuffy. At first, she didn't believe that Ryan had really gone. She found herself checking everywhere, behind doors, under the bed. Ridiculous, she chided herself. Like searching for a stubborn child during a game of hide-and-seek. *Remember that time when Sophie was two and hid herself in the tumble dryer?* Jesus. *He's gone,* she told herself, *just breathe. Calm down. He's gone.*

She drew the curtains, letting the light in, and pushed open the windows to clear the air. The girls ran about the place, hugging their toys and bouncing on their beds, as if they'd been away from home for years, and it hit her: *They thought we were losing our home again, that we weren't coming back.*

The emergency barring order will be in place for eight working days. With Saoirse by her side at the courthouse, the process was relatively quick. She had phoned Grace to tell her what was happening, left her a voicemail, and was surprised to see her standing outside the courthouse when they came out. Grace has issued a letter to Ryan through his solicitor, informing him that he is no longer allowed access to Ciara's home. Once the eight days expires, he may collect the children for access visits, take them out for the day and then bring them home. They are still waiting for his response.

At her dining-room table, between the marmalade jar and spaghetti-streaked place mats, Diego takes out an IELTS paper and she turns to a new page in her notebook. A now familiar rhythm.

Halfway through the mock speaking exam, she makes tea and splits open a pack of chocolate digestives. After they've talked for a while, she dusts biscuit crumbs off her hands. "Right, let's go over the speaking exam part two. *Describe something you own which is very important to you. You should say: where you got it from, how long you have had it, what you use it for and explain why it is important to you.* Okay, Diego. Five minutes starts...now."

He clears his throat. "I will speak about my watch. It was give to me by my mum when I was eighteen. When she give me I was so surprised. It was my birthday morning..."

Diego's low, mellow voice slips away. She's only half-listening. "...and so I always wear and please God I never lose. I am loving my watch so much. Phew." He checks his phone. "I was speak for too long?"

"No, that was... that was perfect. Really good. But just one thing." She's taking a sheet of paper, writing one word on the center. "Love. You can't use the verb to love in the present continuous."

"So is not 'I'm loving you?' Is only possible 'I love you'?"

"Yes."

His hand beside hers on the page is close enough to touch, but neither of them moves. He says, "I was worry about you, that last night, Ciara. You sure you are safe?"

"I'm sorry. I shouldn't have told you to leave. I didn't want him to start a fight with you, to hurt you. Or to make things worse for me—it was selfish, stupid."

Those old feelings again, shame and guilt, but before she sinks further, he says, "Ciara, you are not selfish and you are not stupid. You did what you have to do. That's it, okay? You and your kids is most important. I'm just some student. Coming your home, bothering you. English maybe getting worse, not better."

She shakes her head. "Would you stop." There are things she wants to say, but something holds her back—fear. Of getting it wrong again, and seeing a man change character before her eyes? She remembers that night when she kissed Diego, the heat spreading through her body when he held her close.

He's studying her face and seems to make a decision. "Ciara, I want ask you help with something."

"What? You want to pretend to be my husband?"

He laughs, takes off his glasses, rubs the bridge of his nose where they have left a red mark. "You maybe think is stupid or—how do you say? Daft?—but you know my friend Rodrigo and Luana? They organize a holiday house. I go with them. To Mayo. You know this place?"

"Mayo is beautiful."

"Come with us?"

"What?"

"Ciara, honest. This holiday, it's so bad timing. I will be speaking Portuguese with those guys for five whole days. And Rodrigo also, he tries to go for IELTS next week. No good for him too. So I want ask you to come. There's a spare room. Another guy he dropped out. I asked Rodrigo and Luana already, they would love you join us."

"To Mayo?"

"Yes."

"To force you and Rodrigo to speak English?" She's smiling now.

"Why not? Bring Sophie, Ella, Noah, bring everybody. A holiday. I think, Ciara, you really need. No?"

Rain coming in sideways, she drives out of Foxford, up the main road to Castlebar. She turns right, into the sudden shade of an oak-lined driveway. The road snakes past an eighteenth-century gray-faced manor, then traces the curve of an artificial lake. She parks outside a low-roofed lakeside cabin, and steps out into the patter of rain on wet leaves. Gravel crunches underfoot. Banksides of curling ferns, tree trunks brightened by coats of furry moss. Drizzle sparkles the surface of the lake. *And breathe.*

Diego strolls out of the cabin, eating a bread roll, wide-armed, smiling.

"How can you guys afford to rent this place?" she asks him. "It's gorgeous."

He grins, his mouth full, swallows. "Last-minute deal. I don't tell you? Rodrigo, he's rich. Why Irish people think all Brazilians is cleaners?"

She steps into Diego's open arms. His lips on her cheeks.

"The kids are in the car, we have to listen to another story from the *Gruffalo* CD or there will be carnage."

"Sure. You go, Luana made coffee in the kitchen. I get your bags."

Storm lamps hang over a long pine table, which Luana and Rodrigo have filled with fresh baguettes, roasted chicken, brie, rocket salad, sweet cherry tomatoes, apple crumble. Over lunch, they swap stories about the journey—half an hour behind a tractor coming out of Ballina—and when she speaks up to contribute, it's as if she might never stop speaking. Words trip over each other.

"I saw boats on the river," Sophie says.

"And I saw a whale," Ella adds.

There's laughter. Tea, milk.

For the past five years, her expectations of judgment have usually been met. When she's expected sullen disapproval or berating, she has rarely been wrong. But this is different. The disapproval isn't there. Neither is the awkwardness. Instead, there's a cup of tea handed to her. Juice for the kids. And what Diego and his friends are saying—with their tea, laughter, biscuits, hugs—is that *it's okay to make a bad decision*. You don't have to live your life in the shadow of one poor choice. What they are saying is that it's okay.

Later, Noah asleep in the travel cot, the girls settled in front of a cartoon, Luana hands her a glass of white wine. "Here you go."

"Can I help you cook?"

"No way." She wafts Ciara out of the kitchen. "Just chill."

By the lakeside that evening, brown stone shapes become rabbits. She thinks of Mum, working nights all those years just to put them through school, and how she used to tell them about the rabbits she saw on her way home each morning. *Right in the center of the city, imagine!* For a second, she misses her Mum so much, her chest hurts.

They stay up past midnight, playing Bananagrams and drinking rum on the back porch. The game becomes louder as the night wears on. "*Tit* is not a proper word, Diego."

"Another fucking zed!"

"Ciara, you're cheating."

"No, no, she not cheating. She just speak English. Not like you, Rodrigo."

She's sitting with one leg bent, slouched against the chair in an old college-days pose she hasn't adopted in years. Laughter in her belly. The surprising bubble of it. The relief of it.

Her mum and Sinéad know they are safe, so she's keeping her phone turned off. Under ancient sycamores and elms, she watches her daughters careening down plush green lawns, past the *KEEP OFF THE GRASS* signs.

At lunchtime, they walk up to the local café and order stone-baked pizzas, tumblers of iced water, coffee.

Rodrigo is fishing on the lake. Diego sits next to him, practicing his memorized lines. "*That is an excellent point. I would like to elaborate further by saying. That raises the important question of— It's a highly topical issue at the moment due to the—*"

Day three in Mayo, she has finally got all three children to bed. No small triumph.

Now she pulls the tie from her hair, shakes it loose, scalp tingling. Her breath falls calm, relaxed. In a few minutes she'll go down to the kitchen still warm with the cooking smells of the lasagna that Luana made earlier. She will put on the kettle. Her body is already anticipating the restful sleep to come, she feels as a physical presence the lack of anxiety. Her lungs are bigger now, and so is the room in her head.

Before, she was chained to the spot, with sirens blaring and headlight beams racing toward her. Now, tasks that once grated and dragged seem stupidly easy. She's able to focus on the moment without having to pre-empt the next storm.

Maeve said, "Listen to your body. Everything else can be twisted, but the body knows the truth."

Now she's breathing properly, air reaching places that have been recoiled in hurt and shock.

She's reminded of being back in Sheffield, in her mum's house. Down the ladder stairs. Wandering into the kitchen, where socks are drying on the radiator, and a candle is burning low. Mum on the phone, laughing. Her and Sinéad raiding the biscuit tin, sitting at the kitchen table for a chat. News. Always news. Gossip and stories. Half-watching the telly.

Late that night, she turns her phone on. An email. She's surprised to see her sister's name. Sinéad doesn't write emails.

Ciara I am sorry that I told him to fuck off.

I AM SORRY.

I really didn't mean to. The words leapt out of me.

It was just the way he was smiling at me, mocking me. I couldn't help it. I am really sorry.

Ciara, I love you so much. I admire you so much. The way you happily jumped on a plane, traveled the world. Holidays with you were always the best. Remember Rome, that place near the Trevi fountain where we fibbed and said we were part of that American tour so they let us into that classy club for free? Remember in Barcelona when you'd just broken up with that Spanish lad and you played "Unchained Melody" about fifty million times until I threw the CD out the window? And then we decided to go drinking in the Tequila Bar, only Spanish shots of tequila are not the same as Irish or English shots oh dear God remember that cheesy salsa club we ended up in and that fella that was trying to convince me to run away with him to Morocco holy fuck.

I still have flyers for those spoken word nights. I went to every single one of your gigs even that time at the Fox and Hen, when only two people showed up and you cried and we all got chips and went to the 80s night at the Republic and did Jägerbombs until we both threw up. You were there that night when I met Pete. You told me he was a bit geeky but probably harmless and that's about right, three kids later and apart from Pete you were the first to hold each of them. And you stopped me from naming Nathan "Prince" (thank you on his behalf).

My boys love their Auntie Ciara and it's hard to explain to them sometimes why you're not about, and you're not the auntie they remember and I know you try to be, and I see you trying and it hurts. I know you're trying.

Remember that time you broke Mum's china duck and you were certain you could fix it with Pritt stick and Sellotape and the time you took up cross-country running and the wee skinny legs on you, that day at Monsildale, all covered in muck, bawling crying but you wouldn't stop running. (By the way, you think Sophie looks like Mum? She doesn't. She looks like you—that's where she gets that stubbornness from too. That determination. I guess what I'm saying is that you still have that in you.)

Remember on your last teaching placement. That time we stayed up till 3am to help you paint the bloody Amazon Rainforest poster, and then we realized it didn't fit in your bloody tiny Micra, and I had to wake Pete up to come and attach it to the roof of his van the next morning. Remember stopping at McDonald's for coffee and driving up to Sacred Heart Primary with the rainforest on the roof. The kids' faces, when they saw you unloading the thing. Those kids loved you.

Sometimes I feel guilty I didn't say more. When you met Ryan it was all so fast, but I was happy for you. He was so handsome wasn't he? So funny and smart. And the lovely accent. You'd always done things differently. Followed your heart. You'd always wanted to live in Ireland, and that first time I came to visit you seemed so happy. Wee Sophie in your arms. When I started to feel you withdrawing, getting so quiet. I should have said something sooner. But it's hard to know what to say. We weren't there to see what was going on.

Remember that first Christmas you brought him home after Sophie was born? Dear Lord. He sulked and didn't speak, and Mum asked him to give you a wee hand with the weans. Him calling the family meeting to discuss our behavior. Lecturing us. I've never been so mortified. And I saw it right then in Mum's living room, how scared you were of him. You wouldn't stand up to him. I remember crying that night and Pete saying what's wrong what's wrong, and not being really able to explain. I've seen what he does to you and I've never really been able to put it into words.

And I just wanted to say I'm sorry Ciara. I'm sorry if I made things worse for you. I should have kept my gob shut. But I'm here for you. I'm always here for you. Remember a while back, when I said you didn't have any friends? Well that's a load of crap. I'm your friend, okay? I'm your friend and always will be.

Love Sinéad x

On the beach, the windbreaker is a new concept for the Brazilians. Ciara had to explain how to stake it in place with a mallet. Sophie and Ella eat their sandwiches, leaning back against the soft bulge of the tarpaulin. Noah is trying to sit up by himself, wobbling over each time like a tipsy old fella. Cold sea surging around her legs, the gritty bite of sandwiches on the beach; these were the sensations of her childhood. Diego looks confused when she explains this. "You was wearing coats? And wellington boots? On a *beach*?" She remembers sitting on the beach at Caraguatatuba, on white sand that scalded the soles of her feet, where women wore impossible bikinis, sipping from green coconuts with a straw. As if reading her thoughts, Diego smiles. "Irish beach and Brazilian beach. It's different experience."

There's a man selling kites by the lifeguard station. Inflatable dragons, stingrays, princesses and an orca that ripples and floats on the wind, as if jumping invisible waves.

"Look!" Ella shouts, "There's a whale in the sky!"

Rodrigo and Diego attempt to wrestle a pop-up tent back into its case. Luana swears at them in Portuguese, fishes out the instructions. *Match point A to point B. Then stand on point H and match point C to point D. Easily slip your tent into its carrier.*

Here it is again. The laughter. "Idiots!" Luana flops down on the sand.

Fish and chips from a van in the Aldi car park in Ballina. *The nation's best kept secret*, doused in salt, vinegar, garlic mayo. The cod flakes, melts. Brown bags of salty chips torn open and left on the table to share. Luana, Rodrigo and Diego sometimes repeat the same stories, tales becoming so familiar they feel like her own memories. And nobody says *yeah, you already told me that*. Nobody says *hmmm*. Nobody says *yeah really* in a flat, uninterested voice. Instead, there are questions. Teasing. Laughter

The alarm bells have stopped.

The white panic has stopped.

The constant forward-planning, incessant pre-empting, stopped.

What happens is this: she can hear herself think.

I am coming back to life.

Kids asleep, she's sitting by the lake with Luana, telling her, "I left my husband and lived in a hotel for nine months, and have now taken on the lease of a house I cannot afford."

Luana knows which questions to ask. Which questions not to. She asks for how long. She doesn't ask why.

It's such a bright evening. One of those nights when the air feels crisp, like cool, clear, open water. Tonight has the feel of summer parties from college days, when the pale night stretched its fingers, already touching morning. It hits her again, this feeling of rewinding. Coming to her senses. Without a bruise, without a cut, fear sat in her house for so long that without it, she feels buoyant. Untethered. Like moonwalking.

This is what happens, when the fog lifts. Moods are okay, tiredness is okay.

Night four, the three kids bawl at different pitches and refuse to fall asleep until after ten. When she finally collapses onto the sofa with the others, Rodrigo hands her a cold beer, and pulls a sympathetic face.

Mornings, Diego makes the coffee.

Luana and Rodrigo entertain the girls with silly dance moves they delight in copying. Diego holds Noah for her while she has a shower. Luana packs the beach bags into the car. Is this all love is? People helping each other?

That overused Corinthians reading at her wedding. Love is patient, love is kind. But perhaps the Corinthians got it completely wrong. Perhaps it's the other way round. Kindness is love. That's all there is. There's nothing else.

I am so kind, Ryan used to spit at her. *I am being so fucking kind. You could not meet a kinder person.*

Already his words are starting to dissolve, insubstantial against the wet towels, muddy boots, cool wine, melty ice cream, restful nights.

Falcons live on the estate between the mountains. A dewy morning, she takes the girls up to the aviary for a tour. Sophie listens, her eyes wide. When the falconer asks for a volunteer to hold the peregrine falcon, she shoots her hand up. Other tourists laugh. At the size of her, with her dark determined eyes. The falconer kneels, slips a massive leather glove onto Sophie's skinny arm, and hands her the bird. Yellow feet. Steel talons. It lifts its brown wings, showing soft white plumage peppered with black dashes. "This is the fastest bird on the planet," the falconer says. Sophie is holding very still.

That night, Sophie stays up late, talking about the birds. Noah is asleep in the travel cot, bottom lip sucked under, and Ella is snoring softly in the double bed as usual. Ciara climbs into Sophie's pull-out bed, stuffed unicorns scattering. Sophie lays her head against her mum's chest. "What would happen if one of those birds got lost? And what would happen if it flew as high as the moon? And what would happen if one bird had two nests?"

There's healing in this conversation. She can feel the positive energy ebb and flow between them, as Sophie starts talking about owls camouflaging in the snow. Later, after Sophie has gone to sleep, Ciara gets into the double bed, snuggles under the duvet and takes out the novel she brought with her. It's such a joy to return to reading, to allow herself to be transported.

Their last night in the West, they've booked a table for an early dinner in the hotel marquee. While they are waiting for the food to arrive, the girls run out onto the sloping lawns. They run and roll. Noah bounces in her arms, keen to join his sisters.

After dinner, when it gets late, she brings the kids back to the cabin. For once, the three of them fall asleep early, and she tiptoes back downstairs.

No sign of the others. They must be still at the hotel bar. She pours a glass of white wine and takes it outside, sits on the veranda by the lake. Back to Dublin tomorrow. To reality.

The evening is still. Insects catch the golden light, like floating embers. Diego steps out onto the veranda. He's wearing a white shirt, unbuttoned at the neck. "So peaceful," he says, putting his bottle of Brahma on the windowsill. Music plays softly from his phone.

"What is that song?" she asks, "I used to hear that a lot in São Paulo."

He laughs. "That is one of the greatest songs. DJ Avan's 'Sé.' "

"What does the chorus mean? Something about learning?"

"Yeah, it means something like, *It's easier to learn Japanese in Braille than to know what you're thinking.*"

There's a pause. She knows him well enough to ask, "What's up?"

"You know I apply for the master's in New York? Well, I got in. They say I need still the IELTS, but if I get it, I can start. In September."

A pain in her heart, a swift stab of longing, quickly cut down by reason—she knew this would happen, she's been helping him toward these exams, of course he has to leave. "That's great!" she says.

"Yeah. It's good, I guess."

"But you're not happy?"

He shrugs. "I dunno. If I want leave Dublin, you know."

All week, she's felt herself and Diego drawing closer. The casual way he touches her arm when he brushes past her, or how she leans against him when they are on the sofa, talking in the evenings. Late at night, she's imagined all sorts of steamy scenarios with him that now make her blush. Still, there's a fear she can't seem to get past—of misjudging things, of losing herself again, getting trapped. No. She has to keep a clear head.

He's waiting for her to say something. This moment between them is about to pass. She hesitates, then steps closer, rests her head on his chest. Passion averted, diverted into something else, he folds his arms around her. She can hear his heartbeat through his shirt.

The next afternoon, on the way back from Mayo, she brings Sophie, Ella and Noah up Three Rock Mountain. At the peak, the satellite dishes she used to see from their hotel window. Last time she came here with Ryan, they both had a tight grip on the kids' hands, as if to stop something happening to them. *When in reality,* she thinks, *the thing that kept happening to them was us. Our marriage was the thing that kept happening, and that would have kept happening over and over.*

Now she's letting go of her daughters' hands, letting them zig-zag way ahead in clopping light-up wellies, past mossy boulders, ivy-wrapped trees and yellowing brambles. Letting them trip over roots, rocks, slippery leaves, letting them reach out. Noah, tied to her waist, is getting too big for the sling. He bounces as if trying to propel himself after his sisters.

"MAMMY." Hugging hot throbbing bodies alive with the excitement of space and sky and trees as big as giants. Kissing warm clammy cheeks, she's letting the girls push away from her and run.

35

"So you got my email." There's a smile in her sister's voice.

"Sinéad, you didn't have to. I'm so sorry. I shouldn't have—"

"Look. It's okay. Main thing is that you're safe." A pause, in which she knows Sinéad is about to ask her something. Finally her sister says, "So . . . me and mum were talking. Why don't you come over for a day? And before you start . . . I know Sophie and Ella can't come. But why don't you just come over by yourself. Get Cathy to mind the kids?"

Another three days of the barring order, before she will have to face seeing Ryan again for access. She could do it, could go over. "I don't know . . ."

Sinéad says, "I didn't want to worry you Ciara, but Mum's not been that well . . . she's in hospital for more tests. The heart thing again."

A memory so vivid it catches her breath. Rhona sitting at the kitchen table, her head in her hands. Ciara, sixteen, on her way to meet her friends at Sheffield ice rink. Tartan mini skirt, black biker boots. Breezing past the kitchen table on her way out the door. Seeing Rhona, but not stopping. Deliberately not asking. Fuming onto the Number 16 bus that tipped down into the city.

Hard white leather skates. Blisters stinging her heels within a few wobbly laps of the ice. Circling while anxiety rose, until she couldn't take it anymore and skated away from her friends, out into the center of the rink, and stood there alone, breath knocked out of her, snotty tears ruining her makeup. Skaters drew circles around her, like the Spirograph she had as a child. *Mum. Was she still sitting at the kitchen table? Was she okay?* She should have stopped, should have hugged her mum, talked to her. And now she'd never be able to reach her. Never be able to skate back across this plastic ice, without falling.

On the phone, Sinéad says, "Hello? You still there?"

"I'm here. I'll look up the flights."

Two days later, at Dublin Airport, she crosses the Departures Hall, toward the security gate. Walking in the echo of that April day, their plastic bags full of washing. This time, wheeling a small black cabin case, she passes easily through security, buys a coffee and sits at the gate, reading. She finds herself looking at the photo page on her passport. A grim picture, taken five years ago. She looks harassed, pallid. Her name in caps: CIARA FAY. She should change it back. CIARA DEVINE. It would make certain things more complicated, having a different surname from her children. But wouldn't it be worth it, to rid herself of his name.

She takes out her Walkman, turns on *Buntús Cainte. Seo duit é. Ní raibh tú i bhfad. Rith me go dtí an síopa agus arís.*

Just after nine, her flight boards. She takes a window seat and a woman with curly hair and a dark office suit sits beside her. Engines grumbling, the small plane charges down the runway, tilts into the air, and within minutes they're over the Irish Sea.

At Manchester, she walks the long travelator through glass tunnels to reach the train station. A billboard is advertising the latest exhibit at the museum, "Dinosaurs Discovered." A pang at the thought of Sophie and her pterodactyls. Without her children, how is she meant to walk through this tunnel, get to the airport, board a train and make it back to her home city, to Mum? Yet somehow she does, and somehow she's sitting on a train racing through the familiar Yorkshire countryside and her heart aches. The accents around her, unfamiliar now. As out of place as she first felt in Dublin.

Sinéad is waiting on the platform at Sheffield with her eldest son, Nathan, who is wearing a Sheffield Owls hoodie, a long fringe over his eyes. When she steps off the train, her sister hugs her and starts crying and talking at once. "I didn't think you'd come over, I kept waiting on a call to say you'd changed your mind or something had happened, Mum's up to the nines excited about this, she's up there in the Northern General telling everyone you're coming over."

After a while, Nathan says, "Mum? Are we going?"

"Nathan! Hug your auntie."

"Hey," Nathan scuffs his runners on the platform. He looks like photos of her granddad when he was young. "Now are we going? Mum?"

Sheffield has changed. Even the entrance to the station is now glass-fronted, airy. Sinéad has parked her jeep in the taxi rank, gives the finger to two angry taxi drivers gesticulating at her, beeping their horns. "We'll go straight to the Northern," she says.

Ciara's phone pings. A message from Cathy. A photo of the three kids playing up the garden, rolling around on the Donegal blanket. Her breasts hurt. Noah. His little face. The ache for him. The pump is in her handbag, but she can't figure out how she will get the chance to use it. Stopped at a traffic light, Sinéad glances at her, sees the phone. She says, "They'll be grand, hun, don't worry. It's good for you. To be home."

The ward smells of soup. At first all she sees is a room full of old people lying in bed. It takes a minute before she realizes one of them is Rhona. In her head, her mum is preserved at around fifty. Black bob, dark eyeliner. In reality, her mum's hair is now almost white. Is this the final act of love, refusing to see someone aging?

The cannula in the back of Rhona's hand, the bubble of IV fluids makes her think of Ella, that night in Temple Street. The heart monitor, green peaks and troughs scribbling above Mum's head. Her hair swept back from her forehead, sticking up at all angles, like a toddler woken from a nap.

When she sees them, Rhona sits up. "All this fuss. Honest to God. What are you like? Going to all the hassle, and the state of me. I don't even have my face on. I said to our Sinéad, I said tell wee Ciara not to be coming the whole way over. I'm grand sure."

Sinéad throws Ciara a look, shakes her head. "Two days," she mock-whispers. "Two whole days she's been talking about you coming over, nonstop, to anyone who will listen."

Her mother grins girlishly, and Ciara remembers bursting in the door from the skating rink that night, carrying the cold on her shoulders. Bus fumes and cigarette smoke. Late autumn, city lights an orange blur behind her. Bursting into the bright kitchen on Bate Street, expecting to find her mum still sitting with her head in her hands. Instead, the iron was steaming, Whitney crooning on the radio. Rhona was wearing her favorite red shoulder-padded jumper, her hands busy folding starchy sheets. "There you are, Ciara love. Dinner's nearly ready."

In the good room, Sinéad and her friends were fighting over the remote, *Top of the Pops* and *Neighbours* flicking back and forth. Ciara's heart, that of an athlete overrunning the finish line. She sat on the narrow stairs, under the tick of the brass hall clock, as the fear dissipated, leaving her drained and suddenly ravenous.

Now, Rhona points to the bedside chair. "Come and sit down. Ah Nathan love, the height of you."

Nathan has noticeably softened in his granny's presence. He smiles, hands in pockets.

Sinéad rubs his arm. "Nate's been awful worried, haven't you love."

For a horrible second it looks like Nathan might cry. He can't, he can't. She sees that about him, how upset he would be with himself if he lets himself crumble. He bends over his granny, her hands on his shoulders. Sinéad isn't even bothering to wipe the tears running down her chin. Ciara knows what her nephew is feeling in that hug. Her soft hands, her warmth. Finally, Nathan stands.

"Go on and get yourself some chocolate, and bring us three teas." Sinéad has slipped him a tenner. "Go on there now, love."

Once he's loped off, Rhona says, "Honest to God, what are youse like? Upsetting the young fella and everything. Sure I'm not dead."

Sinéad has produced a shred of balled-up tissue from her pocket, blows her nose noisily. "I know, mum, but it's just..."

"The doctor said I'm doing extremely well."

"Ah mum. He didn't exactly say that in fairness. He said you were very lucky."

"He said I've the irregular heartbeat, but sure half the ones at Weight Watchers have that. Once we get that sorted, I'll be flying. Another couple of nights he reckons, that's all. Anyway, Ciara, come here to me love." Her mum is holding both her hands. "You're okay now, are you? You got him out? Just awful what he did, moving in on you like that. Terrible. You'll not let it happen again?"

"No, Mum. It's never happening again. It's over now."

Rhona seems to be reading her face. She says, "It's not what you wanted, love, and I'm sorry. You didn't deserve any of it."

Ciara holds her mother's hand, and they talk some more. She shows her photos of the girls and Noah, and what she really wants to say is—*Mum, you were always enough. The three of us were enough.* All those fake doubts and insecurities cultivated by Ryan have fallen away.

"You'll need another nightie, Mum. And pants." Sinéad is on her phone now, making a list. "We'll head off in a minute and pop into Primark."

Rhona tuts, "You'll do no such thing. Wasting money. I've perfectly decent nighties at home."

"Mum—"

"Knickers in the top drawer, you know yourself love. You have a key, Sinéad, don't you? Sure pop over with Ciara and then come back here to me."

They've dropped Nathan off at soccer practice and driven over to Crookes. Outside her childhood home, the spill of the city. Seven hills, pale with distance. The dirty-white streak of the fake ski slope. Disused power-station chimneys. Even in summer, the air feels colder, sharper here than Dublin. The Ladbrokes bookies has been replaced by an upmarket nail salon. The corner shop has become a Spar. The launderette has turned into a health-food store. The bus stop is still there, and the street carries the same swirling grit and exhaust fumes. Sinéad opens the kitchen door and they're greeted by the tang of fresh paint. She sees Ciara's face. "Mum's been decorating."

"Decorating? For what?"

Sinéad puts her eyes to heaven. "Wait till you see."

Up the ladder-steep stairs, two of the rooms are bare. Her old room, and Sinéad's. They used to have bunk beds up against the back wall, music posters and photos lining the narrow wardrobe. Now, Rhona has repainted the rooms a sunny custard yellow. Rainbow curtains. Two single beds. New mattresses still in plastic wrapping. Beside the bed, a cot.

"This was Nathan's." Sinéad runs her hand along the pine cot frame. "Little bit worn, but it's grand. You'd need a new mattress for it just." Her sister looks up. "I know. I keep saying to Mum it's not that easy. You can't just up and leave without his permission. He's their dad. And your home's over there now. But you know what she's like. There's no talking to her."

"I would if I could."

"I know, hun. But you're a long time over there, that's the other thing as well." Sinéad sighs. "I'll get those nighties. Did you say you needed to pump?"

Alone in her old childhood bedroom, Ciara places the suction pump to her breast, starts up the motor. The whirring tug of it. Straight away, a thin line of white milk streams into the bottle. Her breasts hot, heavy.

Lunchtime, the girls will be eating their sandwiches, elbows on the table, slurping their juice. Hopefully Noah is taking the bottle she left for him. She can see his little face screwed up in disgust at the plastic teat.

The view from this window feels like the only thing in her life that hasn't changed. A patchwork of gardens. Mrs. Wallace's mossy greenhouse. The alleyway, then the steep staircase of red rooftops leading into the valley. Beyond this, the hills. How could she have thought home was anywhere but here? Even as the thought occurs, there's the restless feeling of wanting to be elsewhere. The excitement of leaving this bedroom, matched only by the thrill of returning. Ryan's hands on her hips in the Leadmill club. *I'm Irish yeah*. She didn't stand a chance.

She's felt such anger at the way Mum laid so much on her. But isn't she doing the same with her own daughters? Doesn't she lift Ella from her bed sometimes, carry her into the double bed beside her? She kids herself that her daughter will probably wake soon anyway, when really she just wants the comfort of Ella's floppy, sleeping body. Of not having to wake up alone.

Your daughters need you to be okay. That's what they need, more than anything.

It's dark when she returns to Manchester Airport. She spent the afternoon at the hospital with Rhona, sitting by her mother's bed and walking with her, round the hospital car park, past the smoking area and the ambulance dock. She had the feeling of watching each moment, feeling time rushing past her. Early evening, Sinéad drove her back to the station and parked in the taxi rank. On the platform they cried into each other's hair. "We're all so worried about you," Sinéad said. "Mum's been so worried."

"It's okay," she told her. "Things are going to get better now."

Walking into the airport, she looks down at her phone. Cathy has sent a video of Sophie blowing raspberries on Noah's neck, him chortling with laughter, Ella spinning around in her fairy tutu. Ciara smiles, heart full of giddy joy at the thought of returning to them. At Duty Free, she buys a pack of hair clips for each of the girls, and a cheap rattle for Noah.

On the plane, she keeps the blind open. Something thrilling, liberating about having taken this trip. The plane tilts upward, cruises briefly, and then tips down toward Ireland. Cabin crew barely have time to make it up and down the aisle with the food cart. If you ordered tea, it wouldn't have time to cool. Her two worlds, so close. Cabin lights are dimmed, and Dublin comes into view. Lights shaped like open shackles around the bay.

36

Pink shooting stars sweep up into Sophie's dark hair. "What's this?" Ryan says. "You got new hair clips, Soph?"

His tone is nonchalant, but Ciara knows better. The barring order ended last night, and today he's picking the children up for his access day. Grace says she can apply for another order if needs be, but not for another month. She can file for another court date to reassess the access arrangements, but there will be a wait. Sophie is balancing on one leg, talking about something that happened at playschool, but Ryan asks her again, "Where'd you get those, Sophie?"

"From Mammy!" Sophie says. "From when she went on the big plane to see Granny and Auntie Sinéad!"

Ciara is standing in the hallway behind the kids, holding their bag of toys and spare clothes, ready to hand over to Ryan. She looks down, pretends to be rooting around the shoe rack for Ella's runners.

"Hang on." Ryan is glaring at her. "You went to England? Without telling me?"

"Just for a day." Ciara tries to keep her voice light. "To see Mum. She's not been well."

Ryan steps over the threshold. He's in her hallway now, moving closer. "So let me get this straight. You went and got this stupid barring order. You stopped me from seeing my children for ten whole days. And meanwhile—meanwhile you were not—even—in—the—fucking—*country*?"

"Just for one day. I was back by bedtime. They were with Cathy."

"Cathy?" That stony stare again. "That random woman from the hotel? Why the hell didn't you leave them with me? I'm their father!"

She's become aware of Sophie hugging her waist, looking up at her. Even though Ryan is the one raising his voice, Sophie's stare is locked on Ciara's face, waiting for her mum to fix things. Ciara says, "Ryan, I don't want to fight like this in front of the kids. Can we talk about this later?"

Ryan's face is livid. His jaw clicks. "Where's Noah?"

"He's asleep. I thought we'd better not wake him—"

He gives a dark laugh, "Oh no, not this time. I want my son."

They have only been gone for half an hour when the messages start.

Just shitting all over my rights as a father, abducting my children and then abandoning them with some crazy homeless bitch.

She throws the phone down on the sofa as if it's scalding. It pings again. Assumpta.

Absolutely evil, what you're doing to Ryan-Patrick. His father and I are utterly appalled, and may you burn in hell for your selfish actions. Those poor children being raised by an evil mother, their only chance of salvation is through the kindness, love and patience of Ryan-Patrick, God love him.

Another message. A number she doesn't recognize. A friend of Ryan's?

You should be fucking grateful to have a man like that in your life—strong enough to put up with you and your family's bullshit. You seduced him into marriage, used him as nothing but a sperm donor. Shame on you. Cruel bitch. Making yourself out to be so victimized. Keep your misery for those stupid books you read. You think you're so smart with all your fucking "literature." Your meant to be a teacher but you dont have a caring bone in your body. Ryan is those kids only chance of not ending up a fuck-up like you and your mother.

She can't move. Words, a toxin coursing through her. Just words, just stupid words. So why does it feel like she's been slapped?

In her living room, the clock hand moves between butterflies where the numbers should be. On the rug, a jumble of Sylvanian animals. Ella's slippers.

After a while, Ciara manages to sit on the arm of the sofa and make a call. As soon as Sinéad answers and hears her voice, she says, "What's wrong?"

"He found out. About me going over to Sheffield."

"And? Ciara. You're entitled to go places. To see your family. To have a life. Why can't he accept that?"

"Sinéad, listen. He's raging. And he has the kids for the day. And him and his family have been sending me all these messages, and I can't..."

She's half expecting one of her sister's usual indignant responses—*tell them to go fuck themselves* or *bunch of arseholes.*

Instead Sinéad is quiet. "He senses you're breaking away. The barring order. Your trip to the West. Coming over here. He knows he's losing control."

For a second neither of them speaks. A car goes past her house. Children's voices. A mum trailing two youngsters on tricycles with fluttering streamers.

Mid-morning, sunlight has moved from the living room. She's trying to keep herself busy. It would be easier to distract herself by going out for a walk somewhere, but she doesn't want to leave the house in case he brings the kids back early. She wipes down the kitchen table, sweeping away remnants of breakfast, congealed Rice Krispies, patches of dried milk. When that's done, she bundles a load of clothes into the washing machine and starts the cycle, grateful for the low grumble softening the silence. She brushes the floors. Mops them.

There have been no more messages.

Her phone in her pocket is a constant presence. Worry is a wall she's pushing back against, but she cannot give in to the panic.

Time creeps. Her breasts fill, harden. She tries to pump, but she's too stressed and it's just sore. Giving up on the blasted pump, she tries to read, her latest from the library, Alice Munro's *Runaway*, but the words blur before her eyes. She's reading without taking anything in. She reaches for her Walkman. In Lesson 30 of *Buntús Cainte*, Pádraig and Séamus are talking about their gardens. Nil na prátaí go léir bainte agam. Bhí an talamh rófhliuch... It's no use. She's not even listening.

The day stretches into late afternoon. He is meant to bring them back at five o'clock. If she can just make time pass until then.

In the garden, she pulls dandelions from the flowerbeds. Daddy lions, Ella calls them. Look at all those daddy lions. When the growl of her stomach can no longer be ignored, she makes a cheese sandwich, grabs an apple. She eats outside, sitting cross-legged on the grass, like she would with the kids.

Five o'clock. Five-thirty.

At six, when the children are not home, she phones Ryan.

Voicemail.

Her defenses are breaking. She's been fighting the panic all day, but now it's becoming bigger than she is.

Six-thirty.

She phones Cathy. Says she'll pay for a taxi. Half an hour later Cathy arrives with Lucy. "I'll stay here, in case they come back. You head over to wherever he's staying. He must have them there."

Ryan's friend Cian answers the door in sweatpants and a hoody. "All right, Ciara?"

Is she imagining the smirk on his face? She thinks of that message. Was he the one who sent it?

"Is Ryan here?" she asks. "And the kids?"

"Ryan?" That smirk again. "Sure we haven't seen Ryan in weeks. Is he not at home with you?"

Eight-ten.

She cannot give in to the part of her that wants to break.

Wants to lie on this pavement and claw at the concrete and scream. She phones Cathy, who tells her they haven't come home yet, no. Sinéad suggests their old home in Glasnevin.

"He doesn't live there anymore, remember? He was evicted, that's why he moved into the houseshare, why he was trying to move in with me, I should have let him, should have just—"

"Go and check," Sinéad says. "Go now and check."

Their old house is in darkness. Perhaps someone else lives here now. She rings the bell. No answer. She tries her key. It still works.

In the hall, all is quiet. She flicks on the lights and cannot make sense of what she is seeing. A lucid dream. Ryan's black fleece jacket is hanging from the coat hooks by the door. Sophie's cardigan, the one with the love-heart buttons, lies strewn on the floor, arms askew. She scoops it up, heart banging.

"Hello?"

"Landlord told me to leave. A houseshare, wouldn't be suitable for the kids. Leaving me homeless, leaving me with nowhere to go!"

In the front room, the usual mess of toys—leftover toys, ones she forgot to bring with them. Dinner plates on the kitchen table. Garlic-bread crusts. Again, she feels taken aback. This cannot be real.

"Hello?"

A muffled thud from somewhere upstairs.

She takes the stairs two at a time, stifling the scream rising within her. A faint light, coming from Sophie and Ella's old bedroom. Two shapes under the unicorn duvet. She pulls back the covers, and there's high-pitched screaming and Ella shouts, "IT'S MAMMY!" They hurl themselves at her, crying and grabbing.

"We didn't know who was coming in, we thought it was a monster!" Sophie bawls. "Daddy went out and we thought, we thought, we thought, we thought, we—"

Sophie has wet herself. Ciara hugs her tight, kisses her face, whispering, "Shhh, shhh, honey, honey it's okay."

She manages to prize the girls off her for long enough to dart into the other bedrooms.

Nothing.

Noah's cot, empty.

Back in the girls' room, they cling to her again. She tries to keep her voice level. "Where's Noah? Girls, where's Noah?"

Ella has her head buried deep in her mum's shoulder. She can't make out what she's saying. She tries to get Ella to say it again. "Where's Noah, love? Where's Noah?"

Her daughter pulls her closer, whispers into her ear, "Noah's with Daddy."

"Why on earth would Ryan-Patrick be here?" On the phone, Assumpta's voice is indignant. "I don't know why you would think that. Lord have mercy, the poor man, having to listen to rubbish like this." She imagines Assumpta pulling on her dressing gown, sitting up in bed, waking her husband.

"The nerve. Phoning me, after the way you've been treating my poor son. Sure he's probably nipped to the shops. Did you leave enough food for the baby? I'd say you maybe didn't."

"Assumpta. He was raging at me earlier. Now he's taken my child—"

"His child—"

She hangs up and calls the Gardaí.

Think, Ciara, think. Where is he likely to have gone? Where?

Knotted together on the wet bed, she's holding Sophie and Ella, her body curled around her daughters. "It's okay, it's okay."

In her head, she's back in their new house, and she's in her childhood bedroom and she's in Room 124. And now she's not here at all. She is levitating and the house is far below, with its undulating red-gray tiles and the iridescent flecks of light in the quartz pillars by the porch. And the whole street shrinks into a miniature railway set. Tiny cars, neatly spaced trees around an oval green. It all seems so peaceful from up here. Each house looks like a haven, lamp lit, snuggled together as if for warmth.

Think, think. Where has he gone? Her house has become a labyrinth. Her staircase, an endlessly repeating Escher sketch. Just like it was on all those nights. So many nights, she thought she would never get out of this house alive. Sophie's skinny arms around her neck. Ella hugging her waist. Her daughters, shocked into a loud silence.

Was that a car outside?

She scrambles to her feet, her daughters still tangled around her. Tries to unknot Ella and Sophie's hands from her arms and legs, but they bawl. "We're coming too!" Down the stairs. Heart thumping.

The doorbell.

Through frosted glass panels on the front door, the pulse of blue light.

Two Gardaí are standing in her living room. One, a man with a Northern accent, a beard and freckles. "Can I put the heat on for you, love? The weans are wild cold."

The other, a woman with short henna-red hair and black-rimmed glasses. "How often does your ex-husband come over? And this hasn't happened before, is that right? And how old is the baby?"

Words make it real.

The woman guard is crouching down to talk to the girls. Asking her to check them for any injuries. White bellies under lifted PJ tops. Sopping wet PJ bottoms. Tousled hair, her hands feeling their heads for any bumps. Wide eyes. She's trying not to scare them. Tries to keep her voice level. "Where did Daddy go, loves? Did either of you superstars see where Daddy might have gone? And what about baby Noah?"

"He was crying," Sophie says. "He didn't want the bottle so he spitted it."

"Noah wanted boobies," Ella says authoritatively, hugging Hoppy.

The other guard tells her they have sent a patrol car over to her new house, in case Ryan goes back there. Ciara phones Cathy, asks her to come over with clean clothes for the girls. She'll give her money for another taxi, it doesn't matter. The savings, the rent, none of it matters now.

Ten forty-five.

While she's sitting with the girls, the two guards step outside. Through the patio glass, she watches them search the garden. What are they looking for? *Don't even think. Don't even allow yourself to think.* The slide door left open, security lights on. The guards are running torches along the back wall.

Somehow night bleeds into a thin, heartless daylight. She phones Sinéad, tells her not to tell Mum. Ten minutes later, her mother is on the phone. "Louise is on her way down to you, will be there in a couple of hours. Tell them to get it on the radio. Ciara? Are you listening? Tell them to put it on the telly. Have you given them a photo of Noah? Ciara?"

Sinéad is already on her way to the airport.

Her girls, awake for the day now, tearful and clingy, cold hands in their dinosaur PJs, nestled in front of the TV.

She sends the same text to everyone in her contacts.

Noah is missing. He is with Ryan. Please if you see Ryan or hear from him, please phone me.

Women begin to fill her house. Louise, beautifully pregnant, takes the girls from her and sits them at the kitchen table with coloring books, playdough, Barbies. Olivia and Maggie arrive with fresh loaves, cheese, fruit, chocolate buttons for the girls. Cathy sits with her, watching the guards speaking to each other in low voices. Ciara keeps phoning. Keeps texting.

Please Ryan, will you just tell me that he's safe?

Lunchtime.

Mid-afternoon.

Time, measured by the light fading from her living room.

She goes past hunger, her damp top stuck to her skin, rank with the stale smell of sweat and sour milk.

Diego arrives, hugs her and kisses her head, paces around saying *fuck* so much that she has to ask him to leave. "I sorry, I sorry. That little baby. I phone everyone. I tell everyone to search, okay?" He stands on the patio, smoking furiously and talking on the phone in loud Portuguese, hands making wild gestures.

Ella and Sophie have tired of Louise's distractions. They come to their mum, scramble onto the sofa beside her. Ciara holds them close. Her eyes burn.

One more try.

Ryan (87 outgoing calls)

"I'm going out."

"Ciara, are you sure?" Louise, kneeling in the dining room helping the girls build a Duplo house.

Ciara shrugs, helpless. "I can't just sit here. I have to do something."

It's Sunday evening now, just after five o'clock. Twenty-four hours since Noah should have been home.

"Just keep your phone on," the female garda says. "If we hear anything we'll call you straight away."

Sophie and Ella don't want her to leave. They cling to her legs at the doorway. "I'll be back soon," she tells them. "Mammy's coming back soon."

The roads are almost empty.

She drives slowly, taking in every car, every tall man walking down the street. Every side alley.

Across the city. Up through Blanchardstown. On a whim,

she stops at the shopping center. Shops are already shuttered, the place half-deserted. She walks, checking faces, but it's only teenagers and couples waiting for cinema show times.

She drives through the Phoenix Park. Slows each time she sees the shape of a man with a stroller, or an infant tied in a sling. But the soft gray sling Noah loves so much was left in her old bedroom. And his stroller was left in the kitchen. What is Ryan carrying Noah in?

Driving back into the city, she can't stop her mind from leaping. Those two girls in Menorca, found in a duffel bag on the ocean floor. Their parents had separated, their mum had just started seeing someone new. That other woman and her three children in Australia. Her ex set their car alight. Her family said she had just started trying to rebuild her life. *You're terrified of him. That's his voice in your head.* Little Noah sleeping with his clammy cheek on her breast. Mum's arms, the comfort of her hug.

On the quays, she pulls over near the Four Courts.

The tears have begun. Hopeless. Beyond despair. Panic completely flooding her. She might stop breathing.

The trill of her phone.

"Ciara, we've just had an update. Ryan's car has been spotted parked on a side street off Aungier Street. No sign of your husband or the baby."

"I know where he is."

She abandons her car on double yellow lines.

Whitefriar Street Church. Where they buried St. Valentine's heart.

Gold statues guard the entrance, a serpent coiled around a woman's bare feet. A long entrance hall slopes upward, past Jesus on his crucifix, surrounded by kneeling saints. She hurries, watched by the eyes of priests and bishops in photographs and paintings along the walls. With both hands, she pushes through the double doors, lets them swing closed behind her.

The heavy scent of melted candle wax.

A vaulted space. Vast domed ceiling. A priest on the altar, his hands held over a gold chalice, his voice reverberating. "Through your goodness take this bread we have to offer, work of human hands..."

Every Sunday evening, they used to come here. She remembers secretly studying Ryan's profile during Mass, then walking out into the darkness holding hands. They'd talk and laugh the whole way up Camden Street, flirting and joking with each other over steaming bowls of soup and noodles, or sometimes eating in companionable silence and—the best part—going home together. Home, wrapped in the security of love, before the criticisms and accusations, before the nights when she was woken by rough hands, before the first time he told her to fuck off in front of her children.

Anger. A sudden wave.

To her left, a shrine to the Immaculate Conception. To her right, a sign points the way to St. Valentine. Tall stained-glass windows are letting in columns of evening sun. There's etiquette in these places, she knows that. If you're late for Mass, you creep quietly down the side aisle. You genuflect to the altar.

Ciara starts striding down the middle of the central aisle. Rows and rows of people. Candles flicker, red and white. The priest is frowning at her, but his lips are still moving. "Before the night he was betrayed, Jesus took the wine and said this is my blood..."

Noah is in here somewhere. She knows it. She's never been more certain.

She scans each row, checks the mahogany pews, the red leather kneelers.

Alabaster icons follow her progress with their serene expressions. Lips curved into calm, unnatural smiles. St. Valentine is terrifying. White hair, meaty hands holding the stem of—what? A rose? His eyes bore holes.

She is so close to the altar now, she can see the priest's thin fingers holding the white disc of the host. Altar boys fidget on their bench.

Ryan will have his phone on silent. Of course he will. But still, she's taking out her mobile, standing still and dialing.

A loud ringtone. People turn toward a spot at the end of a pew.

Noah. She knows by the women's soft smiles. *Ah bless.*

She moves quickly past the altar, up the side aisle and there he is. Ryan, holding Noah in his arms, fumbling with his phone and whispering apologies to the elderly couple beside him.

He looks up and sees her, taken aback. Is that a flicker of guilt? Quickly replaced by an expression of defiance.

"Give him back." Again, that anger. She refuses to whisper.

Ryan's face is ashen. He's holding Noah tight against him.

All she can see is the back of her baby's head. Tears are running down her face.

Ryan hisses without looking at her. "How is this different to what you did? You took my kids away from me."

Is he breathing? Is Noah breathing?

"You didn't want him," Ryan says.

"That's not true."

"You didn't care. You had him living in that filthy hotel. How could you do that to him?"

"Where else could I go? I had nowhere to go."

"Oh yeah? That was your choice. You could have been at home, where you belonged but oh no, that wasn't good enough."

"Just stop—"

"He's better off with me. I'm his father. Take the girls. I'll leave you alone from now on. Just let me have my son."

A voice from over her shoulder. "Sorry, but we are going to have to ask you to leave." In her peripheral vision, she sees a young altar server. She ignores him, but he persists. "Could you just maybe step outside to sort this out?"

"No."

All eyes are on her now. She turns back to face Ryan. The organ begins to play, the low groan of it filling the whole space, drowning her. "You think I wanted this? Any of this? You think I left for no reason? No one does that. No one. You know why I left."

"What? What are you even—"

"You know exactly what I mean." She holds his eyes until he looks away.

He's scoffing at her now, glancing around, embarrassed. "You're insane."

Ryan? Go to hell.

Whose is that voice in her head? A voice so loud that she's not sure if she said the words or only thought them. Then she realizes. That voice shouting in her head? *That voice is me.*

She's stepping closer to him now, right up to him. As close as lovers. She puts her arms around Ryan, smells his musty sweat in his old hoodie. His stubble scratches her cheek. A nativity cameo. Mother, father, infant. Ryan's head bowed over her. She slips her arms under his, around Noah's body, and lifts. Her defiance against his. Her resolve against his. She is stronger than he has ever given her credit for. She lifts Noah up and away, in the way the night nurses used to lift the babies from her arms in the hospital. Sophie. Ella. Noah. She feels Ryan's arms let go.

He's staring at her, furious. Then he pushes past her and strides toward the door.

Cradling Noah, she sinks onto the pew. People are standing now, shuffling up to the altar to receive communion, and the organ music has softened into a hymn about God's love. To her right, a statue of Madonna and Child, their smooth faces both carved from one piece of oak.

She lifts her son close to her face. His eyes are closed, his body floppy. His cheeks are warm, his tiny hands cold. And she's fumbling with her phone and asking the woman beside her could you please phone this number please, tell them where we are and could you please just wait by the entrance and tell the guards we're here, and could you please phone for an ambulance please, there are other people around her now, women's voices, men's voices, the priest in his green and white and gold—do we need any assistance here? And she's kissing Noah's face to try and rouse him, and her hair is falling around him and this cannot be happening, cannot happen, and she lets out an anguished cry and finally, finally, finally she feels her baby wake.

VI

ANSEO

SUMMER 2019

37

He's been up half the night, but now she lays Noah in his cot and stands back, watching him sleeping. It's a habit she's not sure she'll ever get out of. Staring at her baby, drinking him in. The pout of his lips. The flutter of his lashes on his cheeks. After a few minutes, she tucks him under his blanket. Pulling her dressing gown over her pajamas, she tiptoes from the room and down the stairs.

Summer morning not yet bright, she unlocks the patio and steps into the garden. Her bare toes stop at the edge of the lawn. Chase is out there. Somewhere in the cool dawn. A shard of shadow in the dark firs. She has kept him for the past eight weeks. Ever since Eoin phoned from Daylight Animal Rescue to say he'd found Chase tied to the railings. Eoin was so angry that day. "These people who rescue animals! Only to return them in a worse state than they were found in! Nothing but a pure bleeding ego trip!"

She told him she had no idea the crow had been left there. Eoin said there was a note tied to the bird's foot, *KILL OR DIAL THIS NUMBER*. The number was hers.

Eoin had softened by the time he brought Chase over to her

garden in an old cat carrier. He'd grasped the situation. They watched the bird hobble about the lawn for a while. "Poor girl," Eoin had said, "couldn't fly away even if she wanted to."

"She?"

Chase's feathers were mangy, balding. Her feet oozed with open sores where the rope had cut into her. Eoin didn't think she had much of a chance, but when he called back yesterday he was surprised. Chase's talons have healed. Her wings have filled in with black feathers. Eoin repeated what he'd said before, that this probably wouldn't work, but he conceded the bird is as ready as she will ever be. Before leaving, Eoin drained his teacup and left it on the counter. "We've kittens," he said, "if the kids would like to come and see?"

Now Chase swoops down to her, rope thudding against the patio. She remembers the day Ryan brought this bird home in an old paint bucket. A nest fallen from the sky. This is what Ryan presented her with. *This is what you have done,* the gesture seemed to say. Look at the handiwork, the twigs selected and interwoven. Scraps of wool and dog hair. A nest, where they thought they'd be safe. Anger too, in the way the twigs had been bent together. She remembers her students' stories about Japanese crows who'd taken to building nests out of wires on the Tokyo rail lines, causing total blackouts. That day, Ryan's eyes were watching, waiting, testing. Who would she be if she tried to save these nestlings? Who would she be if she didn't?

Chase is looking at her with one eye. She paces and scratches the wall. Her feathers are still dull, mottled. But her eyes shine, pieces of polished jet.

Ciara's fingers close around the handles of the scissors hidden in the pocket of her dressing gown.

"There now, there now," she says to the bird, pulling at the fraying rope. When she gets closer, Chase lets out a loud squawk—more like a bark. Ciara jumps back. Shit. She gingerly reaches over, trying to avoid the sharp beak now making stabs at her hand. With one cut, she severs the knots on the bird's scaly feet, then quickly withdraws her hand and backs away. The bird stands still. Then she lifts her feet, lets out a single cry, and opens her wings.

"Mammy?" Sophie steps into the garden behind her. She's wearing her dinosaur PJs with the word DINO-SNORE printed on them. "Where's Chase?"

"He's flown away to see his friends, love."

"You put him free?"

She checks her daughter's face. This could go either way. "Yes, love. He wanted to be free. You're not meant to keep crows as pets."

"Or penguins."

"Or penguins is right."

She looks now at the fraying rope. Black feathers. Bird-shit scum. She'll have to hose this whole place down. After that, maybe they'll plant some wildflowers. Oxeye daisies, poppies, selfheal. A robin sits on the plastic slide, regarding them with sidelong wisdom.

At the last court hearing, the judge granted her permission to leave the state. Given Ryan's reckless behavior, leaving the girls alone that night. In the light of testimonies from Ciara, Rhona and Sinéad. Access is now strictly limited. She's free to go anywhere. Why she hasn't done so yet, her mother can't understand. She has been phoning daily, asking when they are moving over. Ciara thinks about her teenage bedroom. That new mattress in its plastic cover. It would be so easy to return to Sheffield and live in her mum's house, but something is holding her back. When she thinks about leaving Dublin, there's an ache in her. A sting of nostalgia. She doesn't want her kids growing up with a homesick mother, thinking home is somewhere else. *Home is right here.* If there's only one gift she can give them, it's this.

Autumn is coming. With it, new beginnings. In September, she will start teaching in Kiltale Primary. Half an hour from their house in Clonee, the whitewashed school sits at a crossroads, down a tunnel of trees. The principal who interviewed her seemed friendly. Eyeing the crucifix above the board, she didn't mention that she's a single parent, or anything else. The school has a place for Sophie too. Her new pleated tartan skirts are lined up in the wardrobe. White shirts with folded collars. A unicorn backpack, filled with books. *First Phonics. Figure It Out.* New shoes with a tiny silver buckle. Thank God her HAP payment came through just in time. Nights when the children are asleep, she sits up late, learning Irish.

A few words are starting to stick, verbs and the first few phrases. Slán Abhaile means safe home. Anseo means here.

Diego says maybe he should start learning Irish instead of English, maybe he'd be better at it. When he came over last Friday night, Sophie had built a Duplo house on the table and refused to dismantle it. So, they sat on the sofa, books scattered on the carpet, and did a full run through of IELTS speaking exam parts one and two. Again. And again. Better each time, more concise. His words, closer to what he wanted to say. His voice, husky by the end of the third test. He'd been on night shifts at the Eden for the past week, and was getting very little sleep in his crowded apartment during the day. He was rubbing his eyes, the odd word of Portuguese slipping in. "Will we leave it?" she said, "you're wrecked."

"I am broken," he said. But he didn't close his IELTS book. She knew the feeling, of wanting something so badly, being so committed to a dream that you are willing to ignore the physical reality. Tiredness, soreness, pushed aside.

"Half-time," she said. "I'll stick the kettle on."

When she returned to the room, he was asleep, slumped against the sofa, like a man felled by a stun gun. One hand resting on his English dictionary. Destroyed by language.

She put the two mugs of tea on coasters on the red plastic coffee table, kicked off her runners and slid onto the sofa beside him. She leant back and snuggled against him. Daylight was leaving the room, and she could feel the quiet breath of the house around her, the warmth of his body beside her on the sofa.

Much later, at the first patter of rain against her window and he woke and went to move. She took his hand. "Stay?"

It was Saoirse at the refuge who advised her to start journaling. Her notebook is almost full now. Sentences, phrases that woke her in the middle of the night sometimes, her uncertain handwriting becoming faster, stronger, filling up the pages. She sees now that writing out a story is unknotting it.

Flattening the scroll. Deciphering the codex. Making it clear. Put words into the right order and this is what you can do: break the spell.

Sophie says, "Pancakes for breakfast, Mammy?"

Ella has skipped out of the house now. Her girls are hop-scotching along the patio, the balls of their feet in damp socks leaving heart-shaped prints.

"All right then, missus. Pancakes it is, so."

"Yes! Can we have Nutella on them?"

Before going back into the house, Ciara checks the sky just once. *She'll be imprinted on you. Unreleasable. She'll never fly away.* But there's no sign of the crow, only the start of another summer day. From the pines behind her house, a ripple of birdsong. Rhona has always said the dawn chorus is a way for birds to tell each other they have survived the night. Ciara has no notion if this is true or not, but she can't help liking the idea. That joyous flutter of song is a flag wave. *I'm still here. I made it through.* Above the treetops, a veil of white clouds reaches upward, and further still, high over the houses, a single swift soars and dives as if in defiance of gravity, trying to race its shadow, or to somehow catch the light.

Acknowledgments

Nesting began when I was commissioned to write a three-thousand-word story on the theme of "independence" for RTÉ Radio One. I will be forever thankful to Clíodhna Ní Anluain for commissioning that story (although I think I have gone slightly over the word count at this point). Early on in my research, I was fortunate enough to come across the work of Dr. Melanie Nowicki, who generously took time to discuss the research behind her paper "The Hotelisation of the Housing Crisis," and answered even my most random questions about the lived experiences of emergency accommodation in Ireland. Melanie, thank you so much. I'm also grateful for the work of Don Hennessy, whose book *How He Gets Inside Her Head* provides the most astute exposé of the tactics employed in intimate partner abuse, and whose follow up *Steps to Freedom* is quite simply a lifeline for so many women. Focus Ireland have funded seminal research which was key in linking the threads of this story together. I am also deeply grateful for the advice of Threshold and Women's Aid.

To my wonderful editors Sophie Missing and Betsy Gleick, thank you for your kindness toward this book and its writer. This novel benefited immeasurably from the careful reading of Emily Howes, Elske Rahill, Sean O'Farrell and Djinn von Noorden—thank you all so much. Thanks also to my writing friends Becky, Ally, Abi, Madelon, Aoi, Fabian, Jenni, Joyce, Sam, Natasha and Emily for keeping the flame alive, and to Tom Morris for suggesting I send this novel to Eleanor Birne, my incredible agent, now at Rogers, Coleridge and White. Thanks to everyone who has championed this book at Scribner UK; Polly Osborn, Becky McCarthy, Joe Christie, Ella Fox-Martens, Hayley McMullan, Amy Fulwood, Mat Watterson, Heather Hogan, Sian Wilson and to the team at Algonquin U.S.

To my daughters. My love for you is woven through every page of this story. With your chat and laughter, stories and songs, you pulled me back from some of the darker places this story took me to. If I hugged you a little closer on certain nights, maybe one day you will understand why. To Mum, Dad, Alice and John—thanks for minding us, and for believing in me.

To every person sleeping in emergency accommodation tonight, in particular the 4,027 children. To those in family hubs, hostels, hotels and refuges, and those sleeping in friends' spare rooms and on sofas, hidden from official statistics. To anyone trapped in a place that does not feel like home, and anyone who has ever been asked the question "why don't you just leave?" This book is for you.

February 2024